DON'T MISS THE OTHER
SISTERS IN CRIME COLLECTIONS . . .
Available from Berkley Books

Sisters in Crime: LINDA BARNES, SUE GRAFTON, FAYE KELLERMAN, LIA MATERA, SARA PARETSKY, ELIZABETH PETERS, NANCY PICKARD, and others

Sisters in Crime 2: MARY HIGGINS CLARK, JOAN HESS, SUE GRAFTON, SUSAN DUNLAP, CAROLYN G. HART, LIA MATERA, NANCY PICKARD, and others

Sisters in Crime 3: LILIAN JACKSON BRAUN, DOROTHY SALISBURY DAVIS, LINDA GRANT, FAYE KELLERMAN, SARA PARETSKY, and others

Sisters in Crime 4: SUE GRAFTON, MARCIA MULLER, WENDY HORNSBY, SARAH SHANKMAN, JOAN HESS, LINDA GRANT, and others

Berkley Books Edited by Marilyn Wallace

SISTERS IN CRIME
SISTERS IN CRIME 2
SISTERS IN CRIME 3
SISTERS IN CRIME 4
SISTERS IN CRIME 5

SISTERS IN CRIME 5

Edited by Marilyn Wallace

BERKLEY BOOKS, NEW YORK

SISTERS IN CRIME 5

A Berkley Book / published by arrangement with
the editor

PRINTING HISTORY
Berkley edition / November 1992

ISBN: 0-425-13506-3

A BERKLEY BOOK ® TM 757,375
Berkley Books are published by The Berkley Publishing Group,
200 Madison Avenue, New York, New York 10016.
The name "BERKLEY" and the "B" logo
are trademarks belonging to Berkley Publishing Corporation.

PRINTED IN THE UNITED STATES OF AMERICA

10 9 8 7 6 5 4 3 2

For Anita and David Orlow,
True Friends

Contents

Foreword

The short story renaissance of the nineties is especially apparent to readers of mystery and suspense fiction. While it's true that all short stories are characterized by an economy of incident as well as of language, a consistent sensibility, and a vital change in the main character's situation, whether internal or external, the mystery form has its own (deliciously chilling) requirements.

Mystery short stories add the element of suspense: disaster, or at the very least trouble, will be threatened. In stories of detection, someone must engage in an attempt to uncover the secret. There will be clues, suspects, and the reader will participate along with the protagonist in the discovery process. And in stories of psychological suspense, the reader will experience the main character's tension, the precarious mental, emotional, or physical predicament born of chilling possibilities.

Nevertheless, a mystery short story must first follow all the rules of good fiction and good writing. It is not so much *different*, then, as it is special. And the stories in each volume of *Sisters in Crime* prove just how special mystery short stories can be.

In volume one, Nancy Pickard's "Afraid All the Time" won an American Mystery award, a Macavity, and an Anthony for Best Short Story of 1989, and was nominated for an Edgar and an Agatha. Shelley Singer's "A Terrible Thing" was nominated for an Anthony, and Elizabeth Peters's "The Locked Tomb Mystery" was reprinted in Ed Hoch's *Best Mystery Short Stories of 1989*. From volume two, Susan Dunlap's "The Celestial Buffet" won an Anthony, Joan Hess's "Too Much to Bare" won an Agatha, and Sue Grafton's "A Poison That Leaves No Trace" won a Shamus and was nominated for an Edgar. In volume three, Dorothy Cannell's "The High Cost of Living" was nominated for an

Agatha, and Sarah Shankman's "Say You're Sorry" and my "A Tale of Two Pretties" were nominated for Anthony awards. "Nine Sons," by Wendy Hornsby, was an Edgar winner from volume four.

This volume opens with a Susan Dunlap story, in celebration of her Anthony award. The rest of the stories are arranged by author's last name in reverse alphabetical order, in the interests of fairness (a W's revenge!). Some contributors to this volume are members of the organization Sisters in Crime; others are not.

Edgar Allen Poe awards are given by Mystery Writers of America; Anthonys, named for the late writer/critic Anthony Boucher, are presented at the annual Bouchercon convention; Shamus awards are given by Private Eye Writers of America; American Mystery awards are voted on by the readers of *Mystery Scene* magazine; Macavitys are awarded by Mystery Readers International; and Agathas are given at the Malice Domestic convention celebrating traditional mysteries.

Once again, I'm pleased and grateful to be associated with so many wonderful writers who have provided readers with clever, thoughtful, diverse, and entertaining crime-filled creations.

—Marilyn Wallace
San Anselmo, CA
March 1991

Susan Dunlap, 1990–91 president of Sisters in Crime, has created three memorable series. Berkeley Lieutenant Jill Smith solves crimes in seven novels, most recently Death and Taxes; *amateur detective utility-company meter-reader Vejay Haskell is featured in three books; and Kiernan O'Shaughnessy, former forensic pathologist turned private eye, investigates murder in* Pious Deception *and* Rogue Wave. *Susan's "The Celestial Buffet" (*Sisters in Crime 2*) won an Anthony for Best Short Story of 1990.*

In "A Burning Issue," first published in Alfred Hitchcock's Mystery Magazine, *a woman isn't quite prepared, as even she admits, for the consequences of her actions.*

A BURNING ISSUE

by Susan Dunlap

I AM NOT thorough.

I don't explore every minute detail, every aspect and angle of a subject. Only fanatics do that. But there is a basic amount of preparation required of any adult who seeks to live in relative comfort, without being pummeled by recurrent blows of humiliation. And that preparation is what I fail to do.

It is not that I am unaware of this fault. *Au contraire.* Rarely does a day pass without it being thrust to my attention. There are the small annoyances; grocery lists I tell myself I needn't write down; recipes I skim, only to discover, as my guest sits angrily getting looped in the living room, that the last words are "bake in hot oven (what other kind is there?) for ninety minutes."

Or the time, as a surprise for Andrew, I painted the house. Anyone, I told myself, can paint a house. I do, after all, have two weeks, and it's not a mansion. This time I did not neglect the instructions on the can. I read them. What I did not do was ask if any preparation was necessary. "Everybody knows you need to scrape off the old paint first," Andrew told me later. Almost everybody. I had the second coat halfway on before I realized the house looked like a mint-green moonscape. But all was not lost. The day I finished, it poured. As Andrew said, "You don't use water-based paint outside."

I could go on, but you get the picture. I've often puzzled as to what causes this failing of mine. Is it laziness? Not entirely. Or a short attention span? Perhaps. "You don't prepare thoroughly," Andrew has told me again and again. "Why can't you force yourself?"

That, I don't know. I start to read directions, plodding through word by word, giving time for each phrase to sink into my mind, like a galaxy being swallowed by a black hole. But after two or three paragraphs I'm mouthing hollow words and thinking of Nepal, or field goals, or whatever. And I'm assuring myself that I know enough already that this brief review will stimulate my memory and bring all the details within easy calling range.

In fairness to Andrew, he has accepted my failing. And well he should, since my decision to marry him was one of its more devastating examples.

I met him while planning a series of Man-in-the-Street interviews in Duluth. (Easy, I thought. People love to hold forth on their opinions. Not standing on a Duluth street corner in February they don't.) Amongst the shivering pasty male bodies of Minnesota's northernmost major city, Andrew Greer beamed like a beacon of health. Lightly tanned, lightly muscled, with bright blue eyes that promised unending depths, he could discuss the Packers or Virginia Woolf; he could find a Japanese restaurant open at midnight; he could maneuver his Porsche through the toboggan run of Duluth streets at sixty miles per hour and then talk his way out of the ticket he so deserved. And, most important, my failing, which had enraged so many, amused him.

And so six weeks later (what could I possibly discover in a year that I hadn't found out already?) I married him.

We spent a year in Duluth; bought a Belgian sheepdog to lie around the hearth and protect us. ("Belgian sheepdogs are always on the move," I read later, as Smokey paced through the apartment.) I left the interviewing job (abruptly) and had a brief stint as an administrative assistant, and an even briefer one as a new accounts person in a now defunct bank. And in January Andrew came home aglow. He was being transferred to Atlanta.

I packed our furniture (which is now somewhere near Seattle, I imagine. There was some paragraph about labeling in the moving contract . . .) and we headed south.

It was in Atlanta that I painted the house. And it was in Atlanta that I discovered what I had overlooked in Andrew. For all his interest in literature and sports, his acumen in business, he had one passion that I had ignored. The hints were always there. I could have picked them up. A thorough person would have.

Above all else, Andrew loved sunbathing. Not going to the lake, not swimming, not waterskiing. Sunbathing. He loved the activity (or lack of it) of sitting in the sun with an aluminum reflector propped beneath his chin.

Each day he rushed home at lunch for half an hour's exposure. He oiled his body with his own specifically created castor oil blend, moved the reflector into place, and settled back as Smokey paced from the living room to him and back.

And the weekends were worse—he had all day. He lay there, not reading, no music, begrudging conversation as if the effervescence of words would blotch his tan.

I thought it would pass. I thought he would reach a desirable shade of brown and stop. I thought the threat of skin cancer would deter him. (Castor oil blocks the ultraviolet rays, he told me.) I coaxed, I nagged, I watched as the body that had once been the toast (no pun intended) of Duluth was repeatedly coated with castor oil and cooked till it resembled a rare steak left on the counter overnight.

On the infrequent occasions Andrew left the house before dark, people stared. They moved away, as they might do in proximity of a red leper. But Andrew was oblivious.

Vainly, I tempted him with Braves tickets, symphony seats, the *Complete Works* of Virginia Woolf (in fifty-eight volumes).

In March the days were lengthening. Andrew's firm moved him "out of the public eye." I suggested a psychiatrist (but, of course, they see patients in daylight hours).

By April his firm had encouraged him to work at home. Delighted, Andrew bent over his desk from sunset till midnight, and stumbled exhausted into bed. By nine each morning he was in the sun. The only time he spoke to me was when it rained.

In desperation, I invited the psychiatrist to dinner for an informal go at Andrew. (That was the two-hour late meal, and he the looped shrink.)

Finally, I suggested divorce. I almost filed before my lawyer insisted I read the Georgia statutes, this time carefully. It is *not* a community property state, far from it. And as Andrew pointed out, I was unlikely to be able to support myself.

So the only way left was to kill him. After all, it would matter little to him. If he'd led a good enough life, he would pass on to a place closer to the sun. If not, he could hold his reflector near the fire.

For once, I researched painstakingly, lurking near the poisonous substance books in the public library, checking and rechecking. I found that phenol and its derivatives cause sweating, thirst, cyanosis (a blue coloring of the skin that would hardly be visible on Andrew's well-tanned hide), rapid breathing, coma, and death—all with a fatal dose of two grams. Mixed thickly with Andrew's castor-oil blend, I could use five times that and be assured he would rub it over his body in hourly ministrations before the symptoms were serious enough to interfere with his regimen. If he got his usual nine A.M. start Saturday morning, he would be red over brown over blue, and very dead by sundown.

I hesitated. I'm really not a killer at heart. I hated to think of him in pain. But, given his habit, Andrew was slowly killing himself now. And one day's pain was preferable to the lingering effects of skin cancer.

I poured the phenol into Andrew's castor oil blend, patted Smokey as he paced by, and tossed the used phenol container into the boot of the car as I left.

I don't know where I drove. (I thought I knew where I was going. I thought I wouldn't need a map.) Doubtless I was still in the city limits as Andrew applied the first lethal coating and lifted his reflector into place.

It was warm for April; ninety degrees by noon. I rolled down the window and kept driving. If I'd thought to check on gas stations I wouldn't have run out of gas. If I'd thought to bring my AAA card, I wouldn't have had to hitch a ride into the nearest hamlet.

It was still light and well over a hundred degrees when I pulled up in front of the house. Andrew's contorted body would be sprawled beside his deck chair. I hoped Smokey hadn't made too much fuss.

Cautiously I opened the door. Warily I walked through the living room, as if the ghost of Andrew's reddened corpse were waiting to spring out.

I heard a sound in the study and moved toward it. Andrew sat at his desk.

He looked awful, but not more so than usual.

I ran back to the car and grabbed the phenol container out of the boot. It was too hot to hold. I dropped it, picked up an oil rag, and tried again.

Slowly I read the instructions and the warning: "If applied to skin can cause sweating, thirst, cyanosis, rapid breathing, coma and death." I read on. "Treatments" (a section, for obvious reasons, I had omitted). "Remove by washing skin with water. To dissolve phenol, or retard absorption, mix with castor oil."

I slumped into the back seat. The sun beat down. Why wasn't I more thorough? Glaring at the phenol container, I read the last line on the label: "Caution. Phenol is explosive when exposed to heat or oxidizing agents."

I dropped the oil rag. But, of course, it was too late.

Dorothy Sucher's Dead Men Don't Give Seminars *(an Agatha nominee) and* Dead Men Don't Marry *feature a pair of charming, intelligent, and talented detectives: Sabina Swift, a Washington private investigator, and her young sidekick, Vic Newman. Praised for its rich plotting, polished style, and sharp psychological awareness, Dorothy's fiction is enhanced by her experiences as a psychotherapist, mother, and editor-in-chief of a small town weekly newspaper.*

In "Felis Domestica," *one woman discovers just how to tame her rival.*

FELIS DOMESTICA

by Dorothy Sucher

"JOAN! JOAN! I'M locked in the bathroom!"

There was no answer.

Professor Regina Morgan rattled the doorknob vigorously. "Joan!" she cried.

I suppose she's still making lunch, she thought. "Joan, damn you!" There was nothing to do but wait, and that was something she'd always hated.

How had the door jammed, anyway? She'd been careful, or so she'd thought, not to close it all the way, for she knew there was something wrong with the lock. One of these days she'd get it fixed—right now she had more important things on her mind.

Like David.

"Joan!" she called again. Joan was probably polishing forks, or making sure the plates matched, or something equally foolish—she always wasted her time over nonessentials. It was no wonder she'd never gotten tenure.

Regina had told her, many times, "You've got to *publish,* Joan!" But Joan would only bleat about her service to the college, and the extra miles she'd walked for her students. "All of which is *crap,* darling," Regina would say, while the vague, glazed, stubborn look she knew so well settled on Joan's large plain face.

Why fuss over a lunch? There was no one around to impress. It was only the two of them having a bite, two women, old friends.

Turning away from the door, Regina stepped over to the sink and gazed at her reflection in the mirror. Not bad for thirty-nine, not bad at all, she told herself, raising her sharp, still-firm jaw and smiling seductively at her reflection, that of a lean, tanned woman with intense, slightly prominent eyes and a high forehead sweeping back to a cascade of chestnut hair, the blunt-cut edges brushing one bare, bony shoulder. She was wearing her favorite silk shirt, which had a tendency to slip down over the shoulder, a tendency she encouraged. Sexy lady, she thought, narrowing her eyes at her image in the mirror. She hoped David appreciated what he was getting. Over her shoulder she called, "Joan?"

Still no answer.

"Oh, Joan, why don't you move your fat ass," Regina muttered, and picked up a pair of silver tweezers. Might as well accomplish something, as long as she was stuck in here. She taught three courses, a killing schedule, and there was never enough time to lavish on her body. Of course, that would soon change.

The points of the tiny pincers closed on a hair that marred the perfect arch of her eyebrow, and she yanked it out by the roots, moaning, "Ooh!" at the small, pleasurable pain.

Outside the bathroom, in an armchair facing the door, Joan Bloch silently crossed her thick legs in their beige hose.

Fat ass yourself, she thought, and looked at her watch. The minute and hour hands were about to converge on the twelve. High noon, she thought, and pictured a rangy Gary Cooper striding down a dusty, deserted street at the climactic hour—she was using the film in her Images of the Frontier course this semester. How symbolic.

Joan was an instructor, and Regina a professor, in the Department of American Civilization at Oneida College in upstate New York, where both had worked for fifteen years. The two women had been hired in ways that could hardly have been more different. Regina—quite a catch for a minor college—had been a fresh Ph.D. from one of the Seven Sisters, with a dissertation on a trendy topic, and she'd been snared by the lure of a tenure-track position and a generous salary; whereas Joan, with only a master's degree, had enrolled as an academic galley slave after Labor Day, grateful that a new appointee who was to have taught three freshman courses had failed to show up.

Regina and Joan were the only single women in the department, and as a result they'd become friends; but after ten years their closeness had begun to fray, when Regina developed an allergy to cats—or so she claimed.

Inside the bathroom, Regina finished plucking her eyebrows. She replaced the silver tweezers in their leather case, and as she zipped it up, noticed to her surprise that she was feeling a little short of breath.

"Relax," she told herself. Patience was not her long suit—"I adore instant gratification," was the way she put it, a confession she'd made more than once to men, with pleasurable results—but right now she knew she might as well take it easy, for without help she would be unable to get out of the bathroom. There was no window, and when the door jammed, it could be opened only from outside.

No matter. Joan would come.

Regina relaxed, and began to think about the time, not long before, when Joan had gotten stuck in the very same bathroom during a party. It had been funny, though now that Regina was in the situation herself, it didn't seem all that amusing. For a fleeting moment she wondered if Joan could possibly have shut her in deliberately, to get even.

No. Joan was much too sincere—painfully sincere—much too good, boringly good. A touch of spite would have made her more bearable as a friend.

Regina wouldn't miss her when she went to live in Boston with David. She'd send her a postcard, and after that they'd lose touch; Joan never went to conferences.

Another example of Joan's neglect of the essentials. Not that she could afford to go, really.

Regina felt a tiny twinge of guilt as she recalled how the guests had laughed, how Joan had pleaded to be released from the bathroom, and how she herself had taken her time about it, until the joke had begun to wear thin and the guests to look ill at ease. Though when Regina pictured the expression on Joan's face as she'd stepped out to wild applause, Regina felt an urge to laugh. Joan had been mortified—probably because now it was public knowledge she sometimes took a pee!

Or worse!

A giggle ripped from Regina's throat and was abruptly cut short. Really, she wasn't feeling well.

Outside the bathroom, Joan heard Regina's laughter and felt a momentary disappointment. Regina was going to be fine, then. Just as she'd always thought.

Regina's "allergy to cats" had been very convenient—for Regina. Ever since its inception, Joan, who owned two cats, had to be the one to run over to Regina's house on those snowy nights when neither woman had anything to do but drink wine and watch television, preferably with a friend—how many books could even a college professor read? Such nights were more common in Joan's life than in Regina's, but not infrequent in the latter's either; despite Regina's attractiveness, pickings were lean in the small college town where the two women lived, and most of the men who wandered—and "wandered" was the word for it, as in "wandering husbands," thought Joan—in and out of Regina's life were already married. Now it was always Joan who had to drive home alone over the icy roads late at night, leaving Regina curled up before the fire, although formerly this obligation of friendship had been shared.

Naturally Regina could no longer feed Joan's cats, during Joan's yearly trip to Delray Beach to see her aunt; yet Joan could still water Regina's ferns and wait for her repairmen whenever Regina went out of town to a conference. Regina was forever receiving grants and travel money. She had been away again only this week. In fact, she'd just returned today.

"You can have the run of the house," Regina always said, handing her the key as if conferring a favor. What was *that* supposed to mean? Was she expecting Joan to hold orgies? Move in and revel in having a whole house to herself, instead of a tiny apartment?

Joan *loved* her tiny apartment, she *loved* it, and her darling kitties, and she never stayed one minute longer at Regina's than she had to; incredibly, Regina seemed unaware that the things she expected Joan to do for her were an imposition, a nuisance.

The "allergy" had given Regina a perfect excuse for getting rid of Cattyclysm, and of course Joan had had to adopt him because she couldn't bear to have Regina put him to sleep. Poor Cattyclysm! Regina had become bored with him as soon as he'd outgrown his adorable kittenhood; she'd resented the pitifully few demands he made on her. Cats asked so little, thought Joan—a clean box, food, at a bare minimum *food* on a regular basis, which Cattyclysm hadn't always received—Regina really hadn't an ounce of nurturing in her!

At this thought, a mute and painful cry of Oh David, David, welled up from Joan's heart, as it had been welling at intervals since the last time she'd seen him, intervals that were still so frequent that it seemed hardly any time at all since last she'd lain in his arms. David, the only lover Joan had ever had, the lover who'd turned to her in the terrible month before his departure from the college, eight years ago next June.

And now David was going to marry Regina! How was it possible? Regina, the depths of whose selfishness, vanity, ambition—well, Joan seriously doubted anyone had plumbed those depths more thoroughly than she. Not lately of course, but certainly in the early years of their friendship, the two had told each other everything.

And Regina had had plenty to tell.

The door rattled sharply. "Joan, where are you!" Regina cried. "Joan! Joan!"

* * *

Regina asked herself why she was feeling so short of breath, so uneasy. Nothing could happen to her in her own bathroom. Yet the uneasiness mounted. Why didn't Joan come?

Could this feeling be claustrophobia?

No, of course not. She was splendidly sane, unlike Joan, with whom she'd once been stuck in a stalled elevator. Regina had had to spend the whole time calming her friend, though if she'd been alone, she'd simply have curled up on the floor and gone to sleep until help came.

Regina was much too old to develop claustrophobia, out of the blue like that.

Actually, that wasn't true. You *could* develop things, all sorts of things, when you were fairly old—well, she wouldn't call herself old, but take, for instance, her allergies. Suddenly, for no apparent reason, pollens and dust had begun to redden her eyes and make her sneeze. And cats . . .

She shuddered.

Fortunately the shots had helped, but only with the pollens and dust. Not with the cats, not at all. Her allergy to cats was definitely getting worse. She did her best to avoid the wretched things, but cats were so common, and turned up in such unexpected places, and even if you didn't see a cat around, you could never be sure one hadn't just been there, leaving behind a few flakes of its lethal, invisible dander.

As she fought down a rising, irrational anxiety, she noticed she seemed to be wheezing.

Outside the bathroom, Joan sat in her chair and stared unseeingly at the door.

David, she thought.

Over the years his name had become a mantra, an invocation.

She remembered the thin, dark, sensitive face, the voice that was slightly nasal, the biting, sarcastic remarks that only served to hide, she was certain, enormous shyness. He was so brilliant in his unfashionable field. Classics—now *that* took courage, in this day and age.

And then the college had closed down the Classics Department. Wiped it out.

Oh David, David!

Regina had once remarked that David had used Joan and then dumped her, but Joan didn't see it that way. Poor David had gone through hell that last month—not just the firing, but he'd become a pariah on campus, avoided as if the mere fact that he'd lost his position despite having had tenure was a dangerous, possibly contagious disease.

The loss of his professorship had been a "narcissistic wound," Joan's psychiatrist had said, during one of the many, many times they had gone over the significance of the David episode in her life, milking it, wringing it—not dry, exactly, it would never become that for her, she continually moistened and refreshed it, for it was her one great drama—a wound that had stabbed right to the core of his masculine identity. Hearing the doctor explain this, Joan had suddenly understood, with enormous relief, that David's departure from her life hadn't really been a rejection; and that certain disappointing events, or rather non-events, in bed hadn't been his fault, or (as she'd feared) her own, due to her lack of allure. No, it was because he'd suffered a blow to his masculinity.

No wonder he hadn't answered her letters. He'd been devastated, humiliated. He couldn't face her.

Humiliation was something she understood.

"Don't you think he'll get over it someday, possibly?" she had asked her psychiatrist. "Don't you think he might come back?"

He'd smiled gently—he was a kind man, who held a misguided belief that one should never, regardless of the circumstances, deprive anyone of hope—and replied, "Possibly, Joan. Stranger things have been known to happen."

But David *wasn't* coming back! David was going to marry Regina, who'd bumped into him again, after all these years, at a meeting of the Modern Language Association where he'd been giving an invited talk on the Confluence of Ancient and Modern Languages.

And Regina—incredibly, inconceivably!—was going to leave Oneida, to give up her tenure as if it were nothing.

Joan pressed her lips together and her expression hardened as the bathroom door shook and Regina's knuckles rattled against the inside. "Joan!" Regina called, and began pounding rhythmically and loudly on the door.

Soon she would let Regina out, thought Joan. Soon, but not quite yet.

And once she'd done so, Regina would never again be able to use her "allergy" as an excuse for avoiding the things she didn't want to do.

As she had when Joan had invited her to her birthday party.

"Flaunt it!" her psychiatrist had said, as she'd sat weeping in his office because she was going to be forty and she still had nothing—nothing! "Life begins at forty! Throw a party!"

But Regina had refused to attend.

"Sweetie, I can't, you know that. The cats—" She'd shrugged.

"Just this once, Regina. Please!"

"Sorry, darling."

"Just for an hour!"

She had begged. Begged! (That was before Regina had told her about David.)

"Darling, I know it's a bore, but I *can't* go where there are cats—"

"Regina, you're supposed to be my friend."

"I'm allergic, how many times do I have to tell you?"

"It's psychological, Regina." Joan could hardly believe she'd finally said it. She'd thought it a thousand times, and now she'd said it aloud, possibly because deep down she knew that if Regina came to her party, the others would, too, but otherwise they might not.

"You think everything is psychological!"

"Isn't it?"

"Really, Joan, is it so hard to grasp the concept that cats give me asthma? And asthma means you can't breathe?"

Joan had turned away. "An hour at my party wouldn't kill you."

"Oh, for God's sake. Cats *could* kill me. I could die in fifteen minutes, of anaphylaxis."

"I never heard of it. And please don't overdramatize. Look, suppose I leave the cats with a neighbor. Will you come then?"

"Joan. Your place *reeks* of cats; they drop their dander everywhere!"

"My cats are very clean."

"*Three* of them, in that tiny apartment!"

"Three including Cattyclysm, in case you've forgotten."

"I never asked you to take him, Joan. Look, sweetie, simmer down. I'd *love* to come to your little party but"—and she'd thrown back her head and laughed—"I have to admit I'm not *dying* to come!"

Nobody had come, except for the landlady and two of the departmental secretaries. But it didn't matter, who cared about a party, it was over, in the past.

What did matter was that Joan had determined to prove—*now*, today—once and for all and conclusively, that Regina's allergy to cats was all in her head.

"Joan! Joan! Get me out of here!"

Calm down, Regina told herself. Calm down. She lowered her fists and backed away from the door, coughing.

Think about David, she told herself. David, who had ended up at Harvard with two books to his credit, one a popular success, the other a textbook that would bring in a steady income for years. He'd landed on his feet, amazingly.

He was still a nerd, though.

She frowned. Not a word she cared for, "nerd," a neologism, a word she'd never use in class—she paused, thinking she might try it, fling it at her class one day to make them laugh, charm them, shake them out of their preconceived ideas about professors. . . . She shrugged, doing her best to ignore a mounting uneasiness, a creeping, gnawing. . . .

She clutched her small breasts, forcing herself to imagine marriage to David. Sexually it would be a disaster, she already knew. But sex wasn't what she wanted from him. She wanted to move to Boston, stop teaching, live the good life for a change. She would have a lover on the side. It was never hard to find one; there wasn't an ounce of flab on her body, and that was what men cared about.

Definitely, she was wheezing.

She closed the lid of the toilet seat and sat down. Relax, she told herself.

She knew very well her allergy to cats wasn't psychological, yet she'd read that once you'd developed asthma, it was possible for all kinds of things to trigger it. Including emotional upsets.

So calm down, she told herself. Yet the feeling of uneasiness persisted. If anything, it seemed to be getting worse—a strange, profound anxiety, like a stirring, a quaking, almost a dissolution in the depths of her organism.

"Joan!" she cried. She wanted to leap up and pound her fists on the door again, but she restrained herself.

Why did everyone think allergies were psychological? It was infuriating! Incredible, the way the damned Freudians had brainwashed the entire population, without a shred of scientific proof. Take her dear friend Joan, who could yak on endlessly about what her analyst had said. Regina had met the man at parties and he was a nothing; but Joan adored him, probably because he was the only man in her life. You could hardly count David, who was a fantasy figure by now, practically a figment of Joan's imagination.

The wheezing had worsened.

She could breathe *in*, but she was having trouble breathing *out*, and she knew what that meant. Deep inside her lungs, the tiny bronchioles were going into spasm, constricting, tightening—

Her chest began to heave.

Could she be allergic to something in the bathroom?

But what? A sudden, new allergy to . . . to—she looked around wildly—to the soap!

She seized it and threw it into the trash bin.

To the shampoo, maybe! The lotions, the cosmetics—

With trembling fingers she swept them into the bin and then thrust the bin into the cabinet under the sink and shut the door.

There, that was better—wasn't it?

No, she felt worse, if anything.

Of course! Why hadn't she thought of it before? She would take her allergy medicine!

She flung open the medicine cabinet, but the pills weren't there.

What had become of them? They were always on the second shelf!

One by one, she grabbed at the vials, the bottles, scanning the labels and, disappointed, letting them fall to the floor. Gone! Gone! How could that be?

"Joan!" she cried, and noticed that her voice was weakening.

"Yes, Regina?"

"Oh Joan, you're there! Finally! Thank God! I'm locked in, let me out!"

Joan folded her arms but did not rise immediately. "Why? Don't you like it in there?"

"What do you mean? Of course I don't like it in here! Oh—" Regina's mind was becoming confused, but she seemed to remember having said something like that herself, just in fun, when Joan had shut herself inside the bathroom during the party. "Joan, please—"

Should I tell her now, Joan wondered, or wait until after I let her out?

What would be the most satisfying time to tell her what a fraud she is, what a liar, what a selfish, manipulative bitch? Or possibly, just possibly, she's only a pitiful, self-deluding neurotic whose so-called allergy to cats—dear precious things, sweet little fuzzballs, only a horrible person could hate them as Regina did—was all, all, all in her head!

I'll tell her later, Joan decided. Why not savor the anticipation a little longer? After all, once she'd *told* Regina, made her finally face the truth about herself—why, the fun would be over, wouldn't it?

"You're getting even!" Regina gasped from inside the bathroom. "Joan, don't be petty, I'm sorry, I apologize, I *never* should have left you in here so *let me out*!" The plea would have been a scream, if her tortured lungs had held enough air.

Of course their friendship would be over too, after this practical joke—wasn't that what it was?—but that hardly mattered, since Joan knew Regina far too well to imagine she would bother to stay in touch once she moved to Boston.

I've proved you a liar, my *dear* Regina, Joan was going to tell her to her face. While you were at the conference I finally *did* give myself the run of your house, in fact I moved right in, with my three darling kitties, and we stayed the whole time you were gone. Wouldn't you have had a fit if you'd known!

Slyly, she smiled.

I brought their bowls with me, naturally, and their Kitti-Snax. *And* their litter box. I put everything right in your lovely peach bathroom. I hated to leave my babies in such cramped quarters, but I did keep them company as much as I could. Would you believe I graded fifty-seven freshman papers, sitting right there on your seat with the peach plush cover?

"Joan, please let me out."

"Soon," said Joan calmly. "There's no rush. All we're going to do is have lunch."

"Yes, there's a rush. I'm sick, very sick. I'm allergic to something in this bathroom—"

Joan jerked forward. "What? You're sick?"

"Very sick, very very sick. Open the door." Regina's voice was slurred. "Please—I need to go—to the hospital."

Joan's heart started pounding. "You mean, you're sick, *really* sick?" She stood up. Reluctantly, she took a step toward the bathroom. "Regina, my God—" She paused, irresolute.

"I need a shot—of adrenaline—" Regina's voice was a whisper.

"I just can't believe— What have I—" Joan took another couple of steps, slowly.

She had come to the door. Her large, square hand reached out until her fingertips grazed the knob. Again she hesitated.

Behind the door Regina mouthed, "Joan," and sagged to the floor.

Joan's hand closed around the knob, lingered there, and finally withdrew. She tiptoed back to the armchair and resumed her seat, glancing at her watch.

Twelve past noon. What was it Regina had said, that time when Joan had hardly been paying attention?

Oh yes.

"I could die in fifteen minutes."

Gillian Roberts introduced schoolteacher-sleuth Amanda Pepper in Caught Dead in Philadelphia, *winner of the 1987 Anthony for Best First Mystery. Amanda, who teaches at a private Philadelphia high school and has a developing relationship with homicide detective C. K. Mackenzie, also appears in* Philly Stakes *and* I'd Rather Be in Philadelphia. *Roberts is the* nom de mystère *of mainstream writer Judith Greber, whose most recent work,* As Good As It Gets, *chronicles a quarter century of a marriage.*

In "What's a Woman to Do," first impressions count for a lot for a woman in a small town.

WHAT'S A WOMAN TO DO?

by Gillian Roberts

IT WAS AGAINST the rules, eating when you were on duty at the front desk, but he was starving and who would know, anyway? Nobody else on the force would be back for an hour, and this wasn't the kind of town where citizens burst in, needing to see the police.

Easy for the Chief to say it didn't look good to eat out here. Meanwhile, he was stuffing creamed chicken in his face at the Rotary meeting. Besides, nobody was around for it to look bad to.

Will Pritchett extracted his salami and cheese from the bottom drawer of his desk. Delicious. Extra mayo, too. He took a satisfying bite and read the paper. Guy down in Texas had blown away a dozen people. Will gobbled the news story even more eagerly than the sandwich.

Being a cop in a place like Texas where people get pissed and take out an entire luncheonette would be something, all right. It would be like being a *cop*, not like this job had turned out to be.

He was supposed to be filing, but he looked at the bank of metal cabinets with contempt. He hadn't gone to *clerk* academy.

He'd wanted to be a real cop, to curl himself around a doorway, gun at the ready, to handcuff people and read them their rights. Instead, he got stuck with the scut work. Sure, somebody had to do it, like the Chief said, but why him?

The only sounds in the stuffy room were Will's sighs, the wheezing, ancient air conditioner and the tick of the clock, pushing out one more minute. He shuddered. More like a morgue than a police station. Nothing ever happened here.

She clamped her purse under her right arm and walked resolutely, humming "Feelings," head high despite the wilting heat. Years ago, on a day like today, somebody had actually fried an egg on the sidewalk outside her office. The newspaper came and photographed it. Of course, later on, she'd had to clean up the mess herself. Nobody had any real consideration, even back then.

She felt like that sidewalk egg, edges curling and crisping in the sweltering midday heat. The weather pushed at her nowadays with twice the force it had when she was young. Everything did. She was tired. Of coping. Of trying. Of an entire lifetime of taking care of everything by herself. Had to. Nobody helped anybody. Not even when you were young and reasonably attractive and certainly not when you were a gray-haired old lady.

What was done was done. She could live with what she'd had to do, had been doing, in fact, for a lifetime, but what she couldn't live with was having it all be useless. If people would only be considerate. Leave her in peace. She clutched the navy patent handbag closer, pulled at the flower-sprigged dress where it clung damply to her midriff and directed her canvas shoes toward the police station.

The front door squealed, admitting—of all people—Old Doc Maple, the ogre of his adolescence. A lady dentist was a double humiliation, a combination mother and Nazi torturer, tsking if you hadn't brushed enough for her, poking your mouth with crochet hooks, exhaling the hospital smell of cloves with every breath.

If there was one person in the entire town who would definitely rat to the Chief that he'd been eating a salami sandwich while on duty—it was prissy Missy Doctor Hilda Maple. Will shoved meat, cheese, bread, lettuce and wax paper into the bottom desk drawer, and turned to face his caller.

She stood behind the mahogany banister separating the citizens from the force, lumpy in the kind of dress nobody wore, eyes glinting behind tiny glasses perched on her nose. Standard issue Little Old Lady.

He didn't like her. Who would? Such a prig that at Halloween, she gave out toothbrushes and lectures on dental hygiene. He didn't know if she thought she was giving tricks or treats.

"Help you, Dr. Maple?" Pritchett glanced at the clock. Had to get the filing done, but he wasn't going to let her think he was some kind of clerk. He settled behind his desk.

Hilda Maple pulled a handkerchief with embroidered daisies out of her purse. Her hands looked large and strong, the better to yank the teeth out of your skull. He wondered what Little Old Lady terror had freaked her. Fear of night prowlers? A request for bigger street lights? A lost pet?

"I've come to confess, Willie," she said.

Sergeant, he wanted to snap. *Will. William. Never* Willie anymore. What did she think, that he was still her little helpless victim? But confess, she'd said. The old biddy was making a joke for probably the first time in her life. He should ease up. He pulled out a chair for her. "What awful thing'd you do, ma'am? Jaywalk? Or—I know—you're really the Texas Terror and you shot all those people at the luncheonette! Hold on while I get those handcuffs."

She frowned and sat down primly, eyeing him like he was a giant tooth and she was going to find a soft spot she could drill into. He wiped all expression off his face and returned her stare until she looked down at her hands. The balance of power had shifted. Doc was old and little Willie Pritchett was a grown-up cop now and this was his turf and his call.

"This is not a joke," she said. "I am here to confess."

"Right." He folded his hands over his middle and waited. He felt a smile tug at his lips.

"The problem is," she said, "my crime was perfect."

Impossible to keep a straight face. She had little pink cheeks, marshmallow fluff hair, a voice like sugar sparkles and tiny feet in white canvas shoes. Not quite a hardened mastermind of the perfect crime. He hid his grin with his hand and stroked his moustache, to look concerned.

"To whom do I confess?" she asked.

"What you see is what you get. Unless you want to wait until Captain and the rest get back. But for now, I am the law." Portis was out sick, the Chief was out lunching and the rest were gone. There'd been a burglary near the shopping center and kids turning on hydrants on Hollyhock Circle, plus, a child on Twentieth was missing—or more likely misplaced, because in this town, there were more hysterical mothers than there were criminals. God, what he wouldn't give for one good solid kidnapping.

"How are you, Willie?" she asked. "As I recall, you had problems with caries and plaque. I hope you're flossing and practicing good maintenance. You don't want gum disease."

She certainly hadn't changed. He glared. His mouth was no longer her damned business. "What really brings you here, ma'am?" he asked.

She stood up again, ramrod straight. He saw moisture marks under her arm, and it pleased him, made up for her posture.

"I do not believe it is improper or excessive for a respectable homeowner to expect a decent night's sleep." She pulled her head back and into her wrinkled neck, like a turtle. She was waiting for him to say something back.

It was like being in school again, breath held, every eye on him as he silently prayed the question, the teacher and the whole classroom would disappear.

"Don't you agree?" She talked like somebody tasting every word before letting go of it.

"Sure." Sure. Whatever she wanted. The old hen was bonkers.

He'd answered right. She smiled, showing good teeth, like a commercial for herself. "You're only given one set," she used to say, clove breath suffocating little Willie, prisoner on her torture chair. "Cherish it."

"With too little sleep, I get shaky," she now said. "A dentist can't have trembling hands. Could drill right through somebody's cheek if you get the shakes."

"You still practicing, then?" Let her know that not only had he stopped being her patient, but then he didn't keep track of her. Old biddy should have retired by now, anyway. Age, not insomnia, had given her the shakes.

"I'm trying to practice, but how can I if I can't sleep? My home's impossible now, which is why I want to move to one of your cells. I assume it's quiet here at night, that you enforce the rules, do you not?"

"Whoooah. Let me get this straight. You want me to lock you up?" Why did he get all the cranks? Last time it was the guy whose weather stripping talked to him. Now her. "Listen," he said, "is this some kind of— Is Candid Camera out there or something?"

"I believe that constitutionally, as an admitted criminal, I am entitled to a bed here."

Too little sleep and you crack up. He'd seen it in a torture movie. Or it was just age, that old-timer's disease. "Miz Maple, if you're not sleeping good, the doctor could prescribe pills."

"No pill drowns out rock and roll. Nor do earplugs." She bit hard on the edge of every syllable. "They rehearse all night long."

"Who does?"

"The Johnson Five." She said it like it was some world-famous group and like she didn't have a clue how funny it sounded.

He couldn't wait to tell the guys. The Johnson Five. Too much. Wonder if one of the Johnsons was named Michael and moonwalked and had his face redone every other week.

The old lady closed her eyes for so long, he thought maybe she was catching some of those missed Z's.

He remembered her street. Nice houses. A little past their prime, maybe, but big, on comfortable old-fashioned lots. Much better than he had. "So you're here about this . . . Johnson Five?"

She studied her hands.

"Ma'am?" He half didn't know what to call her. "Doc" had always sounded wrong for a teensy little lady. Kids called her "The Dockess," but that wouldn't do for a professional encounter. "Ma'am?" he asked again.

"Hmmm?"

Not only senile, but deaf. The noises she heard started in her head. "You're here because . . . ?"

"They rehearse in their garage. Back of the property. Every night."

"Then you're here to make a complaint? Disturbing the peace?"

She shook her head. "What's the point? It's Lacey's dog all over again."

She was whacko and he was hungry and the air conditioner made the place stink and still be hot and even more than that, damn but he was sick of being a baby-sitter instead of a cop.

"Big, mean skinny thing, Lacey's dog was." She sounded as if she'd told herself the story exactly the same way, lots of times. It made him queasy, like he was a Peeping Tom or something.

"Some mix of breeds that should never have happened," she continued, stiff-lipped. "Mind you, I *like* dogs. But not that big-headed, long-legged, mud-colored thing."

"Lucky thing it's long gone, then," he said. "You were a good judge of that dog's character, considering what he wound up doing."

"Never shut up. A car, a bird, dandelion fluff went by, it went crazy. I'm not a rich woman and I'm not young anymore. My practice isn't what it was. I couldn't pull up stakes and start over again."

"Lacey's dog is *dead*," he reminded her. His words had no effect. She moved ahead dully, noticing nothing else, like a sleepwalker he'd seen on a movie of the week. He checked the clock. Captain would be back soon and royally pissed if none of the filing was done.

"I tried to befriend it. I *like* animals. But it growled, and squinched its yellow eyes. Couldn't go out and enjoy my garden without it barking and yowling and jumping at the chain link, making it rattle and bang until my head pounded and my hands shook."

"Yes, ma'am, well, now, that sounds real bad, but it's *over*. A dead dog can't bother you. Besides, you came here about something else, am I right?"

"That Johnson Five. Just as bad as that dog ever was. Not sleeping again and afraid just like then that I'll drill right through somebody's cheek, or pull the wrong tooth. Lacey's dog all over again!"

The phone rang, and Will grabbed for it, grateful for a reprieve. Weren't allowed to be rude to them. Didn't dare. Even in a nowhere town like this, people were savvy about police harassment charges. Chief gave pep talks about what he called Gross Insensitivity. "Remember that we are civil *servants*," he always said.

"Sergeant Pritchett speaking," Will said smartly. Old Lady Maple looked impressed. She wasn't the only one with a title, after all. But the caller was only Chuck's wife, asking Will to remind her husband to pick up a cabbage on the way home. Will wrote out the message, hoping Doc couldn't read well upside down. Even the idea of cabbage, a vegetable he didn't like, made his mouth water for the salami and cheese in the bottom drawer. Then suddenly, his heart lurched. God help him—what if the mayo had leaked onto something important! Forms were stacked in that drawer, weren't they? Damn!

"You look startled. Emergency?" she asked after he'd hung up the phone.

"It'll wait." He used his favorite tough, seen-it-all voice. "But not too long," he added as warning. Because his ass would be in a sling if Captain found him wasting his time with an old biddy. "So, ma'am," he said. "As I understand it, you're still upset about Lacey's dog."

"Did you ever notice her dentures?" Doc asked.

"The dog had false teeth?"

"Lacey did! Terrible clackers. Maybe they gave her a grudge against dentists, or against life. If you can't chew good, you can't live good is what I always say."

"Ma'am?" He wished he could grab her, shake her a little, get her marbles in place.

"Oh, yes. There'd be a lot less need for head doctors if more people saw tooth doctors, is what I always say."

"About this problem of yours—"

" 'He's my watchdog!' Lacey'd screech if I complained, and with every word, her upper plate practically fell out of her mouth. I said her dog could watch plenty good from inside her house. She told me to buy earplugs. Her plates wobbled and clacked. I offered to make a new set for free. Bad teeth, bad chewing, bad digestion, bad temper, is what I say."

"Dr. Maple, Miss Lacey isn't around anymore, and neither is her dog. In all truth, I don't see the point of—"

"That *is* the point. I tried. I'm a *nice* person. Nothing worked. Then I called you."

"Me? I've only been on the force a year, ma'am, and Miss Lacey—"

"I mean I filed a complaint with the police. I can prove that part at least. You people keep records, don't you?"

Here it was, then, years later, some kind of lawsuit, like Captain always warned about. Old hen had marched over in her tennis shoes to sue the bejesus out of the department while he was all alone here.

She pulled her little body up even straighter. "You people said there was nothing you could do. Law requires more than one complaint, you said, and I was the only one. Only remove dogs who've attacked somebody, you said."

"Look, the laws are there so people can't make wild accu—"

"The lady who lived on the other side of Lacey was deaf. Still is. Speaks with her hands, you know. The whole row of houses backs onto the big stone retaining wall, so who else is there to hear?" Her voice was less sugar and spice and more like twigs crackling in a fire. "Lacey said that if anything happened to that dog, she'd see that I went to jail. I believed her. You people knew I hated him. Even the deaf woman knew. Isn't that enough proof?"

Proof of what? That she had a complaint against the department? That she was batty? "You know, ma'am Doctor, you said you came about a problem you had *now*." Wanted to be locked up because she couldn't sleep, wasn't that it? He was a trained listener, but this was too much. Her mind wandered all over hell and back. Old Toni Lacey and her dog had been dead and not much missed for a couple years now. "How can we help you?" She was normal enough looking on the outside, but inside, all loose wires. Women went rotten dangerously fast, much quicker than men. This one shouldn't be allowed to handle sharp instruments anymore.

"I don't expect you to help me. Nobody has before. Not once. Always leave me to take care of it on my own. That's why I'm saying this time, give me a quiet cell and a good mattress. I'm too old to do it again."

"Do what? File a complaint?"

She shook her fluff of hair and pursed her mouth. "Take matters in my own hands, you know. Like the other times."

"And which times were they, ma'am?" She looked planted into the floor and likely to stay for days. He smiled to warm her up, then clamped his mouth shut because he wasn't sure the condition of his teeth would pass her inspection. "Ma'am," he said, more loudly than intended, "don't mean to be rude, but hope you don't mind if I work while you talk. Have to take care of some papers." There, that sounded important enough.

He walked to the bank of files and half turned from her as he pulled a stapled set of forms out of the wire basket on top of one cabinet. "Continue," he said. "I'm listening." All ears. Right.

"What happened is this. One day when Lacey went to the market, I put steak next to the fence. Her stupid animal came right over."

Oh how he'd dreamed about chasing robbers, finding clues. Being a hero. Not about sweating and filing and enduring a growling stomach while listening to whackos with nobody but him to talk to. Because he was a civil *servant*.

"Soon as his neck was near the chain link, I gave him a shot."

"Wait a minute." He looked over at her. Her purse was under

her right arm and her hands were folded in front like a schoolgirl reciting a well-practiced piece. "Who'd you shoot again?"

"The dog."

But Lacey's dog hadn't been shot. Best to simply ignore the woman and get the filing done or the Chief would blame him, like always, even though it wasn't his fault. He looked at the file in his hand. McHooley. Never had gotten it straight if the "Mc" names went before or after the regular "M's."

"When he was out cold," the dentist continued, "I skittled over there into her yard. I must confess, I was rather excited. This was pretty much the professional challenge of my career, you see. I'd prepared a really good mold. Had to work fast, of course, because that stuff hardens like that." She snapped her fingers. "Otherwise, people gag too much. Don't know if you need it that fast for a dog, actually. Don't know if a dog's gag reflex is the same."

He shoved McHooley at the back of the M's while he wondered if he'd really heard the Dockess say she'd put mold on the dog and it hardened and gagged.

"Left him by the fence to sleep off the anesthesia. That was the first quiet afternoon in my garden in a long, long time." She paused and took a deep breath. "Excuse me," she said. "Willie?"

Will turned and faced her directly.

"Shouldn't I be writing this out or dictating it into a machine?"

"Well, ah . . ." What form did they use for hogwash and imaginary confessions? And then, where would he file it? "We'll do that in just a while," Will said. "Meanwhile, I'm trying to get a sense of just what kind of complaint you have." Because I am a *civil* servant.

"But I don't have a complaint. I'm confessing!" Her voice was suddenly shrill.

He rolled his eyes. They'd taught this in training. Lonely people need to feel big, confess crimes they didn't commit. But the cases they talked about at the academy had style. Those people claimed they were serial killers, hijackers, major-league embezzlers. Even the L.O.L's imagination was feeble, ending at her garden fence and a moldy dog the Humane Society had put to sleep years ago.

"Sure, of course," he said, "but all the same, um, why don't we run through your . . . confession . . . once. Kind of a . . . rehearsal. So it's fresh and clear in your mind. It's standard procedure."

"And that is exactly what's wrong with this country today! Bureaucratic rules and routines! Inefficiency! Duplication, everything in triplicate. But all right, then. The dog slept it off most of the afternoon, but he was back to himself by dark, and he barked all night long."

Will tsked sympathetically. Anybody still complaining about being kept up by a long-dead dog needed handling with kid gloves.

"However," she said with her schoolmarm enunciation, "that particular night, I didn't mind his barking because I didn't intend to sleep, anyway. I worked straight through in my lab. Years before, I had learned to run in essence my own laboratory. I had a run-in with a lab man because I was female. Sexual harassment didn't start with the young women of today."

Exactly what he wanted, a noontime lecture on women's rights.

"But," she said, "the lab man was long ago, in a different city and there's no point in discussing him."

Maybe, just to shake her up, shut her up, he should do what she wanted: book her and throw her in a cell. But the Chief would kill him. He could just see the headlines about police brutality with a photo of Hilda Maple behind bars, her white hair like fake Christmas snow.

"The point of the lab man, however," she said, "is that way back when, I learned to do my own lab work, and to do it perfectly. I'm a perfectionist, you see. That night in particular, my work was superb. I wished I could have shown them off. In fact, today, the thought struck me that when I'm incarcerated, I might write it up for a professional journal."

Lady, lady, you need a shrink and I need food. He wondered if he should call an ambulance, have her institutionalized for her own good and the safety of all the little victims she still tortured.

"The next day, I went over," the light little voice continued. "Lacey was making tea. She told me to get out, threatened to pour boiling water on me. I tried reasoning with her. I *like* people. I'm a *good* neighbor. But she was impossible, so I just plain grabbed her and stuck in the needle. Same stuff I gave the dog. First, she opened up to scream. I tell you, the sight of those ill-fitting, shoddy false teeth of hers made *me* want to scream. Her eyes got fluttery and closed, and I clamped those doggie dentures onto her neck and let them bite down, hard. Very hard."

"Dentures? False teeth for dogs?"

"Well, not *for* the dog, really. But if dogs wore them, these would have been the best. I am a perfectionist."

"Now listen, ma'am—"

"I know what you're about to say. There's more to it than a bite mark. Forensic science, am I right?"

He had no idea what she was talking about. Besides, Nichols had misspelled a name again. Was anybody really named Shcwartz? He'd file it the way it said, and then guess who would get in trouble when the file couldn't be found?

"I know you people check things out, so I'd collected some of the dog's saliva, too, when I took the impression. Your labs would question the authenticity of the bite otherwise."

He looked at her. She looked so earnest. So sincere. Was it maybe possible that she had really made a set of dog teeth and bitten old Lacey to death?

"If you check your files there, you'll see that everything I'm telling you is accurate," she said mildly.

She melted back into Mrs. Santa with her halo of cotton batting. God! She'd had him going for a second. Of course her story would mesh with the files. She'd had years to work on it. It meant nothing. Nothing meant anything except his getting the filing done. He was in enough trouble with the Chief already without dragging the Case of the Crazy Lady Dentist in front of him, creating more work for everybody and more filing for himself.

"When she was quite dead, I took her teapot." Doc Maple's voice was eager and precise. "The one she was going to throw on me. I poured some of the steaming water on the floor, then I opened the door. The monstrous dog started at me, but I had steak ready again and as soon as he took it, I shot the needle in him, too, and he went ga-ga. I poured the rest of the boiling water on his paw. I was sorry about that, but it was necessary. It must have stung when he woke up. Then I dropped the kettle on the floor and put the pot holder next to it."

Two years since old lady Lacey died. Maybe living next door to all the hullabaloo at the time had given Doc Maple a—what was it? he'd just read about it—a trauma. Maybe she was in post-traumatic shock. He sighed and turned around.

"And you know the rest of the story," she said.

Everybody did. It was ancient history. Lacey and her dog were long since buried next to each other, like Lacey had requested in her will. There'd been a lot of flak about that, you can bet. Even an editorial in the paper. After all, Miss Lacey had made that request before her dog turned. But people said to leave it for pet and master heaven, where the dog could forgive Lacey for pouring boiling water on his paw and Lacey could forgive him for reacting with his teeth on—or in, really—her neck.

"Yes, indeed, I know that story," Will said, standing straight, sucking in his gut and allowing himself a slight professional scowl. Enough was enough.

"But what I said was *true*!"

"Of course it was." He went back to his desk, worry gnawing at him as much as hunger did. He gently open the bottom desk drawer and saw his worst fears confirmed. Leaking mayonnaise had made the Form 15-A's transparent. Damn. How would he explain this one? He closed the drawer and turned back to her. "Look, ma'am," he said briskly, "we need some proof, some evidence of your, ah, alleged crime."

She shook her head. "I destroyed everything when it happened. I had no idea I'd ever want to be caught."

"Well, then." His stomach growled.

"You won't give me a cell?"

"Oh, Doc Maple. Come on. They're for criminals."

She turned and walked away.

"But you came here about that band!" he called after her. "Didn't you want to file a complaint?"

"What's the use? It still takes two complaints and the deaf

woman is still there on the other side and the wall is still in the back. All my life I've known that if I wanted something done, I'd have to do it myself. I was hoping this one time would be different." She sighed. "Never mind, then." She pushed the door open and was gone.

Imagine that. He stared at the door as if her afterimage were still on it. Hallucinating that she'd killed somebody with false teeth. Once a dentist, always a dentist. Wait till he told the guys. But what would he do with those greasy forms?

She should have known better. Did she think that knights still roamed the land looking to save damsels in distress? Even if they did, men in armor didn't rush to the aid of gray-haired damsels. Nobody did. She'd have to do it herself. Again.

She didn't count the ones when she was really young, or even the dorm roommate and that god-awful woman in the apartment next to hers, the one who screamed all the time. You couldn't blame the police for not helping with those problems because she hadn't even asked them to. She was pretty cocky about taking care of everything herself back in those days.

As for the lab man, who could she have asked for help? There weren't even laws against that sort of thing back then, the dirty things he said, the way he "accidentally on purpose" bumped and rubbed against her. A woman was on her own in those days. It still made her smile to have poisoned him with a dentifrice. Sodium perborate, and how appropriate. A cleaning agent to permanently clean—and close—a filthy mouth.

After the roommate and the screamer and the lab man, she'd rented a house in a new neighborhood and expected peace and quiet, but she never got her wishes, no matter how simple they were. Because in that house, there'd been Charlie Mallory next door with his so-called antique car collection. Hammering, battering, and gunning of motors! She'd gone to the police that time, but they were as dim and insensitive a group as they were here, so she took care of it. Charlie was gone all day long, so tinkering with his precious car wasn't much of a problem. She knew physics and chemistry. Dentists had scientific minds, after all.

The explosion left a mess, though. They buried what was left of Charlie, and that should have been that, but car debris was all over, even in her backyard. Then the landlord, who owned both houses, raised her rent for repairs. Wasn't fair and she didn't like the bombed-out look next door, so she'd moved here, where she was positive things would be better. Except then, bad luck again when Lacey got her dog.

It would have been nice if the police hadn't left it to her to take care of the Lacey problem, but on the other hand, she'd had the chance to rise to the challenge and be creative. The dentures were much more inventive than the poisons and the bomb had been.

She sighed. Maybe she'd peaked with those false teeth. Certainly didn't have as good an idea about the Johnson Five. No cars, and the Johnsons' only pets were tropical fish. But there was that pool they'd dug—and what a racket the workers had made! A swimming accident, perhaps, while drugged? Everybody knew about teenagers, especially the musical ones. Laughing gas, maybe?

Why did people keep doing this to her? Keep creating these situations?

The drummer first. Definitely the worst of them.

Or maybe electrocution in the pool? They kept speakers and guitars with wires and all manner of things too close to the water.

It was possible that they'd replace the drummer, that the rest of them would have to go, too.

Perhaps a car accident? A few of them all at once, that way, and heaven knew they drove too fast, that kind, so maybe . . .

But even after she took care of all five Johnsons, there'd still be more to do. She was sick and tired of the police's insensitivity. Patronizing her that way, that stupid Willie with the film on his teeth!

What good were laws if they didn't apply to the important things? And who needed police if they didn't enforce anything? She'd be doing a public service, getting rid of them, easing the tax rolls.

Willie had always been obnoxious, even as a child. He'd be a good place to start—right after the Johnsons.

Little Willie Pritchett shouldn't be much of a problem. She remembered how he'd come into her office years ago, bits of food still lodged between his teeth. Always eating, that one. And even today, she'd seen him shove a sandwich in the desk drawer, seen the glob of mayonnaise caught on his poorly shaved chin. A piggy man. So food it would be. At work. Something he could sneak. Something quick . . .

She walked carefully, brow slightly wrinkled, a little old lady in a flowered dress and tennis shoes humming "Feelings." Nobody noticed her.

Sara Paretsky, founder and first president of Sisters in Crime, is the creator of V. I. Warshawski, a tough, Chicago-based private investigator with strong ties to the neighborhood in which she grew up and a keen personal sense of justice. The seven books in the V. I. Warshawski series include Blood Shot, *winner of a British Crime Writers Silver Dagger award and an Anthony nominee, and, most recently,* Guardian Angel. *Sara is also the editor of* Eye of a Woman, *an anthology of short stories by women, all featuring women sleuths.*

In "The Takamoku Joseki,*" first published in* Alfred Hitchcock's Mystery Magazine, *V. I. Warshawski learns a new game and solves a murder at the same time.*

THE TAKAMOKU *JOSEKI*

by Sara Paretsky

Written for S. Courtenay Wright
Christmas Day, 1982

I

MR. AND MRS. Takamoku were a quiet, hardworking couple. Although they had lived in Chicago since the 1940s, when they were relocated from an Arizona detention camp, they spoke only halting English. Occasionally I ran into Mrs. Takamoku in the foyer of the old three-flat we both lived in on Belmont, or at the corner grocery store. We would exchange a few stilted sentences. She knew I lived alone in my third-floor apartment, and she worried about it, although her manners were too perfect for her to come right out and tell me to get myself a husband.

As time passed, I learned about her son, Akira, and her daughter, Yoshio, both professionals living on the West Coast. I always inquired after them, which pleased her.

With great difficulty I got her to understand that I was a private detective. This troubled her; she often wanted to know if I were doing something dangerous, and would shake her head and frown as she asked. I didn't see Mr. Takamoku often. He worked for a printer and usually left long before me in the morning.

Unlike the De Paul students who formed an ever-changing collage on the second floor, the Takamokus did little entertaining, or at least little noisy entertaining. Every Sunday afternoon a procession of Asians came to their apartment, spent a quiet afternoon, and left. One or more Caucasians would join them, incongruous by their height and color. After a while, I recognized the regulars: a tall, bearded white man, and six or seven Japanese and Koreans.

One Sunday evening in late November I was eating sushi and drinking sake in a storefront restaurant on Halsted. The Takamokus came in as I was finishing my first little pot of sake. I smiled and waved at them, and watched with idle amusement as they conferred earnestly, darting glances at me. While they argued, a waitress brought them bowls of noodles and a plate of sushi; they were clearly regular customers with regular tastes.

At last, Mr. Takamoku came over to my table. I invited him and his wife to join me.

"Thank you, thank you," he said in an agony of embarrassment. "We only have question for you, not to disturb you."

"You're not disturbing me. What do you want to know?"

"You are familiar with American customs." That was a statement, not a question. I nodded, wondering what was coming.

"When a guest behaves badly in the house, what does an American do?"

I gave him my full attention. I had no idea what he was asking, but he would never have brought it up just to be frivolous.

"It depends," I said carefully. "Did they break up your sofa or spill tea?"

Mr. Takamoku looked at me steadily, fishing for a cigarette. Then he shook his head, slowly. "Not as much as breaking furniture. Not as little as tea on sofa. In between."

"I'd give him a second chance."

A slight crease erased itself from Mr. Takamoku's forehead. "A second chance. A very good idea. A second chance."

He went back to his wife and ate his noodles with the noisy appreciation that showed good Japanese manners. I had another pot of sake and finished about the same time as the Takamokus; we left the restaurant together. I topped them by a good five inches and perhaps twenty pounds, so I slowed my pace to a crawl to keep step with them.

Mrs. Takamoku smiled. "You are familiar with Go?" she asked, giggling nervously.

"I'm not sure," I said cautiously, wondering if they wanted me to conjugate an intransitive irregular verb.

"It's a game. You have time to stop and see?"

"Sure," I agreed, just as Mr. Takamoku broke in with vigorous objections.

I couldn't tell whether he didn't want to inconvenience me or didn't want me intruding. However, Mrs. Takamoku insisted, so I stopped at the first floor and went into the apartment with her.

The living room was almost bare. The lack of furniture drew the eye to a beautiful Japanese doll on a stand in one corner, with a bowl of dried flowers in front of her. The only other furnishings were six little tables in a row. They were quite thick and stood low on carved wooden legs. Their tops, about eighteen inches square, were crisscrossed with black lines which formed dozens of little squares. Two covered wooden bowls stood on each table.

"Go-ban," Mrs. Takamoku said, pointing to one of the tables.

I shook my head in incomprehension.

Mr. Takamoku picked up a covered bowl. It was filled with smooth white disks, the size of nickels but much thicker. I held one up and saw beautiful shades and shadows in it.

"Clamshell," Mr. Takamoku said. "They cut, then polish." He picked up a second bowl, filled with black disks. "Shale."

He knelt on a cushion in front of one of the tables and rapidly placed black and white disks on intersections of the lines. A pattern emerged.

"This is Go. Black plays, then white, then black, then white. Each tries to make territory, to make eyes." He showed me an "eye"—a clear space surrounded by black stones. "White cannot play here. Black is safe. Now white must play someplace else."

"I see." I didn't really, but I didn't think it mattered.

"This afternoon, someone knock stones from table, turn upside down, and scrape with knife."

"This table?" I asked, tapping the one he was playing on.

"Yes." He swept the stones off swiftly but carefully, and put them in their little pots. He turned the board over. In the middle was a hole, carved and sanded. The wood was very thick—I suppose the hole gave it resonance.

I knelt beside him and looked. I was probably thirty years younger, but I couldn't tuck my knees under me with his grace and ease: I sat cross-legged. A faint scratch marred the sanded bottom.

"Was he American?"

Mr. and Mrs. Takamoku exchanged a look. "Japanese, but born in America," she said. "Like Akira and Yoshio."

I shook my head. "I don't understand. It's not an American custom." I climbed awkwardly back to my feet. Mr. Takamoku stood with one easy movement. He and Mrs. Takamoku thanked me profusely. I assured them it was nothing and went to bed.

II

The next Sunday was a cold, gray day with a hint of snow. I sat in front of the television, in my living room, drinking coffee, dividing my attention between November's income and watching the Bears. Both were equally feeble. I was trying to decide on something friendlier to do when a knock sounded on my door. The outside buzzer hadn't rung. I got up, stacking loose papers on one arm of the chair and balancing the coffee cup on the other.

Through the peephole I could see Mrs. Takamoku. I opened the door. Her wrinkled ivory face was agitated, her eyes dilated. "Oh, good, good, you are here. You must come." She tugged at my hand.

I pulled her gently into the apartment. "What's wrong? Let me get you a drink."

"No, no." She wrung her hands in agitation, repeating that I must come, I must come.

I collected my keys and went down the worn, uncarpeted stairs with her. Her living room was filled with cigarette smoke and a crowd of anxious men. Mr. Takamoku detached himself from the group and hurried over to his wife and me. He clasped my hand and pumped it up and down.

"Good. Good you came. You are a detective, yes? You will see the police do not arrest Naoe and me."

"What's wrong, Mr. Takamoku?"

"He's dead. He's killed. Naoe and I were in camp during World War. They will arrest us."

"Who's dead?"

He shrugged helplessly. "I don't know name."

I pushed through the group. A white man lay sprawled on the floor. His face had contorted in dreadful pain as he died, so it was hard to guess his age. His fair hair was thick and unmarked with gray; he must have been relatively young.

A small dribble of vomit trailed from his clenched teeth. I sniffed at it cautiously. Probably hydrocyanic acid. Not far from his body lay a teacup, a Japanese cup without handles. The contents sprayed out from it like a Rorschach. Without touching it, I sniffed again. The fumes were still discernible.

I got up. "Has anyone left since this happened?"

The tall, bearded Caucasian I'd noticed on previous Sundays looked around and said "No" in an authoritative voice.

"And have you called the police?"

Mrs. Takamoku gave an agitated cry. "No police. No. You are detective. You find murderer yourself."

I shook my head and took her gently by the hand. "If we don't call the police, they will put us all in jail for concealing a murder. You must tell them."

The bearded man said, "I'll do that."

"Who are you?"

"I'm Charles Welland. I'm a physicist at the University of Chicago, but on Sundays I'm a Go player."

"I see . . . I'm V. I. Warshawski. I live upstairs. I'm a private investigator. The police look very dimly on all citizens who don't report murders, but especially on P.I.'s."

Welland went into the dining room, where the Takamokus kept their phone. I told the Takamokus and their guests that no one could leave before the police gave them permission, then followed Welland to make sure he didn't call anyone besides the police, or take the opportunity to get rid of a vial of poison.

The Go players seemed resigned, albeit very nervous. All of them smoked ferociously; the thick air grew bluer. They split into small groups, five Japanese together, four Koreans in another clump. A lone Chinese fiddled with the stones on one of the Gobans.

None of them spoke English well enough to give a clear account of how the young man died. When Welland came back, I asked him for a detailed report.

The physicist claimed not to know his name. The dead man had only been coming to the Go club the last month or two.

"Did someone bring him? Or did he just show up one day?"

Welland shrugged. "He just showed up. Word gets around among Go players. I'm sure he told me his name—it just didn't stick. I think he worked for Hansen Electronic, the big computer firm."

I asked if everyone there was a regular player. Welland knew all of them by sight, if not by name. They didn't all come every Sunday, but none of the others was a newcomer.

"I see. Okay. What happened today?"

Welland scratched his beard. He had bushy, arched eyebrows which jumped up to punctuate his stronger statements. I thought that was pretty sexy. I pulled my mind back to what he was saying.

"I got here around one-thirty. I think three games were in progress. This guy"—he jerked his thumb toward the dead man—"arrived a bit later. He and I played a game. Then Mr. Hito arrived and the two of them had a game. Dr. Han showed up, and he and I were playing when the whole thing happened. Mrs. Takamoku sets out tea and snacks. We all wander around and help ourselves. About four, this guy took a swallow of tea, gave a terrible cry, and died."

"Is there anything important about the game they were playing?"

Welland looked at the board. A handful of black-and-white stones stood on the corner points. He shook his head. "They'd just started. It looks like our dead friend was trying one of the Takamoku *joseki*. That's a complicated one—I've never seen it used in actual play before."

"What's that? Anything to do with Mr. Takamoku?"

"The *joseki* are the beginning moves in the corners. Takamoku is this one"—he pointed at the far side—"where black plays on the five-four point—the point where the fourth and fifth lines intersect. It wasn't named for our host. That's just coincidence."

III

Sergeant McGonnigal didn't find out much more than I did. A thickset young detective, he had a lot of experience and treated his frightened audience gently. He was a little less kind to me, demanding roughly why I was there, what my connection with the dead man was, who my client was. It didn't cheer him up any to hear I was working for the Takamokus, but he let me stay with them while he questioned them. He sent for a young Korean officer to interrogate the Koreans in the group. Welland, who spoke fluent Japanese, translated the Japanese interviews. Dr. Han, the lone Chinese, struggled along on his own.

McGonnigal learned that the dead man's name was Peter Folger. He learned that people were milling around all the time watching each other play. He also learned that no one paid attention to anything but the game they were playing, or watching.

"The Japanese say the Go player forgets his father's funeral," Welland explained. "It's a game of tremendous concentration."

No one admitted knowing Folger outside the Go club. No one knew how he found out that the Takamokus hosted Go every Sunday.

My clients hovered tensely in the background, convinced that

McGonnigal would arrest them at any minute. But they could add nothing to the story. Anyone who wanted to play was welcome at their apartment on Sunday afternoon. Why should he show a credential? If he knew how to play, that was the proof.

McGonnigal pounced on that. Was Folger a good player? Everyone looked around and nodded. Yes, not the best—that was clearly Dr. Han or Mr. Kim, one of the Koreans—but quite good enough. Perhaps first *kyu*, whatever that was.

After two hours of this, McGonnigal decided he was getting nowhere. Someone in the room must have had a connection with Folger, but we weren't going to find it by questioning the group. We'd have to dig into their backgrounds.

A uniformed man started collecting addresses while McGonnigal went to his car to radio for plainclothes reinforcements. He wanted everyone in the room tailed and wanted to call from a private phone. A useless precaution, I thought: the innocent wouldn't know they were being followed, and the guilty would expect it.

McGonnigal returned shortly, his face angry. He had a bland-faced, square-jawed man in tow, Derek Hatfield of the FBI. He did computer fraud for them. Our paths had crossed a few times on white-collar crime. I'd found him smart and knowledgeable, but also humorless and overbearing.

"Hello, Derek," I said, without getting up from the cushion I was sitting on. "What brings you here?"

"He had the place under surveillance," McGonnigal said, biting off the words. "He won't tell me who he was looking for."

Derek walked over to Folger's body, covered now with a sheet, which he pulled back. He looked at Folger's face and nodded. "I'm going to have to phone my office for instructions."

"Just a minute," McGonnigal said. "You know the guy, right? You tell me what you were watching him for."

Derek raised his eyebrows haughtily. "I'll have to make a call first."

"Don't be an ass, Hatfield," I said. "You think you're impressing us with how mysterious the FBI is, but you're not, really. You know your boss will tell you to cooperate with the city if it's murder. And we might be able to clear this thing up right now, glory for everyone. We know Folger worked for Hansen Electronic. He wasn't one of your guys working undercover, was he?"

Hatfield glared at me. "I can't answer that."

"Look," I said reasonably. "Either he worked for you and was investigating problems at Hansen, or he worked for them and you suspected he was involved in some kind of fraud. I know there's a lot of talk about Hansen's new Series J computer—was he passing secrets?"

Hatfield put his hands in his pockets and scowled in thought. At last he said, to McGonnigal, "Is there some place we can go and talk?"

I asked Mrs. Takamoku if we could use her kitchen for a few minutes. Her lips moved nervously, but she took Hatfield and me down the hall. Her apartment was laid out like mine and the kitchens were similar, at least in appliances. Hers was spotless; mine had that lived-in look.

McGonnigal told the uniformed man not to let anyone leave or make any phone calls, and followed us.

Hatfield leaned against the back door. I perched on a bar stool next to a high wooden table. McGonnigal stood in the doorway leading to the hall.

"You got someone here named Miyake?" Hatfield asked.

McGonnigal looked through the sheaf of notes in his hand and shook his head.

"Anyone here work for Kawamoto?"

Kawamoto is a big Japanese electronics firm, one of Mitsubishi's peers and a strong rival of Hansen in the megacomputer market.

"Hatfield, are you trying to tell us that Folger was passing Series J secrets to someone from Kawamoto over the Go boards here?"

Hatfield shifted uncomfortably. "We only got onto it three weeks ago. Folger was just a go-between. We offered him immunity if he would finger the guy from Kawamoto. He couldn't describe him well enough for us to make a pickup. He was going to shake hands with him or touch him in some way as they left the building."

"The Judas trick," I remarked.

"Huh?" Hatfield looked puzzled.

McGonnigal smiled for the first time that afternoon. "The man I kiss is the one you want. You should've gone to Catholic school, Hatfield."

"Yeah. Anyway, Folger must've told this guy Miyake we were closing in." Hatfield shook his head disgustedly. "Miyake must be part of that group, just using an assumed name. We got a tail put on all of them." He straightened up and started back toward the hall.

"How was Folger passing the information?" I asked.

"It was on microdots."

"Stay where you are. I might be able to tell you which one is Miyake without leaving the building."

Of course, both Hatfield and McGonnigal started yelling at me at once. Why was I suppressing evidence, what did I know, they'd have me arrested.

"Calm down, boys," I said. "I don't have any evidence. But now that I know the crime, I think I know how it was done. I just need to talk to my clients."

Mr. and Mrs. Takamoku looked at me anxiously when I came back to the living room. I got them to follow me into the hall. "They're not going to arrest you," I assured them. "But I need to know who turned over the Go board last week. Is he here today?"

They talked briefly in Japanese, then Mr. Takamoku said, "We should not betray guest. But murder is much worse. Man in orange shirt, named Hamai."

Hamai, or Miyake, as Hatfield called him, resisted valiantly. When the police started to put handcuffs on him, he popped a gelatin capsule into his mouth. He was dead almost before they realized what he had done.

Hatfield, impersonal as always, searched his body for the microdot. Hamai had stuck it to his upper lip, where it looked like a mole against his dark skin.

IV

"How did you know?" McGonnigal grumbled, after the bodies had been carted off and the Takamokus' efforts to turn their life savings over to me successfully averted.

"He turned over a Go board here last week. That troubled my clients enough that they asked me about it. Once I knew we were looking for the transfer of information, it was obvious that Folger had stuck the dot in the hole under the board. Hamai couldn't get at it, so he had to turn the whole board over. Today, Folger must have put it in a more accessible spot."

Hatfield left to make his top-secret report. McGonnigal followed his uniformed men out of the apartment. Welland held the door for me.

"Was his name Hamai or Miyake?"

"Oh, I think his real name was Hamai—that's what all his identification said. He must have used a false name with Folger. After all, he knew you guys never pay attention to each other's names—you probably wouldn't even notice what Folger called him. If you could figure out who Folger was."

Welland smiled; his busy eyebrows danced. "How about a drink? I'd like to salute a lady clever enough to solve the Takamoku *joseki* unaided."

I looked at my watch. Three hours ago I'd been trying to think of something friendlier to do than watch the Bears get pummeled. This sounded like a good bet. I slipped my hand through his arm and went outside with him.

Sister Carol Anne O'Marie, a teacher in Catholic schools in California and Arizona for twenty years, counts among her honors a second place prize in the cable car bell ringing contest in San Francisco. Currently the director of a shelter for homeless women, called A Friendly Place, Sister Carol Anne is an advocate, in fiction and in life, of the positive value of humor. Her four novels, most recently Murder in Ordinary Time, *all feature Sister Mary Helen, "a seventysomething nun who continually stumbles into murders."*

In "A Friendly Place," Sister Mary Helen confirms the value of a good laugh . . . and discovers the limits of friendliness.

A FRIENDLY PLACE

by Sister Carol Anne O'Marie, CSJ

"IT'S ONLY FOR a week, Sister Mary Helen. Please!" Sister Agnes's high-pitched voice penetrated the telephone wires. "Are you still there, Mary Helen? You are still there, aren't you?"

"Yes, of course, I'm here. It's just that you took me by surprise. Now again, Agnes—and slow down this time—what exactly do you want me to do?"

"Oh, thank God! I was afraid that we were cut off, or worse yet, that you hung up. What I want you to do is nothing really. Just be here with me. As a backup more than anything else."

"A backup for what?"

"Sister Barbara was called to jury duty and, it being summer, many of our volunteers are on vacation. So what I need is a warm body to be here with me, just in case. . . ." She let the sentence trail off, and Mary Helen did not care to ask, "In case of what?"

For several years, Sister Agnes and Sister Barbara with a loyal band of volunteers had successfully run A Friendly Place, a daytime drop-in center for homeless women in downtown Oakland.

To Mary Helen's way of thinking, the center had proved to be very friendly, indeed, since it served as many as a thousand women a month.

Although, since it opened, the center had experienced little more violence than one smashed chair and a few BB holes in the front windows, it didn't take much imagination to know that the potential was not very far away. Especially during these long, hot summer days. Of course, Agnes should not be there alone.

Sister Mary Helen was just about to accept the invitation, but Agnes's words tumbled on. "I realize that you are retired now and that this might be an imposition."

Mary Helen's spine stiffened and she adjusted her bifocals. Retired, indeed! Several years ago, just after her seventy-fifth birthday, she had moved to Mount St. Francis College for Women, her order's college in San Francisco, and she hadn't had an idle day since, what with her work in the college's alumnae office. Then, there were those bizarre murders that she'd stumbled across. If the truth be known, she was happy to get away from Mount St. Francis, even if only for one week. She would call it her vacation.

"Of course, you could come to the center a little later in the day, if you need extra rest," Agnes added.

"I'll come!" Mary Helen snapped before Agnes said another word. For all of her sincerity and good works, tiny Sister Agnes was one of those people who could talk you into something and then, before you knew it, right out of it again. Mary Helen figured that "over-talk" was the occupational hazard of the very enthusiastic.

"You will?" Agnes sounded surprised.

"Of course, I will," Mary Helen answered and quickly hung up the phone.

On Monday morning, armed with her suitcase and several paperback murder mysteries for nighttime reading, Sister Mary Helen drove the convent's green Nova across the lower deck of the San Francisco–Oakland Bay Bridge.

Watching the sun dance on the Oakland hills, she knew that she had made the right decision. Her spirits rose. Although the city was a mere five miles east of San Francisco, the difference in the weather was striking. Whereas San Francisco summers were notoriously foggy, Oakland, stretching along the mainland side of the Bay, could always be counted on for sunshine. Furthermore, it was years since Sister Mary Helen had lived in a small convent or worked with the economically poor. She looked forward to both, even though it was only for one short week.

Following Agnes's directions, Mary Helen took the West Grand Avenue exit off the bridge and found herself in Oakland. As she neared the downtown, the old nun knew that she was in the right neighborhood. Several men pushed shopping carts piled high with debris. An ageless woman, layered with clothes, clung to a large, black plastic bag. A scantily dressed young girl stood against a telephone pole waving her arms and cheerfully calling to the passing cars.

Mary Helen felt a twinge of uneasiness as she drove by a small triangular park littered with papers, broken glass and sleeping bodies. What kind of a world am I getting into? she thought. As if to answer, two men on the curb cursed each other in loud, strident tones.

Just ahead, Mary Helen spotted a group of women gathered in front of a squat sandstone building. A quick address check assured her that she had arrived at A Friendly Place. Without too much trouble, she found the fenced-off lot where Agnes had insisted that she park the Nova.

A massive black woman with a long red wig cascading over her bare shoulders stood in front of the center. With a quick motion, she crushed out her cigarette; then she adjusted the elastic-waisted shirt that, stretched to its limits, covered her enormous bosom like a strapless halter.

"How-do?" Sister Mary Helen said, ringing the front doorbell. She hoped that she wasn't staring, but she could hardly take her eyes off the woman who stood at least six feet tall.

"You don't need to ring that thing, honey," the woman said. "All you needs to do is pull." She demonstrated. "See?"

"I'm Glenda," she said to introduce herself, then gave Mary Helen an amazingly sweet smile. "You all follow me."

Without a moment's hesitation, Mary Helen followed. She didn't know what she had expected, but it was certainly not what she saw. The center's main room was bright and cheerful and filled with small tables and chairs and vases of fresh flowers. There was art on the walls and soft music in the background. Women sat at the tables reading, working jigsaw puzzles, or chatting with one another. Everything about the place was genuinely friendly.

"Oh, here you are. Welcome!" Agnes scurried across the crowded room and gave Mary Helen an expansive hug. "Let me show you around," she said and took Mary Helen on a quick yet thorough tour.

"Minute I saw her, I knew she was a Sister," Glenda announced when the two nuns reentered the main room.

The other women turned to watch Sister Mary Helen.

"Didn't I know you was a Sister, Babe?" Glenda giggled and winked at her.

The old nun, who could not remember the last time, if ever, that she had been addressed as "Babe," winked back. "You surely did," she said.

Glenda hooted. To Mary Helen's amazement, from that moment on, most of the women, "guests" as Agnes called them, seemed to accept her unquestioningly.

By the afternoon, Mary Helen realized that her main job at Agnes's Friendly Place was to listen. Tiny, quick Agnes covered the area like a miniature defensive linebacker, replenishing the coffeepot and snack tray, doling out towels for showers, soap for the washing machines, extra socks and T-shirts, giving hugs, and even answering the telephone before it reached the third ring.

And so she listened to Caroline, who talked to herself and everyone else in a kind of jibberish, and to Betty, with the impassive face and the hard, dark eyes that smoldered with rage. She listened to Letitia, who sat alone and leafed through magazines, and to Greta, who filled her plastic sack with bits of bread to feed the birds.

She listened with real interest because she found these women genuinely interesting.

She was especially fascinated by Glenda with the long red wig. By Tuesday afternoon, it was apparent to Mary Helen that Glenda always sat at the same table. Shortly after she arrived each morning, her friends, Jackie, Dorothy and Passion, ambled in to join her. As soon as they poured their coffee, the four women began to talk long, hard, and very quietly about "our business." Although Mary Helen caught only snatches of their conversation, she couldn't help but wonder just exactly what their business was.

What was it that they had in common? Certainly not looks. Jackie was a stout woman with one walleye and skin the color of coffee with cream. Dorothy was painfully thin, with a pasty-white face and a cast on her right arm. She didn't speak much. Passion, whose ebony skin shone, was set off from the others by the enormous emerald-green earring that she wore in her left nostril.

Soon after the center opened on Thursday morning, Mary Helen was surprised to hear Glenda call from her table, "Come on over here, will you, Babe? We needs to talk to you about our business."

Mary Helen crossed the room, trying not to look thrilled. All week long she had been dying to be included in their conversation. She itched to know what possible business kept them talking to one another for all those hours.

"Get yourself a cup of coffee, Babe," Glenda suggested.

"We wants to talk to you." Passion studied her face while Jackie and Dorothy, looking wary, made room at the table.

"We was thinking, Babe," Glenda began, "you be a Sister, so you got no money of your own. Right?"

Mary Helen nodded.

"You all share what you got with the other Sisters. You spread it around. Right?"

"Right," Mary Helen agreed, wondering just where this conversation was leading. She did not have to wait long. Glenda was not given to subtleties.

Like a teacher about to drive home the point, the large woman hunched forward and lowered her voice. "My old daddy says that money is like horse shit—'scuse me, Sister—spread it around and it does some good, leave it piling up and it just stinks." Glenda paused to let that much sink in.

"Now, Babe, we been talking and we been planning for months. What we wants to do is to rob that shiny new bank. You know, the one on Fourteenth and Broadway."

Glenda looked up, undoubtedly checking Mary Helen's face for a reaction. Since Mary Helen was too shocked to even register one, Glenda continued, "But how? That's our problem. Then, you comes along, Babe"—Glenda smiled sweetly—"with that old green car of yours, and takes Sister Barbara's place for a while and it's just like an answer."

Dorothy's pale face broke into a grin.

Sister Mary Helen was aghast. "Rob a . . . ," she blurted out. Before she could get any further, Passion's strong black hand came down on hers. The dark eyes narrowed, silently warning Mary Helen to lower her voice. "Be careful, Babe, we don't wants Betty to hear. You understand?"

"Betty?" Mary Helen whispered. "Why can't Betty hear?"

"You don't know about that girl," Jackie said. "She'd steal the sweet right out of sugar. We don't want her nowhere near our bank robbery. Nowhere. Why, she'd sooner cut you than look at you. Cut her own mother-in-law." Jackie focused her one good eye on Mary Helen. "Cut her face, forty stitches' worth."

Mary Helen shuddered.

"Her mother-in-law be my sister," Passion hissed savagely.

"Now, Babe, we looks up to you and we looks out for you. Right?" Ignoring the tension, Glenda brought the meeting back on target. "We be friends. 'Cause we respects you, you can help us. You can drive the getaway car."

"Glenda, you must be joking," Mary Helen sputtered.

"No, Babe, I'm serious as an old judge. Will you drive your car for us? Then, we can get some of that money that's just piling up and spread it, kinda like you nuns do. Won't take you but a minute. We ladies is all dirt poor, so we don't need that much. Just enough to get us a studio apartment and some good food. And the police? They'd never suspect you." She giggled.

Four sets of eyes, actually three and a half, studied Mary Helen hopefully, waiting for her answer. She took a sip of her coffee. Her stomach rolled. Suddenly the air conditioner felt icy cold. This could not be happening to her. She wondered if her old novice mistress, God rest her, would believe Glenda's interpretation of the vow of poverty. She wondered if Glenda, herself, believed it. This entire conversation was like something right out of one of those slapstick situation comedies on television, the ones that Mary Helen detested. But the intense stares told her that these women were not joking. They were deadly earnest.

"Nuns don't rob banks, then share the money," she began in her best "nun's voice," "and neither should you. It is wrong. It is dangerous. It is against the law." She paused to see if any of her reasons had deterred her listeners. They hadn't.

She fumbled for a further reason. Something that might hit home. "Why, it isn't . . . it isn't even friendly," she said in desperation.

From the tense silence that followed and the unflinching eyes, Mary Helen knew that she had not changed anyone's mind.

"Will you drive for us, Babe?" Glenda asked again.

"No, I will not," Mary Helen said and waited for a reaction. There was none. At least, no verbal outbursts.

Glenda merely sighed. "We mean you no disrespect, Babe." The enormous woman smiled a sweet, resigned smile. "We was just desperate, I guess. We still friends?"

Mary Helen nodded. "Of course," she said, gathering up her cup. As she put it in the sink, she tried to shake off the gnawing sensation that something had just died.

On Friday morning, Glenda came into the center alone. She stayed for only a few minutes, used the phone, then left. Although Mary Helen knew it was ridiculous, she felt sad.

For heaven's sake, she chided herself, while she washed up the dirty cups, I am here to help these homeless women better their lives, not to assist them in further complicating them. Despite her own common sense, she could not rid herself of that terrible feeling of loss.

A little after ten o'clock, Betty burst into the main room. "You seen Glenda?" she demanded.

"She was in here just a few minutes ago," the old nun answered. "But she didn't stay."

Betty's dark eyes flared with rage.

"Do you need something?"

Without answering, Betty stormed out of A Friendly Place, leaving Mary Helen a bit shaken. What in the name of all that's good and holy was that about? she wondered.

Just then, tiny Sister Agnes zipped across the room holding an empty cream pitcher. "Oh dear, Mary Helen, we are out of milk," she announced. "Our guests hate coffee without milk. Would you mind running out to the store and picking up a gallon?"

"Not at all," Mary Helen said. Actually she was relieved to get away from A Friendly Place for a few minutes; away from Glenda's request and Betty's rage and Caroline's jibberish. A trip to the supermarket might help her to put things back into perspective.

She fumbled in her pocketbook. No car keys. She searched her jacket pockets. Nothing. She dumped the contents of her purse on top of Agnes's already cluttered desk and sorted through them. But there were no keys.

"Agnes, please come here," she called from the office, trying to steady her voice and to sound calm and pleasant.

"What is it?" Despite Mary Helen's efforts, Agnes had picked up the tone of urgency. Her eyes were wide.

"My car keys. Someone has taken the keys to the green Nova."

Agnes frowned and pursed her lips. "Who and why?" she said, trying undoubtedly to sort out the culprit and the motive.

Mary Helen had no such problem. She knew who. Glenda or one of her cohorts. And she knew why. To rob that shiny new bank at Fourteenth and Broadway.

She hurried out of the center to the fenced-off parking lot. Just maybe, they hadn't yet taken the car. Mary Helen groaned. Her parking spot was empty.

"Let me use your car keys," she said to a flabbergasted Agnes, who was putting a heaping plate of donuts on the refreshment table. "I think if I'm not too late, I can stop it."

"Stop what?" Agnes asked, rummaging in her pocket. "Mary

Helen, what is going on? All I wanted was a gallon of milk. Now you think someone has your car keys."

"I'm not really sure." Mary Helen hedged. There was no sense worrying Agnes unnecessarily. "I'll be back in a few minutes," she said.

The bank was easy to spot. A parking place in downtown Oakland posed a little more of a problem. Nervously, she circled the block twice, then decided to take her chances in a loading zone.

Half-running, half-walking, Mary Helen pushed her way down the hot, crowded street, intent on reaching the bank before the four women did. There was no predicting what they would do if someone tried to stop them. To her, they seemed harmless enough, but they were desperate, and when desperation drives people . . . She tried to block the possibilities from her mind.

Panting, she shoved open the plate-glass door of the large building and stepped inside. The interior of the bank was cool and dark and as quiet as a church. Patrons, avoiding one another's eyes, stood in long, silent lines, patiently waiting their turns at the windows.

Mary Helen scanned the vast lobby, looking for any one of the familiar foursome. To her surprise, the person she saw was Betty. Betty was next in line. Slowly, Betty moved across the polished marble floor toward a vacant window. Her hand was driven deep into the pocket of her windbreaker. The sharp outline of a knife blade pressed against the fabric.

Sister Mary Helen's head throbbed. What should she do? Move toward the same window? Warn the teller? Shout to the armed guard?

Before she could decide, the plate-glass doors of the bank burst open. The left one hit the bank guard squarely in his forehead, and Mary Helen watched, horrified, as the man crumpled, unconscious, to the floor.

"There she is," Glenda shouted, unaware of the fallen guard. "Stop her," she pleaded, her red wig askew.

Wide-eyed, the bank manager rose from behind his spacious desk. Jackie cannoned across the room. "She's in our bank!" she screeched, pointing her finger toward Betty. "This is our bank! She is robbing our bank!"

Betty spun around. Crouching, she jerked her hand from her pocket and brandished the knife. Its blade glinted in the fluorescent light.

The two women circled each other, eyes locked. The room was so still that Mary Helen could hear the hum of the electric clock on the wall. All at once, Betty lunged. The swish of the blade whistled in the silence. Jackie jumped and stumbled backward. Betty lunged again, this time ripping Jackie's sleeve.

Tellers and customers stood frozen. Mary Helen felt her heart bouncing like a ball in her chest. The room moved around her. As if in slow motion, she watched Jackie dodge to the right, then jerk back, only to trip over the velvet rope. She heard the awful thud as Jackie's head cracked against the marble floor.

With a grunt of surprise, Betty pounced. Eyes blazing, she hovered over the cowering woman. With a cruel smile, she squared her feet. Holding the knife with both hands, Betty raised it high above her head. Her body tensed, ready to strike.

Dorothy dove forward and hit the blade with her cast. "No, you don't, girl," she shrieked. The knife flew from Betty's hand and skittered like a pebble across the floor. Passion scooped it up.

Glenda launched across the room and grabbed a shocked Betty from behind. Her thick arm circled Betty's neck. With a grunt, she squeezed the woman to her enormous bosom and held tight.

Passion was right there, the tip of the knife blade held close to the emerald in her nose.

"You thinks we should cut her, Glenda, Babe?" Passion's eyes never left Betty's. "She a thief."

Betty, a smirk on her face, stared back in angry defiance.

"Want me to cut her right down her ugly face?" Passion taunted, running the tip of the blade across Betty's cheek. "Like she cuts my sister?"

Betty narrowed her eyes. In horror, Mary Helen heard her cough up phlegm. She watched as Betty puffed out her thin cheeks and set her mouth.

Holy Mother of God, Mary Helen thought, she is going to

spit—spit right in Passion's face. There was no telling what might happen then.

"No, don't," she shouted. Her words echoed in the large, silent room, then died away. "Don't cut her," Mary Helen begged. "It's not . . . It's not . . ." She fumbled for a reason, for a word. Her mind was blank. "It's not . . ." Lord, help me, she prayed. The words just blurted out. "It's not friendly!"

"If that don't beat all!" Glenda's raucous laughter dispersed the tension. The bank manager, the tellers, even some of the customers sprang into action. Within minutes, Betty was subdued, the police called, the guard on his way to the hospital and the bank manager ready for an explanation.

Several hours later, the "fearsome foursome," as Mary Helen was now wont to think of them, and the old nun stood on the crowded corner of Fourteenth and Broadway.

"If that don't beat all," Glenda repeated and laughed again.

"Imagine the bank manager giving us a reward!" Dorothy's pale face was flushed with color. "We come to rob and we end up heroes."

"I'm going to get me a studio apartment." Passion beamed, and her eyes shone like the stone in her nose. Jackie was still speechless.

"Thank you, Babe," Glenda said, with that amazingly sweet smile.

And, Mary Helen knew, without any one of them saying so, that the friendship she'd feared was lost had only been misplaced for a time.

"All's well that ends well, I guess," she said, wrestling in her own conscience about how much she really should have told the police when they arrived. Actually, the policemen had asked her very few questions. She had answered them, of course, but she had given them no unsolicited information. They were, after all, policemen, not her confessors, so she need not bare her soul.

Fortunately for the women, when the lieutenant finally arrived, he had taken her for a bumbling old lady. Not that she blamed him, under the circumstances. To call assault with a deadly weapon during an attempted bank robbery "not friendly" did not speak well for having all your wits about you.

The four women, however, were another matter altogether. "That was very foolish," she announced in her stiffest nun's voice. "Very foolish, indeed. Not to mention morally wrong. You fully intended to rob that bank. And would have, too, if Betty hadn't shown up ahead of you. Thanks be to God, the bank guard only has a concussion." She looked from one woman to the next. "Furthermore, you stole my car, deceived me, and, frankly, I am disappointed in you. I thought we were friends."

"I'm sorry, Babe." Glenda was the first to speak. "We didn't mean you no disrespect. Honest we didn't. We was going to share the money, like you nuns do."

"We were going to bring your car back right away." Dorothy was insulted. "We weren't going to keep it. If you didn't go looking for it, you never would have known it was gone."

"Not until the police came looking for me," Mary Helen said, "but that is not the point. The point is what you attempted to do is wrong. And don't give me that malarkey about sharing the money like nuns do. We are all too smart for that. You know perfectly well that nuns don't get money from robbing banks."

"We was desperate." Jackie's eyes filled with tears. "You don't know how desperate we was."

Mary Helen had to admit that what Jackie said was true. She really did not know what it was to be as desperate as these women were with no homes, no jobs, no families to offer support, with almost no hope of ever having a brighter tomorrow.

The group walked along Fourteenth Street, each lost in her own thoughts. "Don't be mad with us, Sister." Passion broke the silence. "We be sorry. Now, we be rich, too." She squealed aloud. "But we be sorry. We promise never to try that again."

"That's right, Babe." Glenda put her thick arm around Mary Helen's shoulders. "Never, not never again."

When they reached the spot where Sister Mary Helen had parked Agnes's car, a great pink ticket fluttered from beneath the windshield wiper. Mary Helen groaned. "How in the world am I going to explain this to Sister Agnes?" she said.

Glenda snatched the paper from under the windshield wiper, tore it into pieces and tossed them into the air. Mary Helen watched them flutter onto the cement like cherry blossoms. "Now, you don't need to tell her nothing," Glenda said.

"And what do you suggest that I tell the police department?"

"You tell 'em just exactly what you told us." Glenda's laughter filled the warm summer air. "It works, Babe. Right? You tell them that their ticket is not . . . How you say that?"

Mary Helen listened in amazement as Glenda mimicked her best "nun's voice." "It is just not friendly," Glenda pontificated. "Not even one bit friendly!"

Joyce Carol Oates is one of America's most influential contemporary writers, teachers, and critics. Her novels, essays, poetry, and short stories have earned her a permanent place of honor in American letters. Winner of the National Book Award, the O. Henry Prize for the short story, the Rea Award for the short story, and a member of the American Academy-Institute of Arts and Letters, she also has written four novels of psychological suspense, most recently Snake Eyes, *under the name of Rosamond Smith.*

In "Extenuating Circumstances," a young woman's monologue reveals the depth of her torment, and her terrible response.

EXTENUATING CIRCUMSTANCES

by Joyce Carol Oates

BECAUSE IT WAS a mercy. Because God even in His cruelty will sometimes grant mercy.

Because Venus was in the sign of Sagittarius.

Because you laughed at me, my faith in the stars. My hope.

Because he cried, you do not know how he cried.

Because at such times his little face was so twisted and hot, his nose running with mucus, his eyes so hurt.

Because in such he was his mother, and not you. Because I wanted to spare him such shame.

Because he remembered you, he knew the word *Daddy*.

Because watching TV he would point to a man and say *Daddy*—?

Because this summer has gone on so long, and no rain. The heat lightning flashing at night, without thunder.

Because in the silence, at night, the summer insects scream.

Because by day there are earth-moving machines and grinders operating hour upon hour razing the woods next to the playground. Because the red dust got into our eyes, our mouths.

Because he would whimper *Mommy*?—in that way that tore my heart.

Because last Monday the washing machine broke down, I heard a loud thumping that scared me, the dirty soapy water would not drain out. Because in the light of the bulb overhead he saw me holding the wet sheets in my hand crying *What can I do? What can I do*?

Because the sleeping pills they give me now are made of flour and chalk, I am certain.

Because I loved you more than you loved me even from the first when your eyes moved on me like candle flame.

Because I did not know this yet, yes I knew it but cast it from my mind.

Because there was shame in it. Loving you knowing you would not love me enough.

Because my job applications are laughed at for misspellings and torn to pieces as soon as I leave.

Because they will not believe me when listing my skills. Because since he was born my body is misshapen, the pain is always there.

Because I see that it was not his fault and even in that I could not spare him.

Because even at the time when he was conceived (in those early days we were so happy! so happy I am certain! lying together on top of the bed the corduroy bedspread in that narrow jiggly bed hearing the rain on the roof that slanted down so you had to stoop being so tall and from outside on the street the roof with its dark shingles looking always wet was like a lowered brow over the windows on the third floor and the windows like squinting eyes and we would come home together from the University meeting at the Hardee's corner you from the geology lab or the library and me from Accounting where my eyes ached because of the lights with their dim flicker no one else could see and I was so happy your arm around my waist and mine around yours like any couple, like any college girl with her boyfriend, and walking *home*, yes it was *home*, I thought always it was *home*, we would look up at the windows of the apartment laughing saying who do you think lives there? what are their names? who are they? that cozy secret-looking room under the eaves where the roof came down, came down dripping black runny water I hear now drumming on this roof but only if I fall asleep during the day with my clothes on so tired so exhausted and when I wake up there is no rain, only the earth-moving machines and grinders in the woods so I must acknowledge *It is another time, it is time*) yes I knew.

Because you did not want him to be born.

Because he cried so I could hear him through the shut door, through all the doors.

Because I did not want him to be *Mommy*, I wanted him to be *Daddy* in his strength.

Because this washcloth in my hand was in my hand when I saw how it must be.

Because the checks come to me from the lawyer's office not from you. Because in tearing open the envelopes my fingers shaking and my eyes showing such hope I revealed myself naked to myself so many times.

Because to this shame he was a witness, he saw.

Because he was too young at two years to know. Because even so he knew.

Because his birthday was a sign, falling in the midst of Pisces.

Because in certain things he *was* his father, that knowledge in eyes that went beyond me in mockery of me.

Because one day he would laugh too as you have done.

Because there is no listing for your telephone and the operators will not tell me. Because in any of the places I know to find you, you cannot be found.

Because your sister has lied to my face, to mislead me. Because she who was once my friend, I believed, was never my friend.

Because I feared loving him too much, and in that weakness failing to protect him from hurt.

Because his crying tore my heart but angered me too so I feared laying hands upon him wild and unplanned.

Because he flinched seeing me. That nerve jumping in his eye.

Because he was always hurting himself, he was so clumsy falling off the swing hitting his head against the metal post so one of the other mothers saw and cried out *Oh! Oh look your son is bleeding!* and that time in the kitchen whining and pulling at me in a bad temper reaching up to grab the pot handle and almost overturning the boiling water in his face so I lost control slapping him shaking him by the arm *Bad! Bad! Bad! Bad!* my voice rising in fury not caring who heard.

Because that day in the courtroom you refused to look at me your face shut like a fist against me and your lawyer too, like I was dirt beneath your shoes. Like maybe he was not even your son but you would sign the papers as if he was, you are so superior.

Because the courtroom was not like any courtroom I had a right to expect, not a big dignified courtroom like on TV just a room with a judge's desk and three rows of six seats each and not a single window and even here that flickering light that yellowish-sickish fluorescent tubing making my eyes ache so I wore my dark glasses giving the judge a false impression of me, and I was sniffing, wiping my nose, every question they asked me I'd hear myself giggle so nervous and ashamed even stammering over my age and my name so you looked with scorn at me, all of you.

Because they were on your side, I could not prevent it.

Because in granting me child support payments, you had a right to move away. Because I could not follow.

Because he wet his pants, where he should not have, for his age.

Because it would be blamed on me. It *was* blamed on me.

Because my own mother screamed at me over the phone. She could not help me with my life she said, no one can help you with your life, we were screaming such things to each other as left us breathless and crying and I slammed down the receiver knowing that I had no mother and after the first grief I knew *It is better, so.*

Because he would learn that someday, and the knowledge of it would hurt him.

Because he had my hair coloring, and my eyes. That left eye, the weakness in it.

Because that time it almost happened, the boiling water overturned onto him, I saw how easy it would be. How, if he could be prevented from screaming, the neighbors would not know.

Because yes they would know, but only when I wanted them to know.

Because you would know then. Only when I wanted you to know.

Because then I could speak to you in this way, maybe in a letter which your lawyer would forward to you, or your sister, maybe over the telephone or even face to face. Because then you could not escape.

Because though you did not love him you could not escape him.

Because I have begun to bleed for six days quite heavily, and will then spot for another three or four. Because soaking the blood in wads of toilet paper sitting on the toilet my hands shaking I think of you who never bleed.

Because I am a proud woman, I scorn your charity.

Because I am not a worthy mother. Because I am so tired.

Because the machines digging in the earth and grinding trees are a torment by day, and the screaming insects by night.

Because there is no sleep.

Because he would only sleep, these past few months, if he could be with me in my bed.

Because he whimpered *Mommy!—Mommy don't!*

Because he flinched from me when there was no cause.

Because the pharmacist took the prescription and was gone such a long time, I knew he was telephoning someone.

Because at the drugstore where I have shopped for a year and a half they pretended not to know my name.

Because in the grocery store the cashiers stared smiling at me and at him pulling at my arm spilling tears down his face.

Because they whispered and laughed behind me, I have too much pride to respond.

Because he was with me at such times, he was a witness to such.

Because he had no one but his Mommy and his Mommy had no one but him. Which is so lonely.

Because I had gained seven pounds from last Sunday to this, the waist of my slacks is so tight. Because I hate the fat of my body.

Because looking at me naked now you would show disgust.

Because I *was* beautiful for you, why wasn't that enough?

Because that day the sky was dense with clouds the color of raw liver but yet there was no rain. Heat lightning flashing with no sound making me so nervous but no rain.

Because his left eye was weak, it would always be so unless he had an operation to strengthen the muscle.

Because I did not want to cause him pain and terror in his sleep.

Because you would pay for it, the check from the lawyer with no note.

Because you hated him, your son.

Because he was *our* son, you hated him.

Because you moved away. To the far side of the country I have reason to believe.

Because in my arms after crying he would lie so still, only one heart beating between us.

Because I knew I could not spare him from hurt.

Because the playground hurt our ears, raised red dust to get into our eyes and mouths.

Because I was so tired of scrubbing him clean, between his toes and beneath his nails, the insides of his ears, his neck, the many secret places of filth.

Because I felt the ache of cramps again in my belly, I was in a panic my period had begun so soon.

Because I could not spare him the older children laughing.

Because after the first terrible pain he would be beyond pain.

Because in this there is mercy.

Because God's mercy is for him, and not for me.

Because there was no one here to stop me.

Because my neighbors' TV was on so loud, I knew they could not hear even if he screamed through the washcloth.

Because you were not here to stop me, were you.

Because finally there is no one to stop us.

Because finally there is no one to save us.

Because my own mother betrayed me.

Because the rent would be due again on Tuesday which is the first of September. And by then I will be gone.

Because his body was not heavy to carry and to wrap in the down comforter, you remember that comforter, I know.

Because the washcloth soaked in his saliva will dry on the line and show no sign.

Because to heal there must be forgetfulness and oblivion.

Because he cried when he should not have cried but did not cry when he should.

Because the water came slowly to boil in the big pan, vibrating and humming on the front burner.

Because the kitchen was damp with steam from the windows shut so tight, the temperature must have been 100° F.

Because he did not struggle. And when he did, it was too late.

Because I wore rubber gloves to spare myself being scalded.

Because I knew I must not panic, and did not.

Because I loved him. Because love hurts so bad.

Because I wanted to tell you these things. Just like this.

T. J. MacGregor's Dark Fields, *nominated for a 1986 Shamus, is one of seven novels featuring husband-and-wife investigators Mike McCleary and Quin St. James, whose cases often involve high stakes and high passions. The most recent McCleary/St. James exploits are chronicled in* Spree. *T. J. also writes as Trish Janeshutz (*In Shadow, Hidden Lake*) and Alison Drake (*Tango Key, Black Moon*), providing readers with tense, suspenseful tales that explore unexplained phenomena and the dark side of human experience.*

In "Wild Card," tension mounts as a psychic gets closer and closer to uncovering hidden facts.

WILD CARD

by T. J. MacGregor

I AM SURROUNDED by toys. A beach ball and a Barbie doll, a stuffed bear with a missing eye, colorful plastic hoops of varying sizes that fit together to form a chain. There's a pretty quilt with frayed borders that is decorated with rainbows, and a little red radio that plays "It's a Small, Small World."

"Are you comfortable?" Newton asks anxiously, his arms dropping to his sides as he sits forward at his desk. "Would you like some coffee? A Coke? Anything?"

"Coffee would be great." It's three A.M. and coffee is the last thing I want, but I think he'll settle down once he's burned off some of that nervous energy. "With cream."

He rises quickly, grateful for something to do. His office is no larger than a cardboard box, and he crosses the room in three or four strides. He's a tall man, several inches over six feet, and moves like a bullet, his shoulders slightly stooped. On his messy desk is a photograph in an oval frame, like a locket, of him with his wife and son. The three of them are laughing, as though they have just shared some private joke. He and his son look like different versions of the same man, both of them with dark hair and eyes and square chins. The wife is blond, blue-eyed, diminutive.

Earlier, he picked up the photograph, turned it over in his hands, thinking, What if . . . His stake in this has become quite personal.

I have no children. But for me, this process is always personal, even when it fails.

I pick up the brown bear with the missing eye and hug him against my chest. He's soft, of course; little bears always are. But when I squeeze him, he feels almost human. I press my hands to either side of his face. His missing eye seems tragic somehow, that great blank space where the bit of glass should be. The gaze of the surviving eye, that iris like a drop of honey, is fixed, relentless. I start to choke up. I want to heal the bear, protect him, hide him from the bad hand.

"Here's your coffee, Claire."

I'm staring at Newman's shoes, penny loafers, probably from Sears. I nod about the coffee, but don't let go of the bear. I hear Newman's chair squeak as he sits down. I can smell the coffee. "Something about the mother's boyfriend," I tell him.

A seed of doubt pokes up at the end of that statement. Boyfriend or husband? Why "boyfriend" instead of lover? Does he live with Jessie and her mother?

"What about him?" Newman asks.

I hear his pen scratching across paper. I hear the whir of his recorder.

"He tore off the bear's eye to punish her."

I let go of the bear, and he tumbles out of my lap, head over heels, and lands on his back. That singular eye stares up at me, and I want to weep.

The beach ball: Newton passes it to me. He knows the routine. Keep things moving.

The ball's skin is hard, red and white, with a black streak that circles its circumference, a little equator. Jessie loves her ball. Her perfect hands cup and stroke it, explore it like a globe. Now the ball is flying, and she reaches up for it, longs for it, cries for it, and something slams against the side of her head, over her ear, I can feel it. The ball is gone. There is only pain and a terrible silence.

"She's deaf in one ear. Because he struck her. The boyfriend struck her when she cried about the ball."

"Which ear?" Newton asks.

"Left. The left."

We've worked together often enough so that he doesn't question my certainty on this point. But his job requires that he confirm it. He picks up the phone, punches out a number. He speaks softly into the receiver, too softly for me to hear. I let go of the ball, and it bounces away from me, the black equator spinning. It strikes the front of Newton's desk and stops. I reach for my coffee. It's thick and rich and still warm. It pools in my stomach, burning like acid, and when I look at the ball again, it is only that, a ball without a story.

I stand, stretch, kick off my shoes and walk barefoot around the tiny room, grounding myself. Outside, it has begun to thunder and lightning. This will be a violent South Florida thunderstorm; the stink of ozone permeates the dark air.

"Okay," Newton says.

As though something is settled. He seems more relaxed now, and I suspect he confirmed that Jessie is, indeed, deaf in one ear and that her mother's boyfriend either lives with them or might as well. I want to ask, but don't. There are certain rules that Newton and I follow. We don't break them. We never even speak of them. When he calls, he merely asks if I'm free, and we both know what that means.

Someday, I may ask him what he thinks of me. But I probably won't like the answer. I make him uneasy. What Newton doesn't realize is that every day he does what I do. He simply has another name for it. Hunch. Instinct. The difference between us is merely one of orientation. I read stories with my hands; he reads them in the very air he breathes.

"You feel like taking a dri—" He stops, watching me as I pick up the Barbie doll.

Jessie is three. I don't remember being three, but I remember Barbie dolls. I had two of them. Between them, they had a dozen outfits, a dozen different hairdos, a dozen faces. They had furniture and dreams and long talks at slumber parties. They were my friends. This doll is Jessie's friend. She misses holding her, dressing her, sharing with her. Jessie is wet and chilled, in a dark, hidden place, and wishes Barbie were with her.

"Claire?"

I realize I am huddled in a corner of the room, clutching the doll, whimpering and rocking. Distantly, like voices in a dream, I hear a man and a woman shouting, arguing about me.

"Claire, hey, listen, I think—"

Yes, I know what he thinks. That we should take a break. That I'm too close to it. His apprehension shows in the lines of his pleasant face, in the way he stands over me, arms folded across his chest as if to protect himself from something. I don't blame him. I'm the X in the equation, the wild card.

I release Barbie and slide slowly up the wall, my heart knotted in my chest. Rain taps the windows. A boom of thunder is followed almost instantly by lightning that burns a path across the dark wet glass.

"Let's go for that drive, Newt."

We leave by the rear door, like thieves. He has lent me a raincoat, and it flaps at my knees as we sprint across the parking lot to his Honda. The rain is cool and sharp, a sure sign that the storm is ushering in the first cold front of this year's winter.

I don't do this for a living. I couldn't. I sell real estate. It's a seasonal market here in Florida, with our busiest time right about now, in that stretch between Thanksgiving and Christmas. But I make my own hours, and when Newton calls, time and sometimes even seasons cease to matter very much.

The Honda's wipers whip across the windshield, leaving half moons of clarity in their wake. I am holding the pretty quilt with frayed borders. I taste the residue of coffee on my tongue.

"Just tell me where to go," Newton says.

Where to go. I press my face into the quilt. The little-girl smells make my cheeks ache. My right side throbs, and when I breathe, I want to double up in pain. Mommy is worried, probably crying. But I don't care. I'm scared. It's raining and I'm scared.

I shut my eyes against the quilt, blocking out the rhythmic monotony of the wipers. Static issues from Newton's radio, then a voice. He turns down the volume. The rain falls harder.

Where to go.

"One of her ribs is fractured. He hit her. She ran away. Do you have a map?"

Newton reaches across my legs to the glove compartment. He's happily married to his college sweetheart. He has been a cop for ten years. His son is eight. He's a good father and a decent man, uncorrupted by what he has seen in a decade in this business. He isn't surprised by what I've said.

But I know the optimist in him was hoping for some other explanation, a drifter, perhaps, a repeat offender or, at the very least, a child who'd simply wandered out of the yard and gotten lost. He knows the nightmare, the monster, is us, but he doesn't want to acknowledge it yet. We are nothing less than the culmination of the choices we make.

I study the map and locate where we are, where Jessie lives, where she was last seen. And I keep clutching the blanket, stroking it, plundering its tales, its brief history. The quilt speaks, but the map does not.

"Do you get anything?" he asks.

The conduit is rather like an electrical pulse, connecting me to her, her to me, us to each other. But it isn't consistently clear, and never is it so specific that it offers an address.

"Dark, wet, round, hard, scared."

"Round? What do you mean by round?"

"Round, I don't know. Something round. Maybe an opening."

"A door? A window?"

"Something hard." I strain, reaching through the wet dark. "A pipe. Yeah, a pipe, that's it. She's in a pipe."

He grabs the map, turns on a light. "A construction site, that's got to be it. There's a new apartment going up about four blocks from where she lives. Does that sound right, Claire?"

"I don't know."

He reminds me that although Jessie's mother reported her missing only an hour ago, she has not been seen for eighteen hours. It means there are no search parties yet, that officially the child isn't even missing. "Please," he says, "try."

But the pain distracts me. Her pain. It's worse when I breathe. The boundaries between us have long since blurred. Her fingers move and mine twitch in response. Something wet and sticky oozes from a corner of her mouth; it becomes my mouth.

"She's badly hurt, Newton. I think the busted rib has punctured her lung."

"We'll try the construction site."

He drives too quickly through the wet, deserted streets, speaking to someone on the radio. The boyfriend will be brought in for questioning. The mother will be encouraged to press charges. Health and Rehabilitative Services will get involved. This is not a pretty story. The most I hope for is that we'll find her and the ending will be better than most.

The wind rises, hurling rain against the windshield, where it smears like spit before the wipers whip it away. Trees crowd the sides of the road, a gang of thugs. The quilt is bunched against my chest, vomiting images of Jessie hiding beneath it, the boyfriend drunk, the mother screaming.

The car screeches into a turn, and a wash of light exposes us like an X ray: Newton is hunched over the steering wheel, trying to see, and I am huddled against the door, trying to breathe. I'm sure now that what I'm looking at is the opening of a pipe and Jessie is inside it, peering out. But a construction site doesn't seem quite right.

Newton downshifts, the car bounces, the tires spew gravel. Then we are outside, and I have no clear memory of stopping, of leaving the car. We shout her name. Rain pelts the hood of my raincoat, my face, my eyes. The wind gasps at my ankles and shakes the wire mesh fence that surrounds the construction site. A spill of light from the sodium vapor lamps illumines tractors, trucks, wet dunes of dirt, the shell of an unfinished building. Rods made of steel and iron and blocks of cement are scattered everywhere, like the refuse of a gang war. There are pipes, but none is large enough to crawl into.

We keep calling for her. I clutch the quilt more tightly, begging it to release something vital. But it has nothing more to tell me; its story is finished. Pain bursts in my right side, and as I stumble, Newton grabs my arm, steadying me. Black dots swirl across the insides of my eyes, my peripheral vision grows fuzzy, a spasm of coughing eats up my meager reserves of energy.

"What is it?" Newton grips me by both arms, his face so close to mine, I can see beads of water rolling down the bridge of his nose.

"She's . . . fading fast."

And then Jessie offers me something, a small gift of water, not puddles or rivulets from the rain, but water like a river that is standing still. I tear across the dunes and plains of this forsaken place, shouting her name, headed for the canal that runs behind the construction site. Newton races after me. The burning in my side is so deep now, so terrible, it short-circuits everything inside me. I stumble again and sink to my knees in the wet dirt. Newton helps me up, grasps my hand, and we move on.

The light is dimmer back here, little more than a thin varnish the color of nicotine. But it's enough to detect the small hills of dirt and rock that rise along the edge of the canal's wall. We lumber like giants, he and I, calling for her, peering over the side into the murky, rain-dimpled waters. I see no protrusions from the wall, no pipes.

I lost her quilt when we left the car and feel I am losing her as well. The borders between us are not quite as blurred now; she is withdrawing, untangling herself from me. Even her pain is leaving me.

We are past the building's shell, where the canal turns away from the mangroves on its far side. I spot a shallow slope of dirt and pebbles that leads to a prayer rug of sand. Six inches of pipe jut from the wall. I scramble over the top and land on my knees in the sand. It's soft as sponge. The beam of my flashlight doesn't reveal much inside the pipe. It's too long, too dark, too wet.

"Jessie?" My voice echoes down the corridor of concrete. A

spider the size of my palm scampers through the pool of light, the echo of my voice dies, and there's no response.

"Maybe it wasn't a pipe you saw, Claire."

Maybe: I detest the word. It punctuates the process, breaks it up as a prism does light, sows endless doubts. Six months ago, a *maybe* spelled the difference for a sixteen-year-old girl, a runaway who died in a Miami crack house. *Maybe* is lethal. I'm going in.

"Keep shouting for her," I tell Newton, and crawl into the pipe.

I don't like enclosed spaces. I especially don't like them wet and dark. I move in a squat, one leg, then the other, keeping my hands free. The beam of light seems impoverished in this darkness. The pipe narrows and I'm forced onto my hands and knees. A spider's web slides across my nose, my cheeks. I jerk back, bang my head on the ceiling. The flashlight slips from my grasp and rolls away from me, clattering, spilling light in thin, pathetic layers.

When it stops four feet later, it illumines an arm, thin and pale, then another arm, then hair tangled like floating seaweed. She is lying where the pipe bends, an elbow of concrete that connects to other elbows, perhaps all the way to the sea. I shout for Newton to get on the radio, call an ambulance. He shouts back.

I quickly unzip my raincoat and lift Jessie against me as I rock back on my heels and settle against the curve of the pipe. Her head lolls against my chest. She whimpers with pain as I pull the sides of my raincoat over her, around her, protecting her as she once tried to protect the little bear.

For a moment that is all too brief, the boundaries between us melt again, and her story is there, whole and untouched. The boyfriend, the mother, the child, a trinity that is crippled, and here, her pain, her fear, her innocence.

Then we are two again, holding onto each other, the rain as distant as some childhood memory. "It's okay, Jessie," I whisper. "It's going to be okay."

And for her, it will be. Of that much I'm sure.

Janet LaPierre's Unquiet Grave, *a Macavity nominee, introduced readers to the fictional town of Port Silva, California, and to high school teacher Meg Halloran and Police Chief Vince Gutierrez. Rich with sensitive portrayals of characters who lead lives of sometimes not-so-quiet desperation, attuned to the issues and concerns of people trying to cope with a rapidly changing world, Janet's Port Silva series includes* Children's Games, The Cruel Mother, *and, most recently,* Grandmother's House.

In "The Woman Who Knew What She Wanted," the reunion of two college acquaintances points up long-forgotten differences.

THE WOMAN WHO KNEW WHAT SHE WANTED

by Janet LaPierre

THERE WAS SOMETHING about that sunlit figure at the top of the steps—angle of the neat blond head? set of the narrow shoulders? Emily Cochran shook her own curly, graying head and continued her climb toward the door of the Port Silva *Sentinel*, the door through which the smaller woman had just disappeared. This was one of Ben's complaints about growing older: memory overload, bits and pieces of the past returning to blur the present. It would hit her any day now, he kept insisting.

Well, so what? The past wasn't so bad, most of it, she thought as she moved down the hall in the long-legged countrywoman's stride that middle age and twenty or thirty extra pounds hadn't altered in the least. She took her piece into the paper's home/gardens/hobbies office, chatted for a few minutes with editor Janey Johns, and was headed back for the door with her mind on next week's column when a voice brought her up short.

"Emmy? Emmy Erickson, is that you?"

For a moment she truly was confused, because approaching her from the ads desk, hands outstretched, was the past come to life: blond curls, wide green eyes, sleek silk dress wrapping the body that had brought dry throats and sweaty palms to half the Stanford class of '62. "Fiona Lacey," said Emily to this impossible vision. "I don't believe it."

"Well, I don't, either! What on earth are *you* doing here?"

Clearly this was the same old Fee, center of her own universe and everyone else's. "*I* was born and raised here, or actually twenty miles out in the county. And so was Ben. My husband?" she added in response to Fee's questioning gaze. "No, you'd left before Ben and I rediscovered each other. I'm Emily Cochran now. And you're not Lacey, you're . . . Rienzi!" she finished triumphantly. So much for memory failure.

"Oh, Emmy, that's ancient history," said Fee with a dismissive wave of one manicured hand. "Look, I'm finished here; can we go someplace for a cup of tea? It's been so long since I had any plain old girl talk, I swear my *ears* are thirsty!"

"How about the NorthCoaster Brew Pub?" suggested Emily, and was reminded by the smaller woman's frown that Fee, daughter of a drinking mother, never touched booze of any kind. "I know the owner," Emily told her, "and I'm sure he'll be happy to make you a pot of tea."

There was a late-afternoon darts game under way in the pub, the players silent with concentration but their supporters providing raucous commentary. Emily got herself a pint of Gull's Best ale, asked that a pot of tea be brought out, and led Fee to the garden, where old rose bushes sweetened the air with end-of-summer blooms. "October is the perfect time for a visit to Port Silva," Emily said with a sigh as she sat down and stretched out her bare legs to the sun. "Fog is our specialty the rest of the year. Now tell me what brings you to my little town."

"I was just utterly weary of southern California," said Fee. "And then this gentleman I know, who keeps his boat in La Jolla but sails the whole coast, mentioned Port Silva. It sounded like a nice change of scene, and here's my old roommate as a lovely big bonus!"

"Old" and "big" were the operative words here, thought Emily, watching the college-boy waiter try to peer down Fee's cleavage as he delivered teapot and cup. Her own breasts were big shapeless mounds in a bra she should have retired months ago; there was a definite bulge below the waistband of her skirt; and a glance at Fee's trim, tanned arms made her wish she herself had not worn a sleeveless blouse. "It's nice to see you, Fee," she said, a half truth anyway. "You look wonderful, hardly any older than when we were at Stanford."

"The face," said Fee, touching fingertips delicately to her temples, her jawbone, "comes to you courtesy of Jack the Knife, otherwise known as Dr. Herbert Jackson. In return, I put his youngest son through Harvard."

Here was something she *had* forgotten, Emily chided herself: Fee's rare moments of drop-the-mask directness. Those, and a shared interest in music, had kept two very different young women friends, or at least friendly, through two college years.

"However," Fee went on, "the body is my own, and I mean to tell you it takes *effort.* You ought to join a gym and work out, Emmy. If I stay in town for a while, perhaps we could do it together."

"Um," said Emily, picturing the two of them side by side in leotards.

"Or we could play tennis. I've had tons of lessons and I'm not bad. Weren't you on the team in college?"

"Not tennis. Basketball."

"That's right, I saw you play one time. You were absolutely terrifying."

"With three older brothers, you learn early to go for the jugular," said Emily. "But I mostly avoid games now, because I'm such a rotten loser." Why, she wondered, had she admitted this to Fee? It certainly wasn't something she was proud of.

"Well, never mind," said Fee, reaching to pat Emily's hand. "You look comfortable and happy, at least, which is a lot more than can be said for me."

Emily finished her pint and had another while listening to the story of a life totally different from her own. Mark Rienzi, the up-and-coming young lawyer Fee abandoned college to marry, had divorced her after almost ten years because she couldn't have children. "Underneath that lawerly sophistication, Mark was just another macho Italian who believed a real man proved himself by his get, like a bull," Fee said. "And I did try, of course I wanted a sweet little . . . baby! . . . But the doctor thought I might be developing toxemia, like my mother, so that was that."

Mark had provided a generous settlement, but Fee was lonely and soon married a man in his forties who had lived with his wealthy mother until her death. Dear Charlie, she said with a sigh, was a sweet, gentle man who designed computer games. A serious diabetic, he was inclined to lose himself in bouts of creative energy and forget about his disease.

Charlie lasted eight years and left Fee well off. Then came a stretch of what sounded like merry widowhood, and finally another marriage. Strong ale and the sun's warmth were taking the edge off Emily's attention; an Edward this time, sixtyish, a widower with three grown children and a heart condition. Fee had had only four years with Edward.

". . . wonderful years; we went to Europe three times. He said I was the best thing that ever happened to him, and the poor man would be dreadfully upset if he knew how his children have treated me. Well, never mind. The point is, I'm alone again, and I hate being alone."

"You won't be for long," Emily assured her.

Fee shook her head, with a grimace that thinned her lips and made her look nearly her age. "You work hard, take care of yourself, still one day it's like somebody's called time and you're out of the game. See, the good men are all taken. And when one of them comes on the market, widowed or divorced, right away he's got all these juicy thirty-five-year-olds lining up at his door. Emmy, you don't know how lucky you are."

Yes, she did. Emily finished her ale in two swallows and stood up. "Ben will be home now, wondering where I am. Fee, this was fun."

Fee rose gracefully. "Emmy, we've got to stay in touch now we've found each other. Could I take you to lunch tomorrow? or the next day?"

Tomorrow, Wednesday, she was on at the hospital. And Thursday she had several appointments. "Could you make it Friday, Fee?"

"Certainly can. Should I pick you up at home?"

For reasons not clear to her—embarrassment about her big, untidy house maybe?—Emily was reluctant. "No, let's meet, at noon. At The Dock, down on the wharf."

The front door was unlocked, and the French doors to the back deck stood wide. Emily detoured through the kitchen to inspect the beef stew simmering gently in the slow-cooker, then went to join her husband.

Ben Cochran straightened from the deck rail to put an arm across her shoulders and plant a kiss on her cheek. With thick dark hair just beginning to gray and a six-foot-plus frame that time had filled out from skinny to lean, her husband was better-looking at fifty-two than he had been at twenty-five. And although he was too smart not to know that, he wasn't vain enough to find it interesting. "Refill?" she murmured, and took his empty glass.

She mixed another gin and tonic for him and one for herself, noting that the freshly opened gin bottle was down several inches already. And she'd spent the afternoon swilling beer—both of them were turning into drinkers late in life. She carried the glasses out and sat down in her canvas chair next to Ben in his canvas chair, and they stared together at the sun-spangled ocean.

"How are your classes coming?" she asked after a while.

"Good, good, especially the senior politics class. That really ought to be a two-year course; I think next year I'll try to convince the school board . . ." He broke off and took a gulp from his glass.

"Ben, you don't *have* to give up . . ." She caught herself, but not in time.

"I know that, goddammit! Don't patronize me!" His angry

glare faded to a sheepish sidelong glance. "Sorry, Em. I guess gin makes the old man mean."

"You never are!" Irritable sometimes, from disappointment in himself or others, but never mean. By way of distraction she said brightly, "Oh, guess who I ran into downtown today. Fiona Lacey, my Stanford roommate freshman and sophomore years."

"Oh yeah, the blond bimbo."

"Ben, I never said that! Did I?"

"You must have, because I never met the lady."

"I guess maybe she was," said Emily. "But she'd had a rotten childhood—no father and a drunken mother who alternately screamed abuse at her and tried to sell her to any sleaze-bag promoter who'd promise to make her a pop star."

"Um," said Ben, who'd seen a lot of mistreated teenagers in nearly thirty years as a teacher. He got to his feet, drained his drink, and stretched out a hand. "Come on, let's have supper. I made the salad."

Fog was beginning to build in the west, dimming the ocean's glitter and blowing a chilly breath at the land. Emily closed the deck doors and set supper out on the kitchen table. Ben ate with little show of pleasure; now and then he glanced at the high chair against the wall in the corner, and Emily vowed silently to put it in the garage.

Then their glances caught, and he ducked his head. "Sorry, Em. I really miss Julie Ann."

"So do I."

"And I worry about her."

So do I. But she belongs with Liz, with her mother. And we agreed that we have to trust Liz. Emily kept her gaze down and said none of this aloud.

Ben pushed his chair back and stood up, to stretch. "I've been sitting all day. Think I'll go for a walk."

"Give me a minute to change shoes and I'll come along."

"Better not, sweetheart. I'm lousy company tonight."

At eleven-thirty Friday morning the sound of the doorbell startled Emily into dropping the makeup sponge into her bathroom sink. "Just a minute," she called, and moments later opened her front door to find Fee on the porch.

"Hi, Emmy. I was in the neighborhood, so I thought I'd save you the trouble of firing up your car. Nice area," she said, turning to cast a glance up and down the street. "And what an interesting old house. Is it Victorian?"

"More or less." Emily stepped back into the dimness of the entry hall to let Fee move past her. "It was built in 1890 by Ben's mother's father, and it's what the locals call ship's-carpenter's Gothic."

"It's just lovely." Fee looked around in admiration. "But a modern kitchen, how sensible. And a back deck with a whitewater view!"

"You sound like a real-estate lady," remarked Emily. "I'm hungry; shall we go?"

"I did real estate for a while," said Fee, trotting down the walk to keep up with Emily. "But you don't see many tall old wooden houses in southern California. Oh, I forgot to clean up my messy car. Just toss that stuff in the back."

Emily scooped up road maps, a tour book, and a sprawl of glossy magazines—*Vogue, Elle, Glamour,* and *Stanford*, the alumni quarterly—and set them all on the back seat of the pricey-looking red car whose make she didn't know without inspection. "Get to Main and head south," she instructed as she buckled her seat belt, "and I'll direct you from there."

It wasn't until they were seated before one of the big west-facing windows in the restaurant that Fee really looked at Emily. "My God, girl," she said in a whisper. "What happened to your face? Did Ben do that?"

"Don't be ridiculous!" The possibility of this interpretation of her bruises had not occurred to Emily, and she wished ruefully that she'd had a more experienced hand with the damned pancake stuff.

"Emily . . ." Fee closed her mouth and sat back in her chair as a waiter approached.

"I volunteer at the city hospital," said Emily when the man had departed with their order. "Usually in the children's ward. Day before yesterday, this man came in drunk and said he was there to pick up his three-year-old, a skinny little mite he'd beaten unconscious two days earlier. I didn't let him take her."

"Girl, that bleeding heart of yours is going to get you killed yet," said Fee.

Moved perhaps by sympathy for Emily's battered condition, Fee was listener today rather than talker. Between nibbles of salad and salmon, she wanted to know all about Emily's life. Had she finished her journalism degree, and had she worked at that or stayed at home? Had she and Ben spent their entire married life in this little town? What had become of her parents, her brothers? How many children had she, and where were they?

Emily, who was hungry, replied briefly at first; but eventually she got caught up in the sheer novelty of talking about herself, her life, her opinions. "Three children," she told Fee as she finally pushed her empty plate aside. "Julie is almost twenty-eight, has a Stanford MBA, and works in San Francisco. Robbie is twenty-six, with a wife and two little boys; he's a forester, in Arizona."

She sighed and sat back, cradling her nearly empty wineglass. "And Liz, our youngest, is twenty-one; she has a five-year-old daughter, Julie Ann."

"My but *she* must have married young."

Emily shook her head. "Liz had a very . . . troubled adolescence."

Fee caught the waiter's eye and ordered coffee for herself and another glass of chardonnay for Emily. "Listen now," she said when Emily protested, "this is my treat. You look plain tired to death, and I'm the one driving, so just sit here and relax with your old friend."

Emily surveyed the harbor and its forest of masts and fishing booms through a haze of tears. Tired, yes; she had not realized how tired.

Liz, her beautiful baby, had hit adolescence like a car hitting a brick wall. Almost overnight she'd gone from cheerful to sullen, from cooperative to defiant. She'd given up school, music, and softball for truancy, booze, drugs, and random sex. "Liz left home at fourteen," Emily told Fee, "on the back of a motorcycle.

Came home at fifteen, pregnant. Wouldn't hear of an abortion; she had the baby, stayed and took care of her for six months, then disappeared again."

"Leaving you the baby, I bet."

"Yes, thank God." Emily shuddered and took a gulp of wine. "But she kept in touch, off and on, and even turned up at home a few times. About a year and a half ago she called from southern California, said she was sick and scared but couldn't get away from . . . these people. So I went down and got her."

"So you have a daughter and granddaughter living with you."

Emily shook her head. "Liz started college this fall. They moved to Davis just six weeks ago."

"They? She took the baby with her?" At Emily's nod, Fee sighed. "Well. I bet you really miss that little girl. And I bet you worry, that your Liz stays on track."

That was something else she had forgotten. Now and then Fiona Lacey could rise above her own self-absorption to put a small, red-tipped finger right on the pain you'd been hiding even from yourself. How did she do that? And why was she expending all this energy and talent on stodgy old Emily? "Liz is just fine now!" Emily snapped. "She's a good mother."

"Is that how Ben feels, too?"

"Ben was the world's best father, especially when the kids were little. He misses all those babies now, and he could hardly stand it when Liz left with Julie Ann."

"A little girl. If I'd been luckier, I'd have had a sweet, pretty little girl of my own. To dress up. To love and play with." Fee opened her purse and looked at her face in a small mirror. "Well. I was surprised to find you living here in town, Emmy. I'd gotten it into my mind somehow that you were married to a farmer."

Emily gave a bitter little chuckle. "You don't know how funny that is. Ben's a high school history teacher. But he grew up on his father's big dairy farm, and he always helped out there, weekends and summers. His father died this spring, and Ben was the only child."

"*That* will surely make a difference in your lives."

"It already has." Emily put her empty glass down and squared her shoulders. "Fee, thank you for lunch, but I'm really tired. If you don't mind, I'll ask you to take me home."

It wasn't until Fee had dropped her off and departed that Emily realized she had no idea where in town her friend was staying. She didn't know Fee's current last name, either, she thought as she trudged up the porch steps, but *that* she could find out. The Stanford Alumni Association kept meticulous track of its members and the changes in their lives.

The slam of a car door was loud in the Sunday quiet, but Emily barely registered it as she came pounding down the concrete, swerved as if to avoid a guard, pivoted on the ball of one foot, and arched a shot through the basketball hoop at the end of the garage.

"Way to go, Ma!" called a voice from the driveway.

"Liz!" Standing flat-footed, Emily wiped her face against the sleeve of her T-shirt and smiled at her tall blond daughter. "Whoo. The reflexes are still nifty, but . . . whoo-oo! The wind is gone. Oh, sugar, don't hug Grammy yet; she's all sweaty." The little dark-haired girl ignored this, wrapping herself happily around Emily's bare legs.

"Enough, little kid," said Liz to her daughter. "You don't want to trip your poor old grandma up. Ma, can you spare a bed for a couple of days? I don't have a class till Tuesday afternoon, Davis is having another damned heat wave and the air conditioner in the apartment just quit."

"For you two, anytime," said Emily.

"Hey, what happened to your face? Ma, is Pop still all fucked up about Grandpa and the farm?"

"Not so much that he'd hit me."

"Hey, right, he wouldn't dare," said Liz with a grin. She fell into step beside her mother to hear the story of the hospital and the drunk; Julie Ann trailed along well to the rear. As they reached the top of the stairs to the deck, Ben appeared in the doorway.

"Emily, there's . . . Liz? What's happened? Where's Julie Ann?" he added, his voice sharpening.

"Gee, I must have left her in that bar," drawled Liz, taking a hipshot, chin-out pose as she met her father's glare.

"Listen here, young lady . . ."

"Stop it, both of you!" ordered Emily. "I'm going to shower and then go grocery shopping. Liz, why don't you come along? Papa Ben can baby-sit and give Julie Ann her lunch."

"Just remember that he put up with years of misery from you," Emily advised nearly two hours later.

"I was a teenager for Chrissake!"

"And he's a middle-aged man mourning his youth, his father, and the profession he's giving up."

"He doesn't have to do that. He could tell Grandma to hire a permanent manager or sell the place."

"I know he could."

"So make him do that, Ma. I know *you* could."

Emily shook her head as she turned the Honda onto Eucalyptus Lane. "Baby, you forget your daddy's killer conscience. He can't live with himself if he doesn't do what he believes is right."

"So everybody else suffers, especially you. Ma, you ought to . . . Hey, who belongs to that awesome car?"

The little red machine was parked right in front of Liz's dusty Subaru wagon. Emily eased carefully past it and turned into the driveway. "An old friend of mine, from college."

Fee and Ben were on the deck, Ben with a gin and tonic in his hand, Fee with a glass of iced tea beside her and Julie Ann on her lap.

"Emily!" Ben got to his feet, sloshing his drink. "You have a visitor."

Fee smiled up at the two tall women. "I came by after looking at a house Ben told me about yesterday. It's right in the next block, isn't that lovely? And in good condition and very reasonable."

"Yesterday?" said Emily, raising an eyebrow at Ben.

"Ah, I forgot to mention that Fee dropped by yesterday, while you were out."

"Ah," echoed Emily, and went to fix a drink for herself.

"Listen, what she really came for yesterday was to check up on you, make sure you weren't at the mercy of a battering husband." Ben, who had followed her into the kitchen, seemed both astonished and slightly pleased that anyone might harbor such a two-fisted image of him. "You won't mind that I invited her to stay for supper?"

"No, I won't mind."

For Emily the afternoon passed in slow motion, a series of set pieces with Fee at center stage. Fee in a low-necked blue dress, her blond curls bent close to the smooth dark head of Julie Ann. "Oh, my, I just *wish* I had a sweet little girl like you," Fee murmured, as Julie Ann giggled and wrapped the pretty lady's gold chain around and around her own narrow wrist.

Fee sailing breathlessly through the house, proclaiming her admiration for hand-pegged floors, hand-turned balusters, leaded glass windows in the entry hall, and antique wall-sconce lamps in the dining room. "It's an absolute treasure," she told Ben with a brilliant smile.

Fee, with soft-voiced questions to Liz about school, about her ambitions, about motherhood. About Liz's past (how brave to be so wild and free, to court danger, and did she miss that, didn't she find life dull without it?). Liz was polite, then engaged, then puzzled. And finally sullen, announcing that she was going out for a while if her mother wouldn't mind baby-sitting. Emily noted that Ben let this plan slide right past, with none of his usual questions about destinations and schedules.

Dinner was late because it was necessary to get Julie Ann to bed, and not particularly good because Emily had been sipping gin and tonic all afternoon. As the three of them picked at overcooked chicken, Fee managed to get Ben talking about his elderly, querulous mother, who insisted that he come to run the family dairy farm instead of selling it for enough money to keep her and Ben's whole family in comfort for the rest of their lives.

You could honor an elderly parent without indulging her every whim, Fee suggested. It wasn't selfish to want to choose your own path. And a person approaching fifty (delicate shudder) had better seize life while he or she still could.

All arguments Emily herself had offered, endlessly and to no avail. She thought the small hand resting now and again on Ben's bare forearm looked to be tipped in blood—whose?

Pat, pat went the dainty little paw. Had Ben ever seen the Tower of London? Fee wondered aloud. Or Versailles? And Rome was a must for a lover of history, although she herself preferred Florence.

Emily cleared the table and then stood over the sink hand-washing dishes, letting steam warm her face and the sound of running water drown out voices from the dining room. Strong Emily, who had faced down hoodlums and pimps, who only four days ago had physically subdued a two-hundred-pound drunk, now had a knife-twisting pain in her gut that could only be panic.

"Em?" called Ben, and he came into the kitchen with Fee on his heels. "It's a pretty night out; let's all go for a walk on the beach."

"And leave Julie Ann alone?" she snapped. Ben hunched his shoulders and put a hand to his mouth like a guilty child. Or, she amended, like a sad and worried man being pulled at by two—no, three—women. Five, if you counted Liz and Julie Ann. "You two go ahead," she said quietly. "I'm not quite finished here anyway."

"You sure? Emily, are you all right?" Ben asked.

"Just tired. Fee, I'm sure I'll see you again soon."

"It was lovely of you to have me. Listen, Em, I'd like to get to know this area, and I surely need some exercise; what about a good long hike? Didn't you tell me the other day that there's a place you like to walk?"

"Em hikes along the headlands north of town," said Ben.

"Lovely! Would Tuesday be okay, Em? I'll pick up some deli things for a picnic."

"What happened?" Ben burst into the living room late Tuesday afternoon, his face ashen and his eyes white-rimmed. "Mrs. Jensen next door says you were nearly killed. Why didn't somebody call me at school?"

Emily sat low in a corner of the couch, her right leg elevated on a footstool with the ankle cradled in an ice pack. "Because I'm all right. And Liz was here; she decided to stay over another day."

"You don't look all right; you look like a truck hit you. Em, what *happened*?" As Emily drew a deep breath and Liz choked back a sob, Ben's eye fell on the uniformed policeman seated in the closest wing chair. "Hank, what the hell is going on?"

"Emily here was in an accident, out on the headlands, with a Mrs. Fiona Wellington. I just arrived myself, right behind the ambulance," said Captain Hank Svoboda, brushing a big hand across his bristle-cut gray hair as he turned his gaze on Emily. "Come to tell her the S.O.B. that hit her at the hospital is back in jail, won't be beating on women or little kids for a while anyway. Emily, you up to talking about today?"

"Of course. Fee—Mrs. Wellington—wanted to see the headlands, so we agreed to hike there. She brought a picnic lunch and we ate at the fishing access by Steeler Creek."

"Anything to drink?" asked Svoboda.

"I had two glasses of wine. Fee doesn't drink."

"But she brought the wine?"

"Yes," said Emily, pleased to have a straightforward fact for this man she'd known her whole life. "Anyway, after lunch we just . . . walked, for a long ways, and talked. We were right on the edge; the rock squirrels were full of chatter and Fee kept looking down to see them.

"Then—I'll try to remember how it went." As she let her unfocused gaze rest on some point beyond her stretched-out leg, she felt Ben settle to the couch beside her and take her hand.

"We were above The Jumble, there where the tallest rocks are so close in. The path dips down along the cliff face at that point, maybe—what, eighteen inches wide? I was leading and Fee was close behind me. I thought she said something, but it was high tide, waves crashing against the rocks.

"So I think I slowed and started to turn, to hear her. Then she must have tripped, came against me hard; I had all my weight on my right foot and it twisted." Right foot giving way, knee and shoulder and the side of her face scraping rough rock. Left leg flung wide—for balance? "Fee . . . tumbled right past me, it actually looked slow but I didn't reach out in time. Maybe it was the wine," she said in a voice that grated. "Or maybe it's just that I'm old and my reflexes are gone."

Liz had been watching her mother intently. Now their gazes met, and the girl's blue eyes widened for a long moment before closing in a slow, catlike blink.

"Anyway, she fell and I didn't stop her. And I couldn't"—she gestured at her leg—"go after her."

Hank Svoboda shook his head. "Wouldn't have helped, Emily, not in those rocks at high tide. Just have got you killed, too. Now, is there anything you can tell us about this lady? Like who we should contact, once we recover her body?"

"Her mother is in a nursing home in San Diego," Emily replied, "and I don't think she had anyone else. Fee was widowed twice, and both times there was trouble made by relatives, suggestions that she had some responsibility in the deaths. She was still involved in a battle with her last husband's surviving children over his estate, and I think she was running out of money."

"Emily, how did you learn all that?" asked Ben, astonished.

By calling the alumni association, to learn that Fee had been a member for years and so would have received the earlier issue of the quarterly magazine, the one with the boxed article on the Cochrans: death of Arthur H., Stanford '32, leaving one of California's biggest private dairy farms to Benjamin A., Stanford '60, who was married to Emily Erickson, class of '62. And then, armed with Fee's married names and various addresses, she had called old connections from school and from her many years of work as stringer for various California newspapers.

"Fee liked to talk" was all Emily said.

"That bluff'd be a pretty good place for suicide, supposing that was what a person had in mind," said Svoboda.

Fiona Lacey a suicide? Never in the world, not thirty years ago and not now. "The idea just never occurred to me, or I certainly wouldn't have gone out there with her." Emily's voice shook, and Ben quickly put his arm across her shoulders.

"Ma, she was a *stranger* for Chrissake! Somebody you hadn't seen since *college*." Liz, her fair skin blotched from crying, knelt beside the couch but turned her furious gaze on the policeman. "Listen, my mother is the strongest, bravest person in the world! If anyone could have saved that woman . . . well, I just know she did her best!"

Emily blinked hard and looked at her daughter, bright and beautiful and very close to being safe. She pressed closer against Ben and felt the steady thump of his heart. There were times, she thought, when the best and kindest people were terribly vulnerable, could be led to take a wrong step or be pushed down a wrong path and be afterward forever sorry, damaged perhaps beyond mending. And a person who loved them should not stand by and let that happen. "It's true," she admitted. "I did my best."

Rochelle Majer Krich won an Anthony in 1991 for Best Paperback Original for Where's Mommy Now?, *"a toothsome blend of deceit, infidelity, and murder" (*Publishers Weekly*). Her forthcoming novels include* Till Death Do Us Part, Fair Game, *and* Still Waters. *By focusing on the terrors that lurk just below the surface of the lives of ordinary people, she creates stories that have readers looking over their shoulders to check the room—and the chair beside them—for danger.*

In "A Golden Opportunity," a woman wonders whether the secret of marriage is sometimes to accept your mate's position.

A GOLDEN OPPORTUNITY

by Rochelle Majer Krich

"NOW LOOK WHAT you've done!" George Pearson shrilled.

Wincing, Myra followed her husband's stubby finger to the rectangular beige rug that sat on the white ceramic tile floor at the side entrance to their house. Two footprints were faintly visible on the rug's shaggy pile.

"I'm sorry," Myra said. "I wiped my feet on the outdoor mat and the step."

"I just washed this yesterday. It came out so nice, too." George held out his hand. "Give me your jacket. I don't want you tracking mud all over the floor and on the carpet."

Myra clenched her teeth. When he'd retired eight years ago, George had become a house-husband. Initially, Myra, who still worked, had looked forward to the convenience, but George had become compulsive, and her dream had quickly turned into a nightmare.

Myra removed her navy blue blazer and handed it to George. He headed for the front-entry guest closet. She knew that once out of sight, he would check the pockets, although she wasn't sure what he expected to find in the blazer of a seventy-two-year-old woman. Birth control pills? He'd find a candy wrapper, a parking stub, a Tums. If Myra had secrets, she wouldn't keep them in her pockets. Forty-nine years of marriage had taught her that.

Holding onto the doorjamb, Myra bent down and removed her Rockport pumps. In the laundry room, she scrubbed the grooved soles of each shoe with a stiff brush until the offending dirt was gone. She left the shoes to dry on a shelf above the washing machine. Then she rinsed the dirt until it was swallowed by the drain.

In her stockings, she padded back into the kitchen. George was worrying at an invisible spot on the white Formica counter.

"I cleaned the shoes," Myra said.

Without looking at her, he said, "If you wash the rug too often, the latex backing starts to peel. Then the rug slips. I could fall and break my neck."

Myra pictured George hurrying across the kitchen toward the laundry room. One slippered foot steps onto the mat. The mat slides. George slides with it. He tries to grab the doorknob to break his fall. His hand clutches the air. His legs fly up and scissor. He lands, bony rump first, with a heavy thud. His head hits the tile floor with a frightening, final thwack.

"I'm sorry," Myra repeated. "I'll wash up."

"Supper's ready," George said. "Minute roast. I hope you didn't snack before you left the office."

He was staring at her, and she repressed the urge to run her tongue around her lips and remove any traitorous vestiges of the Pepperidge Farm Sausalito cookie she'd savored an hour ago. "Just a cup of coffee. I'm very hungry." George was pouting now, probably about to ask her how many cups of coffee she'd consumed today, and she thought again how the grooved flesh that radiated from his pencil-thin mouth looked like corrugated cardboard. "I love your minute roast," she added.

"I don't know why you have to go in," George said. "The boys run the office. They don't need you there."

Myra and George had this conversation every day. After his retirement, their sons had taken over the realty firm he and Myra had started. Myra had stayed. She liked going in, being with the boys, and she knew they liked having her there. They'd told her so often enough. George had been resentful, of course, and she'd contemplated, instead, doing volunteer work at Cedars Sinai Medical Center to placate him, but George had said no thank you; she'd be bringing home all kinds of invisible viruses. What did she want to do, kill him?

"I'll be right back." Myra left George in the kitchen and went to the guest bathroom down the hall. The new wallpaper had a seashell pattern on a light green background—sea-foam green, George had said when he'd brought home the sample. On the white Corian sink countertop, there were miniature cream-colored soaps in the shape of seashells sitting in a larger ceramic sea-foam–green shell. Myra ignored those and reached into the cabinet under the counter for the Jergens liquid soap dispenser. She squirted a dollop of soap into one palm, replaced the dispenser, then added water until she created a lather. After washing her hands, she rinsed them in the sink until she was sure the almond scent of the Jergens had disappeared. She liked almonds, but hated Jergens and marzipan. She'd told George that, but he'd said that was ridiculous. If you liked almonds, you liked almonds.

She shut off the water and reached under the counter for the roll of paper towels. She used one sheet to dry her hands, the other to wipe the faucet, the countertop, and the sink. There was Windex glass cleaner inside the cabinet, but she saw that she wouldn't need it today.

She took a brush from a cabinet drawer and ran it through her hair. The pink of her scalp was starting to peek through the gray-white layered waves, but she wasn't unhappy with her hair or with the face in the mirror. It was a comfortable face and, she liked to think, a kind one; it had been a true companion over the years, never betraying her with false promises.

George had tried to convince Myra to dye her hair, but she'd refused. George used Grecian Formula to dye the fringe of hair that bordered his scalp. He used it on his eyebrows too. He was self-conscious about his age and the liver spots that had sprouted on his face and hands and scalp and back. The creams he sneaked into the house had done nothing to erase the spots, but George had taken to erasing a year now and then. He was seventy-three, a year older than Myra, but he'd convinced himself that he was sixty-eight. The children knew better than to contradict him.

Myra put the brush back into the drawer and wiped the sink and counter one more time. There was a fluted sea-foam–green wastebasket in the bathroom, but she threw both used paper towels into the trash can in the service porch. She noticed that the rug had been whisked away.

George was sitting at the round table, reading a paperback. He kept the book hidden behind a brown vinyl cover, but Myra knew it was a mildly pornographic romance, the kind that made him mutter "Disgusting!" and "Perverted!" but made his eyes gleam and his lips work animatedly as he devoured the pages. George read with his lips but denied doing it.

At Myra's entrance, he shut the book (he used the brown bookmark attached to the vinyl cover to keep his place) and put it to the left of his plate.

"The roast smells great," Myra said and smiled. She sat at her place of almost fifty years, filled her glass with ginger ale, and took a sip. "Cheers," she said, and waited a second for George to lift his glass, knowing that he wouldn't. It was a joke they'd shared when they were first married, when they hadn't been able to afford wine, let alone champagne. The ginger ale had tickled her nose and he'd laughed then, and his mouth had been smooth and full and hadn't looked like corrugated cardboard. His hair, thick and wavy, had been a rich, reddish brown, the color of autumn leaves. Ginger ale had been fine then, had been wonderful then.

"I hope it wasn't tar," George said. "Tar doesn't come out."

"It wasn't tar," Myra said quietly.

"How do you know?"

"I know it wasn't tar." She drained her glass and put it down too quickly, knocking it against her plate. It made the mildest clink, but she didn't have to look up to know that George had slipped on his mask of suffering.

She picked up her knife and fork and started cutting the minute roast, separating the meat from the veins. She knew his eyes were on her.

"They still think I don't know about the party," George said, exhaling smugness and irritation.

Their fiftieth anniversary was ten days away. For over a year, George had insisted to the children that he didn't want a golden wedding anniversary celebration. "I don't need a party," he'd said, "just because our other friends have them and Andrea's kids made her fiftieth in a hotel. I don't want you kids to spend your money on me." But of course, Eddie and Joel and Lois were planning a party. George had wheedled the information out of Joel's youngest. And Myra had bought a Rolex watch for George. He'd hinted enough. Myra was grateful that he'd pointed out the style he liked in a magazine. George usually didn't like the gifts she or the kids bought him.

"Don't let on that you know, George," Myra said. "The kids want to surprise us."

"They want to surprise *you*, not me. What do they care about me? They forced me to retire. Why don't they just forget about me until the funeral?"

"They love you, George. And they didn't force you to retire. It was your idea." Not that the boys had been unhappy. Or Myra. Or any of the staff.

"I hate surprise parties. What if they invite the Hemmings? I hate Jim Hemming. He's a goddamn snide son of a bitch. He'll just stand there, snickering about how he's three years older than I am and still works every day. Jogs three miles a day. Plays tennis twice a week. Of course, his kids didn't force him out of the business."

Count to ten, Myra told herself. "The kids know you don't like the Hemmings, George. They probably won't invite them."

"Oh, yeah? How will they explain not inviting them, huh? They're our neighbors, or hadn't you noticed? And that son of a bitch Hemming will tell everyone we didn't invite him 'cause I'm jealous of him." George lifted a forkful of mashed potatoes to his mouth.

"The boys will know what to say. Don't worry about it. It'll be a wonderful party, George. Our golden wedding anniversary, a golden opportunity to see all our friends and family." Myra smiled.

"Golden opportunity!" George snorted. "The bastard will ruin it. He ruins everything. He'll invite Jim Hemming just to torture me."

"The bastard" was Paul, Lois's husband. He'd been "the bastard" for as long as Myra could remember, ever since he and Lois had started dating seriously. Maybe it was because Paul hadn't complimented George enough on his business acumen the first time he'd had dinner in the Pearson home. That's what George had said that night. "The bastard," he'd said. "Thinks just because he's going to law school that he's better'n me. Didn't pay attention to one word I said."

But Myra knew that if it hadn't been that, it would've been something else. Through the years there had been a litany of complaints. "The bastard" was tightfisted, didn't give Lois nearly enough money to run the household. He was talking behind George's back to everyone, ridiculing him. He hardly invited George and Myra to the house. He kept Lois from coming to see her father more often. He was keeping the children from George, too, encouraging them to favor his own parents. The children rarely came to the house, George pointed out, whereas they visited "the bastard's" parents every weekend.

Long ago, when the grandchildren were young, Myra had mentioned once that it wasn't much fun for them to come visit when they and their parents had to worry every minute about irritating George or touching his chess sets or books or games. There was a box of toys in the spare bedroom where Myra slept when she had a cold ("You know how easily I catch cold," George would say, and she couldn't argue with that), toys that had belonged to Joel and Eddie and Lois. But even with those, the children had had to be careful.

Grandpa George didn't like noise.

Grandpa George didn't like a mess.

The children were adults now and didn't need toys or supervision, but the familial patterns had long been established. And everybody knew that the reverse side of the oblong hemp Welcome mat still warned Don't Touch.

Paul was not alone in arousing George's ire. George had myriad epithets, usually foul, for the many people who crossed him: his youngest sister, Andrea, for marrying wealth and, in George's eyes, nursing their mother through her final illness so that she would get the Florida condominium that had been promised to George; his two other sisters for not siding with George; his brothers-in-law for reasons that changed with his moods; the Oriental girl at the checkout stand at Hughes' Market on Beverly and Doheny for purposely making the bags too heavy and positioning the eggs so that they were sure to crack; the reverend's wife, for failing to visit George during his last bout of the flu because he and Myra weren't among the wealthiest members of the church; the reverend for not taking a stronger hand with his wife; Cynthia Hemming, Jim's new, young wife, for once passing by George without saying hello and clearly marrying Jim for his money.

Cynthia Hemming was "a slut" and "a whore," but not "the slut." "The slut" was Sally, Joel's wife, a devoted mother and, to hear Joel tell it, a loving, considerate wife. Her crime was that she was a strikingly pretty blonde who indiscriminately lavished innocent affection on the entire family, including her "bastard" brother-in-law Paul and all the others—and there were many—who had earned George's dislike. And she had once foolishly commented that Jim Hemming was a handsome, friendly man. Sally had tried, in the beginning, to be affectionate toward George too, but George had discouraged her.

George could discourage anyone, Myra thought. She sighed as she remembered their early dates, how he had drawn her to him when they'd necked in the front seat of his green Chevy, remembered the tingling sensation of her mouth opening under his, of his hands finding their way under her sweater, teasing her breasts. His brown eyes had been liquid pools of heat.

Or so she'd thought.

Later, she'd realized that with George, it had been desperation, not passion. He'd been a lonely, solitary figure when they'd started dating. She had been his lifeline to a normal life. A mutual friend had introduced them. (Who? Myra wondered now; she couldn't remember.) She'd been eager to settle down, have a family. Naive. "I'll cherish you forever," he'd said.

The minute roast was a little chewy, and she'd missed a vein. It tasted like rubber, but Myra knew better than to spit it out. She swallowed, but the chunk of meat wouldn't go all the way down. She pushed back her chair and stood.

"Where are you going?" George asked. "Your plate is full."

"Water," she croaked. She took her glass and hurried to the kitchen sink. She drank the water in huge gulps until it drowned the meat and flushed it down her esophagus.

"You're not going to vomit, are you, Myra?" he called. "Because if you are, use the toilet, not the sink."

"I'm not going to vomit," she said. She waited until the burning sensation in her throat and chest subsided, then brought her glass back to the table and resumed her place. "I thought I was choking."

George frowned. "The meat is soft. Don't blame it on the meat."

"It's not the meat. I took too big a bite, that's all."

"Well, then," he said, and nodded, as he always did when he was right. Which was always. "Andrea won't be here, I know. She told me last week she's going to the Bahamas, and why would she give that up for her older brother's fiftieth wedding anniversary?"

"Maybe she'll surprise you." It was unlikely, Myra knew. Andrea and George couldn't be in a room for five minutes before George started in about the condominium.

"I don't even want her to come. I suppose *your* sister and brother will come from New York."

Myra tensed. She'd been expecting this assault, had tried to imagine which direction it would take. "I suppose so. I'm sure the kids will invite them. It's been a long time since we've seen them."

Six years, she realized. Thirty-seven years ago, the realty company George had been working for had offered him a wonderful opportunity if he'd move to Los Angeles. She'd wanted to stay in New York, close to her family, but George had insisted on taking the position. After five years, he'd quit and, with Myra's help, started his own company.

"I won't have them in this house," George said. "If you were planning on having them stay here, you can just forget it."

"They'll probably stay at Joel's house. He has extra rooms."

"Oh, sure! So people can say I'm a rotten brother-in-law!" George stabbed the air with his fork. "I won't have people talking about me, Myra. And you know goddamn well it isn't true. It simply is not true!" George's chest was heaving. His cheeks were puffed with anger.

"We'll work something out."

"How?" he demanded. "We *can't* work it out. They'll have to stay here, that's all, and I'll hate every minute of it, every goddamned minute! Your brother's bad enough. He's a slob. He leaves hair in the sink and pubic hair on the soap bar, and he pees all over the toilet rim and never, ever cleans up after himself! You'll have to take care of that if he comes. I won't be his servant, Myra."

"I'll take care of it," Myra said.

"But your sister! She hates me; you know that. And I can't have someone in my house who hates me. I wouldn't sleep a wink, worrying about what she might do to me."

Myra suppressed a sigh. "Rose doesn't hate you, George."

"She hates me!" George insisted. "She's hated me ever since she knew you were serious about me. She never thought I was good enough for you. She's sick and perverted and I won't have her sleeping in this house! You have no idea . . ."

George's eyes were brown slits now, Myra thought, little worms that were writhing in the sockets of his face. His nostrils had enlarged and were enormous cavities spewing smoke and steam. The Dragon Man, she called him, but never to his face. The mouth was open, but instead of fire, a ribbon of hate was emerging, an endless ribbon that undulated across the table and wrapped itself around Myra's neck again and again, tighter and tighter, until she thought she couldn't breathe.

She wanted to tell him to shut up, to shut the hell up, but she couldn't get the air down to her diaphragm, and she knew that arguing with him was pointless. So was leaving the table. He'd only run after her, follow her to the bathroom, and pound on the door if she locked herself in. *"Myra! I am talking to you!"* And she knew that if she let the Dragon Man rant and foam, he would eventually calm down and Rose and Carl would be allowed to come.

So Myra did what she'd learned to do over the forty-nine years, eleven months, and twenty-one days of their marriage: She stopped listening. She concentrated on the minute roast on her plate, making sure this time to cut away the vein. Then she worked on the mashed potatoes, and finally, on the broccoli, which was overdone and khaki green, the way George liked it. By the time she finished, she could hear that the storm of words had turned into a drizzle.

". . . probably bring us a cheap piece of crystal she picked up in some bargain store or got as a gift, which I have no intention of letting you put on display, not even when they're here, so don't think for one second that I will."

"Of course not," Myra said.

"Well, then," George said and nodded. "And you'd better tell your sister I'm tired of her comments about the way I dress. There's nothing wrong with my suits."

"Of course not, George. You're an impeccable dresser."

"There's no reason I have to get a new suit for the party. I can wear the gray pinstripe."

"The gray pinstripe is very handsome, George. I've always liked that suit on you."

"It's old. It's old, Myra, and it's dated. The lapels are too narrow. I'm sure you and Rose talk about it."

"Why don't you treat yourself to something new?" Myra said. "I'll go with you, if you like." She gritted her teeth. Shopping with George was a special hell. He was rude to salespeople, snickered at them, made disparaging comments in front of them about the fabric, the prices, the style.

"I thought you said you liked the gray pinstripe. So you were just saying that? Is that it, Myra? Maybe you like the way Jim Hemming dresses better."

There were so many traps; it was impossible to sidestep all of them. "I like the suit, George, but I think you're right. It's a special day, a golden opportunity. You should get a new one." She placed her fork and knife on the plate and stood up. "I'm going to get a grapefruit. Do you want half?"

George shook his head and lifted another piece of roast to his mouth.

Myra went into the kitchen. She rinsed her plate and utensils and placed them in the dishwasher. She took the wooden cutting board from underneath the sink and placed it on the counter. Then she took a grapefruit from the refrigerator and put it on the board.

"This meat is delicious, Myra," he called. "I don't know what you were complaining about."

She was overwhelmed with hate so sharp that it sliced through her. She shut her eyes for a moment, imagining what it would be like to shut that mouth forever. When she opened her eyes, she realized that she'd squashed the grapefruit with her hand. It was a red grapefruit, and its ruby liquid had dripped onto her fingers and the floor and the mat directly in front of the sink. She used a paper towel to wipe up the stains on the floor. Those on the mat, she flooded with water until they disappeared.

With a sharp knife, she punctured the porous skin, then severed the fruit in half. She used a different, serrated knife to separate the ruddy triangles of pulp from their membranes. When she was finished, she carefully wrapped one half—the less mangled one—with Saran Wrap and placed it in the refrigerator. The other half she slid onto a plate. Before she left the kitchen, she rinsed the cutting board and knives and returned them to their respective places. She also wiped the counter.

Something crashed.

"George?" she called. She hurried to the breakfast room. George's dinner plate and glass were on the tile floor—a collage of china and glass fragments and mashed potatoes and broccoli and meat. The gravy had trailed along the floor, into the grout.

Myra looked up. "What are you—" Her eyes widened in shock. "Oh, my God!" she whispered.

George's face was grapefruit-red. His eyes were bulging with fear. His mouth was open, but there was no ribbon now, no smoke.

No noise.

Myra's heart beat rapidly. Her mouth was dry. She swallowed.

George gestured frantically to his mouth and shook his head. He clutched his throat. Tears were streaming down his face.

Myra felt sorry for George, but her feet were rooted to the tile floor. Myra wanted to help George, but she didn't want to hear about the meat or the soiled mat or the suit. She didn't want to hear him rant about "the bastard" and "the slut" and Andrea and Rose and Carl and Jim Hemming and the grocery clerk and the mailman and their accountant and her mother, who had been dead for twelve years and had suffered the slings and arrows of outrageous George while Myra stood helplessly by.

Myra wanted to help George, she really did; he was the father of their children, the man she'd lived with for almost fifty years.

But she wanted the silence more.

She loved the silence. The silence soothed her, caressed her, lulled her. The silence stroked her with long, delicate, sensual fingers as George hadn't done in a long time, as George would never do.

Myra backed out of the room and returned to her grapefruit. She heard the chair screeching across the tile floor, knew that George was pushing himself away from the table. She swallowed a section of the fruit; it slid down her throat. She ate another segment. She heard the phone being knocked off the wall. A part of her brain realized that George's fingerprints would be on it. That was good.

She heard the thud that was George's body hitting the tile floor. She panicked for a minute—what if the fall dislodged the piece of minute roast—she *knew* it was the minute roast—from his throat?

She'd have to kill him.

She'd have no choice.

She walked back to the breakfast room. George was on the

floor, his head lying in the mashed potatoes. His face was blue; his tongue was protruding. His eyes were bulging, not with fear, but with death.

Myra returned to the kitchen and finished her grapefruit. She threw the shell into the trash, rinsed and dried the plate and spoon, and put them away. Then she went to the bathroom off their bedroom and showered. She'd been tempted to use one of the guest towels, the thick sea-foam–green Martex towels George had bought at Saks, but she knew nothing should be different. There would be time for sea-foam–green towels. There would be time for everything. After the shower, she used the towel to wipe the shower door and hung it neatly to dry.

Wearing a fresh blouse and slacks, Myra went to the breakfast room and discovered the body. Seeing George again was enough to make her agitation real, and when she called the paramedics, using the second line on the den phone, her voice was shaking.

Instead of a golden wedding anniversary party, there was a funeral. Rose and Carl came with their spouses and stayed with Myra in the house. Rose brought a crystal vase. Myra put it on the fireplace mantel and told her it looked lovely.

"George would have liked it," she said quietly.

Everybody said that Myra Pearson was holding up pretty well, considering.

Gabrielle Kraft, whose Jerry Zalman is featured in four novels, including Edgar nominee Bullshot *and, most recently,* Bloody Mary, *has been an executive story editor and story analyst at major film studios. Now she writes from the safety of the northwest, about the wages of pride and the struggle for power in LaLa Land. She describes her short stories as ". . . the dark side of the Zalman series; if Zalman's is a lollipop view of L.A., the stories are sour pickles."*

In "One Hit Wonder," a has-been recording star tries for a comeback and rebounds into a situation he never bargained for.

ONE HIT WONDER

by Gabrielle Kraft

YOU PROBABLY DON'T remember me, but ten years ago I was very big. Matter of fact, in the record business I was what we call a one hit wonder. You know, the kind of guy you see on talk shows doing a medley of his hit? That was me, Ricky Curtis.

Remember "Ooo Baby Oooo"? Remember? "Ooo baby oooo, it's you that I do, it's you I truly do?" That was me, Ricky Curtis, crooning the insistent vocal you couldn't get out of your head, me with the moronic whine you loved to hate. Big? Hell, I was huge. "Ooo Baby Oooo" was a monster hit, triple platinum with a million bullets. That was Ricky Curtis, remember me now?

My God, it was great. You can't imagine how it feels, being on top. And it was so easy! I wrote "Ooo Baby Oooo" in minutes, while I was waiting for my teenage bride to put on her makeup, and the next day I played it for my boss at the recording studio where I had a job sweeping up. He loved it. We recorded it with some girl backup singers the next week, and it was alakazam Ricky.

For one long, brilliantly dappled summer, America knew my name and sang the words to my tune. People hummed me and sang me and whistled me, and my voice drifted out of car radios through the airwaves and into the minds of the world. For three sun-drenched months, I was a king and in my twenty-two-year-old wisdom I thought I would live forever.

Then, unaccountably, it was over. Because I didn't have a follow-up record, I was a one hit wonder and my just-add-water career evaporated like steam from a cup of coffee. I was ripped apart by confusion and I didn't know what to do next. Should I try to write more songs like "Ooo Baby Oooo"? I couldn't. Not because I didn't want to, but because I didn't know how. You see, I'd had visions of myself as a troubadour, a road-show Bob Dylan, a man with a message. A guy with heart. I hadn't envisioned myself as a man with a teenage tune wafting out across the shopping malls of the land, and "Ooo Baby Oooo" was merely a fluke, a twisting mirage in the desert. I was battered by doubt, and so, I did nothing. I froze, paralyzed in the klieg lights of L.A. like a drunk in a cop's high beams.

The upshot of my paralysis was that I lost my slot. My ten-second window of opportunity passed, and like a million other one hit wonders, I fell off the edge of the earth. I was yesterday's news. I couldn't get arrested, couldn't get a job. Not even with the golden oldies shows that go out on the tired road every summer, cleaning up the rock-and-roll dregs in the small towns, playing the little county fairs, not the big ones with Willie and Waylon, but the little ones with the racing pigs. I was an instant dinosaur, a joke, a thing of the past.

It hit me hard, being a has-been who never really was, and I couldn't understand what I'd done wrong. I'd signed over my publishing rights to my manager and dribbled away my money. In my confusion I started to drink too much—luckily I was too broke to afford cocaine. I drifted around L.A., hanging out in the clubs nursing a drink, telling my then-agent that I was "getting my head together," telling my then-wife that prosperity would burst over us like fireworks on the glorious Fourth and I'd have another big hit record any day now. Telling myself that I was a deadbeat washout at twenty-two.

Fade out, fade in. Times change and ten years pass, and Ricky Curtis, the one hit wonder, is now a bartender at Eddie Style's Club Dingo above the Sunset Strip, shoving drinks across a huge marble bar stained a dark faux-malachite-green, smiling and giving a *c'est la vie* shrug if a well-heeled customer realizes that he's a guy who had a hit record once upon a sad old time.

But inside, I seethed. I smoldered. I didn't know what to do and so I did nothing. You don't know how it feels, to be so close to winning, to have your hand on the lottery ticket as it dissolves into dust, to feel the wheel of the red Ferrari one second before it slams into the wall. To smell success, taste the elixir of fame on your tongue, and then stand foolishly as your future rushes down the gutter in a swirl of brown, greasy water because of your inability to make a decision.

So I worked for Eddie Style. I had no choice. I groveled for tips and tugged my spiky forelock like the rest of the serfs; I smiled and nodded, but in the abyss I called my heart there was only anger. My rage at the crappy hand I'd been dealt grew like a horrible cancer eating me alive, and at night I dreamed of the Spartan boy and the fox.

I'd wake up every morning and think about money. Who had it, how to get it, why I didn't have it. In this town, the deals, the plans, the schemes to make money mutate with each new dawn. But I said nothing. I had nothing to say. I smiled, slid drinks across the bar and watched the wealthy enjoying themselves, waiting for crumbs to fall off the table. In a joint like the Dingo where the rich kids come out to play at night and the record business execs plant their cloven hooves in the trough at will, a few crumbs always fall your way.

Like when Eddie Style offered me a hundred thou to kill his wife.

Edward Woffard Stanhope III, known as Eddie Style to his friends and foes alike, owned the Club Dingo, and he was also a very rich guy. Not from the Dingo, or movie money, not record business money, not drug money, not at all. Eddie Style had something you rarely see if you float around the tattered edges of L.A. nightlife the way I do. Eddie Style had inherited money.

Edward Stanhope III, aka Eddie Style, came from a long line of thieves, but since they were big thieves, nobody called them thieves; they called them Founding Fathers, or Society, or the Best People. Eddie's granddad, Edward Woffard Stanhope Numero Uno, known as "Steady," was one of the guys who helped loot the Owens Valley of its water, real *Chinatown* stuff. You know Stanhope Boulevard over in West Hollywood? Well, Eddie Style called it Me Street, that's the kind of money we're talking about here.

Trouble was, Eddie Style had bad taste in wives. He was a skinny little guy, and he wasn't very bright in spite of the fact that the accumulated wealth of the Stanhope family weighed heavy on his narrow shoulders. Plus, he liked tall women. They were always blond, willowy, fiscally insatiable and smarter than he was. Chrissie and Lynda, the first two, had siphoned off a hefty chunk of the Stanhope change, and Suzanne, the third blond beauty, had teeth like an alligator. At least, according to Eddie. I didn't know. They'd only been married two years and she didn't come around the Dingo. It was going to take another big slice of the pie to divest himself of Suzanne, and Eddie was getting cagey in his old age. After all, he wouldn't come into any more dough until his mother croaked, and she was only fifty-seven. He had a few siblings and half siblings and such scattered around, so a major outlay of capital on a greedy ex-wife didn't seem prudent.

So, one night after closing, he and I are mopping up the bar—I'm mopping up the bar, he's chasing down mimosas—and he starts complaining about his marital situation, just like he's done a thousand nights before.

"Suzanne's a nice girl," he sighed, "but she's expensive." His voice echoed through the empty room, bouncing off the upended chairs on the café tables, the ghostly stage and the rock-and-roll memorabilia encased in Plexiglas.

"You don't say?" In my present line of work, I've learned that noncommittal responses are the best choice, and I switch back and forth between "You don't say" and "No kidding" and "Takes all kinds." Oils the waters of drunken conversation.

"I *do* say. Ricky boy, I've been married three times," he said ruefully, "so I ought to know better by now. You see a girl, you think she's . . ." He narrowed his eyes, looked down the bar to the empty stage at the end of the room and gave an embarrassed shrug. "I dunno . . . the answer to a question you can't quite form in your mind. A hope you can't name."

"Takes all kinds." I nodded and kept on mopping the bar. Like I said, the Dingo was empty, Eddie Style was in a philosophical mood, and I had a rule about keeping my trap shut.

But he wouldn't quit. "You get married and you realize she's just another broad who cares more about getting her legs waxed than she does about you. I can't afford a divorce," he said, pinging the edge of his glass with his forefinger. It was middle C. "I don't have enough money to pay her off."

I felt my brain start to boil. He didn't have enough money! What a laugh! Isn't that the way the song always goes in this town? I love you baby, but not enough. I have money but not enough. To me, Eddie Style was loaded. He owned the Club Dingo, he drove a classic Mercedes with a license plate that read STYLEY, he lived in a house in the Hills, he wore Armani suits for business and Hawaiian shirts when he was in a casual mood. Oh yeah, Eddie Style had it all and Ricky Curtis had nothing.

"See, Ricky boy," he nattered as he took a slug of his fourth mimosa. "Guy like you, no responsibilities, you think life's a ball. Hey, you come to work, you go home, it's all yours. Me, I got the weight of my damn ancestors pushing on me like a rock. I feel crushed by my own history."

"Sisyphus," I said, wringing out the bar towel. After my divorce I'd gone to a few night classes at UCLA in hopes of meeting a girl with brains. Some fat chance. Even in Myths and Legends: A Perspective for Today, all the girls knew "Ooo Baby Oooo."

"Whatever," Eddie sighed. Ping on his glass again. "I can't take much more of this kinda life." He gestured absently at his darkened domain. "If only she'd die . . ." He looked up at me and shot a loud ping through the empty club. His lids peeled back from his eyes like skin from an onion, and he gave me a wise smile. "If only somebody'd give her a shove . . ."

"Hold on," I told him. "Wait a minute, Eddie. . . ."

He didn't say anything else, but it was too late. I could smell dark blood seeping over the layer of expensive crud that permeated the Dingo. He'd planted the idea in my brain, and it was putting out feelers like a science-fiction monster sprouting a thousand eyes.

For three nights I lay in my bed, drinking vodka, staring out the window of my one-bedroom apartment on Ivar, at the boarded-up crack house across the street, and thinking about money. If I had money, I could take a few months off, vacation in Mexico and jump start my life. I had no future as a bartender at the Club Dingo. If I stayed where I was—as I was—I would never change, and I *had* to revitalize my life or I would shrivel and die. If I could get out of L.A., lie on the beach for a month or two, maybe I could start writing songs again, maybe I could have another hit. Maybe *something* would happen to me. Maybe I'd get lucky. The way I saw things, it was her or me.

Three days later Eddie made me the offer. A hundred thou, cash, no problems. He'd give me the keys to the house; I could pick the time and place and kill her any way I wanted.

"Look, Ricky boy, you've got a gun, right?" he said.

"A thirty-eight." I shrugged. "L.A.'s a crazy town."

"Great. Just shoot her, OK? Whack her over the head, I don't care. Do it fast so she won't feel anything. Make it look like a robbery, steal some jewelry. She's got it lying all over her dressing table; she won't use the damn safe. Christ, I gave her enough stuff the first year we were married to fill a vault; just take some of it, do what you want. Throw it down the drain, it doesn't matter. I just gotta get rid of her, OK?"

"OK, Eddie," I said. By the time he asked me to kill her, it was easy. I'd thought it all out; I knew he was going to ask me, and I knew I was going to do it. Ultimately, it came down to this. If murder was the only way to finance another chance, I would become a killer. I saw it as a career move.

I told him I'd do it. Eddie gave me a set of keys to his house and planned to be at the Dingo all night on Wednesday, my night off. He said it would be a good time to kill Suzanne, anxiously pointing out that he wasn't trying to tell me my job. It was all up to me.

I drove up to his house in the Hills; I'd been there for the Club Dingo Christmas party, so I was vaguely familiar with the layout. It was a Neutra house from the thirties, a huge white block hanging over the edge of the brown canyon like an albino vulture, and as I parked my dirty Toyota next to the red Rolls that Suzanne drove, I felt strong, like I had a rod of iron inside my heart. Suzanne would die, and I would rise like the phoenix from her ashes. I saw it as an even trade—my new life for her old life.

I opened the front door with Eddie's key and went inside, padding silently on my British Knights. My plan was to look around, then go upstairs to the bedroom and shoot her. Eddie said she watched TV most nights, used it to put her to sleep like I used vodka.

The entry was long, and there was a low, flat stairway leading down to the sunken living room. The drapes were pulled back, and I could see all of Los Angeles spread out through the floor-to-ceiling windows that lined the far wall. The shifting shapes of moving blue water in the pool below were reflected on the glass, and in that suspended moment I knew what it meant to live in a world of smoke and mirrors.

"Who the hell are you?" a woman snapped.

It was Suzanne and she had a gun. Dumb little thing, a tiny silver .25 that looked like it came from Le Chic Shooter, but it was a gun all the same. Eddie never mentioned that she had a gun, and I was angry. I hadn't expected it. I hadn't expected her either.

I'd met her at the Christmas party, so I knew she was gorgeous, but I'd been pretty drunk at the time and I wasn't paying attention. Suzanne Stanhope, nobody called her Suzie Style, was a dream in white. She was as tall as I was, and she had legs that would give a lifer fits.

"Eddie sent me," I said brightly. "He forgot his datebook. Didn't he call you? He said he was gonna . . ." I let my voice trail off and hoped I looked slack-jawed and stupid. I thought it was a damn good improvisation, and my ingratiating grin must have helped, because she lowered the gun.

"You're the bartender, the one who used to be a singer, right?" she asked. "Now I recognize you." She loosened up, but she didn't put down the gun.

This was going to be easy. I'd bust her in the head, steal the jewelry and be a new man by morning. I smiled, amazed that one woman could be so beautiful.

She was wearing a white dress, loose, soft material that clung to her body when she moved, and the worst part was, she wasn't even trying to be beautiful. Here she was, probably lying around in bed watching TV, painting her toenails, and she looked like she was going to the Oscars. Once again I saw the futility of life in L.A. without money.

"Tell Eddie I could have shot you," she said, very mild. "He'll get a kick out of that." She still had the little silver gun in her hand, but she was holding it like a pencil, gesturing with it.

"Sure will, Mrs. Stanhope," I said, grinning like an intelligent ape.

"Oh, cut the crap, will you? Just call me Suzanne." She looked me over, and I got the feeling she'd seen better in the cold case. "You want a drink, bartender? What's your name, anyway?"

"Ricky Curtis."

"Rick, huh?" She frowned and started humming my song. "How does that thing go?" she asked.

I hummed "Ooo Baby Oooo" for her. Her hair was shoulder length, blond, not brassy. Blue eyes with crinkles in the corners like she didn't give a damn what she laughed at. "Ooo baby oooo, it's you that I do . . . ," I hummed.

"So how come you don't sing anymore, Rick?" she asked as she led me down the steps into the sunken living room. I could see the lights of the city twinkling down below and idly wondered if, on a clear day, I'd be able to see my apartment on Ivar or the boarded-up crack house across the street.

"How come nobody asks me?" I said.

She went behind the bar, laughing as she poured herself a

drink. Sounded like wind chimes. She put the little gun down on the marble bar, and it made a hollow clink.

"Vodka," I told her.

She poured me a shot in a heavy glass, and I drank it off. I had a strange feeling, and I didn't know why. I knew Eddie Style was rich, but this was unlike anything I'd ever seen before. The sheer weight of the Stanhope money was crushing me into the ground. Heavy gravity. I felt like I was on Mars.

She sipped her drink and looked thoughtfully out the huge windows, past the pale translucent lozenge of the pool toward the city lights below. "It's nice here," she said. "Too bad Eddie doesn't appreciate it. He'd have a better life if he appreciated what he has, instead of running around like a dog. The Dingo is aptly named, don't you think, Rick?"

I wanted another drink. I wanted to be drunk when I killed her, so I wouldn't feel it. I hadn't planned on killing a person, just a . . . a what? Just a blond body? Just a lump in the bed that could be anything? I hadn't counted on looking into her clear blue eyes as the light went out of them. I pushed my glass across the counter, motioning for another drink.

"So why are you here, Rick?" she asked softly. "It was a good story about the datebook but Eddie's too frazzled to keep one. I'm surprised you didn't know that about him. Maybe you two aren't as close as you think."

I didn't know what she meant. Was she kidding me? I couldn't tell. What was going on? I had that old familiar feeling of confusion, and once again, I was in over my head. Did she *know* I was there to kill her? I couldn't let her think that, so I did the next best thing. I confessed to a lesser crime.

"I'm broke," I said shortly, "and Eddie said the house was empty. I was here at the Christmas party and I figured I could bag some silver out of the back of the drawer. Maybe nobody would miss a few forks. It was a dumb idea but it's tap city and Eddie has more than he needs. Of everything," I said, looking directly at her. "You gonna call the cops?"

"Robbery? That's an exciting thought," she said, clinking the ice in her glass as she leaned her head back and popped an ice cube in her mouth. She took it out with her fingers and ran it over her lips. "You value Eddie's things, his lifestyle. Too bad he doesn't."

"In this town it's hard to appreciate what you have," I said slowly, wondering how her lips would feel, how cold they really were. "Everybody always wants what they can't get."

"Don't they," she said meaningfully as she dropped the ice cube back in her glass. "What do *you* want, Rick? Since you brought it up."

"Me? I want money," I said. As the phrase popped out of my mouth I realized how pathetic it sounded. Like a teenager wanting to be a rock star, I wanted money. That's the trouble with L.A. Being a bartender isn't a bad gig, but in L.A., it's just a rest stop on the freeway to fame, a cute career to spice up your résumé.

"That shouldn't be tough for a good-looking guy like you. Not in this town." She refilled our glasses and led me over to a white couch. There were four of them in an intimate square around a free-form marble table. I felt like I was somebody else. I'd only had a couple short ones and I was wondering what she wanted in a man. I wondered if she was lonely.

"Sit down," she said, her white dress splitting open to show me those blond legs. "Let's talk, Rick," she said.

"Sure I married him because he's rich, just like he married me because I'm beautiful," she said, running a finger across my stomach. "But I thought there was more to it than that. He was sweet to me at first. He didn't treat me like some whore who spent her life on her knees. Christ, I'm tired of men who want me because I'm beautiful and then don't want me because I'm smart. Am I smart, Rick?" she asked, pulling the sheet around her body as she got out of bed. "Want anything?"

Mars. I was on Mars. You hang around L.A., you think you know the words to the big tune, but you don't. You think you've seen a lot, know it all, but you don't, and as I lay in his bed caressing his wife, I wondered how it would feel to be Eddie Style. Live in his house, sleep with his wife. If I had a room like this, why would I ever leave it? If I had a wife like that, why would I want to kill her? The sheets were smooth, some kind of expensive cotton the rich like; the carpet was soft—was it silk? The glinting perfume bottles on her dressing table were heavy, geometrically cut glass shapes twinkling with a deep interior light far brighter than the city below. If I unstoppered one of those bottles, what would I smell?

She let the sheet drop to the floor as she lowered herself into the bubbling blue marble tub at the far end of the room. I lay in Eddie's bed and watched her as she stretched her head back and exposed a long white highway of throat pointing to a dark and uncharted continent. I thought about killing her and realized it was too late.

"This is insane," I said.

She laughed. "It's so L.A., isn't it? The bartender and the boss's wife, the gardener and the . . ."

"Yeah, I read *Lady Chatterly*. I'm not a complete illiterate," I told her. "What do you want to do about it?"

"Oh, we could get together afternoons in cheesy motels," she said. "Think you'd like that?"

"Sounds great," I said ironically. "Don't you think you'd find cheesy motels boring after a while? Say, after a week or so?" I got up out of bed, went over to the tub and got in with her. The water warmed me to the bone. "You could come live with me in my one-bedroom. You'd fit in just fine. Course, you'd have to leave this house behind," I said as I slipped my hands underneath her body and lifted her on top of me. "And there wouldn't be much time for shopping since you'd have to get a job slinging fries. Think you'd miss the high life?"

"Probably," she gasped.

"Yeah, I think so too. But we can talk about it later, right?"

"Right," she said, clutching at my back with those beautifully sculpted nails. "Yessss."

Of course, I left without killing Suzanne. Then I went back to the Dingo and yelled at Eddie, which was a laugh since I'd been rolling around with his wife all evening. Funny thing, though. As I stared at Eddie Style, sitting on his usual stool at the long faux-malachite bar, I felt contempt for him. He had everything, Eddie did. Money, cars, a beautiful wife. But he didn't know what he had, and that made him a bigger zero than I was. Even with all that money.

"Why the hell didn't you tell me she had a gun?" I snarled over the blast of the head-banging band onstage. I'd never snarled at him before, and it felt good.

"I forgot," he said, very apologetic as he tugged on his mimosa. "Really, Ricky boy, I didn't think about it. It's just a little gun. . . ."

"Easy for you to say," I grumbled. "Don't worry about it, man. I'll take care of it for you."

But I didn't.

I called Suzanne a few days later, she came over to my apartment and we spent the afternoon amusing ourselves.

"Why don't you fix this place up?" she said. "It doesn't have to look like a slum, Rick."

"Sure it does. It *is* a slum," I told her, stroking the long white expanse of her back. "You think it's *La Bohème*? Some sort of arty dungeon? Look out the window, it's a slum."

"Don't complain, you've got me. And," she said as she got out of bed and went over to her purse, "now you've got a nice watch instead of that cheapo."

You think your life changes in grand, sweeping gestures—the day you have your first hit, the day you get married, the day you get divorced—but it doesn't. Your life changes when you stretch out your hand and take a flat velvet-covered jeweler's box with a gold watch inside that costs two or three thousand dollars. Your life changes when you don't care how you got it.

When you're a kid, you never think the situation will arise. You think you'll be a big star, a hero, a rock legend; you don't think you'll be lying in bed in a crummy Hollywood apartment with another guy's wife and she'll be handing you a little gift. Thanks, honey, you were great.

I took the watch. A week later, I took the five hundred bucks she gave me "for groceries." You see the situation I was in? Here

I was, supposed to kill Eddie Style's wife for a hundred thousand dollars, and I was too busy boffing her to get the job done. Me, the guy who was so hungry for cash that his hands vibrated every time he felt the walnut dash on a Mercedes.

I was swept by the same confusion I'd felt after "Ooo Baby Oooo." Once again I was staring out over a precipice into an endless expanse of possibilities, and I didn't know what to do. I was looking at a row of choices lined up like prizes at a carnival, and the barker was offering me any prize I wanted. But which one should I take? The doll? The stuffed monkey? The little toy truck? Reach out and grab it, Ricky boy. How do you make a decision that will determine the course of your life? A thick, oozing paralysis sucked at me like an oil slick.

All I had to do was kill her and I couldn't do it. When she wasn't around I fantasized about taking her out for a drive and tossing her down a dry well out in Palm Desert or giving her a little shove over the cliff as we stared at the sunset over the Pacific. But when she was around, I knew it was impossible. I couldn't kill Suzanne. Her beauty held me like a vise.

Beautiful women don't understand their power; their hold on men is far greater than they comprehend. Women like Suzanne sneer at their beauty; they think it's a happy accident. Mostly they think it's a commodity, sometimes they think it's a gift, but they don't understand what the momentary possession of that beauty does to a man, how it feels to see perfection lying beside you in bed, to stare at flawless grace as it sleeps and you know you can touch it at will.

The flip side of my problem was that a rich guy like Eddie Style didn't understand that possessing a woman like Suzanne made me his equal. Within the four corners that comprise the enclosed world of a bed, a fool like me is equal to generations of Stanhope money.

"So, Ricky boy, when you gonna do that thing?" Eddie asked me late one night, giving me a soft punch on the arm. He's acting like it's a joke, some kind of a scene. Kill my wife, please.

"Don't pressure me, Eddie; you want it done fast, do it yourself." Now that I was a hired gun, I no longer felt the need to kiss the hem of his garment quite so fervently or quite so often. Weird, what power does to you. You start sleeping with a rich guy's wife, you feel like a superhero, an invincible Saturday morning kiddie cartoon. "If you'd told me about the gun, I would have killed her that first night. Now the timing's screwed up."

This was true, and it creased a further wrinkle into my murderous plans. The vacationing couple was back at work at Eddie's big white house in the daytime, so it was no longer possible to slip in and kill Suzanne even if I'd had the guts to do it. Too many people around.

Besides, I was no longer an anonymous cipher, a faceless killer. I was a piece of Suzanne's life, although Eddie didn't know it. Now that she was coming to my apartment for nooners, I knew we'd been seen together. The elderly lady with ten thousand cats who lived across the courtyard and peeked out between her venetian blinds at people coming in and going out, Suzanne's big red Rolls parked on Ivar—there were too many telltale traces of my secret life, traces that would give me away if I *did* kill her.

So there I was, stuck between skinny Eddie Style and his beautiful wife, and it was at this point that a brilliant idea occurred to me. What if I killed Eddie Style? What if I killed the husband and not the wife? Assuming Suzanne approved of the idea, it would have a double-edged effect; it would cement Suzanne to all that Stanhope money and it would cement me to Suzanne. For I had no intention of allowing her to remain untouched by Eddie's death, if I chose to kill him instead of her.

Turnabout.

But would Suzanne take to the idea of killing her husband? Would she see me as a lout, as a sociopathic lunatic, or merely as the opportunistic infection I truly was? Or would she, too, see murder as a career move?

At night I worked at the Dingo, and though I poured drinks, laughed and chatted with the customers, I was changed inside, tempered by my connection to death. Now that I was concentrating on murder, I was no longer a failure, a one hit wonder. I was invaded by the knowledge that I possessed a secret power setting me apart from the faceless ants who surrounded me in the bar. A few weeks ago, I was a shabby, sad wreck tossed up on the shores of Hollywood with the rest of the refuse, the flotsam and jetsam of the entertainment business. Now that I was dreaming about murder, I was on top again, and I had the potential of ultimate power.

A week later I decided to talk to Suzanne about killing Eddie. I had no intention of bringing up the question directly; I was too clever for that. I planned to approach her crabwise, manipulate our pillow talk in the direction of murder. If she picked up the cue, well and good. If not, I'd have to alter my plans where she was concerned.

It was Wednesday, my night off, and Eddie was at the Dingo. I called Suzanne and said I'd be at her house that night. She wasn't too happy that I was coming over, but I let my voice go all silky and told her I felt like a hot bath.

The white Neutra house was lit up by soft floodlights, and as I knocked on the door, it reminded me of the glistening sails of tall ships flooding into a safe harbor bathed in sunshine.

The door opened. It was Eddie Style. "Do you think you should be here, Ricky boy?" he asked, very mildly.

Not a good sign. I had a moment of fear, but I covered it. I was feeling omnipotent, and besides, I had my .38 in my jacket pocket. "You mean we've got to stop meeting like this?" I mocked. Simultaneously, I knew I was in over my head and apprehension started nibbling at my shoes.

He held open the door for me, and I went inside, automatically stepping down into the sunken living room. Suzanne, wearing a white kimono with deep, square sleeves, was sitting on the couch, a drink in her hand. Her nails shone red as an exploding sun and her face was flat, expressionless. All the beauty had drained out of it, and there was only the molded mask of a mannequin staring back at me from behind a thick sheet of expensive plate glass. Who was she?

Confusion swept me, and I was carried off down the river like a dinghy in a flash flood.

"Here we all are," Eddie said. "Drink?"

I nodded yes. "Vodka."

"Ricky boy," he said as he went behind the bar, "I've had you followed and I know you're sleeping with my wife. I'm afraid I can't stand still for that," he said slowly. "When the help gets out of line it makes me look foolish and I simply can't allow it to go unpunished." He reached underneath the bar and pulled out the shiny silver .25 Suzanne pointed at me that first night.

Now the dinghy was caught in a whirlpool. "I'm sorry, Eddie," I said. "These things . . . just happen." I indicated Suzanne. "I'm sorry."

"Ricky boy, I know what you think. I've seen you operate." His voice was cold and he was still holding the gun. "You think because I'm rich you can come along, skim a little cream off the top and I'm so stupid I won't notice. You think you're as good as I am, street-smart Ricky boy, the one hit wonder. Wrong, buddy. Dead wrong. You're not as good as I am and you never will be."

The absurd little gun was firmer in his hand, and I had the cold, cold feeling he was going to shoot me. He'd claim I was a robber, that his faithful minion had betrayed his trust. Who'd dare to call Edward Woffard Stanhope III a liar? With his beautiful wife Suzanne by his side to back up his story, why would anybody try?

I looked at Suzanne. Her face was unmoved. I felt empty and desperate in a way I hadn't felt since I'd started sleeping with her. I'd had a taste of invincibility in her bed, but she was giving me up without a backward glance; I could read the news on the shroud that passed as her face. I felt like a fool. What made me think she'd choose me instead of the unlimited pool of Stanhope money? Once Eddie killed me, she'd have him forever. He'd never be able to divorce her; they'd be locked in the harness until the earth quit spinning and died.

"Eddie, that's not it," I said. I heard the helplessness in my own voice. I sounded tinny, like a playback. "OK, man, it was a mistake to get involved with your wife. I know that. I'm sorry." I was trying to sound contrite, once again the serf tugging his forelock. I walked over to him and shifted my right side, the side with the gun in the pocket, up against the bar so neither of them could see what I was doing. Slowly, I dropped my hand and began to inch my fingers toward the gun.

"Yeah?" he laughed, an eerie sound like wind whining down a tunnel. "Tell me how sorry you are."

Confusion butted heads with omnipotence. This was the time, the moment, my last chance for a comeback, and I gave omnipotence free rein as I kept inching my hand toward the gun in my pocket. "Ever try, Eddie? Ever try and fail? You've never had to work, rich boy. You have it all. The house, the wife, the car. You want to own a nightclub? Buy one. You want your wife killed? Hire it done."

Suzanne gasped out loud. "Killed?" she said slowly. "You wanted me *killed*?" she asked Eddie, her voice thick with distaste.

"He promised me a hundred thou to get rid of you, princess. Ain't that a kick in the head?"

"Rick, you were going to kill me?" she asked. "That first night, you were here to kill me. . . ." Now she was thoughtful, pondering her own murder like a stock portfolio.

Eddie Style said nothing.

My fingers closed on the gun and I turned toward him, slowly. "Think about living without that mass of cash behind you, that blanket of money. Ain't easy, Eddie. But you'll never know 'cause whatever happens, you've always got a fallback position. The rich always do."

It wasn't until I said it that I realized how much I hated him, how much I hated his flaccid face, his thin shoulders that had never seen a goddamn day's work, his weak mind that never had to make a tough decision, his patrician arrogance. I pulled the gun out of my pocket, fired and caught him right between the eyes.

I heard Suzanne shriek as blood sprayed out of the back of Eddie's head, splattering the polished sheen of the mirror on the back bar with a fine mist. His body crashed to the floor, taking a row of heavy highball glasses with it, shattering a few bottles. The smell of blood and gin filled the air. I didn't give a damn.

It was all mine. At last I'd turned myself inside out, and the mildewed scent of failure that had clung to me was gone. I was no longer a grinning monkey at the Club Dingo, but Zeus. A king. I was on top, a winner at last.

"Your turn, love," I said softly. "What's it gonna be? The way

I see things," I said, pocketing the gun as I went over and sat down on the couch beside her, "Eddie just struck out and I'm on deck. He's dead, I'm alive and you're rich. Time to choose up sides for the Series."

She shuddered like a stalled Ford. "You killed him. You killed Eddie." Her voice was quiet and she sounded vaguely surprised.

"Yeah. I did. Now, you got two choices. You can do what I tell you to do or you can die."

"I thought you said two choices, Rick. I only heard one," she said carefully. Her voice had changed, and her face was no longer an expressionless mask. "Can I go look?" she asked as she got up and went behind the bar. She stood there for a minute, looking down at her dead husband; then she bent down and touched his cheek. "What do you want me to do?" she asked me as she straightened up.

"First thing I want, I want you to come over here and wrap your prints around my gun," I told her. "That'll keep you in line just in case you get tired of me, some faraway night when we're under the stars on the Mexican Riviera. I'll keep the gun for insurance."

"Don't you trust me?"

"This is L.A. I don't trust anybody who's ever breathed smog. Then I give you a black eye and leave. I won't hurt you, much. You call the cops and say a bad, bad robber broke in and killed hubby. You'll have a rough few months, but I'll take care of the Dingo and we can meet there once in a while. Maybe next year, we'll get married. Think you'd like a June wedding?"

"You're a cold son of a bitch; how come I didn't notice it before?"

"You weren't interested in my mind, Suzanne. Look, baby, now that Eddie's out of the picture we can have it all. Don't you understand, I can't afford to blow this off. I had one hit, I blew it. Usually, one hit is all you get in this town but I got a second chance tonight and I'm taking it. I'm not gonna get another. Ever."

"Why did he want me killed?" she said, looking down at Eddie's bloody body.

"Do you have to know? Money, OK? Isn't it always money? He said you cost too much and he didn't have enough money to pay you off."

"Greedy hog," she said and made an ugly snorting noise. "But that's what they all say, right, Ricky boy?"

I walked over to her, very fast, and slapped her in the face, very hard. "Never call me Ricky boy again, Suzanne," I said, a tight hold on her arm. "Call me honey or sweetie or baby or call me you jerk, but don't ever call me Ricky boy."

She pulled away from me, rubbing the red spot on her cheek where I'd hit her. "Why'd you have to hit me? I wish the hell you hadn't hit me. . . ." Her voice trailed off like a little girl's as she stepped back, leaned against the bar and buried her hands in the deep sleeves of her white kimono. She looked up at me and I saw death in her eyes. My death.

I saw it all and there was nothing I could do. She smiled and seemed to move very, very slowly, though in the back of my mind I knew everything was happening normally, skipping along in real time. The little silver gun slipped into her hand like a fish eager for the baited hook, and I realized she'd picked it up when she'd knelt down next to Eddie's dead body. She aimed it at me and fired. I watched as the gun leapt back in her hand and the bullet jumped straight for my heart.

I felt the slug sink into my body, only a .25, I told myself, a girl's gun, nothing to worry about. But Suzanne's aim was true. I put my hand to my chest and it felt scorched and fiery, like I'd fallen asleep with the hot water bottle on my naked flesh. I took my hand away and looked at it foolishly. Red. I had a red hand. Where the hell did I get a red hand? I was hot and tired and all of a sudden I thought a nap would do me good. Somewhere far away I heard her voice. . . .

"You were right, Rick. In this town, one hit is all you get."

Karen Kijewski, winner of the 1988 St. Martin's Press/Private Eye Writers of America award for Katwalk *(which also earned Anthony and Shamus awards for Best First Novel), shares several attributes with Kat Colorado, her Sacramento-based private eye. Both are concerned with friendship and independence, and both know the difference between a sidecar and a stinger, having put in their time tending bar. Kat's adventures continue in* Katapult, Kat's Cradle, *and* Copy Kat.

In "Alley Kat," a politician juggling problems with his career and his family comes to Kat for help.

ALLEY KAT

by Karen Kijewski

SHE WAS FIVE-FOOT-SEVEN with thick, curly brown shoulder-length hair, green eyes that were shadowed by heavy makeup, dimples. Hot pink leather miniskirt, pale pink blouse with too many buttons undone, sequined panty hose. Way too much makeup. The woman looked like a hooker, a high-class one, not an alley cat. On the other hand a lot of perfectly respectable women look like that these days.

I narrowed my eyes critically. She put on more lip gloss, a spritz of perfume. Too much perfume. I smiled. Perfect. I slipped on hot pink flats that matched the skirt. The woman was me.

I was headed for a bar but not to drink or hook. To look for a blackmailer. It wasn't my idea of a good time; I was getting paid for it. Paid, but not enough. Pink flats and sequined tights? Not nearly enough.

Manny had walked into my office earlier in the week. "You owe me Colorado." No *Hi?*, no *How you doing?* Rude, huh?

I looked up from the report I was compiling for a corporate client and shook my head.

"No," I said, "I don't. Not even in your dreams."

He had parked his pinstripe-suited lean and hungry body against the door frame, a tall man with a slim girlish figure and a cleft chin. When he smiled, his eyes lit up. With lies. The lies danced around and made promises that wouldn't be kept. I knew this; I still smiled. For a con artist, he's okay.

"Nice try." I rechecked the latest entry on my report.

"You didn't even think about it." He was still smiling, still giving it his best shot.

"I never owe someone I don't trust, and I don't trust politicians."

"I need your help, Kat. My man—"

"Your man?" I asked, sounding puzzled but being obnoxious. I knew of course.

"The senator. We've got a job and it needs honesty, discretion, and speed."

Honesty? Discretion? I stared at him. Yeah. Right. Well, I suppose anyone can memorize words. He had no idea what they meant, of course. I did. That's why I wasn't going to work for him, or for the senator who employed him as a front man, PR person, gofer and worse, no doubt.

"You want to hire a private investigator?"

"You got it." His eyes lit up, pleased that I'd caught on.

"Yellow pages over there." I pointed. He looked less pleased. "Use my phone if it's a local call. Glad to help." I lied, and I let the lies dance in my eyes at his consternation.

"Katy—"

The lies, the dances faded. "Don't do it, Manny." There was an ugly warning note in my voice.

"Please."

I shook my head. He was going back a long time: to Katy, to unfriendly streets growing up, to old ties and blood brothers.

"Just listen to him. After that if you don't want anything to do with it, I butt out. Please, Katy."

Katy again.

"Please."

"Aw *shit*."

"Thanks. Let's take a meeting right now."

"Take a meeting? This is Sacramento, not L.A., Manny."

He ignored me. Why not? He'd won; he had nothing to lose.

"The senator's waiting outside in the car."

I opened my mouth and he shook his head. "He can't afford to be seen going into a private investigator's office. Consider it."

I considered it. And I could afford to be seen in a senator's car? I've got a good reputation in this town. All right, I *had* a good reputation. That was before the hot pink leather miniskirt and matching flats. Don't forget the sequined tights. Rhinestones in my ears too. *Damn.*

Manny escorted me out of the office with all the aplomb of a trainer who's just gotten a recalcitrant seal to jump through the hoop. I didn't clap my hands and bark though; I was hanging onto what was left of my dignity. A senator. *Goddamn.*

It was a small limousine—or is that an oxymoron?—smoky gray, with tinted windows. Manny opened the back door and ushered me in, then got in the driver's seat. There was a privacy panel between the driver and the rest of the limo. Manny closed it.

"Ms. Colorado." The senator leaned across a quarter acre of back seat to shake my hand. "How nice to meet you. Manny says you're the best in town." His eyes swept across me and landed politely on mine, ignoring the Levis, oversized sweater and scuffed Western boots. "I'm delighted you're on the team."

I shook my head. "I'm not. I'm just here to listen." Doubt flickered in his eyes. For a moment he looked like a kid watching a toy being pulled out of his reach. A mean kid.

"Fair enough," he said, obviously not meaning it. But then he was a politician and such things came easily to him. I looked him over: senator-cookie-cutter-stamp-#3 was my guess. Tall, with the build of an ex-jock going to seed, brown hair fading into gray at the temples, expensive well-pressed suit, wing tips, perfect teeth, honest eyes, a sincere smile and an easy charm. The last three radical departures from truth were turned in my direction, but not full force. A good politician knows his audience.

"Serving the people of the state of California is an honor, Ms.

Colorado, a mighty big one." I started to hum "My Country 'Tis of Thee" but caught myself in time and shut up. "But with that great and weighty honor come great and significant drawbacks."

I looked out my window. We had left midtown, where my office is, and were heading in the general direction of Sacramento City College. I turned back to the senator. Reluctantly.

"Shall we cut to the chase, Senator?"

He flushed slightly. "Someone's trying to get my daughter." He said it simply and with real feeling. I found myself responding positively for the first time. Not liking him, no, that was too strong a verb; not disliking him either.

"Get your daughter?"

He flushed deeply this time. "She's a good kid, but young, sometimes a little wild. You know how kids are?" His voice pleaded with me—not just to know but to not judge her harshly, maybe not judge her at all.

His senator-cookie-cutter look was blurred, sad, as though someone had cut the cookie too quickly, too clumsily.

"What happened?" I kept my voice level, neutral.

"She was at a party. Went with girlfriends. A lot of young people were there. Lot of drinking. She . . . she passed out, says she doesn't remember anything until three or four in the morning. Her girlfriends found her in an empty bedroom. Not all her clothes were on. There were other things . . . uh . . . compromising things."

He ran his hands through his perfectly combed, blow-dried and sprayed hair. It looked like hell after that, three or four hairs out of place, easy. He didn't look like a senator now, just like another worried, anxious dad. I started to like him. Almost.

"You have kids?" He didn't look at me, didn't want or expect an answer. "Hell, you do the best you can and you still feel it's not enough, not— She didn't tell us until three days later." He looked at me. "She wouldn't have even then but . . ." I waited it out. ". . . her doctor mentioned it, out of concern of course. We golf together and—you see?"

I saw. The girl had made a mistake, had had too much to drink in what had turned out to be an unsafe environment. Her friends hadn't stuck with her; her doctor had betrayed his oath and her confidence and tattled to his golf buddy. Now he was tattling to me. My moment of almost liking him faded as quickly as a popsicle on a hot day.

"No, I don't see. That's over and done with."

"It's not that easy."

I shrugged. It seemed easy to me. The limo idled at a stoplight and I looked out on William Land Park. The light changed and we started through the park toward the zoo.

"It's not over. There are photos."

"Of?" I asked, but I knew.

"Of her. Of Saundra. Compromising photos."

"And?" I knew that too.

"They want money. Blackmail."

"Extortion."

"Huh?" He looked at me, his all-American nice-guy face caved in like an old man's in the morning without his dentures. "Yeah, whatever."

"What do you want me to do?" Another question I knew the answer to. I was on a roll. Days like this I should be on "Jeopardy" or drive to Tahoe, play blackjack.

"I want them: the pictures, the negatives. He threatened to make them public, to trash Saundra's reputation. I can't have that . . . I . . ."

"Extortion is a felony. Go to the cops."

His head snapped up off his chest, where he had been snuffling manfully in an expensive silk tie.

"No! That's just as bad. I want her protected, not exposed to an investigation, to ridicule, to a public trial. God, no! I want it handled privately, discreetly. I don't care about the costs; I just want to take care of it, of her—"

"And of your career," I finished.

He looked at me, eyes numb with pain, and shook his head stupidly. "Every kid makes mistakes. Your dad's well known, you're held to different standards. It's not right, but it's the way it is. I want to protect my daughter, any father would. My career? You *can't* think that!"

But I did. I was that cynical. A cynical private investigator? Go figure.

"How did he contact you?"

We approached, then passed the entrance to the zoo. The human beast was enough for us apparently.

"He wrote, asked for money, said he'd call and tell me when and where."

"You have the letter, of course."

He shook his head miserably. "No, I threw it away. Stupid, I know, but it was trash, filth. I didn't want it around."

"Handwritten?"

"Typed. No, off a printer. The page had serrated edges."

"Signed?" Of course not. I was just covering all the bases.

"No."

"Dated?"

"No."

"Postmark?"

"I don't know, I threw the envelope away."

Covering ground fast and getting nowhere. Not my favorite kind of investigation.

"Has he called yet?"

"Tomorrow," he said. "You'll be there; I'm glad." His face had filled out again, and he enunciated his words now in a hearty senatorial voice, booming with assurance and heavy on rhetoric, easy on facts. Politics as usual.

"Maybe."

"Maybe? I thought—"

"I need to talk to your daughter first."

"To Saundra? Absolutely not. It's out of the question. I can't have her bothered, disturbed any further by this. *Absolutely* not!"

"All right."

He looked relieved. I looked at his watch; I don't wear one. It was later than I thought; it always is. The senator smiled complacently at me.

"Shall I tell Manny I need to get back to my office, or will you?"

"Your office?" He asked it stupidly.

Should have gone to the zoo after all, I reflected. At least there the monkeys don't talk.

"But we haven't discussed the meeting place, how you'll make the exchange, your fee."

"We haven't," I agreed, "but there's no need since I'm not working for you." I tapped on the glass partition. Manny slid it open. "Drop me off at my office please, Manny."

The silence was loud, the senator's breathing harsh and rapid. Good heart attack or stroke material, I thought. Type A behavior: genetic selection of the nineties. I leaned back into the cushions and closed my eyes. Manny cleared his throat with just the hint of a question mark. Age and politics had made him more subtle. As a kid he'd busted heads and noses. I liked him better then.

The senator pushed buttons on a cellular phone. "Rena, are my wife and daughter home? Yes. Yes. Tell my wife I'm bringing two guests home for lunch. I'll want to speak to my daughter. Shortly. Yes. Twenty minutes." He hung up. No please, no thank you. Good buddy on the (voting) streets, tyrant at home, his commitment to democracy strictly relative. Big surprise there.

"Ms. Colorado?"

"Lunch would be fine."

He suppressed an irritated sound; Manny suppressed a snort. The car pulled up in front of a magnificent home in the Fab Forties. Fab is for fabulous, and that is an understatement.

"I'd like to speak to your daughter before lunch, Senator." I said this as we walked a cobblestone path that trailed through lush jungle-green lawns. California was in its fifth drought year. I held it against him.

"After lunch would be better."

After lunch, after he spoke with her. He still hadn't gotten it: my way or the highway. I said as much and not very diplomatically. He started to protest, then shrugged. A maid anticipated our arrival and opened the door.

The senator ushered me through a stately foyer and into a small and informal sitting room prettily furnished in delicate colors, florals, and breakables. He started to say he would get his daughter, caught my eye and sent the maid.

She came promptly and fit into the room perfectly with a delicate, floral, and breakable air about her. There was a bruised look around her eyes that intimated that she had been hit recently and thought that she would be again. Soon. She didn't look wild to me.

"Saundra, this is Kat Colorado. She's here to help us with . . . with things."

I held out my hand. She was surprised, but recovered quickly and took it. Her hand was light and cool, her grip firm.

"Senator, if you will excuse us?" They both stared at me. Then he left, shutting the door with a snap.

"Wow," she breathed it out slowly. "He *never* does what people tell him. Most people don't even try. Who are you? You don't look like anybody—" She broke off. Anybody important was what she meant, and she was right, I didn't look like it.

"I'm a private investigator."

She colored. Bright raspberry, not delicate floral.

"You're going to investigate this?"

"Yes, and try to resolve it without any more hurt."

"Oh."

"Tell me what happened."

"I . . . I can't. I'm so ashamed. I was wrong, bad . . . I . . ." She looked at me full in the face, so I could read the anguish and shame there.

"No."

"No?"

"Not bad. You were trusting, perhaps foolish, but not bad."

"Stupid!"

"Perhaps. That isn't a crime, or bad. We all make mistakes. Stupid ones."

"Do you?" She asked it with the innocence of youth that thought that grown-ups—I was thirty-three to her nineteen—didn't make mistakes.

"Yes. Want to hear some of them?"

She giggled. She was a young nineteen. I didn't realize they made them like this anymore. Kids seem so grown-up and tough these days with their expensive designer clothes, hard faces and knowing eyes. Or street kids, gang kids, who are kids in name only.

"Tell me," I said again.

Her face closed over. I thought for a moment, then spoke.

"A friend of mine got into trouble once and called me. I went to help her, took my gun." Her eyes widened. "There were two guys there, a lot bigger and badder than we were. I bluffed them and they left. Later I checked my gun. No bullets. I *always* keep it loaded, but there it was. No bullets. And I hadn't checked it beforehand."

Silence.

"That's stupid. *Really* stupid."

"Yes."

"Could you have gotten hurt?"

"Yes."

More silence. Then she spoke.

"I went to this party with these two girls I didn't know very well. I mean, they were just in one of my classes but I liked them. I had too much to drink; I was trying to be cool and keep up. Except I don't drink, hardly ever, and we were drinking kamikazes."

"Uh-oh."

"Yeah. So I remember going into the bedroom where the coats were and pushing them aside to make a place to sleep. That's all until my girlfriends woke me up and we went home."

"Were you dressed when they found you?"

She nodded. "My clothes were pulled out and around, scrunched up and stuff, but they were mostly on."

Mostly.

"Were you hurt in any way? Were you raped?"

"I don't know. And I would know, wouldn't I? Wouldn't I remember?" She wrung her hands in the gesture of an old woman, not a young one.

"It depends a lot on the amount of alcohol you consumed. Were you bruised or scraped? Any hurts? Were there fluid or semen traces?"

An odd look passed across her face, a shadow across the moon. "Not that exactly. The next morning . . . I slept in my clothes that night . . . The next morning . . . it was . . . there was . . . someone drew on me."

"Drew on you?"

"In lipstick. Ugly things." Her eyes dropped. Too much shame. "*Piece of ass* was written on my bottom. In front *dumb c-c-c . . . c-cu . . .* that word. They drew concentric circles, bulls-eyes, around my breasts with drops of blood dripping down my stomach. It was *awful*. I was so ashamed. And scared." She started to cry. If the senator thought his daughter was wild, he was in for a rude shock when he hit reality.

"Don't tell them, my mother and father."

"I thought they knew."

"Not the lipstick part." She stuttered. "I'd die if they did."

"All right."

"And a dagger. There was a dagger over my heart with blood dripping from it. It wasn't a nice joke."

"It wasn't a joke at all. It was an ugly, hurtful thing done by a sick and twisted person."

"The photos . . . are they of that? . . . Is that what . . ." Her voice ran down, like a child's toy with a dying battery.

"I don't know yet."

"You'll find out?"

"I'll do my best."

"And get them back?"

"I'll do my best."

She smiled for the first time.

It was a nice smile, I thought later, but it didn't entirely make up for wearing pink flats. I charged the senator triple my usual rate. That made up for it: the flats, his attitude, his lawn.

"Why are people like that, Kat? Can I call you Kat?"

"Yes. Like what?"

"So mean and ugly, so vicious."

"I don't know, Saundra. Did you know anyone at the party besides your girlfriends?"

"No."

"Then it wasn't you." Unless it was a setup. "It wasn't personal. A lot of people choose to hate what they don't know, or are afraid of, or want to be but don't have the courage to try to become."

"It was so awful, so ugly."

"It was; you aren't."

It was a while before she looked up, before she met my eyes. I could have filed my nails and slapped on a quick coat of polish. But I didn't.

"It's not Saundra, it's Zandi. With a Z and an I."

So there was the wild streak. Wild as a carousel pony. She smiled again. I liked Zandi. I felt okay about taking on the job. I hoped she didn't water the lawns.

"It took me a long time to scrub off the lipstick, Kat." Her voice shook. It would take longer to scrub off the memory. We both knew that.

I picked up my tray and walked my station again, flashing sequined legs and pink-shoe-expense-account feet, seeing if customers needed drinks or appetizers, checking on the possible arrival of blackmailers. So far it was just a typical Thursday happy hour crowd.

With a couple of possibles.

I knew from the phone call yesterday that I was dealing with an amateur. A guy, late teens or early twenties, with, I figured, maybe a drug habit to support and a mean streak that didn't mind supporting it that way. I bluffed him into meeting me at Callie's, a restaurant where I'd worked as a bartender for three years while I was in school.

That was a while ago but I was still a big favorite there and I still couldn't buy a drink. Mike, the owner, had laughed at my request and agreed that if I was dumb enough to work a cocktail shift for free, he was dumb enough to let me. He tried to buy me a drink too, but I took a rain check.

We were supposed to meet at six, the blackmailer and I, but I figured him to be there early, checking the place out, looking for cops or someone like me, someone like me but not in hot pink, sequins, and a waitress smile.

"Okay, Kat, there's another one."

Barb, the usual Thursday night cocktail waitress, was ticking off folks who weren't regulars. I'd asked for her help in that. She didn't know what the deal was, but she loved cloak and dagger, cops and robbers, and "Murder She Wrote," she told me.

"See those two coming in? Never seen 'em before. Definitely not regulars. Him either." We were ogling a tall guy in Levis, a sports jacket, and a Tom Cruise look. "Hoo boy, hope *he* sits in my section.

"The girl on B2? I've seen her once or twice but never alone, always with two, three, four civil service types. And the kid at the stand-up bar? Never seen him; he doesn't fit in here either."

I picked up my tray. "I'll get these." Barb wrinkled her nose at me. Off and on I was working her section as well as mine, though the tips were all hers. A few minutes later I came back with a drink order: gimlet, vodka tonic, margarita, white wine, two drafts. Nobody had said a thing yet about five thousand dollars in old bills. Yeah. It goes like that sometimes. Most times. It was five-thirty.

By five-fifty the possibles list had shortened: the kid at the stand-up bar, the guy in Levis, or someone who wasn't here yet. The kid had body odor, pimples, and bad nerves. He couldn't sit; he couldn't stand still. He twitched and twisted inside his pimply, scaly skin like a snake trying to slough it off. The guy in Levis was cool, deliberate. A watcher, his eyes on everyone who came in, moved around, neared his table. A blackmailer, an anxious lover, or a bored, nosy dude?

Five-fifty-eight. A guy in black leather walked in, and he and the twitchy kid walked out. Black leather finished the kid's beer first. They weren't coming back. Darn. Hate to see a big spender leave.

Barb yawned. "Are we having fun yet?"

"Cover for me, okay? I'm going to go flirt with the guy on A4."

"You get paid for this? You call this work?" There was a teasing note in her voice. "Where do I sign on?"

I smoothed pink leather over my hips. "Would you tell me your secrets?"

"It depends. Maybe if I was a horny guy."

I winked at her. Exactly.

He watched me walk over. I twitched my hips, flashed a thigh full of sequins. His smile was open, welcoming, a guy smile, a waiting look. He was too smart for hungry.

"You need anything?" I asked, ignoring the half-full glass in front of him and putting a spin on "anything." Curveball.

"Company would be nice." He let his eyes appreciate me without sliding, sliming. They were brown with yellow flecks. His hands looked steady, but he had knicked his chin shaving.

"I'm supposed to be working." I smiled a slow, heavy-eyed, sexy smile and licked my lips slightly. What the hell? It worked in the movies.

He smiled back, with his mouth, not his eyes. "Supposed to be?"

I inclined my head.

"What time do you get off?"

I flashed a sequin or two. "Soon, it keeps slowing down like this."

"What's your name?"

"Jane," I lied. "Yours?"

"Dick."

Dick and Jane. We were both lying. And unimaginative.

"So, Jane, maybe we could have a drink later?"

"Oh?" I made my voice saucy, my eyes sassy—not hard for me. "I thought you were waiting for someone, someone special the way you keep looking at the door."

"Business," he said, his eyes still hard, his mouth still smiling, "before pleasure." The pupils were dilated.

"You don't look like a businessman—no tie, no briefcase, no IBM eyes." As I glanced at the large manila envelope on the table, his hand traveled to his left inside breast pocket. He stopped his hand; I stopped my eyes. Someone passed us. His eyes flicked up, then back to me, then to his wristwatch. Five past six.

"What's your business?"

"I'm a photographer."

"Hey, wow, like could you take my picture?"

It was hard getting it out. I had to wrap my tongue around a couple of nasty adverbs and nouns and spit them out before I gagged. Like wow.

"Like I could, yeah." He said the words easily.

"What kind of pictures? For newspapers, magazines? Weddings and stuff?"

"Like that, yeah."

Like I could feel the bile rising in the back of my throat, a mean, ugly, vile taste.

"Of people, sports, human interest, whatever?" I asked through the bile. He felt like my guy. I was ready to jump on a conclusion like a tick on a dog.

"Human interest, yeah, you could call it that. Crime scenes." His eyes smiled.

"Ooooh," I said girlishly through the bile, "blood and stuff?! Wow!"

"And stuff, yeah." His eyes closed down. He looked at his watch, at the envelope, at me.

"You get paid good for that?" I didn't wince, even though I know that people rot in hell for bad grammar.

"Sometimes." He smiled a slow, easy smile, took a sip of his drink. He put the glass down and let his hand rest on the manila envelope. "This lot here is worth five grand to me."

Bingo.

I never met a blackmailer I liked or a con artist who could keep his mouth shut.

"Five thousand, no kidding!"

"No kidding."

"Wow, guess it's a good thing there's a cop here. Shoot, you just never know. And you sure can't be too careful!"

His eyes narrowed, his lips thinned out, his forehead furrowed. Amazing, the power and majesty of the law. "A cop? Where?" His voice was thin too.

"The guy in the middle of the bar."

We both looked at the five-foot-six Walter Mitty guy in polyester I'd picked out at random. He looked like a cop like I look like a Miss Black America beauty pageant contestant. Not *totally* impossible, but not too damn likely. It was get-to-the-bad-boy time, make-him-do-something-stupid time. It was working.

"He doesn't look like a cop."

"I think he's undercover. Undercover guys aren't supposed to look like cops, are they?" I asked it dumb; I looked dumb. If I'd had a dunce cap, I would have worn it. "Hey, gotta work." I winked at him, but he was too jumpy to notice. "See you."

I drifted off and pretended to wipe tables. He stared at the guy at the bar, probably an accountant, a shoe salesman, or a used-car financier. The guy at the bar didn't notice. Why should he? My buddy, Dick the blackmailer, was seriously spooked now. Edgy. Hyper. Frantic. Starting to run scared, scared and stupid. Good.

He unwrapped two or three sticks of gum and popped them in his mouth, chewed frantically. Hey, it beat smoking. I looked at a dirty ashtray on the table I was cleaning and decided to ignore it. After all, I wasn't getting paid for this.

Dick looked around quickly. I drifted out of his line of vision, then watched as he spat the gum into his hand, pulled it into small wads, stuck it on the manila envelope and under the table. He did the same for the envelope in his jacket pocket.

Then he got up and walked toward the telephones and rest rooms. He was going to look around for cops, check things out, make sure the coast was clear. And, if it wasn't clear, he didn't want to be caught with the evidence on him. I was betting that one envelope had prints, the other negatives. It was a bet I didn't want to lose.

I moved quickly, retrieved the envelopes and sandwiched them between the two trays I was carrying. The bar started to fill up suddenly then, the way bars do for no known reason. I picked up Dick's half-empty drink glass—no money out for a tip, I noticed—wiped the table and smiled as a young couple seated themselves there.

They were in love, the hungry, thirsty stage of love; they would be here for a long time. By the time Dick got the table back and figured the envelopes were long gone, I would be too. Perfect. Like wow, dude. I went to the bar and put in the lovebirds' order.

"Hey!" The voice was loud behind me. I turned, then smiled.

"Hey! Hi! Far out, I thought you'd left!"

"Goddamn, what happened to my table, my drink. Goddamn!"

Mr. Charm. No kidding. Mr. Grace-Under-Pressure.

I frowned. "I thought you'd left. Hey, Jimmy, can I have a Stoli rocks on the spill tab?" The bartender made the drink; I garnished it with a lemon twist and handed it to him.

"Here. Here's a drink on me." My tone was formal and slightly past glacial.

"I want my table!"

What style. Five-year-old stuff. Maybe kindergarten, but that was tops.

"That table is occupied. There are plently of others—"

"Get me my table goddammit!"

Five thousand dollars. It had his blood pumping.

I looked at him like I thought he was nuts. "I'm getting the manager."

"No . . . uh . . . *shit!* Never mind." He glared at me.

I smiled a sexy smile, I licked my lips.

I told him off.

Why not? I didn't have a job at stake.

"Hey, forget the drink after work. You're a jerk. A puke. A slimeball with no manners or class." I made a face at him. Speaking of class.

He took it. He had to or leave. Then he found a seat where he could watch every move made at his former table. Look at Dick. See Dick stare. See Dick frown. Too bad, Dick. Too little, too late, Dick.

Two more couples joined the couple at that table. Good. Safety in numbers and confusion. It was going to be a long night. For them. For Dick. Not for me. I counted my take and turned my cash caddy over to the bartender, turned my tables and tips over to Barb, walked to the kitchen with my trays. It took a while to scrape the gum off everything, but I managed. Then I got Mike, the owner-manager, to walk me to my car.

"The guy sitting at B1 in a bad mood?"

"Yeah?"

"He was sitting at A4. Don't let him bother the folks there now."

"Why would he?"

"He thinks he lost something he left at that table."

"And he didn't?"

"Oh no," I said serenely. "He didn't lose it; I stole it."

Mike laughed. I went back to my office to take off sequined tights and look at pictures.

I didn't sleep well that night. It wasn't the tights, the pink flats or the leather miniskirt. And it wasn't the lipstick in the pictures. There wasn't any.

It was uglier than that.

I picked up the phone when it rang at ten-thirty. "Hi, Manny."

"Kat, how did you know it was me?"

"It was the fourteen messages on my machine in the last three hours, Manny. I'm a detective; that was a clue. Good, huh? You hire me, you get your money's worth."

"You get it?"

I didn't play cute, but it was tempting. "I got it. You have the senator and his checkbook sitting in my office, alone, in half an hour."

"Look, Kat, you know—"

"That or nothing." I broke the connection and left the receiver off the hook.

The senator was prompt. He was also uneasy. He brushed his palms back over his styled, sprayed-in-place hair; he shot his cuffs; he looked at his gold Rolex; he looked at me.

"I understand you got the photos. Thank you. Thank you very much."

He said it simply and with dignity. He did it well, but then he was a politician, he'd had practice. I didn't buy it. I hadn't voted for him either. Hadn't. Wouldn't.

"I'm pleased that it's been handled so smoothly and quickly. I'd like to include a bonus in with your fee and expenses. How does a total of two thousand dollars sound?"

I nodded. It sounded good. Excellent. Except for *bonus* read *payoff.*

He held out a hand. "The pictures, may I have them, please?"

I didn't move. I spoke. "I looked at them."

The healthy ruddy color in his face faded slightly. "Let's not get into that, Ms. Colorado."

Oh, what the hell. Let's. Let's take a walk on the wild side.

"Tell me about it, Senator."

"Let's not get into that, Ms. Colorado."

He stood up and made his voice ugly. His hand was out. Male intimidation doesn't work real well on me; it does make me ornery. I looked at his hand. I managed not to tremble.

"You going to hurt me like you did her?"

The air went out of him in a whoosh. He sank back into his chair and followed male intimidation with bribery. Stylish was the word that came to mind. Yeah. Right. Like wow.

"Three thousand dollars, that's my last word."

But not mine.

"It's not often you see a woman so badly beaten with no cuts, broken bones, or bruising visible if she were fully clothed. You did a nice job."

Admiration in my voice. Okay, I was lying. He said nothing. Hadn't been well brought up, I guess. No thank-you-for-the-compliment stuff.

"Well, maybe a couple of cracked ribs, a slight concussion. But cracked ribs don't show, they just hurt like hell, and maybe you hit her on the back of the head—slammed her up against a wall?—but that doesn't show either. Neat, tidy, *very* professional."

More praise on my part. More lies. More nothing on his. I hate these one-sided conversations. I got over it before he did.

"Who took the pictures?"

Silence. I arched my eyebrows in an I-don't-like-to-ask-twice-and-I-still-have-the-pictures gesture. He got it. He was a quick study, no doubt about it.

"A friend of Saundra's. He and Saundra dropped by unexpectedly one evening. It was bad timing. My wife and I had had a little misunderstanding—"

Misunderstanding. That was an innocuous term for felony spousal abuse, the intentional affliction of great bodily harm and—

"Every married couple has their ups and downs." He shrugged. "That goes without saying. I didn't want to air my dirty linen in public. That goes without saying, too."

Dirty linen. How nice, low-key, and innocent. How inaccurate.

"Saundra's—" I caught myself. "Zandi's friend took the pictures?"

"Yes, that goddamned—" He paused, editing out obscenities, I assumed. "He got away before I could get the camera, the film."

"You and Manny set Zandi up at that party with her friends." A statement, not a question. He didn't answer me. He still wasn't holding up his end of the conversation.

"You get someone to get creative with the lipstick or did you do it when she was passed out at home?"

"How *dare* you!"

"And then you let her live with the shame, the humiliation, the fear that she'd been raped. Nice guy. Swell dad. A prince, a real prince."

"Fuck you!"

"Zandi still send you Father's Day cards?"

He flushed. Minimal. Minimal at best.

"You set her up so she could take your fall."

"It wasn't like that. I . . . I had no choice. Those pictures . . . I couldn't afford . . . couldn't take the chance. The investigator I've used before—I couldn't trust him, not with those pictures, he'd have sold them to someone. I couldn't do it myself; I couldn't send Manny out. The kid would've been looking for us. He wouldn't be looking for a woman, for you.

"I needed you because you were honest, but I couldn't tell you the truth; Manny said you wouldn't do it then. I had to have a story you'd go for."

And he called it right. I had. Kat Colorado—all-day sucker.

"You had a choice, Senator; you didn't have to put your daughter through this. She'll live with it for a long time." With it and the betrayal.

He shrugged. "She's young, she'll recover. My career wouldn't have though." He got out his checkbook. "Three thousand?"

I nodded.

"The pictures?"

I handed them over, still in the gum-stained manila envelope. He flipped quickly, unemotionally, through the ugly pictures of the woman beaten, bruised, and frightened by his hands. His wife. She didn't look anything like the smiling woman who stood next to him in publicity photos.

"The negatives aren't here."

"No." I agreed.

"You said you got them."

I agreed to that too.

He stared at me, eyes as mean as those of a starving pit bull who'd just been offered a soyburger. I didn't tremble; that's how tough I am.

"Senator, make that three-thousand-dollar check out to WEAVE."

He looked like he wanted to spit. WEAVE is an acronym for Women Escaping A Violent Environment. They helped abused and battered women and their children. I have a lot of respect for what they do.

"No negatives, no check."

"Wouldn't it be nice if you became a regular contributor," I mused. "The negatives? They're in a safety deposit box."

I paused on that thought. Silence hung in the air like a politician's lies.

"I hope your wife's health is better in the future than it has been," I remarked conversationally. "I'll drop your wife and Zandi a note on my investigation and keep in touch." I'm a pal, a Girl Scout, a real trooper, yessiree.

He looked at me for a long time. I met that look straight on. That's how tough I am.

He wrote the check.

I have green eyes and a conscience. He had green lawns and an ugly soul. But who am I to talk? There was a word for what I'd just engaged in.

Extortion.

Ask me if I lost sleep.

I mailed the check. I told Manny that he couldn't call me Katy ever again. I gave Zandi a hug, a lecture, and the pink flats and sequined tights. Then I went back to Callie's and let Mike buy me a drink. Maybe two. Maybe three.

Okay, I got hammered.

That's how tough I am.

*Joyce Harrington is a New York City advertising executive, and the author of three novels (*Dreemz of the Night, Family Reunion, No One Knows My Name*). Among her many short stories, "The Purple Shroud" won an Edgar and "The Cabin in the Hollow," "Night Crawlers," and "The Au Pair Girl" have been nominated for Edgars. Joyce's fiction, laden with undercurrents of menace, delivers potent emotional impact.*

In "Mirror Image," a woman makes a discovery that allows her to see some things very clearly, indeed.

MIRROR IMAGE

by Joyce Harrington

I FOUND IT at the flea market. The one on Sixty-seventh Street just off First Avenue. I'd been to donate at the Blood Center just a block away and was on my way home. I was feeling both puny and virtuous, and thought I needed something to perk me up and get me back to reality. It could have been anything—a nice string of jasper beads, a kooky teapot, even a really good, ripe tomato from the greenmarket that shared space with the tables of odds and pseudo-antique ends.

But there it was. I saw it winking at me from the other side of the schoolyard as soon as I walked through the gate. I didn't rush right up to it and pounce. No, no. That way lies disappointment, in flea market shopping as in love. Instead, I sauntered around the yard, checking out the tee-shirts and the organic veggies. It's amazing how the organic stuff always looks so wizened and gnarly; I suppose that's how you know you have to pay more for it. I did find a ripe tomato, nonorganic, and bought it before I sidled up to the object of my desire.

And even then, I didn't look right at it. Instead, I examined everything else on the table in front of it. A box of old hat pins, a truly ugly cookie jar in the shape of a pig, a lovely lace pillow that would have been perfect for a bride if I'd known of any brides, and lots more that I can't remember. And then I raised my eyes and looked directly into it.

It was everything I wanted and then some. It was the mirror of my dreams. For years, I had been searching for just such a mirror to replace the totally unsatisfactory one that hung on the wall above my dressing table. You'd think such a thing would be easy to find, but not if you have a dim memory of the mirror that hung above the table when it was younger and your mother sat before it every day and you watched her reflection as she primped and powdered and made herself beautiful.

She was beautiful, even without all the primping. The family always said it was too bad I took after my father instead of her.

I don't know what happened to the original mirror. Maybe it broke somewhere along the way. Maybe one of my aunts took it in the general confusion after Mommy died and Daddy went to prison. All I know is that a few years later, when I found a job and an apartment and moved into Manhattan, my grandmother said I could take anything I wanted from her attic. And the table was there. But not the mirror.

Perhaps I should make something clear before I go any further. My mother was murdered. They said my father killed her. They said it was because all that primping and powdering was for other men. I found her body when I came home from school one day. She was sprawled across her dressing table, now my dressing table, facedown in a puddle of blood and Coty light rachel face powder. I never knew what to believe.

Except for this. I came to believe the mirror saw it all, and if I could ever find that mirror, I would find out the truth.

It was too much to hope that the flea market mirror was the very mirror I had been searching for all my adult life. Still, it was very much like it, a long oval of glass framed in gilded wood with a little cluster of rosebuds at the bottom.

Standing there, in the bright afternoon of the flea market, I stared into the mirror, mentally pleading with it to tell me something. It showed me nothing but my face, the same face I'd lived with for years—pale and round, hung about with frizzles of mousy brown hair, its nose a blob, its mouth a pursed little buttonhole, and its eyes too close together, too small, the color of muddy puddle water.

I bought it anyway. Didn't even haggle at the price, which was more than I could really afford or had with me in cash, but the dealer was willing to take a check. He wrapped it in brown paper, tied it with string, and I carried it home on the First Avenue bus.

I still live in the same apartment in Yorkville that I took when I moved into the city fifteen years ago. It's a rent-controlled walk-up in an old tenement building just off First Avenue. I'm on the third floor, overlooking the street.

Yorkville has changed a lot in fifteen years. One by one, the old German restaurants and shops disappeared; only a few remain. But there is still the Steuben Day parade every September, when the dirndls and lederhosen and the oompah bands converge in a flotilla of school buses from the suburbs, and Eighty-sixth Street, for a day, celebrates its former Teutonic majesty. I usually stay at home that day.

Do I sound cranky? I guess I am. Sorry. It's just that I hate things to change and I hate pretending that they haven't. That's why I've worked at the same place all these fifteen years. I'm in insurance. I do statistics. Not very exciting I suppose, but, as they say, there's safety in numbers. Numbers don't cause you heartache or care how you look. A number won't kill you if you take up with other numbers.

Let's get back to the mirror. I carried it up the stairs on that bright August Saturday afternoon, unwrapped it right away, and hung it on the wall over my dressing table in place of the one that had dissatisfied me for so long.

And I sat down in front of it. And looked into it. What did I see? I saw myself, of course. Nothing strange about that. The mirror didn't speak and I didn't speak to it. None of that "mirror, mirror on the wall" stuff. I gave up fairy tales a long time ago. But I did sit there, gazing and hoping that something would happen, that the mirror might unlock some secret image in my own mind, some remembrance of how things were and what really happened.

I've never believed that my father killed my mother in that brutal way. He was too gentle, too kind. He never argued with her or asked her where she'd been when she stayed out all night. When he died in prison, they said it was from a stroke, but I always thought it was because of a broken heart.

One of her boyfriends might have done it. Oh, yes. She did have boyfriends. Even I knew that. She never tried to keep it a secret. Our whole nosy, gossipy Queens neighborhood knew about it. Or it might have been a burglar, except that nothing was stolen.

The problem was that my father confessed. Absolutely refused to discuss it with anyone, other than to say that he did it and he was sorry and ready to pay for his crime. I can't forget his eyes the last time I saw him. The way he looked at me. So sad, so sorrowful. As if there were things he wanted to say to me but couldn't.

My eyes are like that. Sad and full of secret knowledge, secret even from me. I gazed into my eyes in the mirror, willing some of those secrets to come forth.

Did you know that if you look at yourself in a mirror long enough, things get very weird? Your face begins to be not a face, but something alien, inhuman. It's a bit like repeating a word over and over again until it loses meaning, becomes nonsense.

There are only a few objects on my dressing table—a comb and brush, a jar of moisturizing cream, a manicure scissors, a compact of pressed face powder, a tube of pale pink lipstick. I don't go in much for beautification. It wouldn't do any good. I remember once, when I was very small, trying out all my mother's cosmetics. She laughed when she saw me and made me look at myself in the mirror. "You look like a clown," she said. "Now go wash your face. When you're older, I'll show you how to do it right." She never had the chance.

For a moment, that small, sad clown face appeared in my new old mirror, flickering like an old movie, grinning despite the tears that streaked through the bright circles of rouge on its cheeks.

That was enough for one day.

In the days that followed, I spent more and more time in front of the mirror. I began being late for work. Or if I made it on time, I left early. A few times, I called in sick. No one seemed to notice. Was it because I had become such a fixture around the place that no one cared whether or not I was there as long as my work got done?

The weekends were wonderful. The mirror and I spent many happy hours reliving childhood memories. All I had to do was to remember an event—a trip to the Bronx Zoo with Daddy, a birthday party when I was six, the summer we went to the Jersey shore for a week, all the happy times—and the mirror would show me a fragment of the scene. Sometimes it would show me something about the scene that I hadn't remembered or known about. It was better than having a photo album.

But whenever I tried to conjure up the scene of my mother facedown in a pool of blood at her dressing table, the mirror darkened—not truly dark, but like the sky before a thunderstorm. Its light became threatening, as if warning me to think of something else.

Do you wonder at the absence of other people in my life? There are a few. Women friends from the office to share lunches and occasional shopping trips. One old school friend who lives on the West Side near Lincoln Center; we meet once in a while for dinner and a movie or a concert. But since I got a VCR, there's been less of that. And since I got the mirror, I seldom rent a video. Why should I? The story in my mirror is much more fascinating than any movie, new or old.

And, yes, there have been men. Some of them said they loved me, but I found out bitterly that they didn't. For a few, a very few, I felt what might have been love, but there was something not quite complete about it. Once I even had a wedding planned, but I realized at the last moment that if I married and had children, I would never discover the truth. I would become distracted with other people's demands on me, and I would forget what I needed to find out. Selfish? Perhaps, but I doubt I would have made much of a wife or a mother.

The year was winding down toward the holidays. I was sleeping less, staying up late and rising early to prod at the mirror for the revelation of what I was now convinced it could tell me. I had to buy some new clothes. Nothing seemed to fit anymore. Everything was too big. When I went for my annual physical exam, my doctor seemed mildly concerned about weight loss. I told him I had become a vegetarian, which was almost true. I had no time to cook, but I was content with a piece of fruit or a raw carrot, a slice of bread, a cup of tea. He advised me not to carry it too far, and I assured him I would be careful. I could see that he was thinking anorexia and therapy, but I circumvented that by complaining of insomnia. He gave me a prescription for sleeping pills. I never had it filled. Sleep was the last thing I needed.

No way would I see a shrink. I'd had enough of that right after Mommy died. No one could understand why I wasn't weeping and moaning and falling apart. After all, there I was a virtual orphan and obviously entitled to grieve. My grandmother meant well, but she couldn't possibly understand how I felt. For six months I went to the psychiatrist she selected, until he finally told her I was a waste of his time and her money. I admired him for his honesty.

The anniversary of my mother's death is November 18th. As the time grew near, I began to feel an overwhelming sense of anticipation. I scheduled my vacation for the two weeks surrounding that date and told my supervisor I would be going to Florida. She seemed a bit surprised. I had never gone anywhere before and I wasn't going anywhere now. But I didn't want her calling me up to fill in for someone who had suddenly quit or broken a leg. She'd done it in the past and I had willingly complied. Why not? I had nothing else to do.

But now I had lots to do, getting ready for the great day. On the first day of my vacation, I cleaned my entire apartment. I didn't look into the mirror once, not even when I brushed my hair. It occurred to me that maybe a little benign neglect might have some effect on what the mirror was willing to show me.

The next morning, again without visiting the mirror, I went out and bought armloads of fresh flowers. Chrysanthemums mostly, but some roses, too. I put them around the apartment in every kind of container, being a bit short on vases.

And I put some candles around, too.

Then, when everything was ready, I drew the drapes, lit the candles, and sat down before the mirror. In it, I could see the candles flickering behind me and a yellow mass of flowers. The roses were in front of me, right beside the mirror. I cleared my mind of everything but the memory of that scene at this table and my own ashen teenaged face in the mirror.

For the longest time, nothing happened. The candles burned down, the radiator clanked, and I heard rain pattering on the window.

Then, just as I was about to give it up, my face in the mirror changed. You've heard people say that a magnificent view or a splendid sunset was breathtaking. Really, they have no idea what breathtaking is all about. I literally could not breathe. I felt as if some great, heavy, clammy *thing* were squeezing my chest, squeezing the air out of my lungs. Paralyzing me. All I could do was stare at that new face in the mirror.

It was my mother's face. Her mass of auburn hair, her creamy skin just faintly touched with a rosy flush, her alarmingly green eyes fringed with jet black lashes that seemed a yard long. She held a mascara wand in one hand.

She was looking out of the mirror at me, her eyes scornful and her lips forming words I couldn't hear but which I knew to be proud and full of ridicule. She wasn't talking to me, of course. She was talking to a person somewhere in that long-ago room, out of range of the mirror. The person who killed her.

I think I must have blanked out then, because the next thing I knew, I was in the kitchen, standing by the open refrigerator and wolfing down whatever came to hand. I had never been so hungry. And I ached all over. It was as if I'd been doing hard physical labor for a long, long time, without eating.

When I'd eaten everything that was edible and thrown out the moldy odds and ends, I suddenly felt very sleepy. I didn't want to sleep, but I couldn't help it. I was gone almost before I hit the pillow.

I don't know how long I slept, because I don't know what time it was when I collapsed. No dreams, or at least none that I could remember. I was still a bit achy, but the ravenous hunger had left me. In fact, I was a bit queasy from all the stuff I'd eaten earlier and there was a vile taste in my mouth. My bedside clock-radio said 12:15 A.M. Middle of the night.

I crawled off the bed and sat down at my dressing table. She was still there, as if she'd been waiting for me. Her eyes flashed and her lips moved, but I still couldn't hear what she was saying. Too bad I'd never learned how to read lips.

Then I saw something moving in the room behind her. It was so real I turned around to see what, or who, was there. Of course there was no one there. There were only the chrysanthemums and the candles that had guttered out hours ago. My room.

The room reflected in the mirror was some other room. Her room, in the house in Queens we'd lived in all those years ago. The details were hazy, but there was definitely someone back there. A shadowy someone who held something bright and shiny in one hand.

And my mother kept talking and sneering at that someone without ever turning around. Surely she saw that shiny thing, that knife, that was coming closer and closer. Why didn't she turn around, get up, do something to stop it? She didn't have to keep talking like that, did she? She didn't have to keep telling me how silly I was being, how stupid it was to pull a trick like that, how she'd have me committed to a loony bin if I didn't put that knife down instantly and apologize for saying all those nasty things about her.

Me? She was talking to me? No. No, that's not the way it happened. The mirror was wrong. I never said anything nasty to my mother. I *loved* my mother.

But the mirror showed the knife flashing again and again and the blood spurting, and some of it splashed onto the mirror and I had to wipe it off.

There was blood on my hands. The mirror was streaked with it. My mother's face was gone. There was only my own face, my own horrified eyes staring back at me.

I went into the bathroom to wash my hands.

Jean Hager's mysteries, three Mitch Bushyhead novels (most recently Ghostland*), and a new series featuring Molly Bearpaw (*Ravenmocker*), focus on traditional Cherokee culture and history. Jean says, "I wrote forty novels in several genres . . . before finally writing the book I always wanted to write. That was* The Grandfather Medicine, *the first book in my Mitch Bushyhead series." Making the case for writing what you really care about, the book won an Oklahoma Writers Federation Tepee Award for Best Novel.*

In "Country Hospitality," a beleaguered woman finds that remembering her country manners works to her benefit.

COUNTRY HOSPITALITY

by Jean Hager

"How could anyone be so cruel as to do a thing like this, today of all days?" Lori Simpson stared at the bare table in a corner of the living room. Two hours ago, when they'd left for Ed Thorndyke's funeral, it had held Emma Thorndyke's twenty-five-inch television set. Now the set was gone, along with the heirloom silver tea service that had graced the oak buffet in the adjoining dining room.

Lori went to the door and called to her husband, who was smoking a cigarette in the yard. "Dave, come quick! Emma had a burglar while we were gone."

Dave stamped out his smoke and hurried inside.

"I don't know how they got in," Lori told him. "The door was locked and bolted."

Dave walked down the hall and returned shortly to say, "They climbed in the back bedroom window—Emma must have left it unlocked. The screen's been cut."

In the meantime, Emma had gone ahead to the kitchen. She'd entered the house first, turned a ghastly white and, shocked speechless, merely pointed at the table and the buffet. Now, a high-pitched wail came from the back of the house. *"Oh, no!"* Emma had recovered her powers of speech.

Lori hurried to her neighbor's aid. Emma stood in the middle of the big country kitchen, gaping at the remains of a pecan pie and a chocolate cake strewn across the counter and floor, part of the meal delivered that morning by the members of Emma's garden club. There was also a puddle of milk in front of the refrigerator. The empty milk carton had been tossed in the sink.

Lori took Emma's arm and led her to a chair. "Come, dear. You'd better sit down."

Dave peered at the mess from the doorway. "Nervy lot, weren't they? Taking time to finish off most of a cake and a pie."

"And a half gallon of milk," Emma said weakly. "That carton was full."

"It's almost as if," Lori said, frowning, "they were thumbing their noses."

Dave snorted. "That's exactly what they were doing."

Emma buried her face in her hands. "Call the sheriff," Lori said, watching Emma with a worried expression.

"A lot of good that'll do," Dave muttered, but he went back to the living room to make the call.

Emma squeezed her eyes shut to keep back tears. She'd thought she was all cried out, but this, after burying her husband of forty-six years, was just too much. And Dave was right. The sheriff would come out, look around, mutter a bit, leave, and that would be the end of it. He and two deputies covered the entire county, and it was well known that they resented the newcomers who by building homes at the lake had added to the population base for which the sheriff and his men were responsible. Most of the rural residents of the county had lived there all their lives, and they got first call on the sheriff's time and attention, over the outsiders from the city.

Dave came back to the kitchen. "I talked to the dispatcher. Somebody will get here as soon as they can."

Lori sighed. "If they don't come right away, they won't be able to find Emma's things before they're disposed of. It's not as if we don't know who did this."

Emma, having conquered her tears, lifted her lined face. "Bo and Frank Cramer." The Cramer brothers were a constant aggravation to the lake community. Speeding past on their motorcycles at all hours of the night. Throwing beer cans on porches. Yelling taunts.

Early in the season, the residents had complained to the sheriff, who had admitted that the Cramer "boys" were "a little wild since their old man died, but they're not criminals." And there was no law against riding motorcycles on the public road. As for the beer cans, could they prove the Cramers were responsible? He'd promised to have a talk with Bo and Frank, two hulking "boys" in their twenties, who'd earned the right to the benefit of every doubt by being local football stars in their high school days. If, indeed, the sheriff had talked to the Cramers, it had had no effect.

Shortly after that, the red-barn storage shed behind a new lake house had burned to the ground in the middle of the night. The family had noticed the flames shortly after being awakened by the Cramers' motorcycles roaring by. The Cramers, of course, denied any knowledge of the fire.

There had been other incidents, as well. Obscenities had been spray-painted across the back of one house. Two family pets had disappeared. All four tires on a car left parked close to the road all night had been slashed. But this was the first burglary. The Cramers must have seen the funeral announcement in the newspaper and known that none of the Thorndykes' neighbors would be home to see them breaking in.

"Dave," Lori said, "I'm going to clean up this mess and stay with Emma for a while."

"I'll go home and change, then. Emma, why don't you come spend the night in our spare room."

She shook her head, dislodging a strand of gray hair from the fat bun at the nape of her neck. "I won't be driven from my home." Her bottom lip quivered a little as she said it.

"Go and lie down until the sheriff comes," Lori said kindly. "I'll have the kitchen put back to rights in no time."

Emma stood. "I'd better see if anything else is missing." She went into the front bedroom, and Lori and Dave exchanged a helpless look. "Maybe she'll agree to my staying here tonight," Lori said.

"Wanta bet?" Dave gave his wife a peck on the cheek. "Talk to her again about moving back to the city when the rest of us go."

Emma and Ed Thorndyke had built this house as a permanent home when Ed retired from the university; they'd moved into it the previous April. In June, Ed had been diagnosed with bone cancer. The disease had progressed quickly, and now, less than three months later, he was dead.

As soon as they knew Ed wasn't going to make it, Lori had tried to talk to Emma about the inadvisability of her staying alone at the lake over the winter. All the other residents, most of whom were professors at the university eighty miles away, lived there only from May to mid-September, returning to the city in time for the fall semester.

But Emma had not wanted to listen to Lori's arguments. "This is the house Ed and I always wanted," she'd said. "We spent years planning every detail. It's our dream home, and it's where I want to be."

"I'll speak to her," Lori promised her husband. "After what's happened today, maybe she won't be so set on staying."

Dave left and Lori cleaned up the kitchen. Then she went to check on Emma, who had changed her dark silk dress for a cotton robe and her hose and black shoes for house slippers. Emma was standing in front of the dresser with a pair of diamond earrings resting in the palm of her hand.

"They took my silver-handled brushes, but they didn't find these. They'd dropped down behind a drawer in my jewelry box." Her fingers closed around the earrings. "Ed gave them to me on our first anniversary. They're clip-ons. That was before I had my ears pierced." She hadn't worn the earrings in years, fearing that one of them would slip off unnoticed. "I always meant to have them reset on posts, but I never got around to it." Suddenly, her eyes swam with tears. "I'd better find a good hiding place for them."

Lori had just succeeded in getting Emma to lie down when the sheriff arrived, and she had to get up and talk to him. As far as Emma could tell, nothing but the TV set, tea service, and brushes was missing.

"They only take things they can sell easily," the sheriff said. "I'll send a description of the missing items to the area pawnshops. Maybe they'll turn up." He gave a disgruntled shake of his head. "We never had this kind of thing around here before all these strangers moved in."

Lori clamped her lips shut to keep from giving the sheriff a piece of her mind in front of Emma, and followed him outside to say, "Strangers didn't do this. It was those Cramers."

"Did anybody see them?"

"We were all at the funeral."

"I'll go by their place on my way back to town, but I can't conduct a search without a warrant, Mrs. Simpson. And I can't get a warrant on the basis of your suspicions."

Furious, Lori went back inside. Emma was sitting in the big easy chair in the living room. "You should go back to bed."

"I'm too restless."

"I'll fix you something to eat, then."

Emma didn't protest, but she only picked at the food and, finally, set the plate aside.

"Emma," Lori said, "I think you should reconsider staying here all winter. Surely you can see now that it would be foolish. Dave and I are leaving in two weeks. Everybody else will be gone before then."

"You have another house to go to. I don't."

"You could store your furniture for the winter and rent a small furnished apartment. It wouldn't cost that much."

Emma glanced around her, at the antique Victorian sofa which she had reupholstered herself, the oak and walnut tables which she and Ed had lovingly refinished, and pretty lace curtains. "I would hate the inconvenience of pulling up stakes every autumn and again every spring," she murmured, her gaze lingering on a framed needlepoint bouquet of flowers. She'd made it during the many hours she'd sat with Ed in his last weeks. "Ed always loved the lake so much. I feel close to him here."

"Forgive me, Emma, but I have to say this. The Cramers aren't going to leave you alone. Once the rest of us are gone, there's no telling what those savages might do."

"They've already taken the things they can sell easily."

Lori expelled an exasperated breath. "Emma—"

"Don't badger me, Lori." Emma's voice caught. "I'm capable of making my own decisions."

Lori gave her a long look. "If you insist on staying, at least get a gun and learn how to use it."

"I'll think about it." Emma put her head back and closed her eyes, effectively ending the conversation.

Two days later, Emma returned to working in the flower garden. More than any other activity, gardening distracted her from her grief. She and Ed had planned the colors and arrangement of plants in the garden as carefully as they'd drawn the house plans. There were red dahlias and petunias, pink tuberous begonias, dark purple smoke tree, rust-colored Helenium, yellow rudbeckia, and white "Emerald Isle." In a separate backyard bed, yellow and white and lavender chrysanthemums were in bloom, spilling over the borders.

It took several days to weed the beds and till the soil around the plants for the last time before winter. Then she filled a wheelbarrow with rich, black compost from the compost heap and mulched the perennials to protect them during the coming cold months.

She left for last the roses, which had been Ed's pride and joy. Emma had suggested that they plant only a few since roses were susceptible to so many different diseases and required a great deal of care. But Ed had said they were beautiful enough to be worth whatever care was required.

Since Emma had last worked with the roses, a few of the leaves had developed black spot. She pulled on protective gloves, got her collection of rose pesticides, and dusted all the leaves. Then she used a spray designed to kill various insects. Finally, she uncapped the bottle of liquid nicotine and treated the plants for aphids. Ed had always said there was nothing as effective against aphids as nicotine.

As she worked in the garden, she saw neighbor after neighbor drive away from the lake for the last time that season, hauling furniture and belongings that might tempt burglars to break in. What a nuisance, she thought, having to lug all that back and forth.

Emma considered what it would be like when she was there all alone. Lori Simpson was right. She should make plans to protect herself.

The Cramers hadn't been seen or heard from since the day of the funeral, but Emma knew they were just lying low, waiting for the lake residents to leave. Emma considered Lori's suggestion that she purchase a gun, but not for long. She was terrified of firearms. She wouldn't be able to rest easy just knowing one was in the house. As for pointing one at an intruder, Emma thought she would probably be paralyzed by fear, her finger frozen stiff, unable to pull the trigger. Or she'd shoot herself in the foot. So she discarded the idea of a gun and thought some more.

The Simpsons left the third week of September, after Lori had tried one last time to get Emma to go with them. Emma saw them off, standing on her front porch, waving. As soon as their car disappeared around a bend in the road, Emma backed her station wagon out of the garage and drove to the small community six miles away.

She went to the Western Auto Store. "I need some large cardboard boxes," she told Keith Bartell, the manager. "For packing my late husband's clothes. Plenty of good wear left in them, so I'll give them to some worthy charity."

"That's mighty generous of you, Mrs. Thorndyke," Bartell said. "Come on in the storeroom. I've got some nice big ones back there."

"Oh, my, yes," Emma exclaimed when she saw the pile of boxes. "I'll take that one. Must have held one of those giant-screen TVs."

"Yes, ma'am." Bartell lifted the box from the pile. "You need more?"

"I could use a couple of smaller ones. What about one of those VCR cartons? And the one that says 'microwave oven' on the side."

Bartell loaded the boxes into the back of Emma's station wagon. It was almost dark by the time Emma got home. She hauled the boxes onto the front porch and placed them with the words identifying the items they'd contained facing toward the road.

After dinner, she got out her recipe file and made an Italian Cream Cake, the one that had won the blue ribbon at the county fair. She decorated it with swirls of fluffy burnt-sugar frosting studded with pecans and maraschino cherries. Ed had always said Emma's cakes were works of art. She set the cake on the dining table, covered it with a transparent cover, and went to bed.

That night the sound of motorcycles woke her. They roared up and down the road in front of the house for more than an hour. Several times, she heard beer cans hitting the porch. She lay, trembling the whole time, with the covers pulled up to her chin, and wondered how many such nights she could endure.

The next day, she disposed of the beer cans, but the cartons stayed on the porch, and that night, the motorcycles came again. This time, they rolled right up in the yard and deep male voices shouted obscenities. They were getting braver. But, finally, they roared away. Emma crept out of bed and put on her robe. She sat in the living room in the dark and didn't fall asleep until dawn.

That night she didn't go to bed at all. She didn't even put on her nightgown. She dressed in a clean pair of gardening slacks and a long-sleeved shirt and settled down in the easy chair with a quilt wrapped around her.

The motorcycles woke her at one A.M. The "boys" drove up to the house and killed the engines. Their heavy boots clomped across the porch, and one of them banged on the door.

"Emma, you got company!"

She threw back the quilt and rose from the chair. She heard a thud, thud, thud. They were kicking the door.

"Let us in, you old bag, before we break the door down."

She turned on a table lamp with fingers that shook. It took every ounce of courage she could summon to unlock the door. She opened it a crack.

"Please go away and leave me alone."

Bo, the older brother, was in front. He shoved the door back and brushed Emma out of the way. "Aw, now, Emma, that ain't very friendly. You're living in the country now. Gotta show some country hospitality to your neighbors." Frank followed his brother inside. They were well over six feet and looked like professional wrestlers in their leather jackets. Emma cringed against the wall.

"What do you want?" she squeaked.

Frank had stomped into Emma's bedroom, and she could hear him rummaging through her dresser drawers. Bo was looking around the living room. "Where's that nice new TV?"

"I don't have a TV. I—I was robbed."

"You don't say!" Bo cackled. "Where'd you put it, Emma? I saw the box it came in on your porch. Noticed you gotcha a new VCR, too."

"Oh, no. I got those boxes to pack Ed's clothes in."

Bo frowned and clomped through the dining room and into the kitchen, flipping on lights as he went. "Don't see no new microwave, either."

"I told you—"

"Bo!" Frank came back to the living room. "She had thirty-six dollars in her purse. There ain't nothing else worth bothering with in the bedrooms except these." He held Emma's beautiful diamond earrings in the light from the table lamp. "Good-sized rocks. She had 'em hid under her mattress."

"Please . . ." Emma's voice broke. "Those were an anniversary present from my husband. Please don't take them."

Frank pocketed the earrings. "You must be having a bad dream, Emma. We never took nothing. Ain't that right, Bo?"

"Right. Emma ain't even gonna mention this little visit to the sheriff. Out here all by her lonesome, she wouldn't wanta get her only neighbors mad at her. She'll need her neighbors in case her house catches fire or something terrible like that. Ain't that right, Emma?" It was a clear threat.

She nodded, unable to speak.

"Lookee at that cake!" Frank walked into the dining room and lifted the cake cover. He went into the kitchen and came back with a knife.

"Oh, please don't cut the cake!" Emma pleaded. "It's for my garden club."

"What'd I tell you about country hospitality, Emma," Bo clucked. "Your garden club won't mind sharing."

Frank cut out a third of the cake and handed it to Bo, then cut another third for himself. "See there, we left some for your old ladies."

They stuffed the cake in their mouths, like two hogs, dropping crumbs and frosting on the carpet. Emma stood behind the easy chair, clutching the cushion. She was shaking so badly that she thought she might collapse if she didn't hold onto something.

"She ain't got no new appliances," Bo said, wiping the frosting off his mouth with a corner of Emma's lace tablecloth. "Those boxes are for her old man's clothes. Let's blow."

At the door, Bo said, "Remember, Emma, this visit is our little secret. Right?"

"Right," Emma said quickly. Then they were gone. As they drove away, she sank into the easy chair and waited for her heart to stop racing. Then she bolted the door and cleaned up the mess left by the Cramers, feeding the remainder of the cake to the garbage disposal. At dawn, she dragged the three cardboard boxes around back and burned them in the big oil drum that served as a trash barrel.

Two days later, the sheriff's car turned into Emma's driveway. She stepped out on the porch. "Mornin', Miz Thorndyke," the sheriff said as he got out. He had a grocery sack in one arm. "Got something here you'll be happy to see."

"Well, come on in. Would you like a cup of coffee?"

"No, ma'am, I don't have time." He lifted her silver teapot

from the sack. "Here's your tea service and brushes. We haven't found the TV. They must've pawned it already."

Emma accepted the teapot and the sack and set them on the coffee table. "Oh, I'm so pleased to have these back. I don't care about the TV. My insurance will buy a new one, as soon as I get around to making a claim. Where on earth did you find these?"

"In Bo and Frank Cramer's house." The sheriff shook his head sadly. "Never would've believed those boys would turn so bad."

"I don't understand. Lori Simpson said you didn't have enough evidence for a search warrant."

"Didn't need a search warrant. Bo and Frank were supposed to do some work for a rancher out west of town yesterday. They didn't show up, and finally yesterday afternoon he went out to their place to see what the holdup was. The house was locked, but he could see Frank through a window, stretched out on the bed. Couldn't raise 'em, so he called me. We broke in and found 'em both deader'n doornails. Been dead for hours, it looked like. Maybe a day or two."

Emma gasped and her hand flew to her mouth.

"Have you seen them around lately?"

"Not for some time. Actually, I haven't seen them since before the funeral. It . . . it must have been an accident. Were they cleaning guns or something?"

"No. We couldn't tell from looking what killed 'em so the coroner did an autopsy. Called me this morning. Damndest thing I ever heard of. Said the boys died of nicotine poisoning."

Emma's mouth dropped open. "How strange. You mean people can actually smoke enough to poison themselves?"

"They didn't smoke themselves to death, Miz Thorndyke. Coroner thinks they must've got hold of some poisoned moonshine. We found a couple of empty jugs in their trash heap. I don't reckon we'll ever find out where they got it."

"What a shame."

"Yes, ma'am. Well, I've got work to do. Oh, I almost forgot." He pulled Emma's diamond earrings from his shirt pocket. "Found these in the Cramers' house, too. They wouldn't happen to be yours, would they?"

It was all Emma could do to shake her head, but it had to be done. "No. See, those are clip-ons." She fingered the tiny gold stud in one ear. "I have pierced ears."

"Didn't think so. If they'd been taken in your robbery, you'd have noticed they were gone by now and reported it." He returned the earrings to his pocket. "I'll be going then. If we find your TV, I'll bring it out to you."

"Thank you, Sheriff. Next time you're in the neighborhood, stop and I'll give you a cup of coffee and a nice piece of pie or cake. I always have something baked, in case anyone drops by."

"Mighty nice of you, ma'am."

Emma smiled at him. "It's just plain old country hospitality."

Jaqueline Girdner's Kate Jasper has appeared in Adjusted to Death, The Last Resort, *and* Murder Most Mellow. *A vegetarian, tai-chi-practicing divorcée who owns Jest Gifts, a gag gift company, and lives among the New Age sensibilities of Marin County, Kate is a lively, appealing addition to the roster of contemporary sleuths. Jaqueline, herself a resident of Marin County, has worked as a psychiatric aide and practiced family law, and is a self-described "incorrigible entrepreneur."*

In "Don't Eat the Red Herring," a mystery writer realizes how stiff the competition for some writing contests may be.

DON'T EAT THE RED HERRING

by Jaqueline Girdner

"NO!" ARDITH DECLARED abruptly. She stood to make her point, pushing her chair back impatiently. She was a rangy, dry-looking woman with the kind of face you rarely saw outside of old sepia-toned photographs of pioneer wives. Hers was a Donner Party kind of face. She ran her hand through frizzy gray hair before continuing.

"John's own karma isn't enough punishment. The s.o.b. needs to die, and he needs to die painfully." The tone of her voice was as harsh as her face. She paused again, her pale lashless eyes glinting with the fervor that usually accompanied her animal rights lectures or her court appearances. I had seen her once in court. She was good. She went for the kill. Now her thin lips curved in a smile.

"I've got it," she said. "If you must give John a chance, throw him in a lion's pen at the zoo. Let destiny play a part. See if he gets out alive."

She sat back down and surveyed our faces, looking for agreement.

Bonnie shook her head. "I don't think it would really work," she objected, her voice high and whining. "How do you get John into the zoo, much less the lion's pen? It sounds like a lot of work to set up."

Bonnie was an altogether different type from Ardith. She was a rose of a woman, plump, pink-cheeked and succulent. And thorny. She tapped her red-lacquered fingernails and considered John's death.

"Why don't you just poison him?" she said. "But give him a chance. Put DDT in one of two glasses of wine. If he chooses the wrong glass, he's dead." She sliced a finger across her throat, flashing red nails. "But John probably wouldn't choose the wrong glass. Rats like him always come out on top," she added bitterly.

I sighed. I knew she was thinking of her own husband again, her ex-husband actually. He had thrown her over for a twenty-year-old after a decade of marriage. That was five years ago. And now Bonnie's alimony was running out. I couldn't figure out why she'd never found another man. She was certainly attractive enough. And there are lots of sweethearts out there. Take my husband Victor, for instance—what a sweetheart! I brushed away the romantic thought. It was time to get back to business.

"Just shoot him," I said brusquely. I was tired of this discussion. I was tired of a lot of things.

"I can't just shoot him, Dee," said Clara dreamily.

Saint Clara the Good. Her large, ethereal blue eyes were all you noticed in her tiny face. And she was bone thin, so thin that I sometimes wondered if she had already ascended to angelhood and mistakenly left this small remainder earthbound. But let me tell you, angels can be a pain in the rear sometimes. Why she was even attempting to write murder mysteries was beyond me. And I was tired of critiquing her latest manuscript.

"I created an evil character like John for a reason," Clara continued, her voice a mere breath. She clasped her spindly white hands together. "A lesson in karma. If my heroine kills him, what is the message? What would that teach?"

"Get with it!" barked Ardith. "Readers don't want spiritual

teaching. They want the bad guy to get what's coming to him. If your heroine can't do the dirty deed, arrange for the police or someone else he's messed with to do it. You owe a definite conclusion to your readers."

"Readers," I snorted. A blast of reality would end this discussion. "What readers? None of us is published."

Ardith and Bonnie both sighed. But not Clara. She just sat there with a dreamy expression on her face I couldn't fathom. It had taken four years of being in this mystery writers critique group with her for me to realize she wasn't on drugs. She was—I can barely stand to say it—"high on life."

Clara's misguided serenity was more than balanced by the remainder of the group. Ardith, for one, was perpetually angry. If she wasn't angry about animals' rights or some other damn thing, she was angry about not getting her work published. She had "something to say, by God," and no one wanted to listen.

Bonnie was bitter. She had hoped to have a career in writing by the time her alimony ran out. She needed the money. But the publishing world had turned its back on her as coldly as her ex-husband had.

I was just tired myself, tired of rejection letters and tired of the never-ending search for the right agent, the right plot, the right series character and the right opportunity. Not being published was like having an earache. The intensity of the pain took every ounce of my attention. My husband, Victor, a marketing executive and a realist, kept telling me that my failure to be published was simply the law of supply and demand at work. There were too many mystery writers and too few publishing opportunities. "So what are you going to do about it, Dee?" he would ask me. Then, when I looked blank, he'd give me a comforting hug. "Something will come up," he'd say. My husband—what a sweetheart! Only he could make me believe that I would be published someday.

Bonnie's whine broke into my ruminations. "Oh, forget it," she said. "Let's just eat."

Our potluck was strictly vegetarian. By a quirk of fate—or perhaps simply our residence in the California Bay area, home of food as a personal statement—we were all hard-core vegetarians.

And we didn't just shun red meat. We ate no fish or chicken either, thank you.

Ardith's refusal to eat animal products was politically inspired. Clara's motives were spiritual. Bonnie's abstinence grew out of her belief that a vegetarian diet kept her weight down. And I was under doctor's orders, a "holistic" doctor but a doctor nevertheless. Originally our critique group had included three carnivorous mystery writers. But they had drifted off, still unpublished—and unimpressed with the food.

"Okay," Ardith mumbled minutes later through her mouthful of brown rice. "We gotta talk about it. Are we going tomorrow night or not?"

"It" was the American Mystery Writers annual convention, to be held in San Francisco, only miles away. A gala dinner and awards ceremony was planned. The awards were for the published mystery writers, of course. That grated on all of us. Except for Clara.

"Of course we're going," she said blithely. "We all have tickets, don't we?"

"I don't know if I can take it," Bonnie complained. "The speeches. The congratulations—"

"The food," I finished for her. The only dish that had been free of animal products last year was the bread. Even the salad had contained bacon bits. Real bacon bits, the waiter had assured me.

"Eat something beforehand," Ardith advised. "That's what I always do—"

"It's not really the food though," Bonnie objected. "It's all those writers who have made it and . . . and I still haven't." Her voice trailed off into a tearful whine. "It's just not fair!"

"Supply and demand," I muttered.

Bonnie sniffled loudly, not comforted by the explanation.

"We could bomb the place," Ardith suggested. She smiled to show she was joking. Her bared teeth were sharp and white. "It'd cut the supply in half. Increase the demand."

That was a cheery thought.

Bonnie clapped her hands gleefully. "I love it," she said, her voice suddenly free of tears.

Even Clara giggled at the proposal, then attempted to hide her giggle with a napkin.

We finished our brown rice and vegetables convivially.

By the time the four of us were sitting at a rear table in the largest meeting room of the San Francisco Center Stage Hotel, we weren't cheerful anymore. Or convivial. The room was filled with the chatter, shrieks and laughter of the partying writers. But somehow our group remained untouched by the gaiety. I wished my husband, Victor, had found the time to come with me.

I looked at my watch. It was nine o'clock and the meal had yet to be served. I had read the posted menu on the way in. It was cute, murderously cute. Hearts of Enemies Salad and Red Herring Soup led off. Pasta with Blood Sauce followed. The entree was Skewered Beef. And Devil's Food Cake with Whipped and Chained Cream finished the meal. I coerced a translation from a passing red-jacketed waiter.

"Green salad, Manhattan clam chowder, pasta marinara, beef shish kebabs and chocolate cake with whipped cream, lady," he rattled off before hurrying away.

Bonnie sighed and got up to go to the bathroom for the fourth time.

"Got a bladder infection or what?" snarled Ardith. So much for group solidarity.

Bonnie ignored her and made her way through the crowd toward the elevator.

Even Clara seemed impatient that night. "The vibrations are unsettling here," she whispered as she stood. "I'm going to find a quiet place and meditate."

"Well, I'm going to find a cigarette," Ardith snapped. Too bad. She hadn't smoked in over two years. She glared a challenge at me. I shrugged my shoulders, too tired to argue her out of it. She stomped away, leaving me alone at our table.

I pasted a smile on my face as if I were delighted with my own company, then got up to go to the bathroom myself. But I was waylaid before I got there by Linda, a former member of our critique group.

"How are things going?" I asked her cautiously. She had manifested an unrivaled ability for complaint when she had been a member of our group. But she wasn't complaining tonight.

"Oh, Dee," she breathed, her plump carnivorous face shining with happiness. "I did it. I got a publishing contract."

"That's great!" I said, instantly happy for her. But in a moment jealousy snuck in. I shook it away. "Tell me all about it," I said.

A half-an-hour-of-success-story later I returned to our table. My head was filled with Linda's story. She had even given me her new agent's name. Maybe there was hope for me yet. Ardith sat alone at the table, scowling and smelling of smoke.

"Linda got a publishing contract—" I began.

"I don't wanna hear about it!" she barked. At least she was honest.

We sat in uncompanionable silence until Bonnie came back to the table. Bonnie gave Ardith's angry face one quick glance and dropped into her chair without a word.

Clara arrived a moment later, just as the green salad was served. At least it didn't have any bacon bits in it this time. We ate it quickly and quietly. In fact, no one at our table spoke at all through the Manhattan clam chowder, which we left untouched, the pasta, which we swallowed gloomily, or the skewered beef, which Ardith pointedly removed from our table. I decided to leave before the chocolate cake, before the speeches and awards. I was tired again.

I was asleep when the phone rang at midnight. Victor rolled over and groaned. My turn. I gave him a kiss on the forehead and shuffled across the room to pick up the receiver.

"People are getting sick," came Clara's thin voice over the line.

"What people, where?" I asked sleepily. She did tend to go on and on about universal suffering.

"Here, at the Center Stage Hotel," she answered. "People are throwing up all over the place."

"Too much to drink," I diagnosed impatiently. I yawned. "Did you call me in the middle of the night to tell me that writers get drunk? This isn't news, you know."

I could barely hear Clara's reply. "They're really sick," she whispered urgently. "And I'm scared."

"Are you okay?" I asked, suddenly awake.

"Yes, I'm fine. And so are Bonnie and Ardith." She paused. "But Dee, some of the others are acting like they're dying."

As it turned out, they were dying. In twenty-four hours thirty mystery writers had died from triphosphormethanol poisoning. A day later the death toll had risen to forty-nine. The newspapers greeted the occasion with glorious alliteration.

"AMERICAN AUTHORS ANNIHILATED AT ANNUAL ASSEMBLY," "DEADLY DINNER FOR DEATH-MONGERS," and "MYSTERY MAVEN MASSACRE MAY BE MURDER," they screamed.

Underneath the headlines bits of the story emerged. The Red Herring Soup, aka Manhattan clam chowder, had been the culprit. It had been spiked with a lethal helping of triphosphormethanol, a liquid phosphorous compound used in the production of rodenticides and fireworks. How it had found its way into the soup was still a question. But the police were seeking an anonymous waiter who had been scurrying around the kitchen officiously before the dinner. He had apparently disappeared by serving time. And he had been seen sprinkling something into the soup. He was described as being of medium height and weight, with curly blond hair and a blond mustache. No one had gotten a good look at him.

I put down the newspaper I had been holding. Ardith was tall for a woman. Did that make her medium height for a man? Or was Bonnie's medium woman's height tall enough to fit the description with heels? Clara was tiny, but she might have used stilts. No, I told myself quickly, if Clara wasn't capable of murder in her writing, she could hardly be capable of mass murder in real life. But she had left the table for at least half an hour. So had Ardith and Bonnie for that matter. And I knew from reading their manuscripts that they all had imagination. Certainly any one of the three had more than enough imagination to become a blond, curly-headed waiter with a mustache for the time it took to poison the Red Herring Soup. And any one of them had vegetarianism as an excuse for passing it up when it came time to eat.

At first I investigated. My characters always did—why shouldn't I? And I was nervous. What if one of my friends were a murderer?

I talked to Victor about triphosphormethanol. He knew a little about the compound. One of his best accounts was a chemical company. Victor told me the compound wasn't all that hard to come by. I visited Bonnie next, and noted a thick volume about poisons on her kitchen table. Of course, a poison reference book wasn't all that unusual for a mystery author. And Bonnie always had been fond of chemical weapons in her work.

I didn't find anything physically incriminating at Ardith's house. But her lecture of the day gave me pause. She explained impatiently to me that the death of fifty human writers was nothing compared to the slaughter of untold numbers of innocent animals that are gobbled up daily as hamburgers.

Clara had a box of sparklers left over from Fourth of July celebrations under her sink. An odd place to keep them, I thought. But they looked intact to my untrained eye. They certainly didn't appear to be missing any triphosphormethanol, if they had contained any to begin with. Karma was Clara's explanation for the tragedy. I should have known.

I probably would have continued my investigations, the murders having remained unsolved. In fact, I got all tingly just thinking of the publicity value if I, a mystery writer, were to be the one to discover the poisoner's identity. But I simply didn't have any spare time after a month had passed. I had a publishing contract!

Supply was down and demand was up. I had contacted Linda's agent a week after the dinner. Linda had unfortunately perished at the infamous affair. But Linda's agent was only too happy to have me as a new client. She quickly sold not only the manuscript I had finished that year, but two more novels as yet unwritten. I was busy all right! Bonnie and Ardith were busy too. They made their book deals a few months after mine. Clara still hadn't sold a mystery. But she had sold a semi-autobiographical metaphysical novel on the meaning of death. Close enough.

It was more than two years after the American Mystery Writers massacre when I finally found the missing evidence. My agent was flying in to meet me that day. She wanted to explain the movie deal she was negotiating for my latest mystery. She was talking big bucks now! And I was jittery. In less than one hour we would be talking about a deal that could support me—and Victor—for life.

I needed a quick project to calm myself down. I decided to clean out the top shelf of our bedroom closet, a shelf I could only reach by ladder. It hadn't been cleaned since we had moved into the house. It was time. I scrambled up the ladder and began pulling down the shelf's disorderly contents at random. Victor was such a pack rat! Halfway across the shelf, behind a box of abandoned ankle weights and worn-out jogging shoes, I found an unfamiliar canvas backpack. I zipped it open. I saw red, a red waiter's jacket. And nestled beneath the jacket were a blond curly wig and mustache.

I swayed on top of the ladder, stunned by my find. My husband was a mass murderer. And he had killed them all for my sake. I had to do something! But I only had half an hour until my agent arrived. That just wasn't enough time.

I would have to find the perfect way to thank Victor later.

My husband—what a sweetheart!

Diane Mott Davidson's Gertrude ("Goldy") Bear first appeared in Catering to Nobody, *an Agatha, Anthony, and Macavity nominee for Best First Novel of 1990, and continues to ply her culinary trade and solve puzzling murders in* Dying for Chocolate. *Diane has come a long way in her knowledge of food since her days as a young newlywed. "When we splurged and bought steak," she says, "I put it in the oven at three hundred fifty degrees for an hour. That was what you did with everything else." Goldy has certainly benefited from Diane's experiences!*

In "Cold Turkey," Goldy finds more than she's bargained for in her refrigerator—and is less than happy about it.

COLD TURKEY

by Diane Mott Davidson

I DID NOT expect to find Edith Blanton's body in my walk-in refrigerator. The day had been bad enough already. My first thought after the shock was *I'm going to have to throw all this food away.*

My mind reeled. I couldn't get a dial tone to call for help. Reconstruct, I ordered myself as I ran to a neighbor's. The police are going to want to know everything. My neighbor pressed 9-1-1. I talked. Hung up. I immediately worried about my eleven-year-old son, Arch. Where was he? I looked at my watch: ten past eight. He was spending the night somewhere. Oh yes, Dungeons and Dragons weekend party at a friend's house. I made a discreet phone call to make sure he was okay. I did not mention the body. If I had, he and his friends would have wanted to troop over to see it.

Then I flopped down in a wing-back chair and tried to think.

I had talked to Edith Blanton that morning. She had called with a batch of demanding questions. Was I ready to cater the Episcopal Church Women's Luncheon, to be held the next day? Irritation had blossomed like a headache. Butterball Blanton, as she was known everywhere but to her face, was a busybody. I'd given the shortest possible answers. The menu was set, the food prepared. Chicken and artichoke heart pot pie. Molded strawberry salad. Tossed greens with vinaigrette. Parkerhouse rolls. Lemon sponge cake. Not on your diet, I had wanted to add, but did not.

Now Goldy, she'd gone on, *you have that petition we're circulating around the church, don't you?* I checked for raisins for a Waldorf salad and said, Which petition is that? Edith made an impatient noise in her throat. *The one outlawing guitar music.* Sigh. I said I had it around somewhere. . . . Actually, I kind of liked ecclesiastical folk music, as long as I personally did not have to sing it. *And Goldy, you're not serving that Japanese raw fish, are you?* To the churchwomen? Never. *And you didn't use anything from the local farm where they found salmonella, did you?* Oh, enough. Absolutely not, Butt—er . . . Mrs. Blanton, I promised before hanging up.

The phone had rung again immediately: our priest, Father Olson. I said, Surely you're not calling about the luncheon. He said, *Don't call me Shirley.* A comic in a clerical collar. After pleasantries we had gotten around to the real stuff: *How's Marla?* I said that Marla Korman, my best friend, was fine. As far as I knew. Why? *Oh, just checking, hadn't seen her in a while.* Haha, sure. I involuntarily glanced at my appointments calendar. After the churchwomen's luncheon, I was doing a dinner party for Marla. I didn't mention this to the uninvited Father Olson. You see, Episcopal priests can marry. Father Olson was unmarried, which made him interested in Marla. The reverse was not the case, however, which was why he had to call me to find out how she was. But none of this did I mention to Father O., as we called him. Didn't want to hurt his feelings.

My neighbor handed me a cup of tea. I thought again of Edith Blanton's pale calves, of the visible side of her pallid face, of the blood on the refrigerator floor. I pushed the image out of my mind and tried to think again about the day. The police were going to ask a lot of questions. Had I heard from anyone in the church again? Had anyone mentioned a current crisis? What had happened after Father Olson called?

Oh yes. Next had come a frantic knock at the door: something else to do with Marla. This time it was her soon-to-be-ex-boyfriend—lanky, strawberry-blond David McAllister. He had desperation in his voice. *What can I do to show Marla I love her?* Sheesh! Did I look like Ann Landers? I ushered him out to the kitchen, where I started to chop pecans, *also* for the Waldorf salad, *also* for Marla's dinner party, to which the wealthy-but-boring David McAllister *also* had not been invited. Not only that, but he was driving me crazy cracking his knuckles. When he took a breath while talking about how much he adored Marla, I said I was in the middle of a crisis involving petitions, raw eggs and the churchwomen, and ushered him out.

About an hour later I'd left the house. I lifted my head from my neighbor's chair and looked at my watch: quarter after eight. When had I left the house? Around one, only to return seven hours later. The entire afternoon and early evening had been taken up with the second unsuccessful meeting between me, my lawyer, and the people suing me to change the name of my catering business. George Pettigrew and his wife own Three Bears Catering down in Denver. In June it came to their attention that my real, actual name is Goldy (a nickname that has stuck like epoxy glue since childhood) Bear (Germanic in origin, but lamentable nonetheless). What was worse in the Pettigrews' eyes was that my business in the mountain town of Aspen Meadow was called Goldilocks' Catering, Where Everything Is Just Right! We began negotiating three weeks ago, at the beginning of September. The Pettigrews screamed copyright infringement. I tried to convince them that all of us could successfully capitalize on, if not inhabit, the same fairy tale. The meeting this afternoon was another failure, except from the viewpoint of my lawyer, who gets his porridge no matter what.

I nestled my head against one of the wings of my neighbor's chair. Just thinking about the day again was exhausting. For as if all this had not been enough, when I got home I heard a dog in my outdoor trash barrels. At least I thought it was a dog. When I went around the side of the house to check, a *real* bear, large and black, shuffled away from the back of the house and up toward the woods. This is not an uncommon sight in the Colorado high country when fall weather sets in. But combined with the nagging from Edith and the fight with the Pettigrews, it was enough to send me in search of a parfait left over from an elementary school faculty party.

Not on your diet, I thought with a measure of guilt, the diet you just undertook with all sorts of good intentions. Oh well. Diets aren't good for you. Too much deprivation. But on this plan I didn't have to give up sweets; I could have one dessert a day. Of course the brownie I'd had after the lawyer's office fiasco was only a memory. Besides, I was under so much stress. I could just imagine that tall chilled crystal glass, those thick layers of chocolate and vanilla pudding. I opened the refrigerator door full of anticipation. And there in the dark recesses of the closetlike space was Edith, fully clothed, lying limp, sandwiched between the congealed strawberry salad and marinating T-bones.

I'd screamed. Rushed over to the neighbor's where I now sat, staring into a cup of lukewarm tea. I looked at my watch again. 8:20.

My neighbor was scurrying around looking for a blanket in case I went into shock. I was not going into shock; I just needed to talk to somebody. So I phoned Marla. That's what best friends are for, right? To get you through crises? Besides, Marla and I went way back. We had both made the mistake of marrying the same man, not simultaneously. We had survived the divorces from The Jerk and become best friends. I had even coached her in figuring her monetary settlement, sort of like when an NFL team in the playoffs gets films from another team's archenemy.

When Marla finally picked up the phone, I told her Edith Blanton was dead and in my refrigerator. I must have still been incoherent because I added the bit about the bear.

There was a pause while Marla tried to apply logic. Finally she said, "Goldy. I'm on my way over."

"Okay, okay! I'll meet you at my front door. Just be careful."

"Of what? Is this homicide or is it a frigging John Irving novel?"

Before I could say anything she hung up.

My neighbor and I walked slowly back to my house. The police arrived first: two men in uniforms. They took my name and Edith Blanton's. They asked how and when I'd found the body. When they tried to call for an investigative team, they discovered that the reason I hadn't been able to get a dial tone was that my phone was dead. The wires outside had been cut. This would explain why my brand-new, horrendously expensive security system had not worked when Edith and . . . whoever . . . had broken in. The police used their radio. While I was bemoaning my fate, Marla arrived. She was dressed in a sweatsuit sewn with gold spangles: I think they were supposed to represent aspen leaves.

The team arrived and took pictures. The coroner, gray-haired and grim-faced, signaled the removal company to cart out the body bag holding Edith. Marla murmured, "The Butterball bagged."

I said, "Stop."

Marla closed her eyes and fluttered her plump hands. "I know. I'm sorry. But she *was* a bitch. Everybody in the church disliked her."

I harrumphed. The two uniformed policemen told us to quit talking. They told me to go into the living room so the team leader, a female homicide investigator I did not know, could ask some questions. Marla flounced out. She said she was going home to make up the guest bed for me; no way was she allowing me to stay in that house.

The team leader and I settled ourselves on the two chairs in my living room. Out in the kitchen the lab technicians and other investigators were having a field day spreading black graphite fingerprint powder over the food for the churchwomen's luncheon.

The investigator was a burly woman with curly blond hair held back with black barrettes. Her eyes were light brown and impassive, her voice even. She wanted to know my name, if I knew the victim and for how long, was I having problems with her and where I'd been all day. I told her about my activities, about the following day's luncheon and Edith's questions. At their leader's direction, the team took samples of all the food. They also took what they'd found on the refrigerator floor: an anti–guitar-music petition. Through the blobs of congealed strawberry salad and raw egg yolk, you could see there were no names on it. Edith was still clutching the paper after she'd been hit on the head and dragged into the refrigerator.

I said, "Dragged . . . ?"

The investigator bit the inside of her cheek. Then she said, "Please tell me every single thing about your conversation with Edith Blanton."

So we went through it all again, including the bit about the petition. I added that I had not been due to see Edith, er, the deceased until the next day. Moreover, I was not having more problems with her than anybody else in town, especially Father Olson, who, unlike Edith, thought every liturgy should sound like a hootenanny.

The investigator's next question confused me. Did I have a pet? Yes, I had a cat that I had inherited from former employers. However, I added, strangers spooked him. Poor Scout would be cowering under a bed for at least the next three days.

She said, "And the color of the cat is . . . ?"

"Light brown, dark brown and white," I said. "Sort of a Burmese-Siamese mix. I think."

The investigator held out a few strands of hair.

"Does this look familiar? Look like your cat's hair?" It was dark brown and did not look like anything that grew on Scout. In fact, it looked fake.

"'Fraid not," I said.

"Synthetic, anyway, we think. You got any of this kind of material around?"

I shook my head no. "Oh gosh," I said, "the bear." I started to tell her about what I'd seen around the back of the house, but she was looking at her clipboard. She shifted in her chair.

She said, "Wait. Is this a *relative* of yours? Er, Ms. Bear?"

"No, no, no. Have you heard of Three Bears Catering?"

The investigator looked more confused. "Is that you, too? I wouldn't know. They did the policemen's banquet down in Denver last year, and they all wore bear . . . suits. . . ."

She eyed me, the corners of her mouth turned down. She said, "Any chance this bear-person might have been waiting to attack you in your refrigerator? Over the name change problem? And attacked Edith instead? Do they know what you look like?"

"I told you. I spent the afternoon with the Pettigrews," I said through clenched teeth. "They're suing me; why would they want to kill me?"

"You tell me."

At that moment, Marla poked her head into the living room. "I'm back. Can we leave? Or do you have to stay until the kitchen demolition team finishes?"

I looked at the investigator, who shook her head. She said, "We have a lot to do. Should be finished by midnight. At the latest. Also, we gotta take the cut wires from out back and, uh, your back door."

I said, "My back door? Great." I gave Marla a pained look. "I have to stay until they go. Just do me a favor and call somebody to come put in a piece of plywood for the door hole. Also, see if you can find my cat cage. I'm bringing Scout to your house."

Marla nodded and disappeared. The investigator then asked me to go through the whole thing *backward,* beginning with my discovery of Edith. This I did meticulously, as I know the backward-story bit is one way investigators check for lies.

Finally she said, "Haven't I seen you around? Aren't you a friend of Tom Schulz's?"

I smiled. "Homicide Investigator Schulz is a good friend of mine. Unfortunately, he's up snagging inland salmon at Green Lake Reservoir. Now, tell me. Am I a suspect in this or not?"

The investigator's flat brown eyes revealed nothing. After a moment she said, "At this time we don't have enough information to tell about any suspects. But this hair we found in the victim's hand isn't yours. You didn't know your phone lines were cut. And you probably didn't break down your own back door."

Well. I guess that was police talk for *No you're not a suspect.*

The investigator wrote a few last things on her clipboard, then got up to finish with her cohorts in the kitchen. I didn't see her for the next three hours. Marla appeared with the cat cage, and I found Scout crouched under Arch's bed. I coaxed him out while Marla welcomed the emergency fix-it people at the stroke of midnight. The panel on their truck said: *Felony Fix-up—They Trash It, We Patch It.* How comforting. Especially the twenty-four-hour service part.

An hour after the police and Felony Fix-up had left my kitchen looking like a relic of the scorched-earth policy, I sat in Marla's kitchen staring down one of Marla's favorite treats—imported *baba au rhum.* There's something about being awake at one A.M. that makes you think you need something to eat. Still, guilt reared its hideous head.

"What's the matter?" Marla asked. "I thought you loved those. Eat up. It'll help you stop thinking about Edith Blanton."

"Not likely, but I'll try." I inhaled the deep buttered-rum scent. "I shouldn't. I ate Lindt Lindors all summer and I'm supposed to be on a diet."

"One dessert won't hurt you."

"I've already had one dessert."

"So? *Two* won't hurt you." She shook her peaches-and-cream cheeks. "If I'd had to go through what you just did, I'd have six." So saying, she delicately loaded two *babas* onto a Wedgwood dessert plate. "Tomorrow's going to be even worse," she warned. "You'll have to phone the president of the churchwomen first thing and cancel the luncheon. You'll have to call Father Olson. No, never mind, I'll make both calls."

"Why?"

"Because, my dear, I am still hopeful that you'll be able to do my dinner party tomorrow night." Marla pushed away from the table to sashay over to her refrigerator for an aerosol can of whipped cream. "I know it's crass," she said as she shook the can vigorously, "but I still have three people, one of whom is a male I am very interested in, expecting dinner. Shrimp cocktail, steaks, potato soufflé, green beans, Waldorf salad, and chocolate cake.

Remember? Beginning at six o'clock. I can't exactly call them up and say, Well, my caterer found this body in her refrigerator—"

"All right! If I can finish cleaning up the mess tomorrow, we're on." I took a bite of the *baba* and said, "The cops ruined the salad and the cake. You'll have to give me some more of your Jonathan apples. Gee, I don't feel so hot—"

"Don't worry. Sleep in. I have lots of apples. And I'll send a maid over to help you."

"Just not in a bear suit."

"Hey! Speaking of which! Should we give the Pettigrews a call in the morning? Just to hassle them?" She giggled. "Should we give them a call right now?"

"No, no, no," I said loudly over the sound of Marla hosing her *babas* with cream. "The police are bound to talk to them. If they're blameless, I can't afford to have them any angrier at me than they already are. I'm so tired, I don't even want to think about it."

Marla gave me a sympathetic look, got up and made me a cup of espresso laced with rum.

I said, "So who's this guy tomorrow night?"

"Fellow named Tony Kaplan. Just moved here from L.A., where he sold his house for over a million dollars. And it was a small house, too. He's cute. Wants to open a bookstore."

"Not another newcomer who's fantasized about running a bookstore in a mountain town," I said as I took the whipped cream bottle and pressed out a blob on top of my coffee. Immigrants from either coast always felt they had a mission to bring culture to us cowpokes. "Gee," I said. "Almost forgot. Regarding your busy social life, Father Olson called and asked me how you were."

"I hope you told him I was living in sin with a chocolate bar."

"Well, I didn't have time because then David McAllister showed up at my front door. Wanted to know if there was anything he could do to show you he loved you."

Marla tsked. "He asked me the same thing, and I said, Well, you can start with a nice bushel of apples."

"You are cruel." I sipped the coffee. With the rum and the

whipped cream, it was sort of like hot ice cream. "You shouldn't play with his feelings."

"Excuse me, but jealousy is for seventh-graders."

"Too cruel," I said as we got up and placed the dishes in the sink. She escorted me with Scout the cat up to her guest room, then gave me towels; I handed over a key to my front door for her maid. Then I said, "Tell me about Edith Blanton."

Marla plunked down a pair of matching washcloths. She said, "Edith knew everything about everybody. Who in the church had had affairs with whom . . ."

"Oh, that's nice."

Marla pulled up her shoulders in an exaggerated gesture of nonchalance. The sweat-suit spangles shook. "Well, it was," she said. "I mean, everybody was nice to her because they were afraid of what she had on them. They didn't want her to talk. And she got what she wanted, until she took up arms against Father Olson over the guitar music."

"Too bad she couldn't get anything on him."

"Oh, honey," Marla said with an elaborate swirl of her eyes before she turned away and swaggered down the hall to her room. "Don't think she wasn't trying."

The next day Scout and I trekked to the church before going back to my house. Scout meowed morosely the whole way. I told him I had to leave a big sign on the church door, saying that the luncheon had been canceled. He only howled louder when I said it was just in case someone hadn't gotten the word. If I hadn't been concentrating so hard on trying to comfort him, I would have noticed George Pettigrew's truck in the church parking lot. Then I would have been prepared for Pettigrew's smug grin, his hands clutched under his armpits, his foot tapping as I vaulted out of my van. As it was, I nearly had a fit.

"Were you around my house in a bear suit last night?" I demanded. He opened his eyes wide, as if I were crazy. "And *what* are you doing here? Haven't you got enough catering jobs down in Denver?"

"We don't use the bear suits anymore," he replied in a superior tone. "We had a hygiene problem with the hair getting into the food. And as a matter of fact I am doing lunches for two Skyboxes at Mile High Stadium tomorrow. But I can still offer to help out the churchwomen, since their local caterer canceled." His eyes bugged out as he raised his eyebrows. "Bad news travels fast."

Well, the luncheon was not going to happen. To tell him this, I was tempted to use some very unchurchlike language. But at that moment Father Olson pulled up in his 300E Mercedes 4matic. Father O. had told the vestry that a priest needed a four-wheel-drive vehicle to visit parishioners in the mountains; he'd also petitioned for folk-music tapes to give to shut-ins. The vestry had refused to purchase the tapes, but they'd sprung fifty thou for the car.

Father O. came up and put his hands on my shoulders. He gave me his Serious Pastoral Look. "Goldy," he said, "I've been so concerned for you."

"So have I," I said ruefully, with a sideways glance at George Pettigrew, who shrank back in the presence of clerical authority.

I turned my attention back to Father Olson. Marla might want to reconsider. An ecclesiastical career suited Father O., who had come of age in the sixties. He had sincere brown eyes, dark skin and a beard, a cross between Moses and Ravi Shankar.

". . . feel terrible about what's happened to Edith," he was saying, "of course. How can this possibly . . . Oh, you probably don't want to talk about it. . . ."

I said, "You're right."

Fancy cars were pulling into the church parking lot. George Pettigrew unobtrusively withdrew just as a group of women disentangled themselves from their Cadillacs and Mercedes.

"Listen," I said, "I have to split. Can you take care of these women who haven't gotten the bad news? I have a dinner party tonight that I simply can't cancel."

I almost didn't make it. Cries of *Oh here she is; I wonder what she's fixed* erupted like birdcalls. Father Olson gave me the Pastoral Nod. I sidled past the women, hopped back in the van, and managed to get out of the church parking lot without getting into a single conversation.

To my surprise, the maid Marla had sent over had done a superb job cleaning my kitchen. It positively sparkled. Unfortunately, right around the corner was the plywood nailed over the back-door opening: a grim reminder of last night's events.

I set about thawing and marinating more steaks, then got out two dozen frozen Scout's Brownies, my patented contribution to the chocoholics of the world. I had first developed the recipe under the watchful eye of the cat, so I'd named them after him. Marla adored them.

Edith Blanton came to mind as I again got out my recipe for Waldorf salad. Someone, dressed presumably as a bear, had taken the time to cut the phone wires and break in. Why? Had that person been following Edith, meaning to kill her at his first opportunity? Or had Edith surprised a robber? Had he killed her intentionally or accidentally?

I knew one thing for sure. Homicide Investigator Tom Schulz was my friend—well, more than a friend—and he often talked to me about cases up in Aspen Meadow. This would not be true with the current investigator working the Edith Blanton case, no question about it. If I was going to find out what happened, I was on my own.

While washing and cutting celery into julienne sticks, I conjured up a picture of Edith Blanton with her immaculately coiffed head of silver hair, dark green skirt, and Loden jacket. Despite being an energetic busybody, Edith had been a lady. She never would have broken into my house.

I held my breath and opened my refrigerator door. All clean. I reached for a bag of nuts. Although classic Waldorfs called for walnuts, I was partial to fresh, sweet pecans that I mail-ordered from Texas. I chopped a cupful and then softened some raisins in hot water. The bear-person had been in my refrigerator. Why? If you're going to steal food, why wear a disguise?

Because if I had caught him, stealing food or attacking Edith Blanton, I would have recognized him.

So it was someone I knew? Probably.

I went back into the refrigerator. Although only a quarter cup of mayonnaise was required for the Waldorf, it was imperative to use *homemade* mayonnaise, which I would make with a nice fresh raw egg. I would mix the mayonnaise with a little lemon juice, sugar, and heavy cream. . . . Wait a minute.

Two days ago my supplier had brought me eggs from a salmonella-free source in eastern Colorado. I was sure they were brown. So why was I staring at a half dozen nice white eggs?

I picked one up and looked at it. It was an egg, all right. I brought it out into the kitchen and called Alicia, my supplier. The answering service said she was out on a delivery.

"Well, do you happen to know what color eggs she delivered on her run two days ago?"

There was a long pause. The operator finally said, "Is this some kind of *yolk*?"

Oh, hilarious. I hung up. So funny I forgot to laugh.

I would have called a neighbor and borrowed an egg, but I didn't have any guarantees about hers, either. Many locals bought their eggs from a farm outside of town where they *had* found salmonella, and hers might be tainted too.

I felt so frustrated I thawed a brownie in the microwave. This would be my one dessert of the day. Oh, and was it wonderful—thick and dark and chewy. Fireworks of good feeling sparked through my veins.

Okay, I said firmly to my inner self, yesterday when you came into this refrigerator you found a body. There is no way you could possibly remember the color of eggs or anything else that Alicia delivered two days ago. So make the mayo and quit bellyaching.

With this happy thought, I started the food processor whirring and filched another brownie. Mm, mm. When the mayonnaise was done, I finished the Waldorf salad, put it in the refrigerator, and then concentrated on shelling and cooking fat prawns for the shrimp cocktail. When I put the shrimp in to chill, I stared at the refrigerator floor. I still had not answered the first question. Why had Edith been at my house in the first place?

She had been carrying a petition. A *blank* petition. So?

My copy had had a few names on it. Edith was carrying a blank petition because I had said I didn't know where my copy was. She came over with a new one.

So? That still didn't explain how she got in.

When she got here, she didn't get any answer at the front door. But she saw the light filtering from the kitchen, and being the busybody she was, she went around back. The door was open, and she surprised the bear in mid-heist. . . .

Well. Go figure. I packed up all the food and hustled off to Marla's.

"Oh darling, *enfin!*" Marla cried when she swung open her heavy front door. She was wearing a multilayered yellow-and-red chiffon dress that looked like sewn-together scarves. Marla always dressed to match the season, and I was pretty sure I was looking at the designer version of Autumn.

"You don't need to be so dramatic," I said as I trudged past her with the first box.

"Oh! I thought you were Tony." She giggled. "Just kidding."

To my relief she had already set her cherry dining room table with her latest haul from Europe: Limoges china and Baccarat crystal. I started boiling potatoes for the soufflé and washed the beans.

"I want to taste!" Marla cried as she got out a spoon to attack the Waldorf.

"Not on your life!" I said as I snatched the covered bowl away from her. "If we get started eating and chatting there'll be nothing left for your guests."

To my relief the front doorbell rang. Disconsolate, Marla slapped the silver spoon down on the counter and left. From the front hall came the cry "Oh darling, *enfin!*" Tony Kaplan, would-be bookstore proprietor.

The evening was warm, which was a good thing, as Marla and I had decided to risk an outdoor fire on her small barbecue. There were six T-bones—one for each guest and two extra for big appetites. I looked at my watch: six o'clock. Marla had said to serve at seven. The coals would take a bit longer after the sun went down, but since we were near the solstice, that wouldn't be until half past six. The things a caterer has to know.

Tony Kaplan meandered out to the kitchen. Marla was welcoming the other couple. He needed ice for his drink, he said with a laugh. He was a tall, sharp-featured man who hunched his shoulders over when he walked, as if his height bothered him. I introduced myself. He laughed. "Is that your real name?" I told him there was a silver ice bucket in the living room. He just might not have recognized it, as it was in the shape of a sundae. You had to lift up the ice cream part to get to the ice. "Oh, I get it!" There was another explosive laugh, his third. He may have been rich, but his personality left a lot to be desired.

When the coals were going and I had put the soufflé in the oven, my mind turned again to Edith. Who could have possibly wanted to break into my refrigerator? Why not steal the computer I had right there on the counter to keep track of menus?

"We're ready for the shrimp cocktail," Marla stage-whispered into the kitchen.

"Already? But I thought you said—"

"Tony's driving me crazy. If I give him some shrimp, maybe he'll stop chuckling at everything I have to say."

While Marla and her guests were bathing their shrimp with cocktail sauce, I hustled out to check on the coals. To my surprise, a nice coat of white ash had developed. Sometimes things do work. The steaks sizzled enticingly when I placed them on the grill. I ran back inside and got out the salad and started the beans. When I came back out to turn the T-bones, the sun had slid behind the mountains and the air had turned cool.

"Come on, let's go," I ordered the steaks. After a long five minutes the first four were done. I slapped them down on the platter, put the last two on the grill, and came in. In a crystal bowl, I made a basket of lettuce and then spooned the Waldorf salad on top. This I put on a tray along with the butter and rolls. The soufflé had puffed and browned; I whisked it out to the dining room. While I was putting the beans in a china casserole dish, I remembered that I had neglected to get the last two steaks off the fire.

Cancel the *things working* idea, I thought. I ferried the rest of the dishes out to Marla's sideboard, invited the guests to serve themselves buffet-style, and made a beeline back to the kitchen.

I looked out the window: around the steaks the charcoal fire was merrily sending up foot-high flames and clouds of smoke. Bad news. At this dry time of year, sparks were anathema. There was no fire extinguisher in Marla's kitchen. Why should there be? She never cooked. I grabbed a crystal pitcher, started water spurting into it, looked back out the window to check the fire again.

Judas priest. A bear was lurching from one bush in Marla's backyard to the next. In the darkening twilight, I could not tell if it was the same one that had been in my backyard. All I could see was him stopping and then holding his hands as if he were cheering.

I sidestepped to get beside one of Marla's cabinets, then peeked outside. I knew bravery was in order; I just didn't know what that was going to look like. Too bad Scout had never made it as an attack-cat.

The bear-person shows up at my house. The bear-person shows up at Marla's. Why?

Oh damn. The eggs.

"Marla!" I shrieked. I ran out to the dining room. "Don't eat the Waldorf salad! There's a bear in your backyard . . . but I just know it's not a real one. . . . Somebody needs to call the cops! Quick! Tony, could you please go grab this person? It's not a real bear, just somebody in a bear suit. I'm sure he killed Edith Blanton."

For once, Tony did not laugh. He said, "You've got a killer dressed as a bear in the backyard. You want me to go grab him with my bare hands?"

"Yes," I said, "of course! Hurry up!"

"This is a weird dinner party," said Tony.

"Oh, I'll do it!" I shrieked.

I sprinted to the kitchen and vaulted full tilt out Marla's back door. Maybe it *was* a real bear. Then I'd be in trouble for sure. I started running down through the tall grass toward the bush where the bear was hidden. The bear stood up. He made his cheering motion again. But . . .

Ordinary black bears have bad eyesight.

Ordinary black bears don't grow over five feet tall.

This guy was six feet if he was an inch, and his eyes told him I was coming after him.

He turned and trundled off in the opposite direction. I sped up, hampered only by tall grass and occasional rocks. Behind me I could hear shouts—Marla, Tony, whoever. I was not going to turn around. I was bent on my prey.

The bear howled: a gargled human howl. Soon he was at the end of Marla's property, where an enormous rock formation was the only thing between us and the road. The bear ran up on the rocks. Then, unsure of what to do, he jumped down the other side. Within a few seconds I had scrambled up to where he had stood. The bear had landed in the center of the road.

I launched myself. When I landed on his right shoulder, he crumpled. Amazing. The last time I'd seen a bear successfully tackled was when Randy Gradishar had thrown Walter Payton for a six-yard loss in the Chicago backfield.

I leapt up. "You son of a bitch!" I screamed. Then I kicked him in the stomach for good measure.

I reached down to pull off his bear mask. Of course, I was fully expecting to see the no-longer-smug face of George Pettigrew.

But it wasn't George.

Looking up at me was the tormented face of David McAllister. I was stunned. But of course. The hand-paw motion. David McAllister had been doing what he always did when he was nervous: cracking his knuckles.

"David? David? What's going on?"

"I'm sorry, I'm sorry," he blubbered, "I didn't mean to hurt that old woman in your house. I just needed Marla. . . . I thought I was going to lose my mind. . . . I wanted to hurt her . . . and whoever she was seeing. . . . I wanted to make them pay. . . . I'm just so sorry. . . ."

Marla and Tony Kaplan appeared at the top of the rocks.

"Goldy!" Marla shrieked. "Are you okay? The police are on their way. What's that, a person?"

Later, much later, Marla and I sat in her kitchen and started in on the untouched platter of brownies. David McAllister had said he figured Marla had asked for the apples for Waldorf salad because she was having somebody else over. (*He knew you better than you thought,* I told her.) He was crazy with jealousy, and I had been no help. Worse, when he was in my kitchen, he had seen "Marla—dinner party" on my appointments calendar. And here I'd thought all he'd been doing was cracking his knuckles. He cut my wires and broke through my back door. He knew I made everything from scratch. (*He knew us all better than we thought,* Marla said.) So he substituted salmonella-tainted eggs for the mayonnaise, to make Marla and her dinner guests sick. When Edith Blanton surprised him, they struggled, and she fell back on the corner of the marble slab I used for kneading. It was an accident. But because David McAllister had broken into my house before his struggle with Edith, the charge was going to be murder in the first degree.

Marla sank her teeth into her first brownie. "Ooo-ooo," she said. "Yum. I feel better already. Have one."

"I shouldn't. I can't." In fact, I couldn't even look at the brownies; my knees were scraped and my chest hurt where I'd fallen on David McAllister.

"Well, you're probably right. If you hadn't gone after that parfait, you never would have found Butterball, I mean Mrs. Blanton. Which just goes to show, if you're going to give up desserts, you have to do it cold—"

"Don't say it. Don't even think it. And no matter how you cajole, I'm not going to join you in this chocolate indulgence."

Her eyes twinkled like the rings on her fingers. "But that's what I wanted all along!" she protested. "Leave more for me that way! Dark, fudgy, soothing . . ."

"Oh all right," I said. "Just one."

Susan Taylor Chehak's first novel, The Story of Annie D., *was nominated for an Edgar award for Best First Novel of 1989.* Harmony *and* Bader *continue to explore with clarity and sensitivity the lives and secrets of the residents of small Midwest towns, giving readers extraordinary glimpses into the inner—and often disturbing—lives of everyday people. Susan is a graduate of the University of Iowa Writers Workshop and now lives in Los Angeles with her husband and two sons.*

In "Coulda Been You," a mother and daughter learn, to their horror, that certain warnings should be heeded.

COULDA BEEN YOU

by Susan Taylor Chehak

I DON'T KNOW if she could ever come up with the right words to tell just what it is exactly about fall, but I think even before what happened to Dana there seemed to be already a feeling that Katie had acquired, about how that season is a special one, different from any of the other times of the year. And now, when it comes around again, she still looks glad to welcome it back, like an old friend, long gone and hard-missed. I can tell by what I see there in the squinting of her eyes that it still is true, this year the same as last—the shortened days just somehow hold out more promise, more hope, more possibility for change and betterment in life than any other time in any other place. I've been studying Katie, and I think I understand her. I think I can almost read her thoughts. They're printed on the freckles of her face and in the way she holds her body, just as if they were words and sentences, filling up the pages of a book.

A spirit such as Katie's is the kind that quickens to change, and all the more so with September's turnabout weather and mulchy smell. At summer's end, she's filled up to overflowing with a charging ambition, impatient with the empty days of August, anxious to get back to her studies again, and you can tell by the way she talks that her imagination is brimming over with any extravagant plan she can come up with for her future—what she'll do tomorrow, where she'll go, what she'll be when she grows up—every idea trying to crowd out every other thought, struggling to the forefront, fighting for her attention—and, for a while, it seems that there is nothing in the world that Katie can't do.

But, don't make a mistake and confuse it with the kinds of feelings everybody knows go along with New Year's Day. It's not anywhere near to being the same as how a person's likely to be thinking about herself on that morning, working hard to face up to her own hard resolutions and promises for self-improvement, hanging bleary-eyed over a sobering black, hot cup of coffee, with her head pounding from the effects of last night's overindulgence down at the Nite Life Bar and Grill—too much drinking, too much dancing, too many kisses, too much food—and staring out through the kitchen window, past a bitter roil of cigarette smoke, at a view of the land that's been frozen over, too stark and cold for nurturing any dreams at all in a heart and imagination that has already been saturated by the excesses of Thanksgiving and Christmas and even my birthday, which happens to come just before. No, the truth of it is that by the time the months have turned that corner into January, I can already feel that I have earned a serious need for penance and a strict sticking to whatever I can still make out of the path that's been laid out for me in the autumn days that have come before, not go dreaming up any more designs for the dead of winter to come. By then it is enough for a woman just to get by, and stay warm and alive until spring.

In the fall, though, it's different. In the fall, everything still seems possible. Then, anything can be just about to happen; then no project seems too big to tackle or too complicated to find a way to follow through or too impossible to get done. It is a hopeful sort of feeling that gets slapped awake with the sudden, fresh change in the temperature, the chill that sneaks in on the edge of the morning sunshine and sits in the shadows of the early settling dusk at the tail end of the day.

* * *

Last year I had a premonition that was brought on by the brightening of the turning trees, and an anticipation that seemed to be building up with the accumulation of certain smells—of mown hay and dry leaves, of brand-new clothes and polished leather shoes, of schoolbooks and pencil shavings and ink. It was a sense that came on hand in hand with the first days of school, with Katie just ten years old, skinny and scrawny, jumpy and itchy, her long legs mottled by a day's worth of bumps and bruises, and the fine pale curls of her hair so tangled on her head that it took my own two hands to comb through the snarls at the end of the day, when it was time for me to tuck her off to sleep in bed. By then I'd already brought the heavy winter wool blankets down from the trunk where I kept them in the attic, and they'd filled up the house with their smell of mothballs and cedar and must. And I could think of more chores that I'd need to be seeing to soon—the leaves that were carpeting the front lawn raked away and burned, the rose bushes that grew alongside the driveway cut back and bundled in burlap, the screens all brought down and the storm windows polished and put up in their place. Summer was over. There was a world of work to be done.

Katie and her friend Dana were both of them entering together into the fifth grade then. And it was exactly the night after the first day of school when I looked up from the dishes that I'd been washing in the sink, and first I saw my own face reflected back at me in the window glass and then, beyond that, I could see houselights shining down through the trees behind where Dana Franklin lived, and shadows moving past them, people out there prowling around in the woods behind her house. And I remember it clearly, the thought coming to me like a voice was talking out loud from somewhere behind me, speaking right into my ear, and it was saying, "Uh-oh. Uh-oh." Then something else, something I wasn't able to quite catch, garbled words, a warning, I thought, all mixed up with the deep sounds of the men who were outside walking through the woods and calling out Dana's name, and I could feel the idea tugging at me, snagged in the back of my mind like a fish hook, pulling, "Uh-oh." And that was how I knew it that something had happened. And that was how I knew that most likely it was something bad. I don't pretend to have the gift of sight or anything like that. I only had an intuition, that was all.

Katie was upstairs, in her bedroom, in a sulk after the fit she'd thrown. She'd taken off her new school clothes and left them in a messy pile on the floor for me to pick up after her—a green-and-blue-and-black plaid wool skirt and a white cotton blouse with a Peter Pan collar and a blue sweater with a ribbon placket and dark green knee-high socks and black Mary Janes with thin leather straps across the top and tiny pearl buttons on the side. I had even bought her some new pairs of underpants, white cotton with pink and blue flowers and a thin lace ruffle around the elastic waist, so Katie could go off to school knowing that every stitch of cloth that rubbed up next to her skin that day was brand new, fresh off the rack, never been worn by any other body before.

It was fall, just after Labor Day, but it was Indian summer, too, when the weather still hadn't turned quite so cold yet, except in the very earliest morning hours. By noontime the sun was burning as high as it ever had been in July, shining down hot and crisp and dry. And even though Katie was ten going on eleven, and even though she was already in the fifth grade, graduated upstairs to the middle school in the second-floor classrooms with the bigger sixth and seventh graders, who had different teachers and had to travel back and forth through the hallways all day, even so, I still had not allowed her to ride her bike to school in the morning with Dana and then home again in the afternoon. She was still mad at me for it then. She was still holding a grudge against my carefulness, thinking I meant to punish her, when all I wanted was to steer her clear of harm.

"Maybe later in the year, Katie dear," I'd said, standing there at the kitchen sink, up to my elbows in soapsuds and greasy gray water, talking over my shoulder, my back stiffened against what I could guess was going to be her anger straining at the reins of what she thought was just my meanness and stubborn will. "Maybe when it's not so hot out you can."

But, she knew and I knew, when it wasn't too hot anymore, then it would be too cold. Or too wet. Or too snowy. There would be rain or ice. It would be too late or too early. The truth was, I had a thousand million reasons made up about why it was better for me, for her, for everybody in the school, in the city, in the whole wide world around, if she would just let me drive her to school in the mornings—it wasn't so far, and I didn't mind, not one bit—and then be there waiting by my car at the curb in the afternoons again to pick her up outside the door.

Katie had stomped away out of the kitchen, banging her fists on the walls of the house and slamming whatever doors she came to as she went along through the front room and up the stairs to her bed, and that was why she missed the sound of the telephone ringing, and so she wasn't aware of the fact that Dana's mother had called—looking for Dana, who wasn't with us, who hadn't been here—and that Dana was missing and nobody'd seen her and nobody knew where she'd gone.

After the dishes were done, washed and dried and put away, I went upstairs and found Katie lying flat on her back on her bed, staring at the spiderweb pattern of cracks that crawled along the edges of the ceiling over her head, her face solid with an anger that had set it like cement, dry-eyed and thin-lipped and gray. When I sat down next to her, all she could do was moan and roll away, over onto her side, showing me her back—her nubbed shoulders, winged like an angel's underneath the worn pink flowered fabric of her nightgown, the bumpety line of her spine, her hips narrowing down into the girlish round tuck of her behind—while I tried to make it clear to her that the real honest-to-God reason I was not about to let her go off alone to school on her bicycle like everybody else her age was allowed to do was not what she thought—that I didn't trust her or that I didn't want her to have fun or be like the other children or have any friends at all. It was only that I was worried, and that was all. I was afraid she'd have an accident. I was scared that she'd get hurt. I was just too good at imagining a catastrophe that might be about to happen, and I knew I couldn't ever bear it if it did.

"I think probably I'd die, Katie," I told her, "if anything bad ever happened to you." And that still is true. Katie is all I have in the world to take care of besides myself.

* * *

Already we'd had one close call too many for my lifetime. It had happened when Katie was only a baby, hardly even able to toddle on two feet yet, and her father was still living with us then, off and on. I was outside standing on the back porch, leaning against the railing on the hottest summer day, trying to get myself cooled off before I went back to my work, scrubbing floors or washing clothes or some such. I remember I'd been rolling a cube of ice around on my face, letting the small relief of it drip down my neck and onto my shoulders, wishing up the most gentle whisper of a breeze in the branches of the trees that cast their heavy shadows across our yard, dappling the sides of the house and the grass and Katie, too. She was out there by the driveway piddling around in the mud she'd made with the dribble off the end of the garden hose, and then inside the kitchen the telephone started to ring.

I didn't think two times about it. I just left Katie where she was, and I went inside to answer it, hoping that maybe it was her dad calling. I still had some feeling for him then, I guess. And maybe he'd come over, and we could sit out there sharing the heat and passing the afternoon away with some bottles of cold beer. Maybe he'd take me out for a drive after dinner, with the top down on his convertible car.

I only left Katie alone for just a minute, no more, but what I heard sometime shortly after the screen door had slapped itself shut behind me was a terrible screeching of truck brakes trying desperately to stop, and then a low-sounding solid awful whump! Somebody was screaming then, and it was a while before I figured out that it was me. Because I could see there was something that looked pink, like a baby, on the shimmering blacktop of our road, and a truck turned sideways in it, and the only other bare glimpse that I could get of that poor child was its hair, and it looked to me to be the same straw yellow as Katie's had been back then, and I thought, I believed, I understood that it must be her.

I was running along the curled length of our long driveway to the street, and I was screaming out all the way, over and over again, "Oh, no, no, no!" and not even wondering how in the world Katie could have left our yard and toddled down to the road that fast, just so sorry, only wanting to somehow be able to change the fact, to stop the way the day was happening, to turn back the clock only five minutes and then start it up all over again, take back that time and begin back where we'd been before, just thinking about how hot it was and trying to dream up some simple way of keeping cool. And then when the telephone started to ring inside this second time around, wouldn't I know better than to go inside to get it? What would I do but just let it ring and ring and ring?

All the while these thoughts were storming in my head, and I was still making so much noise of my own, still crying out loud—"Oh no, no, no!"—to myself and to Katie and to what I was thinking of then as the figure of God—a big old gray-bearded man frowning down at me, holding a clock of some kind grasped hard and steady in the crook of his knotted-up hand—and it wasn't until I got caught up to the side of that truck and was starting to move around past it to where the driver was standing bent over double with his hands on his knees and his head hanging down, wagging back and forth in disbelief and misery, that I heard the sound of Katie's own sweet voice coming to me like it was nothing else but the singing of an angel, drifting down from behind me, letting me know that she was still up there in the yard, all in one piece, same as ever, untouched, one hand curled around the end of the garden hose, mud spattered on her face, mouth opened wide and crying out because she'd watched me running away from her, and from her point of view it looked like I was off somewhere in a hurry, and leaving her behind.

When I understood then that the body of the child that I could see was lying beside the mangled frame of a bicycle there at the edge of the roadbed was a boy, as dirty and limp as a thrown-away old bag of rags, and too big to be Katie, besides, then it came to me that a miracle had happened and I'd been given a second chance and I knew that a person like me was not likely to ever get a third one, so I'd used up all my good luck in that area, and now I didn't dare risk letting Katie go off on her bike alone because the next time that it happened, well, I wouldn't want to have to say.

"It could have been you, Katie-dear, Katie-did, Katie-do," I sang to her, pulling on her shoulder, turning her over toward me, taking hold of her hand and rolling her fingers around mine. It was only that I loved her so much, I told her. It was only that I could not stand to think she might get hurt.

It took a while, but eventually Katie brought herself around to an understanding of this weakness of mine, and she suffers it now the same way her father used to tolerate my dread of heights. He steered me clear of low windows and high bridges and elevators made out of glass, and now Katie leaves me to worry over her with the belief that my fears for her safety are a shortcoming of mine that she can forgive and work around and learn to accept. It was what happened to Dana that made her see my side of it, finally. It was what happened to Dana that brought her to understand.

"They're out there looking for her now, Katie," I said, still tangling her fingers up with my own. "She's a reckless girl. No telling what they're liable to find."

The house that the Franklins lived in is right behind ours, a square brick box with two dormer windows on the front and a tar-paper roof on top, perched at the crest of a pretty little swell of wooded land. The yard grows wild with weeds and trees, sloping downward to the dirt string of an alleyway that runs between the back sides of both our lots. Sitting in our dark house on that first night of school, when Dana didn't show up for dinner and no one had seen her and nobody knew where she was, Katie and I could look out our big picture window in the kitchen and see the flashlights that were bobbing through the trees in the hands of some of the fathers from around our area who had got together to conduct a search for her.

The ground underneath us here is honeycombed with limestone caves, and so the first idea that occurred to the authorities was that maybe Dana, without Katie there to play with her that afternoon, had gone off exploring in the places all the children had been told time and time again to stay away from. Kids'll do that, they said to Mrs. Franklin. Or maybe she'd been climbing in the trees and she'd slipped and fallen and hit her head and got knocked out. The men tromped around through the woods, hoping for the best, nobody venturing to utter a word like kidnap or abduction, nobody daring to think anything worse than that there'd been an accident and a little girl was missing, bellowing out her name, and going off in a line all the way up into the park and out onto the palisades that soar up over the river to the north.

When it got to be late, and Dana still wasn't found, Katie and I got dressed, and we wrapped ourselves up in blankets and wool coats, and we stood with some of the other onlookers outside, flocked together in the crease of the alley, sharing a thermos of hot coffee and shivering together in the cold autumn chill.

Katie is a tall girl, big for her age, and skinny, too, all elbows and knees, and long fingers and toes. But Dana Franklin was a petite little thing, short in the calves and narrow through the hips, small-boned as a bird. Her legs were pale white, scabbing over on the knees in places where she'd taken a fall from the seat of her bicycle or the wheels of her skates. She'd swing by her knees, with her feet braced against the horizontal bars of the fence, hands hanging, her fingertips tracing snaky patterns in the dry dirt. Her blouse came up to bare her white stomach and her skirt flipped up, too, turned upside down just like an umbrella blown inside out by the strength of the wind, showing her naked legs and the blue-black veins running just under the surface of her skin.

Dana wore her hair in two braids that hung long and thick as ropes on either side of her face, down over her shoulders and onto her back. Her mother had to comb them out for her once a week, on Friday nights or Saturday mornings, when she shampooed Dana's hair and then rebraided it again, and Dana always made a terrible fuss, crying and complaining about it when she did. Katie's hair is thin and blond and curly and fine, and it tangles so easily that all we can do is keep it cut short, cropped up close to her head.

* * *

Dana and Katie had a collection of playing cards that they shared. They'd combed the neighborhood for them over the summer, going from door to door asking the ladies of the houses if they had any old decks of cards they didn't want anymore, and if they did, could Dana and Katie have them?

It seemed that everybody always had an extra deck with some cards missing that they saved tucked away in the corner of a drawer on account of it seemed a shame to throw out the whole pack just because one of them was gone. The girls liked the kind with pictures of dogs and horses on them best. Flowers were all right, too. I remember one set had a watercolor painting of Notre Dame on it. Of course the plain old Bicycle cards, red or blue, were worthless. Dana and Katie kept what they found in an old leather-bound photo album that I had dug out of the attic for them, each card glued in at the corners and protected by a sheet of plastic over the top. It didn't matter what suit or number the card was, only how pretty was the picture on its back.

It was by going from door to door asking for the cards that they came to know the Hamilton boy who had come for the summer to live with his grandparents in their big old house up at the end of the street at the southeast corner of the park.

His name was Milan Hamilton. Milan. What kind of a name is that for a boy? Dana, clasping her hands together, proclaimed that it was the most romantic name she'd ever heard. She said she thought from the first time she saw Milan Hamilton that she knew he was going to be the most different kind of person that she'd ever get a chance in her lifetime to meet. And that was true. He'd been sent here by his parents, who didn't have the time or the inclination to take care of him for themselves.

Milan was the one who answered the door when Dana and Katie came knocking together at the Hamilton house. The Hamiltons own the cereal plant on the edge of the river downtown, and they live in a big house and they have a lot of money and the girls were expecting old Mrs. Hamilton to have a treasure trove of old playing cards to give them when they came to ask. Dana was right about one thing: Milan was a good-looking boy all right. He was fourteen that summer. He had straight black hair that he wore parted in the middle and hanging down long like a curtain on both sides of his face. His eyes were the color of grayish blue that the sky gets sometimes on the darker side of the horizon after the sun's just gone down. Even on a hot day in the middle of the summertime, Milan Hamilton was all dressed up in khaki slacks with sharp creases pressed into them and a starched white cotton shirt with the sleeves rolled down and buttoned at the cuff. He had a big lump of an Adam's apple rolling in his throat and the darkening smudge of a boy's downy mustache beginning to shadow his lip.

He gave the girls the prettiest cards, with a picture of some foreign place where a bridge soared out over a gorge, above a silver shimmer of water, between two sheer drop-off cliffs. It was a brand-new deck, Katie said, unopened, with the cellophane still folded around it. Milan invited the girls to follow him inside the house, and he showed them the way through the living room—with a big black baby grand piano in the corner and glass shelves in the windows that were lined with the pots of violets that Mrs. Hamilton grew, heavy furniture upholstered in a rich dark tapestry fabric, a portrait of old Avery Hamilton hanging on the wall above the fireplace—to the stairs and up to his room. Katie told me that Milan drank coffee out of a cup, black with one teaspoon of sugar stirred in, just like a grown-up, and that while she and Dana were there, he had even smoked a cigarette that he lit with the silver lighter that Dana came to covet.

He had long, thin fingers, with a slight tremble in them. He kept a fan in the window to blow away the smoke, and it stirred the pages of all the books and magazines he had strewn about all over the room, made it look like there was some kind of an extra energy there, held back, just like the quivering of his hands. Damp towels and dirty clothes lay in piles on the floor of Milan's bedroom, left for Mrs. Hamilton's maid to come in and pick up, and there was an old trundle bed in the corner, unmade. When Milan found the cards and held them out for the girls to take, Katie, seeing they were new, told him, no, they only wanted old ones, but Dana jabbed her with her elbow and smiled at Milan and thanked him for his generosity and said she hoped that the three of them could become friends.

He had a long thick rope that he coiled up and carried over his shoulder when he went out walking through the woods behind his house. He tied a big fat knot in one end of it to toss over a high tree limb, and then he shinnied up it like a monkey and pulled the rope up after him. Sitting up there so far off the ground, he said, nobody could touch him. The two girls stood under the tree with their hands on their hips, craning to see him, until Katie got a cramp in her neck that gave her a headache, and she came home.

Katie told me then that Milan Hamilton was different from any other boy she'd known. Different from any other people, for that matter, and not just because his family was rich. He was a gentleman, she said. He'd traveled with his parents. He'd experienced something of the world.

I could look out across the yard and see his window there in the corner of the Hamilton house, and even in the middle of the night the light was on inside it and the shade was pulled down. I thought I could make out his shadow moving back and forth like a moth trapped inside a lamp shade, looking to find a way out.

The search for Dana went on well into the middle of that first night. Her father and the other men combed the woods and the caves, following the trails all the way down to the river. We could hear them talking together outside. The murmur of their voices was carried up to us on the wind.

I took a casserole dish over to the house the next morning. Mrs. Franklin looked like she'd taken on weight in the night, not grown fatter or bigger, only denser, heavier, and she walked slowly, as if it hurt her to move, crossing to the refrigerator and back again. She had something cooking in a pot on the stove, which I found out later was chicken soup that she was planning to feed to Dana when she was found. She was a religious woman, and there were candles burning in glass containers of every color on just about every bare surface, all over the house.

* * *

Katie's father had walked out the door on us some short time after she was born, and he only came back to see her every now and then, with the time between his visits getting longer and longer and the visits themselves getting shorter and shorter until he stopped coming by at all. I didn't miss him too much, but maybe Katie did. When she got to be friends with Dana Franklin, and the two of them started talking about things, sharing their feelings and their views of how the world should be, Katie began to reinvent the story of why she was living with her mother in a house without a man, and she made up the facts of it all over again in her own way, and I would not be the one to call what she told about her circumstances a lie. What child wants to know that it was her own crying and getting in the way that sent her father off? But Katie was just a kid, and her memory was short, so the tales that she told Dana about her father and why he was gone and where he was gone to had no train of thought running through them, there was no consistency, they changed all the time, from one reason to another, depending on what kind of a life Katie and Dana could think to make up for him to have lived. Sometimes it was that he was off on business in Europe, and when he struck it rich there, he'd be back to get us and take us away to live like royalty with him. Or maybe he'd been killed in the war, shot down over Laos or taken prisoner by the Viet Cong and locked up in a bamboo cage and living like an animal in the jungle over all these years.

Katie had in her possession an old wooden humidor box, the kind for keeping cigars and cigarettes fresh, and in it she collected the things that I told her had at one time belonged to her dad. Among other things, there was a silver dollar with a hole drilled in it and hanging on a chain, some receipts that had his name printed on the top and his signature scrawled over the bottom, and a curly bit of seashell that we'd picked up off the beach in Hawaii when we were visiting for a vacation there in the year that we had on our own together, before Katie was born.

"Did she say anything to you?" the men kept asking Katie. "Did she give you any indication at all of where she might be going? Was she unhappy at home? Can you think of any reason she might have had to run away?"

"No," Katie answered. "No. No. No."

One of the detectives was a thin, balding man with black moles on his forehead that I thought looked like they were probably cancerous. He put his big hand, like a paw, on Katie's head, and patted it. He had a sadness in his eyes, I thought, and I figured that must have come from his seeing too much of this sort of thing in the course of his work. Looking at him, I saw that he was wearing a wedding ring, and it occurred to me he was the kind of man who would have made a good father for somebody. I supposed that he must have had daughters of his own at home already, and that was why what had happened to Dana was making him seem so upset.

All that Katie could say was that the last time she'd seen her friend was at school. Dana had been outside playing tag when Mr. Linder saw her standing on the grass that was known as no-man's-land and he'd called to her through the window and punished her by making her sit for a half hour on the hard bench in the hall outside his office. You aren't supposed to step on no-man's-land. They've been trying to grow grass on that patch of ground for years. So by the time Dana left school, everyone else was already gone and she'd had to ride her bike home alone.

And hadn't I looked out my window to see Dana walking her bike along the line of the alley that afternoon? Or did that happen on another day, one I'd mixed up with this one in my mind? And didn't every day seem the same? She'd dropped the bike down on the grass and then headed off into the woods toward the Hamilton house. Katie said Dana had been planning all along to steal that silver lighter that Milan had. She'd had her eye on it from the very first day she saw it trembling in his hand. She wanted to give it to Katie to keep in the humidor box with her other things, and then after a while there would be a story about how it had belonged to her father once and where he got it and how it had ended up there.

But Milan Hamilton was right there in the kitchen with us, and he'd looked at me, and I'd looked at him, and this is why I say I don't believe I have a second sight or anything because I was as surprised and shocked as anybody when the truth came out later, about what had happened to Dana, about what he'd done to her. I didn't suspect anything, looking at his face; I had not an inkling, not a clue, except that later when I thought about it, what I remembered was that he had stared hard out the window at the sky, as if he was trying to find some meaning in the pattern of the clouds that were racing over it. He kept flicking out his tongue and licking at his lips, with a nervousness that chapped his skin to a vivid soreness all around the edges of his mouth. And he had a scratch on his cheek that he said he got from a tree branch that had snapped back and slapped him while he was out with the rest of them searching for Dana in the dark in the woods.

First she'd asked him, nicely, would he give her the silver lighter so she could give it to Katie? And then when he said no, she couldn't have it, she took it anyway, she stole it, she slipped it into the pocket of her shorts when she thought he wasn't looking, and that was what started making him mad, getting him hot, her thinking he was too stupid to see it was gone and too timid to accuse her of trying to steal it right out from under his nose. So, when she denied she had it, his anger was already smoking up into a flame, and when he tried to get it back from her, she fought him until he was burning past his own control, just like a fire that's skipped off the top of a leaf pile and gone skittering away onto the grass, catching there and growing until if you don't stomp it out right away you'll have no chance of stopping it, you'll just have to stand back and watch while the damage is done.

The way the paper told it, Milan sat on the backs of Dana's legs with his full weight, and he crossed her braids over and wrapped them around her neck and twisted them so tight that he just about broke her back with the effort of bending her body backward, toward his own. When he was done, he folded her up and bundled her down inside the space at the bottom of his trundle bed. He slept on top of the mattress that was on top of Dana for three days, with all of us out searching the woods and the caves and along the riverbanks, and he even went along and helped out for a while, trudging alongside her father, standing with the rest of us in the kitchen, looking away, studying the sky.

What I think is that he was hoping it would snow soon. He was looking for winter to blow in early and turn the world cold. Then he could take Dana's body out of the bed and dump it in the woods, let it freeze over out there until spring, by which time he'd be long gone. But it didn't snow, and it wasn't cold, and finally it was the smell that gave him away. He put his fan in the window with the idea of blowing away the odor and mixing it in with the rising of the wind. He locked his door and pushed a chair up against it, and he wouldn't answer and he wouldn't come out, and his grandmother, worried, thinking something had happened to him, called the fire department, and when they broke through the door they found Milan sitting on the bed with his hands in his lap, and he was still looking out the window, he was still studying the patterns of the clouds that were blowing through the sky.

The Franklins moved away from the neighborhood altogether after Dana was buried and Milan Hamilton was locked away in jail. Probably the memories that the place evoked in them were just too much to take. The Hamiltons stayed put, of course. That house has been in their family for going on a hundred years, and although this was the worst thing that ever happened inside it, it was not the only thing. They couldn't very well abandon the place, any more than they could abandon Milan. There was never any question that he'd done it, only about how troubled he was, and crazy, too, and the Hamiltons were a family of businessmen, with plenty of lawyers and doctors that were included in the circle of their acquaintances and friends, so they had the situation pretty well in hand.

The last time I saw Mrs. Franklin, except when her picture ran in the paper during the trial last spring, was on the morning when she left here—Dana had been dead two months already, it was the middle of November, and cold—and she was standing in her yard with her winter coat buttoned up under the folds of her chin and her gloved hands stuffed down into her pockets, her collar standing up and her shoulders hunching against her ears, that heaviness that I had first noticed the morning after Dana disappeared still growing on her, slowing her down. It was cold enough by then to make our breathing come out smoke. She brought one hand out of her pocket, and she pulled off her glove by tugging at the fingertips of it with her teeth, and then she held my own hand inside the warm curl of hers, and looking at it, I remembered how she'd brushed out Dana's braids, her hand moving around the girl's head like the flutter of a bird, snapping with sparks of static electricity that shot like little bits of lightning in her hair.

I stood in the yard there with Mrs. Franklin while her husband closed up their luggage in the trunk of the car and then climbed inside behind the wheel. I took hold of her hand, and I squeezed it, until I felt that Katie was behind me, and I could tell that Mrs. Franklin was looking past me at my daughter, so perfect and pretty she was, starting to round out some and take on what will, in a few years, become her woman's shape. She looked just like an angel with the sunlight shining all around her like a halo of blessed light, and Mrs. Franklin couldn't help but smile to see her as beautiful as she is.

"Coulda been you," she said, not to Katie, but to me. A film of tears had welled up into her eyes, and it seemed to harden there, glazing over as clear and shiny as ice. "You know that, don't you?" Mrs. Franklin was asking me. "Could just as likely have been you," she said.

And when I looked up at the sky I could see and smell and feel it, that the seasons had begun another change. That pretty soon the whole world would be frozen, hard and cold and clean and white, silenced under winter's suffocating muffle of deep and drastic snow.

P. M. Carlson's background in linguistics and psychology is used to wonderful advantage by Maggie Ryan, a bright and lively amateur sleuth, featured in eight books, including 1992 Edgar nominee Murder in the Dog Days, Murder Misread, *and,* Bad Blood. *Actress Bridget Mooney appears in several short stories, including "Father of the Bride; or, A Fate Worse Than Death," a 1988 Agatha nominee.*

In "The Dirty Little Coward That Shot Mr. Howard; or, Such Stuff As Dreams Are Made On," the historians and balladeers who reported that Jesse James (aka Mr. Howard) was shot from behind by Bob and Charley Ford get Bridget's eyewitness account.

THE DIRTY LITTLE COWARD THAT SHOT MR. HOWARD; or, SUCH STUFF AS DREAMS ARE MADE ON

by P. M. Carlson

1

"WHEN HE SHALL die," I quoted to Billy Gashade, "take him and cut him out in little stars,/And he will make the face of heaven so fine,/That all the world will be in love with night."

"Juliet! Bridget, you have a contract to play Juliet!"

I nodded smugly. Aunt Mollie would have been so proud! True, it was only Kansas City, but it was Shakespeare, wasn't it? The leading role! And I reckon a girl has to start somewhere, especially when she's been several months without a salary.

The train for Kansas City had left St. Louis at dinnertime. It was September of 1881, and it was soon dark enough that I couldn't see anything in the window except my own freckled but fashionable reflection. I was wearing my sapphire-blue silk shawl and my splendid bronze-colored natural-form dress with its close-fitting straight skirt layered with bows, but no bustle. My auburn hair—well, Irish red if you insist—was knotted loosely in a perfect Jersey Lily style. And, ever hopeful, I'd just spent my last pennies redeeming my emerald tiara from the pawnbroker, because the Kansas City manager had hinted that after Juliet I might play Lady Macbeth. My old Nellie Grant dress would do for Juliet, but Lady Macbeth is royalty, and requires quality costumes. I knew my genuine emerald tiara would ensure success.

Billy Gashade, in the next seat, was a musician I'd met in a show or two, a pleasing fellow except that he still felt Confederate sympathies fifteen years after Appomattox. Since a dirty Rebel had shot my older brother, I wasn't so sympathetic. But Billy cocked an eyebrow at me and pointed out gently that a lot of Rebels had been hurt by Union soldiers too. "And I adore you even so, Bridget Mooney," he declared.

Well, it's difficult to dislike a fellow who adores you, isn't it? Besides, he was right, the Union soldiers were no better. They'd done in my dear Aunt Mollie. I reckon any argument over which side was worse would end in a tie. So I smiled and changed the subject. "Give us some music, Billy."

Billy reached for his banjo. "I'm working on a song about a famous Missouri lad. Tell me what you think." He strummed his banjo and sang, "Jesse James is a lad who's killed many a man. He robbed the Glendale train. He steals from the rich and he gives to the poor. He has a hand and a heart and a brain."

"Well—" Some said Jesse James was a cruel killer and robber, but in these parts he was a great Confederate hero. Missouri had fought for the Union, but it had been a slave state and rebel guerrillas like the James brothers enjoyed great sympathy even now that they were outlawed. I said judiciously, "I like it, Billy, but not everyone will agree that he was a Robin Hood."

"Was?"

"Didn't another outlaw shoot him after the Glendale robbery?"

"Then why is the Governor still offering a reward?"

"Well, alive or dead, it would be more uplifting to sing about good citizens. Besides," I added, "this train goes through Glendale too. A different song might be in better taste."

Billy grinned and sang "Dixie" just to tease me, but he was a charming singer so I let bygones be bygones and sang with him.

As the evening wore on, however, Billy put away his banjo and settled down for a snooze. I hooked a cigar from his jacket pocket and headed for the front platform of the coach to smoke.

Oh, you needn't tell me! I know proper ladies don't do such things. But it had been such a long time since I'd had money for a cigar. Besides, if he'd wanted to be asked, he shouldn't have gone to sleep, should he?

I couldn't move quickly because my fashionable natural-form suit was very snug around the knees. I minced along the aisle toward the door, pleased at the admiring glances from the men and the envious ones from the better-dressed ladies in the car. But suddenly the train lurched, and I fell like a heap of turnips against a plump lady drinking water from her canteen. As I sat up on the floor, apologizing to the dampened lady, I heard screaming brakes and shots and excited hollering from outside. Then the door was flung wide and the conductor burst in. "Ladies and gentlemen, hide your valuables!" he cried. "We've been boarded!"

"Boarded?" cried the plump lady. "You mean bandits?"

But the conductor jumped over me and rushed through without answering. An excited hubbub arose in the car as everyone began removing their watches and money to hide under cushions.

I suddenly regretted the new styles. The secret pocket I'd sewn into last year's bustle had been roomy and easily accessible. Now, the form-fitting lines of my skirt required me to keep my contract and tiara and Colt buttoned into my bloomers, and rather indelicate gestures were needed to determine that all was well. I took advantage of my sprawled position to pretend that I was merely clambering to my feet.

I straightened up at last and found myself eye to eye with an enormous black revolver.

2

Well, hang it, I've never been able to puzzle out what a proper young lady ought to do when confronted with a gun. In my favorite melodramas the guns are usually pointed at someone else, and the young ladies scream prettily and run upstage out of the way, or perhaps swoon. Now, the scream was easy enough, but running was out of the question in my beautiful bronze-colored skirt. Two other ladies in our car had fainted already, so I decided to try a swoon. I collapsed into the aisle once again.

The man holding the revolver was tall and well built, with nicely cut clothes and a snowy handkerchief tied across his face so we couldn't see his features. I couldn't see much else, either, squinting through my lashes from my recumbent position, except for his handsome cordovan leather boots. "Ladies and gentlemen," he said in a pleasant well-born Missouri voice, "please raise both hands in the air."

The passengers who hadn't swooned hastened to obey him. Two more masked bandits entered the car behind the first. One of them held a pistol to the head of a fellow who, from my lowly point of view, appeared to be the engineer. The new bandits were both scrawnier than the well-built fellow standing at my head. He went on, "As you can see, your engineer's life depends upon your actions. But we have no desire to hurt anyone. Please get out your money and jewelry." He jerked his head. "Collect it, Charley."

The blond bandit stepped over me and passed down the aisle holding out a two-bushel sack for the money and watches of the passengers. When he brought it back, his chief inspected it, shook his head, and said, "Ladies and gentlemen, we must try again." His voice had hardened. "Do you think that I'm a green boy, and won't know that you've been hiding things? I'm Jesse James! Now get out everything!"

The portly man in the first seat held out his palms helplessly. "But I've given you everything!" he exclaimed.

At a nod from the bandit who claimed to be Jesse, blond Charley jerked the man to his feet, struck him on the head with the butt of his gun, tore at his jacket, and came up with a handsome hunting-watch. He dangled it high, then struck the man again, harder. The portly man groaned and sank into the aisle, blood running into his eyes from a gash on his forehead.

All over the car, purses and watches magically reappeared. The second time Charley brought back the bag, it was nearly full.

"Thank you, gentlemen," said the bandit chief in a mild voice. "Now if the ladies would please come out of their fainting spells, we'll be done."

Now, I pride myself on a good swoon. I'd been paid well to lie as though dead for a long scene in *Othello* while the leading man committed a spectacular suicide, and I'd do the same as Juliet. But the bandit in the cordovan boots was not as impressed with my acting as my audiences had been. When I didn't move, he seized the plump lady's canteen and emptied it over my face. I sat up spluttering, water dripping from my Jersey Lily coiffure onto my beautiful sapphire-blue shawl and my bronze-colored dress.

"A pretty recovery." There was a smile in his voice.

"Sir," I said indignantly, "that was not a gentlemanly act!"

The white-masked face looked down a moment. "Alas, my lovely, you are right," he said. "I am driven to knavish deeds." The revolver still held at the ready in his right hand, he knelt and tipped up my damp chin with his left, and for a moment gazed into my eyes. Behind the mask, his own were a penetrating blue, and danced with devilment. He too seemed pleased by what he saw. He murmured, "But then you aren't always a lady, are you, my beauty?" Suddenly, his left hand was reaching under my skirt.

All over the car there were shocked exclamations and shrieks from the ladies. I shrieked too, but I'm bound to admit it wasn't because of the threat to my virtue. My virtue is quite sturdy, thank you, and seldom objects to threats from well-spoken, dashing, blue-eyed fellows. No, I was shrieking because he must have noticed me furtively investigating my nether limbs when he first entered the coach, and now he'd found the secret pockets that held my few possessions. I clutched at them, but he tugged away my bloomers one leg at a time, dropped them into his sack, and handed it back to his henchman.

Charley collected the last items from the other ladies, all of whom had suddenly recovered from their faints. When he brought back the sack for the third time, the cordovan-booted leader nodded, reached into it, and turned to the engineer. "You've been a bully boy. Here's two dollars to buy a drink in the morning. Drink it to Jesse James." He handed the coins to the engineer, took the sack from Charley, and with a jerk of his head signaled the other bandits. Suddenly they were all gone.

And I was right behind them. I might be wet and sputtering, but I needed my things. Luckily the bandit had missed the Bowie knife in my boot. The first thing I did was slit the back seam of my snug, fashionable natural-form skirt.

I know, I know, don't fret! The bows at the back hid most of the damage. And if one is chasing bandits, mincing is not an appropriate gait, is it now?

I tucked the knife back in my boot and leapt through the door to the train platform. Horses were ready beside the tracks; my cordovan-booted friend had already mounted and was spurring his horse up the embankment. As the last outlaw jumped from the platform to his horse, I caught his belt and sprang aboard with him.

"Get off!" he shouted, even as I locked my arms around his waist. The horse leapt into a startled gallop, following the others. The bandit pulled out his revolver, tried to fire, and cursed as he realized it needed reloading. He seized it by the barrel and twisted around to aim a blow at me.

I buried my face against his back to avoid being struck across the nose by the revolver. He smelled sweaty and unwashed. Trying to ignore the stink and the ungentlemanly blows and the jouncing of the horse, I gripped his belt, pulled his second revolver from its holster, cocked it, and jabbed him in the back. I said in my fiercest Lady Macbeth tones, "Knave, I could shoot you right now. But I must see your chief. Let's go!"

He was more attentive with the gun in his scrawny back. He aimed our horse at the fast-moving band disappearing into the hills. It was a long, rough ride, and we were losing ground. But by and by, the other hoofbeats sounded louder, and I rejoiced that we'd catch up after all. So I was astonished when a horse's head appeared at my side, overtaking us from behind. A powerful hand reached forward and twisted my revolver up and out of my grasp. "Pull up, Ed," said a familiar voice.

I tried to slide off the far side of Ed's horse as we halted, but that hand was gripping my wrist now. Ed was quaking and blubbering an apology. His chief laughed. "You're right, Ed, it was stupid. But be off now. It's already settled that Dick and I will count the booty and we all meet in Kansas City tomorrow night. Go on, I'll attend to the entertaining Miss Mooney." He lifted me smoothly from Ed's horse to his own.

Ed took his gun back and rode away, and in a moment there was nothing but the faint dappled moonlight, the crickets, and the tall bandit chief. The handkerchief was still over his face so I couldn't see anything but those restless blue eyes. Well, all right, the light wasn't good enough to make out the color either, but I remembered. I still remember. Yes indeed.

"Sir, how do you know my name?" I asked.

"It's on your contract, my freckled beauty." He spoke kindly even as he patted my skirt for weapons. He had slender, well-shaped hands, except that the tip of one middle finger was missing. Banditry was not an easy profession, I thought sympathetically. Of course the portly man bleeding on the train had not found things easy, either. The bandit chief placed one arm around my waist and spurred the horse to a trot. "Gee-up, Stonewall!" he said and added, "Now, Miss Mooney, why did you come?"

"Please, sir, I'm only asking to have my bloomers back."

He laughed. "Surely a famous actress can purchase more!"

"But I need my contract! And my . . . my . . ."

"Your little jeweled headpiece? And your Colt revolver?" His voice had hardened again.

I said, "Sir, I'm not rich. Was Billy Gashade wrong, then? Jesse James is not like Robin Hood?"

"Not much. Come along, Miss Mooney, to a comfortable place I know. We must reach an understanding, you and I."

3

After scrawny, inhospitable, stinking Ed, it was a delight to ride with the bandit chief. He smelt of good soap and Macassar oil. 'Twas a pity we'd met in such unfortunate circumstances.

The comfortable place he spoke of turned out to be a large fresh-swept barn. He dismounted by the half-open door and helped me down, then led Stonewall, and me, into the barn. We were greeted by the stamping and snorting of three stabled horses. He hitched Stonewall to a rail and unstrapped the sack of booty. "Would you light the lantern on that post, Miss Mooney?"

Well, I was a little nervous about being seen in the light, because of the seam I'd ripped out, and it turned out I was right because it must have given him a clear peep at my boots. No sooner had I lit the lantern than he dropped his sack, leapt to my side, grabbed my wrists with one hand, and jabbed a revolver into my ribs. "Sir!" I complained. "That's not proper!"

"Nor is it proper for ladies to carry knives in their boots!"

"Oh." It was impossible to deny, so I apologized. "I forgot it, sir. I carry it when I travel. For apples and for gentlemen who become too friendly."

"Forgive me, Miss Mooney, but I must be certain you're carrying nothing else. Hold on to this hitching rail and move your feet apart."

Let us glide over the details of the next two minutes. Suffice it to say that at the end I was wearing nothing but my corset and petticoat, and even they had been carefully explored by the bandit chief's nimble fingers. My fine dress and stockings and shawl and boots had all been examined thoroughly and laid neatly aside on the straw. He sniffed Billy's cigar, nodded, and tossed it and my Bowie knife into his sack. He said, "All right, Miss Mooney. Now, my comrade took the southern route but he'll be along in a few moments. It would be best if he didn't see you. You may dress in one of the box stalls."

I picked up my stockings and asked grumpily, "Do you plan to keep my bloomers as a trophy? Will each of your companions receive a strip of muslin?"

"We needn't be that democratic, Miss Mooney." He laughed and pulled my bloomers from the sack. Under them I spotted watches, money, express-company bags, and my contract. He tossed the garment to me.

"Thank you, sir." My bloomers were crumpled and all the pockets were empty. "Though it does seem to me that a gentleman like you could be successful in some other line of business."

He started to answer, then changed the subject. "Tell me, why are you here?"

"I told you, sir! I came to ask you for my things fair and square! And that's more than I can say for the way you and your ruffians took them from me! My contract, my costumes—everything!"

His eyes twinkled. "Not your brave spirit, Miss Mooney."

"Yes, sir, well, I'll swap you that for my things."

He threw his head back and laughed. "No, ma'am! I could never manage *your* spirit! You're the first lady who's ever tried to follow our band."

"I reckon you never stole a theatrical contract before."

"That's true too." He was still chuckling. "Yours is a desperate breed, Miss Mooney. Almost as desperate as mine."

"Well, sir, a poor girl has few paths to fortune. My Aunt Mollie told me never to become entangled with a poor man or I'd always be poor. And the illustrious Mrs. Fanny Kemble advised that a rich one would want me to retire from the stage. And of course I didn't want to be a servant, and probably end on the streets, or in a house of ill repute. No, the stage is best."

He picked up my shawl and ran his fingers over the silk. "You love the stage so much, then?"

"Oh, yes!" Lifting my arm dramatically, I quoted Juliet, "When he shall die,/Take him and cut him out in little stars,/And he will make the face of heaven so fine/That all the world will be in love with night." I clasped my hands, envisioning the applauding crowds and the flowers.

He seemed to be envisioning something too, and cleared his throat. "You want fame, then, Miss Mooney?"

"Yes, sir, of course. And riches. But you've taken my belongings," I reminded him.

"I'm very sorry, Miss Mooney. But my boys have fewer resources than you have. You are rich, truly, with your beauty and your enchanting voice and your sparkling spirit."

It was the kind of talk that could make a girl tingle, but I hadn't come this far to succumb to flattery. I drew myself up as regally as I could in a petticoat, pointed at the sack, and retorted, "Your boys may have fewer resources, but they have more money."

"Well, if ever I need a lady to ride with us, I'll send for you, Miss Mooney."

"Sir! I'm not a bandit!"

The smile was in his voice again. "But we'd be such a bully team! After all, Miss Mooney, you can handle a gun. You can ride. You can playact, that's important. A bandit acts a dozen roles, here tonight, gone tomorrow, as in the theatre. Actors and bandits, we are all spirits, and are melted—how does it go?"

"Melted into air, into thin air," I quoted. "We are such stuff as dreams are made on."

The hands stroking my silk shawl had paused. "Yes. We are such stuff as dreams are made on. You'd enjoy it, Bridget Mooney."

A bully team. He was teasing, I knew. Still, I had a sudden delicious vision of Robin Hood raids on evil bankers and railroad men, thrilling gallops through the night, a secret hideout full of jeweled doors and decanters of wine and dishes of marmalade, a secret bedroom with crimson damask wallpaper and silken sheets and a dashing blue-eyed bandit to keep them rumpled.

But then I could almost hear Aunt Mollie's voice saying, "Lordy me, Bridget, what foolishness!" And of course she was right. Bandits didn't live like that, even if they were rich. Bandits camped outdoors or hid in caves and barns, like this one. Bandits struck men on the head and made them bleed. I sighed and shook my head. "It's not very likely, is it, sir?"

Gently, he touched my hair, his eyes sad. "Not very. And yet—"

Suddenly his head jerked around, and in a blur his hand flashed to his holster and emerged with his revolver. I froze, and in a moment I heard what my alert companion had noted: hoofbeats approaching slowly. I murmured, "I'll be in the stall with the gray horse, sir."

He nodded and tiptoed to the door to peer from the crack. I scooped up my things and scurried into the box stall, closing the plank door behind me. In a moment he said softly, "Good, it's Dick. Do remain silent, Miss Mooney. He's hotheaded at times."

Well, I'm bound to admit, I was vexed! In any well-written melodrama, the playwright would delay the arrival of the henchman until the exciting scene between the kidnapped heroine and the handsome blue-eyed bandit could develop further, at least to the point where she was fighting off his ardent embraces. But in life I seem to be cast in the comic subplot. The horse nuzzled my back as I donned my wretched, damp, bronze-colored dress. By the time Dick arrived, I was crouching by a crack in the stall door. My equine companion and I both peered out at the lighted barn.

Dick was shorter than my friend, with a round face and the air of a dandy. He led a sorrel horse into the barn. His leader took the reins and patted the horse's nose while Dick stepped eagerly to the sack in the middle of the floor. "It's almost full," he said, squatting by it.

His chief was hitching the sorrel next to his own horse. He'd pulled his mask from his face, but I noticed that he didn't turn toward my stall, and when he joined his dandy friend, he sat back in the shadows. "Let's see what we have," he said. He emptied the sack onto the blanket, and the two began sorting the items into piles: bills, coins, watches, rings, brooches, handkerchiefs, scarves. Mine was the only tiara. Dick started to pick it up, but his chief's quick hand suddenly rested on his wrist.

"That's for Zee," he said.

"We should pawn it, Slick," Dick objected. Slick! I liked that better than Jesse, which reeked of blood and cruelty. Dick went on, "Are those emeralds real?"

"Not likely. Came with those papers." Slick nodded at my contract. "Gal's an actress. They're sure to be paste."

Well, did you ever hear such an insult? But dandy Dick nodded and asked, "What would Zee want with it?"

"Well, for Hattie Floyd then."

Dick laughed. He was convinced, as well he might be. I knew the voluptuous Hattie. We'd been girls together back in St. Louis. She had chosen a rather lewd path in life but thanks to my Aunt Mollie's sensible advice had got into a house popular with the higher classes. When I was in St. Louis, I often stopped by for a chat and a giggle, because she was one of the few folks there who didn't natter on about what a drunkard Papa was.

Dick picked up a ring and stroked his mustache. "How's this for the Widow Bolton?"

Slick rocked back on his fine cordovan heels. "Now, you know my cousin favors her."

"The question is, who does *she* favor?" Dick grinned.

Well, I thought Dick's point well taken, but his chief slammed down a fist. "She's not worth a fight. Do you hear?"

Dick's smile faded. "Yeah, yeah, I hear."

"If you and my cousin get to fighting, this whole band is in trouble. I won't have it. There's enough trouble with all the green hands."

"Yeah, well, there's trouble with the old hands too. All killed now, or in jail like Whiskey-Head Ryan. And your brother hiding in Texas."

There was a pulse of danger in the air. Even the horses felt it and were still. But Slick's voice was mild when he said, "They were courageous comrades in the war, as true as steel, Dick Liddil. I honor them."

"So do I. My brothers fought and died with them too!"

"And Whiskey-Head was talking in his cups about Glendale."

"Yeah, he's a good man when he's sober. Let's count the money."

They bent to their work again, but the excitement of the earlier evening had soured. I'd ripped one corner of my shawl, but I pulled the remnants about me and, under cover of the chinking coins, took my things to the far corner of the box stall. The plank walls of the barn were not tight, and cool night air blew through cracks as wide as my fist. I was glad I hadn't snatched my tiara when he'd turned his back out there, because he would have noticed, and I saw no easy way to escape. No, the bandit chief's nobility of soul was still my best chance.

I only wished the man on the train hadn't bled so much.

By and by I heard their voices raised again, and crept back to peer through the crack in the door. Dandy Dick Liddil was saying, "There was more! You know there was more in that safe!"

Slick said, "We don't know that, Dick."

"Well, I know, blast it!" When I saw Dick's hand start for his holster, I clapped a hand over my mouth in dismay. But there was no need for worry, because a flash of dark metal revealed Slick's revolvers already cocked in those quick hands.

"Dick!" he said, and there was such sorrow in his voice that I almost sobbed myself. "We've been through too much together! I rode with your brothers, rest their souls!"

"Yeah." Dick licked his lips, more convinced by the revolvers than by the sentiment. "But— Blast it, Slick, you know I trust you! I just thought there'd be more in the safe, like the Glendale job. More diamonds."

"I thought so too." There was a dangerous edge to my fine friend's voice. "But we were both wrong, weren't we?"

Dick turned his palms up in a gesture of peace. "It's just that the boys will be disappointed. They heard there was ten or twenty thousand in that safe."

"Well, we both counted it. Three thousand. You know how those railroad cheats lie. Maybe they changed it to the next train." He holstered his pistols and picked up a bottle. "Here, drink up and we'll divide the money."

Dick accepted the bottle, loaded half the booty into his saddlebags and led his horse out of the barn. Slick pulled up his mask again and watched him from the door, standing where his busy eyes could also take in my stall. When the hoofbeats died away, he opened my door and picked up my ripped shawl. "Miss Mooney, you will forget this night, won't you?"

"Yes sir. But I'd like my—"

"Hurry, now, we're going to Kansas City."

He saddled the little gray horse for me. As we left, I asked casually, "What's the name of this place?"

He was suddenly stern. "I said, forget this. Let's both of us forget."

We rode through a long confusion of trails I could never retrace, reaching the city just as dawn grayed the skies.

I kept hoping, but Slick didn't give back my tiara or my shawl or even my cigar. Nobility of soul, indeed!

He did give me the contract. He rode with me to the stage door, helped me down, and handed it to me along with four silver dollars. Twice as much as he'd given the engineer. He pressed my hand in his, said, "Farewell, my bandit queen. I wish you fame and fortune," and rode away.

Now, is that your idea of Robin Hood? I sat down on a bench by the stage door and had a good cry because my tiara and sapphire-blue shawl were lost, and I'd never find that romantic barn again. And whoever would have thought a bandit would be so blamed proper? I even found myself envying naughty Hattie Floyd.

But by and by I noticed how hungry I was. I hammered on the stage door until the sleepy-eyed doorkeeper opened it, and I wheedled him into sharing his breakfast of tea and biscuits.

4

Romeo and Juliet was a ripping success. In St. Louis we used to think of Kansas City as uncivilized, populated by the crudest of bushwhackers, but it's not so. The people there, though perhaps untutored, were filled with longing for the higher things in life. They thought that Shakespeare was splendid, and that my Juliet was the most glorious creature they'd ever beheld. Opening night they cheered and stamped and tossed bouquets to me. It was all so thrilling I had tears in my eyes. Flowers came to my dressing room too, with little cards from my admirers. "Miss Mooney, I love you dearly, do you love me?" said one. Another, "To Miss Mooney, who beggars description." Or, "What light through yonder window breaks? It is the unforgettable Miss Mooney." I rather liked that one. At least he knew which play he'd seen. One overeager fellow wrote, "I am a 'Prosperous Farmer' and when my wife dies who is sickly I would kindly beg to propose marriage to you."

The newspapers were delighted too. Major John Newman Edwards went into ecstasies about my Juliet in the Sedalia *Democrat*, and the Kansas City papers admitted they liked the show too. Sid, the theatre manager, was happy as a pig in clover. The second night he knocked on the ladies' dressing room door before the show. "Your admirer from Sedalia wants to speak to you after the show, Bridget! Will you see him?"

"Of course!" In show business one indulges newspapermen.

That night was another triumph, ending with cheers and Rebel yells. I did love Kansas City! Afterward, Major Edwards appeared, a long, tall, shy man, with sad houndlike eyes and a bushy mustache that drooped down to his chin. He escorted me to a private saloon in the St. James Hotel. In the back corner a card game was in progress, the players in shadows around a green baize table lit by a single gas lamp. When we entered, the men turned toward us abruptly, hands reaching toward bulges in their jackets. But Major Edwards seemed unperturbed and bowed me to a velvet sofa near the stove. He sat with a little notebook on his bony knees. With a few furtive glances at the neckline of my Nellie Grant dress, he first asked my opinion of Shakespeare and of Kansas City, then said, "Miss Mooney, I understand that you were on the train that was robbed at Blue Cut."

"Yes, sir, I'm sorry to say that was my misfortune."

His sad eyes snapped up from my neckline to my face. "And do you harbor bitter feelings toward the robbers?"

I opened my mouth to complain about so-called Robin Hoods who stole things and pistol-whipped passengers, but reconsidered at the memory of blue eyes. I said cautiously, "It is a terrible experience to lose one's precious possessions, sir. But there were gentlemen among the robbers who expressed remorse for having been driven to such desperate actions."

Major Edwards's head bobbed up and down enthusiastically. "Very true, Miss Mooney," he said. "Many unjust accusations have been leveled against certain heroes of the late war, who were unjustly branded as outlaws and forced to become fugitives. What can a true man do when cruelly hunted, but turn upon his hunters? Don't you agree?"

"Why, yes," I said, astounded by his sudden fluency.

"Good, good." A tiny smile widened until it disappeared into his drooping mustache. "Miss Mooney, do you think you could identify the highwaymen for the law?"

Well, I'd certainly know dandy Dick Liddil, and smelly Ed, and blond Charley, and of course one other. But Major Edwards's talk about outlaw heroes gave me pause. I shrugged, which drew his eyes to my neckline again, and said, "Alas, sir, they were all masked, you see. How could I ever know them again?"

It seemed to be the right answer. Major Edwards said, "Miss Mooney, there is a man, a friend of mine, who would like to make your acquaintance. He is a businessman, highly respected in these parts, and his name is"—here he consulted his notes—"Mr. T. J. Jackson. Would you consent to a meeting with him?"

My mind went back to the big bouquet of roses that sat next to my dressing room mirror. Mr. T. J. Jackson was the one who had sent the pretty quote about Juliet. What light through yonder window breaks? I wanted to leap up and dance on the piano, yes indeed! But instead I said earnestly, "Sir, I would be happy to make Mr. Jackson's acquaintance, since you recommend him."

Major Edwards beamed. He stood up and led me to the card table and, to my astonishment, introduced Mr. Dick Liddil, who kissed my hand moistly. Next came Mr. Ed Miller. Since someone had apparently made Ed bathe for this occasion, I offered my hand to my one-time riding companion and said, "Delighted, sir." Next came Charley Ford, the blond bandit who'd carried the sack on the train, and his smooth-faced younger brother, Bob, who looked as though he'd just come from Sunday school. Yes indeed.

Finally Major Edwards said, "Miss Mooney, I'd like to present Mr. T. J. Jackson."

He stood then and leaned into the light. And wasn't he a grand businessman! He had a well-cut suit, a lustrous beard, a warm and ready smile, and those lively blue eyes. I found myself trembling at the thought of his trust in me, and of what the consequences might be. He took my hand and said, "Miss Mooney, let me congratulate you on an unforgettable performance."

"Thank you, sir. I'm delighted to make your acquaintance."

"And I yours. Mattie, sing us a song!"

The others had all been watching him, as though waiting for a cue. Now one of the ladies sat down at the piano, and Dick Liddil began to deal out cards. Slick murmured to me, "Come along, Miss Mooney, let's talk a bit."

"Yes, sir, Mr. Jackson. We do have business to discuss."

He bowed and opened a door. In the back of my mind Aunt Mollie was trying to holler something at me, but I told her to hush and climbed the rose-carpeted stairs to a second-floor room. In the lamplight I could see that there was no crimson damask wallpaper, but the bed and window were hung with gold brocade and the sheets seemed smooth enough. A picture of General Lee graced the wall near me. I pushed aside a tasseled curtain to see that the window gave onto a porch roof, then turned to face Slick.

He had closed the door and was watching me, one hand still on the knob. "Well, Bridget Mooney. I had hopes of forgetting you, but you do hang on a man's mind."

"I found you memorable too, Mr. Jackson."

"Not Mr. Jackson, Bridget! Call me . . . maybe Tom?"

"Mr. Jackson, sir, if we reach that level of familiarity, I shall call you Slick, like a loyal comrade. But now I am speaking to Mr. Jackson the businessman."

"Oh?"

"You have taken a very kind interest in my career, sir. The cheering and newspaper articles are most welcome. I am extremely grateful, but . . ."

"But not grateful enough?" Frowning, he walked toward me. There was a crackle of danger in the room. I was very aware of the pistols under his well-cut coat.

I raised my palm. "I know you are a gentleman, sir, forced by injustice to certain acts not in your true nature." He slowed, and I breathed again. "But as a businessman, sir, you know the importance of reputation, in my profession as in others. 'The purest treasure mortal times afford, is spotless reputation.' "

He grinned. "I do love to hear you talk, Bridget Mooney! Yes, of course I know that acting Shakespeare is not the same as saloon singing. Spotlessness shall be arranged. But since we're discussing business, let me point out that I've entrusted something of great value to you too."

"I know." I put a hand on his arm and looked at his sweet unmasked face: the strong cheekbones, the trim beard, the gentle mouth, the questioning blue eyes. I said, "Five thousand dollars for arrest, five thousand for conviction. I'm honored, sir, at the gift of your trust. I won't betray it. Ever."

"You wouldn't live if you did," he said matter-of-factly, then smiled. "It's a knavish profession, my lovely, not for the cowardly. But you shall be a queen. Are we agreed?" He picked up my hand and kissed my fingertips.

Part of me was agreed, yes indeed. I wanted to throw myself into his arms and do all sorts of jolly wicked things, but I knew Aunt Mollie would scold. I said, "Well, sir, as a businessman, you are also aware that any business requires certain equipment, certain investments."

"Your equipment is your beauty, your charming voice, your soaring spirit."

"Yes, sir. As to my voice, I paid hundreds of dollars for the illustrious Mrs. Kemble's tutelage. As to my beauty, I need proper attire." When he began to protest, I added hastily, "Onstage, that is, sir. I'm still speaking to Mr. Jackson the businessman. Mr. Jackson the businessman would not approve of a Lady Macbeth without a crown."

He laughed. "I wondered when you'd get to the cursed tiara!" He reached up to pull a packet from behind the picture of General Lee. "Here it is, sweet Juliet. I kept your blue silk shawl with the torn corner, and your Bowie knife and revolver for sentimental reasons. Here is something in exchange." He took a sparkling ring from the packet and fitted it gently on my third finger. I turned away and drew it down the windowpane. The scratch glittered in the lamplight.

It quite took my breath away. I noticed that it silenced Aunt Mollie for the moment too. She was always a good businesswoman, and perhaps had only been trying to tell me to collect in advance.

He put his hand on my shoulder, the gentlest and deadliest hand in the West. "Are we agreed at last, my bandit queen?"

I turned my head to kiss his fingers, and said, "Remember, you still owe me a cigar."

He laughed and whirled me onto the bed, and he was right, very very right. We were a bully team.

5

It was good times, those next few weeks. Oh, I know you're thinking it was wicked and shameful, and of course it was. In my mind Aunt Mollie stomped around sometimes, telling me how reckless and improper I was being. But hang it, what's a poor girl to do when she's offered riches, and fame, and sweet frolics with a man who thrills her blood? Do you truly expect her to wait for "Prosperous Farmer's" sickly wife to die?

Aunt Mollie didn't have any answers either.

Most days I'd wake up late, and spend the afternoon rehearsing or at the dressmaker's or going to the bank, and the evening as Juliet or Lady Macbeth or Rosalind. Sid was no fool, and though he complained loudly at the terms, he extended my contract. You see, I'd sent Major Edwards's columns to a St. Louis newspaperman named Fishback who owed me a favor—no, it wasn't that way at all! I'll tell you why some other time. Soon the St. Louis papers were talking about "Bridget Mooney, the Bernhardt of Missouri," and other theatres were wooing me. But I had reasons to stay in Kansas City. After the show, I'd join Slick and his friends for a glass of wine, and he'd ask me to recite or sing something. He loved to sing with me, especially hymns, his poor dead father having been a minister. To Slick, outlawed so young, I think I was a dream of the elegant life he should have had amidst well-spoken ladies and gentlemen. But I was a dream he could touch. After the singing, we'd leave the others and— Well, taste and decorum preclude a detailed description. But it was good times, yes indeed.

And yet the sweet blue Kansas City nights were not flawless. The far-off shimmer of danger, like summer lightning, played around the edges of my moon-bright world. Slick always slept with a gun. Not just under his pillow. In his hand. And once when I asked dreamily, "Where was that barn where we first met?" he gripped my shoulder and snapped, "Forget that night!" So I kept mum about it for a while. And he was often away. I'd heard there was a wife somewhere, poor thing. But most often he took trips with Dick Liddil or one of the others, so that I saw him only two or three nights a week. With most men this would be a decided advantage, but hang it, I had such an appetite for Slick.

When we sang hymns, his favorite verse said, "Must I be carried to the skies on flowery beds of ease,/While others fought to win the prize and sailed through bloody seas?" He told me what it meant to him. "We must fight on! The North is robbing us of our birthright. We must keep hitting their banks and railroads. We've sworn to be true till and through death, and we must see to it that our brave comrades didn't die in vain." I knew that Major Edwards and other Rebels sympathized. But I wondered, if his comrades hadn't died in vain, did that mean my brother had? Still, I decided to keep mum about my brother too.

That war would never be over for Slick, I feared. He never slept well. Some nights I'd awaken in the wee hours and find him crouching by the window, gun cocked, eyes searching the empty alley. "What is it?" I'd whisper.

"Nothing. Just a dream." And in a moment he'd be back, laughing and friskier than ever.

Major Edwards, and in fact most Rebels in Missouri, worshiped him—or maybe not him, the idea of him. Jesse James's courage in the war, his refusal to bow to Northern law, his ready smile and quick hands and gentlemanly speech and ability to melt into air, into thin air—it was an idea that was easy to love.

But it was hard to live. And behind the romance and the song, I knew my bandit king still sailed through bloody seas.

Late in September, it got worse. I sidled over to young Bob Ford one evening to ask, "What is it? Why is he in such a mood?"

Bob was a sweet-faced lad, as dazzled by a fine neckline as Major Edwards was. He fidgeted, his hazel eyes shifting in his Sunday-school face. "I can't tell you if he won't, ma'am."

"Bob, please, it might be dangerous for me."

"Or me! He says if three men jump out to shoot him, he can kill them all before he falls. And it's true, I swear!"

I handed him a silver brooch. "Please, Bob!"

Little Bob, though fearful, loved money. He glanced at the door where Slick had just gone storming out and muttered, "It's the Ryan trial, ma'am. Poor Whiskey-Head may be convicted."

I studied the newspapers. The story was that a fellow named Tucker Bassham had been jailed after the James gang's famous Glendale train robbery two years ago. Just recently they'd caught another member of that gang, Whiskey-Head Ryan—I remembered Slick's complaint about Whiskey-Head bragging in his cups. Well, Bassham didn't much like jail, so he decided to turn state's evidence against Whiskey-Head in exchange for his own freedom.

The next night, as Slick stared moodily out through the curtains, I screwed up my courage to ask, "You're worrying about the Ryan trial, aren't you?"

He whirled from the window. "What do you know about it?"

"Well, goodness, Slick, I can read the newspapers! I'm no ninny. And I can tell that you're worrying."

"You're worrying that I'm worrying?" He sounded exasperated. "We'll soon be running in circles! Please, be my sparkling Juliet, speaking beautiful words, shining in the footlights!"

"Thank you, Slick, but that's a rather insubstantial role. And it's difficult to sparkle in this gloom. You can't attend the trial, for reasons we've agreed not to discuss. But I can. I can tell you what happens there."

"I have friends reporting to me."

"Not in beautiful words."

I had my way and rode to the Jackson County Courthouse the next day, dressed in coarse black like any curious rural widow.

He was right about friends. I found the courtroom filled with rowdy local Rebels, and most spoke warmly of the James boys and their friends. I'd doubtless been in one of their barns, but I didn't know which. Slick still snapped whenever I asked.

In this company Tucker Bassham was heavily guarded. He was a raw country man, clumsy in speech but very earnest. His story was that Whiskey-Head Ryan had invited him to join the James gang. He'd declined. A few months later Whiskey-Head returned and ordered Bassham to come along to rob the Glendale train. He obeyed out of fear, he said; and I remembered the bleeding man on the train, and believed him.

But Slick saw only a betrayal of the dream. "That traitor Bassham!" He slammed his fist on the card table and Dick Liddil and I jumped. "My old comrades were true as steel!"

"They fought beside you in the war," I protested. "Bassham was only—"

"Bassham's people were brave guerrillas too! No, he's a traitor and a sneak!" Slick's eyes shone like ice in the winter sun. He started for the door, beckoning for Dick with a jerk of his head. I realized I'd given the wrong lines. He didn't want judicious Portia; he wanted Lady Macbeth, urging him on. I shivered and retired to my lonely room for the night.

But very late, there came a whisper. "Under the greenwood tree, who loves to lie with me?"

He was in his long dark coat and cordovan boots, leaning over my bed. I giggled. "Slick, are you auditioning for our show?"

"Come!" He slid his smoke-scented coat over my nightdress and led me to the back door. The moon was in the west, and I could see in his eyes the same warmth and devilment I remembered from the Blue Cut night. Stonewall stood outside, blowing a little and lightly lathered with exertion. Slick handed me into the saddle and swung up behind me. "Time for a midsummer night's dream, my lovely!"

"But it's October!" I said feebly.

He spurred Stonewall down the road toward the woods. "I'll keep you warm, under the greenwood tree."

He did, he did indeed; and I rejoiced in the return of my own lighthearted bandit chief.

The next day, the newspapers blared that Tucker Bassham's house had been burned down.

Well, that made me sit down and have a good think. It seemed to me that poor old Tucker Bassham wasn't getting a fair shake. But what could I do about it? I was an artiste, not a sheriff or a marshal. And there were all my pretty rings and brooches, and cheers and bouquets, and good notices in the newspapers, and lovely trysts under the greenwood tree.

But Bassham's raw, earnest face haunted my memory.

He continued to give testimony, though Governor Crittenden had to send in arms to keep order. And Slick grew tight with fury behind his banter and songs. So, when the jury declared Whiskey-Head guilty and Bassham was released, I waited only long enough to be sure Slick wasn't going to want me that night, then put on my traveling cape and borrowed a horse from the ones hitched in front of the saloon. I set off for Jackson County.

I know, I know, Aunt Mollie would have said it was reckless too. But she hadn't seen Tucker Bassham, nor Slick's cold eyes.

Of course I'd never betray Slick, and I knew that Bassham couldn't be allowed to cross Jesse James and then resume a normal life. But suppose he merely disappeared? I'd learned that two of the ladies in the front row at the trial were Bassham's cousins, and that they lived on the road from Kansas City. My plan was to deliver a little packet for them to pass on to Bassham, containing two valuable rings together with the sensible advice to leave Missouri immediately and for a good long time.

The moon was sinking toward the western woods when I turned into the lane that led to the ladies' house. At the side of the lane, I thought I saw a shirtsleeve, and reined in my horse. The sleeve was very still. Everything was very still. Did someone need help? I dismounted, leading the horse, and pushed aside a branch to let the moonlight shine on a horrid sight.

Something clamped over my mouth.

I could not cry out. My startled horse cavorted, but my captor did not slacken his grip on my mouth until he had quieted the animal and led us both into the nearest woods. He jerked back the hood of my cape and cursed under his breath. "Bridget!"

He released my mouth. Furtively dropping Bassham's little packet and toeing it into the earth, I whispered, "Slick, I wanted to help!"

"Stay out of this! You'll betray us!"

Well, at such a time, those words were hardly music to my ears. I needed a stronger defense. So I sold smelly Ed. I said, "Betrayal? Slick, you've got betrayal all around! Ed Miller whispers that you stole from the Blue Cut booty before you divided it. And Dick Liddil—"

Some people don't like bad news. There was a puff of breeze, and Jesse James's gun butt slammed into the side of my face.

I woke at noon, tucked into my own bed, with a thundering headache and vague recollections of tightly bound hands and feet amid a nightmare of galloping hoofbeats.

I held up my wrists and saw the red track of rope burns.

Somehow I sat up. The hoofbeats continued. They were inside my head, I realized at last. I was dressed in the clothes I'd worn last night. I lurched to the dressing table, leaned on it with both hands, and blinked into the mirror. My cheek was gashed open over the bone, and a purpling bruise spread above it from temple to eyebrow.

I closed my eyes to avoid the ghastly sight. But a ghastlier one intruded: Tucker Bassham's body in the moonlight last night, with a bullet hole in his earnest forehead.

I felt sicker than an old hound. But I wasn't dead. I clung to that. Killing a woman would betray Jesse's code. Wouldn't it?

Show people are grand, better than family. Sid tut-tutted and declared my wound to be the most spectacular he had encountered in a long career of ministering to tragedians, with the possible exception of a Hamlet he'd hired once, who had foolishly challenged an enraged sow. Sid spent two hours with sticking-plaster and greasepaint, piecing together the remnants of the Bernhardt of Missouri. At the end he gave his handiwork a good squint and decided to dim the footlights as well. I was playing Lady Macbeth that night, and my copper-red costume looked grand in the lower lights. If I had to be a walking target, at least I'd look splendid. Luckily, Jesse did not show himself that night.

Nor the next.

Nor the next.

By mid-November I realized that he was truly gone. Melted into air, into thin air. Through a milkman I finally found Mr. T. J. Jackson's Kansas City home on East Ninth Street. The problem was that Mr. Jackson had moved out a couple of weeks before. A splendid gentleman, the neighbors said, always with a smile and a pleasant word. Yes indeed.

I rented a livery horse and rode the Jackson County hills for a month, but I saw no dashing bandits, no romantic barns. Where was that barn? Things look different by daylight.

I went to see Major Edwards, at the Sedalia *Democrat*. "Mr. Jackson?" he said, and coughed. "I don't know any Mr. Jackson."

"Sir, please, I have very important news for Jesse James."

"Miss Mooney, you don't understand. This is a matter of courage, of fealty sworn till and through death, of honor!"

In fact I did understand because I'm in the dream business too. Just ask "Prosperous Farmer." I said, "Sir, honor and fealty are splendid, you are right. My message has to do with sacred duty." That sounded important, don't you think?

But Major Edwards merely blinked at my neckline. "Miss Mooney, my admiration for your thespian abilities is sincere. Therefore my advice is to play your tragedies on the stage."

"This is not a play, sir! It's real!"

But he wouldn't help. I went back to the theatre. "Prosperous Farmer" and some others remained loyal, but there were fewer Rebel yells now among the cheers at the end, and fewer bouquets. For January Sid decided to book in a wonderful attraction with eleven trained dogs instead of the *Twelfth Night* I proposed. "Next year, Bridget," he said with that shifty-eyed look managers get when receipts fall off. Yet my disappointment was softened by my weariness, and anger, and aching for what might have been, and worry about what was coming.

A St. Louis theatre asked me to come do Lady Macbeth in February. I packed up my tiara and lace parasol and new dresses, all made with bustles this time, and went back to St. Louis. There was someone there I should have seen long since.

6

Hattie Floyd had always had a splendidly ample figure. She was a few years older than I was, and I'd been green with envy of her when I was a girl still waiting to fill out. Now, in her thirties, she was blonder, better-dressed, and rounder than ever, and her hugs were like sinking into a sweet-scented featherbed. "What news, Hattie?" I asked.

"I've got a fellow, Bridget!"

"Um—in your line of work, isn't that to be expected?"

"No, no! Jake is news. We're going to get married, soon as we have enough put away for a house."

Well, I was flummoxed. "You're getting married? And he's not rich?"

"Bridget, honey, I've had the opportunity in life to look over quite a few fellows," she said with dignity. "And Jake is the one. We'll settle down and take in my two orphan nephews, just as soon as we have our cottage. Now tell me about you! The papers say you're rich and famous. But honey, is that a scar?"

"Hattie, did you ever know . . ." I didn't know what name he'd used. ". . . um, Jesse James?"

She smiled and settled back in her velvet chair. "Ah, Slick. Now there's a fellow can spin a dream for you. He told me I'd be his bandit queen. Though I taught him some sweet games too."

She certainly did. I swallowed, and Hattie's eyes sharpened. "I ask for news of you, and you ask about him. Bridget, what have you been up to?"

"Hattie, please, how can I find him again?"

"You can't! The sheriffs can't, the Governor himself can't." She looked into my eyes and saw how bad things were. She said, "Sometimes I hear rumors. Last fall he was in Kansas City."

"He isn't anymore."

"Oh, Bridget, honey, and I thought you had such a sensible heart!"

I couldn't help sniffling. "And I was just becoming famous! Hattie, he's chopped my life to flinders!"

"Didn't do much for your cheek either, honey."

I've always thought that if my poor dear mama had lived, she would have been like Hattie. I sobbed out the story. All of it. She hugged me and clucked at all the right places, and gave me lots of sound advice; but this time it was all too late. "I'll help you, honey," she said at last. "Remember, time heals."

But time was in no hurry to knit up my raveled sleave of care. The St. Louis *Macbeth* closed at the end of February, and I found myself unable to accept more work, unable even to laugh. I bailed Papa out of jail a couple of times, but most of the time I moped along the riverbank under slate-colored skies, watching the gray Mississippi slide by like my gray life.

Then, toward the end of March, Hattie summoned me. "Bridget, come meet my cousin's niece. She works in St. Joseph."

I felt a surge of hope when I saw that the cousin's niece's hair was Irish red like mine. But it turned out she'd never met Jesse. Or Slick, or Tom, or any such man.

"The one I know is Bob," she explained. "Hattie said you'd want to hear. She said you're a grand lady now, and you'd pay."

Hattie was beaming at me, so I unpinned the emerald brooch from the lace fichu at my neck and showed it to her cousin's niece. "If it's useful news, this will be yours."

She looked it over with hungry eyes. We red-haired ladies do love emeralds. She said, "This Bob is a pretty-faced little fellow with a big gun. And he has a brother named Charley."

"That's right! Bob and Charley Ford! What did he say?"

"He likes to brag. He says he knows how to get a big reward from Governor Crittenden if he kills somebody."

Well, sometimes a girl can't help it. I burst into tears and Hattie hugged me while her cousin's niece asked with an anxious glance at my brooch, "Don't cry, darlin'! Should I go on?"

"Yes, yes!" I sniffled. "Who—who's he going to kill?"

"He calls him Slick. He's a murderer." Her Irish eyes were round with awe. "And isn't Bob scared! He says some fellow named Ed accused Slick of holding out diamonds from a robbery. So Slick hunted him down and shot him dead."

Poor smelly Ed! I felt a pang of guilt for accusing him to Jesse in the first place. Oh, I know, I know, it's the wages of sin, and Ed was sinful enough. But if Jesse was shooting everyone he imagined was betraying him— I shivered.

"Where does Bob live?" I asked.

"I don't know," she said. "But I meet him at the Worlds Hotel in St. Joe. And he doesn't use a horse to get there."

She'd earned her brooch. I kissed Hattie, promised to be careful, packed my carpetbag and parasol, and caught the next train to St. Joe. I worried about Jesse the whole way. His band was eroding. Many were in jail. His brother had fled to Texas, Ed Miller was dead, sneaky Bob Ford was thinking about rewards. Was his only remaining friend Dick Liddil?

No, there were the dream-makers. Major Edwards, writing about the outlaw hero, the last stand of the Lost Cause. Or Bridget Mooney with her bandit king. Or Billy Gashade's Robin Hood: "He steals from the rich and he gives to the poor. He has a hand and a heart and a brain." But no soul, Billy, I thought. The rest of us have stolen his soul to use in our own dreams.

The man sitting in the next seat on the train was reading a newspaper. One headline jolted me. Dick Liddil had been arrested in Clay County.

Jesse was down to nothing but dreams.

St. Joseph was a pretty city of soft hills and budding trees. I found my way to the Worlds Hotel, which did not cater to the upper classes. The sour clerk at the desk had never noticed anyone looking like Bob Ford. I went back out in the street to ponder my next move, and saw my long-lost sapphire-blue shawl.

It was around the shoulders of a short, pleasant woman dressed in a dark dress and bonnet and leading two children. "Hurry, Mary," she said; and, to the boy, "Come along, Jesse."

No, I didn't swoon. I only do that professionally. Instead I opened my lace-trimmed parasol and strolled along in the same direction, admiring the flowers in order to stay a few steps behind them. I saw that she'd mended the missing corner of my shawl.

The three walked to a small, neat house behind the hotel, with a plank fence and a roundtop window over the door. There was a good view in all directions, and some woods nearby—just what Major Edwards's heroic fugitive needed. There was a barn, and Charley Ford was currying a horse in the barnyard. It was Stonewall.

I tilted my parasol to hide my face and hair and walked on to the woods. There was a comfortable log where I could be invisible yet see the house. I waited.

Late in the day, Jesse came out to the barn, then washed his hands at the pump. The little boy came dancing out of the house, and Jesse caught him and swung him up in the air. Their laughter drifted down the hill to my brushy hideaway. He put the boy down, drew one of his revolvers, and emptied out the cartridges. He belted the empty gun to the boy's waist. The boy capered around the yard, and Jesse stood there beaming at his little Jesse.

Whose dreams would little Jesse have to live?

They were sweet children. Jesse might not leave them for me, but surely he could provide for us all. How could I convince him? If only he'd told me how to find that other barn near Blue Cut! Finally, I wrote a note.

After a few minutes the woman came to the door and called, "Supper's ready!" Jesse scooped up his son and went in.

As soon as the door slammed, I scurried up the hill and slipped into the barn. Voices and the clinking of dishes came from the house. I pulled out my note and speared it onto a splinter on Stonewall's stall door. Then I ran back to the woods again, my spine shuddering in anticipation of bullets. I'm a dreadful coward.

But nothing happened till dusk, when Jesse came out to the barn with both Ford brothers. A moment later he ran out and looked around, even squinting at my woods a moment. He'd drawn his revolver. I noticed he didn't turn his back on the Fords. He was good at his job, hang it. It was going to be difficult.

Soon they all rode off toward St. Joe. I waited. The Fords came back before midnight. Not Jesse. He wouldn't be back before Sunday night, I reckoned, because he'd travel in the dark, and my note had sent him all the way to that other moonlit barn, near Blue Cut.

Getting back to the Worlds Hotel so late, I had to turn down a large number of ardent proposals from gentlemen on the steps. The bedbugs were unpleasant also; but then, I wasn't in St. Joseph for its cosmopolitan gaiety.

Sunday night, I huddled outside the back corner of the barn, waiting. The woman and her children went to bed early in a back bedroom. The Fords rode away, and returned. The lamps went out. I dozed a little. When at last approaching hoofbeats woke me, the moon was in the west. I didn't want to surprise him if things had gone wrong, so I held my breath as he rode into the yard and swung lightly down from Stonewall.

I could tell from the bounce in his step that he'd fetched them for me. I stepped out slowly, hands up, palms out, for all the world like Lady Macbeth sleepwalking. He dropped the reins and sprang for me. "Bridget, my lovely!" Then I was in his arms again, and there was heyday in my blood. In Jesse's too, I think.

"But Slick, your wife!" I protested feebly.

"She's asleep." But he pushed me into the shadow of the barn door before nuzzling my hair. "Dear Miss Mooney, are you armed?"

"Well, Mr. Jackson—"

"No, no. Mr. Howard. In St. Joe I'm Thomas Howard."

I smiled at him. "No, Mr. Howard, I'm not armed."

Well, of course I was telling the truth! How can you doubt me? There was room for a revolver in my bustle pocket, it's true, but it would have been worse than foolish to bring a weapon to Jesse James's house.

"I must check, all the same," he apologized, but we both were laughing by the time he was done. He said, "Here, help me unsaddle Stonewall. Major Edwards said you had a message about sacred duty. I never dreamed it would be about those diamonds!"

I smiled and didn't correct him. It wasn't yet time to tell him the other news. He asked, "How did you find me?"

"I didn't find you. I found Bob Ford. He talks too much."

Jesse frowned. "He's young. I'd better warn him again."

"Slick, did you get them?"

He hung up the saddle, then reached into his waistcoat and drew out a little bag, made from a scrap of silk knotted at the top. In the moonlight it was silvery. I clapped my hands.

Jesse tucked it back in his waistcoat and began to rub down Stonewall. "Ed Miller thought I stole them, and I had to— And all the time it was Dick, blast him! How did you find out?"

"I saw him reach into the sack, that night in the barn," I said. "You were tying up his horse." I spun him a tale about how Dick had hidden the diamonds outside my stall, but didn't retrieve them because he feared Jesse would discover the betrayal and kill him, as he'd killed Bassham and Ed Miller and all traitors. But after Dick was arrested, I said, he sent word for me to fetch them and pawn them to pay the lawyers.

Jesse led Stonewall to his stall, closed the door, and turned to face me. "But instead you came to me."

"Yes. I came to you. Of course." I gave a tiny shrug.

"Dear Bridget." I could see that Jesse wanted to believe in his loyal bandit queen. Even when you know all about dreams, you want to believe in them. But his next question showed I wasn't out of danger. He asked, "Why didn't you tell me what he'd done?"

"I was frightened, Slick," I said truly. "Look what happened when I told you about Ed Miller."

"Bridget, Bridget." He touched the mark on my cheek, and for an instant we stood in a blaze of reality, two scarred and lonely creatures. Then he cleared his throat and said, "I sent someone to the theatre that next night. To be sure you were all right."

I looked away. That wasn't very polite, but hang it, I still didn't feel like thanking him.

"Bridget, can we be . . . friends again?"

I smiled sidelong at him. "I'm here, Mr. Howard. And I would not be averse to doing a little business right now."

He glanced at the barn, then at the dark windows of the back bedroom, and smiled impishly. Jesse and I both liked our loving edged with danger. "Why not? I have the front sitting room. She knows not to disturb me when I get in late. Come, my bandit queen!" He led me into the house.

A voice called out, "Who's that?"

"It's Slick, Bob. Go back to sleep." We tiptoed to the front room, and he lit a lamp, turning it low, to my relief. It was a plain little room, with a simple bed made up. A rich home would draw suspicion, I realized. I'd been a rare chance for him to flaunt his wealth at a safe distance. He stepped on a chair to adjust a picture on the wall, "The Death of Stonewall Jackson," and I saw him slip something behind it.

Then he took my hand and dropped two diamonds into my palm.

"Why, Mr. Howard!" I whispered, and met his mischievous eyes. "Perhaps you'd like to make certain once again that I'm not carrying a weapon?"

Amid muffled giggles, he made certain I wasn't. Then I made certain he wasn't—though with one revolver on the bed and two more in a gunbelt hung on the bedpost within easy reach of those nimble fingers, it was a hollow endeavor on my part. Still, I was able to ascertain that he wasn't hiding any of the Blue Cut diamonds in his clothes. After that, other exceedingly pleasant activities ensued that we needn't mention, except to say that some of them involved a feather duster.

We ended exhausted and as happy as either of us was ever likely to be, and dozed a little. There was no hurry to tell him he owed me far more than two diamonds. For now, I was back in his good graces—at least I would be if I left before his wife saw me. He had to try to live her dream too, poor fellow.

So, when jocund day stood tiptoe on the misty mountaintops, we both stirred. The first sunbeams shot cheerfully across the room. Jesse smiled at me and rose to pull on his shirt and trousers. Then he picked up his gunbelt from the bedpost, but before buckling it on, he paused, staring at the wall.

I followed his gaze toward the picture of "The Death of Stonewall Jackson." Bright in the morning sun, a blue thread hung from behind the picture frame.

I came scrambling out of bed as he bounded onto a chair,

dropped the gunbelt over the back, and reached behind the picture. He withdrew the little bag and stared at it. In the sunlight the cloth that held the diamonds no longer looked silvery. It was a lovely sapphire blue.

"Your shawl!" he exclaimed. "The corner was torn—*You* stole them! Hid them in that crack in the barn wall—"

His back was still to me, but he turned his head, and for an instant I saw in his face the crumbling of his dream of me. Then his eyes glazed cold and cruel as ice, and I knew the end had come. He was quick as ever, glancing down to grab the gunbelt from the chair back, his hand flashing to his pistol. If he'd been wearing the guns, things would have been very different. But in the extra instant fate allotted me, I snatched up the revolver he'd left on the bed and fired.

There was no time to mourn. When Bob and Charley Ford burst in a moment later, guns drawn, I was struggling into my dress. "What happened?" Bob demanded.

I sobbed, "No real lady would do what he asked!"

"You shot—*you* shot him?" exclaimed Charley. Four guns were leveled at me.

In the back of the house a child wailed. The woman's voice, groggy and fearful at once, called out, "What is it?"

"It's all right, Zee, I was just cleaning my gun," Bob called. Then he said to me, "I bet you did it for the reward!"

"No, no!" Of course I would have loved the reward. But an actress can't afford to be hated by half of Missouri, and the diamonds would suffice. I suggested, "Bob, you take the reward!"

"What?"

"Goodness, *I* don't want it! It would ruin my reputation if people knew I'd been in Jesse James's bedroom! Please, please, for my sake, take the reward!"

They were staring at me. I said, "Look. Here's the gun that shot him. Take it! When his wife gets up, tell her you did it."

Greed was flickering in Bob's eyes. But Charley frowned. "He's not wearing his guns. They'll say we were cowards."

"It's not cowardly, it's good sense!" I said testily. "Do you know a man anywhere who could draw faster than Jesse James?"

"That's true. But he fell from a chair. Why was he on a chair?"

"Hang it, Charley, don't you have an ounce of invention in your head? Say . . . say he took off his coat because it was warm, and he took off his guns because he didn't want anyone to see them through the window. Say he got on the chair to dust the pictures, there's the duster right there! Hang it, say anything!"

I finished buttoning my dress, slipped one of Jesse's pet revolvers into my bustle pocket, and ran to the barn. I saddled Stonewall and lit out for the railroad station while the Fords were still memorizing their lines.

I know, I know. It was sneaky to shoot him when he was unarmed and his back was turned. A proper lady might have waited for him to draw. But I can't quite get the hang of being proper.

Besides, don't you agree it was better for posterity? So there would be no more Tucker Basshams, no more bleeding men on trains. So Jesse's children could grow up to their own dreams. And I needed those diamonds, remember. For all her help I was going to owe Hattie Floyd a cottage, and more.

And posterity needs its dreams too. Admit it, now, doesn't the notion of a bandit king thrill you too? A hero who swears fealty to his comrades till and through death, courageously raids his evil oppressors, romances his ladies with poetic words, kills rather than betray his ideals? Now, the squalid shooting of a pretty woman would have tarnished his name. I provided Jesse with a hero's exit. Legends are fragile, after all—just look at Jesse's brother. Eventually Frank surrendered, was acquitted, and lived on to a bald old age—and do you know a single soul who prefers Frank to our dream of Jesse?

And furthermore—

Oh, I know, I know, you're right. The real reason was, if I hadn't done it, he would have shot me dead. I never claimed to be anything but a dirty little coward.

7

"Let not Caesar's servile minions/Mock the lion thus laid low:/ 'Twas no foeman's hand that slew him,/'Twas his own that struck the blow."

That's what Major Edwards wrote, keeping the legend alive.

In my profession too, we know a good idea when we see one. "Take him and cut him out in little stars,/And he will make the face of heaven so fine,/That all the world will be in love with night." The very week Jesse died, a New York producer announced J. J. McCloskey's new play, *Jesse James, the Bandit King*, and that was only the first of a whole slew of them.

And there was Billy Gashade. It was September again. Hattie had said it was time for me to get back to work, so I'd said my tearful good-byes and was in the St. Louis station waiting for the train to New York. Billy was going back to Kansas City. I offered him a cigar and said, "Watch out for bandits, Billy."

"There's not much trouble from them these days," he said. "Do you want to hear my song, Bridget? It's nearly finished."

"Of course."

It was a good song, and he got the story right, most of it, until he got to the chorus. Billy sang, "Jesse had a wife to mourn for his life,/Two children, they were—"

"Three," I said.

"Three?" Billy's eyebrows crawled up. "Little Jesse, and little Mary, and—?"

"Just get the facts right, Billy," I said crossly. "Three."

Billy nodded and sang again:

"Jesse had a wife to mourn for his life,/Three children, they were brave,/But that dirty little coward that shot Mr. Howard/Has laid poor Jesse in his grave."

Ah, Jesse, Jesse. We sing of you to this day. You were such stuff as dreams are made on.

The trouble was, I was real.

K. K. Beck has created an original sleuth in the person of Iris Cooper, a Roaring Twenties ingenue, Stanford coed, and friend and fellow crime-solver of Jack Clancy, a wisecracking reporter. The entertaining series includes three books, most recently Peril Under the Palms. *Ms. Beck has written six other non-series mysteries (including* The Body in the Volvo*) and has launched a new series featuring Jane da Silva, "a reluctant private investigator and former lounge singer," in* A Hopeless Case.

In "Seascape," Iris, Jack, and a houseful of guests learn a startling but important lesson in art appreciation.

SEASCAPE

by K. K. Beck

IT IS A STRANGE fact of history that Robert Lincoln was present not only at the assassination of his father, Abraham Lincoln, but also years later on the occasions of the fatal shootings of Presidents Garfield and McKinley.

In the same vein, a British nurse found herself shipwrecked three times between the years 1911 and 1915, and was rescued from the Titanic, the Lusitania and the hospital ship Britannic.

Can this be coincidence, or is some other principle at work here? The question was of interest to me, because I was twenty years old and had already been at hand four times when a murderer had struck.

First of all, just a year ago, in 1927, when my aunt and I sailed from Southampton to Montreal on the *Irenia,* a mild-mannered young man was found stabbed in a deck chair. The following spring, I was a guest at the Brockhursts in Hillsborough near Stanford University, where I go to school, and I found a dead lady's maid in a mummy case in my pajamas. (I was wearing my pajamas; poor Florence was wearing step-ins trimmed with Valenciennes lace.) Later that year, Aunt Hermione and I went to Hawaii, and, by moonlight on the beach of Waikiki, my friend Jack Clancy and I encountered the corpse of a respectable Boston lady who appeared to have been bludgeoned by a coconut. Most recently, Aunt Hermione and I had returned from Banff, and there, again, had been murder.

Of course, in each case I had the satisfaction of actually *solving* all the mysteries surrounding these deaths, but the string of crimes did give me pause. Was I in some way attracting criminals because of the pleasure I took in unmasking them? Or was my yearning for excitement somehow responsible? There was no question that while the crimes with which I became involved were shocking, I found sorting them out quite exhilarating.

I had returned to Stanford and was relaxing in Roble Hall, looking with anticipation at my new books. Classes would begin in another week, and although that lovely autumnal nip, with which I had grown up in Oregon, was absent here in California, I had the same eager feeling I always had at the beginning of school. I was, in fact, ready to forget about crime altogether and concentrate on my studies and on being a perfectly happy, carefree coed, enjoying collegiate life.

Then, Bunny Brockhurst telephoned.

I was once almost engaged to Bunny's brother, Clarence, an Egyptologist. Bunny had been engaged to many people, including her parents' chauffeur. She was, quite frankly, a flapper, right down to the silver flask of gin in her pocketbook and her rolled-down stockings, the sort of girl the newspapers characterized as a "madcap debutante."

When she telephoned, however, she didn't sound madcap at all. The call was long distance, from Carmel, but the connection was excellent and the worry in her voice was clear. "Iris," she said, "you must come down and help us as you did before with that business with Florence."

"What has happened?" I asked. The Brockhursts were an eccentric family and I expected anything.

"The police are absolutely *grilling* poor Rodney. My cousin, Rodney Beaumont. You see, Iris, my mother's sister, Aunt Lulu, has fallen off a cliff and they think he pushed her."

"Well, if the police are already there . . . ," I began, although of course I was thrilled at the prospect of finding out all about it.

"Please come, Iris," said Bunny. "The rest of the family are all abroad. Mother and Father and Clarence and Henry. Digging up more dead things over in Egypt. I'm all alone here with my cousins and don't know where to turn."

I wondered at the wisdom of the Brockhursts leaving the rich, beautiful and impetuous Bunny on her own. She was easy prey for cads and fortune hunters. Although she was my age, and old enough to know better, it was my opinion she would need a watchful eye on her until her parents saw her married off to some patient and respectable man.

"I'm sorry to hear about your aunt," I added.

"Thank you," said Bunny, without any evident grief. "She lived a full life. She must have been well over fifty. I can't imagine being that old, can you?"

"No," I said, "but I suppose we'll find out what it's like eventually."

"And at the end she was mixed up with a *man*. At her age, too."

Bunny sounded disgusted, but I could well imagine *her* still at it well into the future, overrouged, her straight Colleen Moore bob dyed jet black, her man-eating instincts intact. "She fell off a cliff, you say?"

"Into the ocean. Painting. She was an artist. She did seascapes. The kind of thing you might find on a box of chocolates. You'll see them when you get here."

"The police might not want me to interfere," I began.

"Iris, please. Poor Rodney is very high-strung. I'm afraid his nerves aren't up to all this. I know he didn't do it. He's my favorite cousin."

I imagined there were plenty of high-strung, cold-blooded killers, capable of pushing their relatives off cliffs, who had been somebody's favorite cousin. It occurred to me that if I did go to Carmel, I might conclude, just as the police had, that Rodney had done it. But perhaps I could be of some comfort to Bunny in any case.

Still, I wondered if it were wise of me to insinuate myself into the affair. Then, Bunny said something that decided me.

"I called your friend Mr. Clancy, too. He says he'll take you down in his machine. Please come."

"All right," I said. "I hope I can be of help. But I'm not sure it's wise to invite Jack. After all, he writes for the *San Francisco Globe*. I would think your family had enough publicity over that other thing."

It occurred to me that even with her family in turmoil, Bunny was up to her old tricks. She'd set her cap for Jack in a very blatant and obvious way before. This time he might not escape her clutches so easily.

"Oh, but he's so amusing. And we might need something physical."

"Heavy lifting, or opening pickle jars, I suppose you mean," I said rather frostily.

Bunny giggled.

"But what having a caveman around has to do with your Aunt Lulu, I can't see," I continued.

"It's all settled then," said Bunny. "Perhaps you'll be here in time to hear about the will. A man is coming down from the city day after tomorrow to tell us what it says."

I had the feeling there might be quite a bit at stake in that will. Aunt Lulu had been Bunny's mother's sister, and I happened to know the Brockhurst fortune came from that side of the family.

Jack picked me up the next day around noon. "Swell of Bunny to count me in," he said, as he tossed my bag into the rumble seat and opened my door. "Since I met you, Iris, my editor has expected me to come up with a baffling murder like clockwork. I know you won't let me down."

"I've been worrying about that," I said, settling in. "Is it normal for me to come upon crime all the time?"

Jack got behind the wheel and began to intone, in his newspaper voice: "What strange forces haunt this pretty young coed, by all appearances a sweet, well-brought-up girl who finds herself nevertheless plunged time and time again into cunningly spun webs of intrigue, deception and death?" He put the car into gear. "My best leads are often in the form of a question."

"Aren't your sentences rather long for newspaper writing?" I said. "All those dependent clauses."

"That's why we have rewrite," said Jack. "I give 'em the juicy stuff, and they worry about the periods."

"At least this one is already dead," I said, getting us back on the subject.

"Iris, you're not getting squeamish on me?" he said, sounding vaguely alarmed.

"I must confess I was thrilled when Bunny called," I said.

He squeezed my knee, laughed and said, "That's my girl. Now sit and relax. I figure this gas buggy'll get us there in three and a half hours. I had my landlady make us a couple of sandwiches so we don't have to stop. You like liverwurst?"

I sighed, and turned to look out the window. I had to face the fact that any affection Jack might have for me was simply because I was a source of lurid newspaper stories.

Aunt Lulu had lived in a large and rambling house in the Carmel Highlands. It was very much in the California style, stucco, with curly red roof tiles and exposed dark beams. It stood on a great rocky bluff.

There was a pleasant and well-cultivated garden around the house, full of vivid geraniums and bougainvillea. The garden was surrounded by a stucco wall. Beyond this wall, the natural landscape prevailed—bare rock, with tenacious, wind-pruned pine trees and golden grasses.

Though quite beautiful in a rather savage way, the bluff was a queer spot for a home. There was an eerie sense of desolation about the place, and something unsettling about the roar of the ocean below. Gulls, buffeted by the winds, bounced around in the sky and let out irritable cries.

We were met at the door by an olive-skinned woman of about forty, wearing a maid's uniform, which seemed somehow too formal for the casual architecture of the place. Her thick blue-black hair was done up in a heavy braid coiled at the nape of her neck. Her large dark eyes were rimmed with red, and I was sure she'd been crying.

I spoke to her in the hushed tones one is supposed to use around the bereaved, and she replied with just a touch of a Spanish accent:

"They are expecting you," she said softly, taking our bags and directing us into a large living room off of the tiled entry hall.

When we entered, Bunny, standing at a table by the window, put down a cocktail shaker and rushed to greet us. "Thank goodness, you're here," she said. "Since we spoke, the police have been back, haranguing poor Rodney. And Thelma, too."

She introduced us to the two other people in the room. Rodney was a tall, thin young man with brilliantined fair hair. He was wearing baggy flannels and a scarlet-and-navy-blue argyle sweater. Thelma, his sister, was equally thin and fair, with grayish blue eyes obscured by a rimless pince-nez, and wearing dark tweeds. Although they looked remarkably alike, they created distinctly different impressions. Rodney had a slackness about him, a weak twist to his mouth. Thelma, who sat ramrod straight, looked shrewd and a little severe.

"Quick," said Bunny, back at the cocktail shaker and agitating its contents with a practiced hand, "we've got to tell you everything before that horrible Nigel comes back."

"Oh, it's useless," said Rodney with a weary sigh, flinging himself back onto the sofa and moaning.

"Who's Nigel?" said Jack.

"Well," said Bunny, drawing in her breath and pouring out a tray of cocktails. "Aunt Lulu never married or had children, just her nieces and nephews. Naturally, we always expected . . ."

"Naturally," I said, leaving her thought unspoken, just in case Bunny was a little reticent about discussing her expectations.

Apparently, however, she wasn't. "We thought we'd get it. She had bags of money. Never wanted to spend too much, because she fancied herself a Bohemian. It's not that we're greedy or anything," said Bunny, with a nervous glance over at Rodney, "but she always told us she was leaving it to us."

"Let me help you," said Jack, going to her side and taking the tray.

"Thank you," she said, batting her eyes vampishly and running a hand over her sleek, dark bob. "I sent the servants away so we can talk frankly. There are just two of them, Dolores and her husband Ignacio."

"And Nigel," said Jack. "Who's Nigel?"

"Nigel's the one we were all afraid she'd leave her money to," said Bunny. "Thelma and Rodney here had come up to try and stop her."

Two bright spots appeared in Thelma's cheeks. "Actually, we came up to warn her that he was an adventurer," she said. "It was for her own good."

"Nigel," said Rodney wearily, "is some kind of a remittance man Aunt Lulu scraped up somewhere. An Englishman who's been sponging off her for ages. Thelma and I made a few discreet inquiries and we found out he's got a wife and five children in Los Angeles."

"She said he lives in the guest house," said Bunny, rolling her eyes. "I think she just stashes him out there when she has houseguests."

"Aunt Lulu felt Nigel understood her art," said Thelma, accepting a cocktail from Jack's tray.

"Well, that gives him one up on me," said Jack. "That is, if these seascapes are examples of her work."

The room was simply arranged with unvarnished dark furniture and roughly woven rugs and draperies. There was a large, modern picture window, and practically every inch of wall space was taken up with seascapes of various sizes.

They seemed to represent years of futile attempts at catching the subtle interplay of light and water. Here was the sea in all its moods from serene to storm-tossed, and bathed in light from pale gray to a deep golden. Yet every canvas had a lifeless, labored quality. Most repellent were the pictures that incorporated garish sunsets.

"Let me get this straight," said Jack with his usual bluntness. "You were afraid the old girl was going to leave it to this Nigel character, so you came up to blow the whistle on him?"

"That's right," said Thelma, looking rather pained.

"It wasn't just the money," said Rodney with a little quiver. "We hated to see poor Aunt Lulu make a fool of herself."

"Naturally," said Jack with a broad smile that appeared patently false. "Like your sister says, it was for her own good."

"What was her reaction?" I asked, simply for form's sake. After all, her reaction was fairly predictable. When people are told things for their own good, they invariably resent it.

"She was quite unreasonable," said Thelma. "She actually said it was none of our business."

"Did she seem surprised?" I asked.

Thelma frowned in concentration. "Not entirely. She said he'd been separated from his wife, who was a Catholic and wouldn't divorce him. But she did seem a little taken aback that there were so *many* children. She said, 'Five?' with rather a start. And then I told her the youngest was three, which, I believe, overlapped with the beginning of her liaison with Nigel."

Perhaps, I thought, after having put up a brave front with her relatives, she'd thrown herself off the cliff in agony at Nigel's treachery.

"She was upset," said Bunny. "She took to her room for a couple of days after that, quit painting and sulked around. And she must have had words with Nigel, because he was lying low. Spent all his time fishing and looking down in the mouth. Then, she snapped out of it and acted as if everything were grand. I think she talked herself into being the fascinating other woman. Her last words on the subject were that we were hopelessly bourgeois for having brought it up, and that we mustn't be shocked at her irregular way of living, as she had the soul of an artist."

Rodney groaned rather than moaned this time. "The soul, perhaps, but not a *shred* of the talent. When she wasn't daubing away on those awful oils, she was trucked out in Grecian draperies for dreary pageants in the woods, several of which I actually attended so as not to hurt the poor thing's feelings. She was a silly woman, and I never should have let you girls talk me into coming here and nagging her about Nigel. You just got her all mad at us."

"How mad was she?" I asked.

"Mad enough to bring up the will," said Bunny, fitting a cigarette into an amber holder, crossing her legs and bouncing one knee saucily. "Said we had been the sole legatees, but because of our having brought up Nigel's wife and kiddies she'd leave it all to him, just to show us."

Rodney whimpered, and took another sip of his cocktail. "We never should have said a *thing*," he said. I thought that it didn't matter now, as Aunt Lulu was dead, presumably without having had time to change her will.

"Well," I said, "I can see why the police might be questioning you. After all, you had a powerful motive."

"Dolores and Ignacio told them about our little scene," said Bunny. "They creep around and listen to everything. And Nigel told them he'd heard her yelling at us. The rat."

"Why do the police seem to think she was pushed?" asked Jack.

"I suppose because she stood out on that bluff and painted her lousy seascapes for years without a mishap," said Rodney sounding very resentful that she hadn't plunged over the edge on a previous occasion.

"Where was everybody when she fell?" I asked.

"I was in bed. To be perfectly honest, I had a hangover," said Bunny. "After Aunt Lulu shouted"—here Bunny assumed a fluty sort of voice—" 'Now that you've had your say about Nigel's family, I'm changing my will,' and flounced out of the room, I headed straight for the bar and mixed up a batch of White Ladies."

"It must have been a shock," said Jack, apparently excusing Bunny's excess.

"Oh, I didn't care about the money. My family's got plenty of that. I felt badly because Thelma and Rodney could use some money. And I'd been down here trying to help them, and we'd made a big mess of it." She tilted back her head and blew a column of smoke up toward the ceiling.

"Rodney and I were here, in the living room, when it happened," said Thelma. "We talked for a while, then Rodney read a book and I darned some of his socks.

"You see Aunt Lulu went out and set up her easel right after breakfast, around nine o'clock. And when Dolores brought her her lunch at noon, she wasn't there. Just her easel, knocked over. Dolores peered down over the cliff and saw her body wedged between some rocks at the bottom."

"So you were in the living room between nine and noon. Together?" I said.

"Yes," said Thelma. "And Bunny was tucked in, as she says. Dolores and Ignacio had driven into town to do some marketing. They came back around noon, and Dolores went out to bring her a tray with lunch."

"Nigel," said Bunny, "was gone all morning fishing. He came back around lunchtime with a couple of fish. He came clomping up the steps from the boathouse whistling; then the police went down and took the boat around to retrieve the body."

"So Thelma and Rodney are providing each other with an alibi," I said.

"And they're providing me with one, too," said Bunny. "My room is right off the living room here. I couldn't have left it without them seeing me. The police even went outside to check the windows, but there's all sorts of shrubbery beneath them that hadn't been disturbed, and there weren't any marks in the soil or anything, which was damp, as it had rained."

"But you didn't see them?" I persisted.

"I was dead to the world," said Bunny cheerfully. "In the arms of Morpheus behind a black sleeping mask."

Just then, the door opened and a trim, middle-aged man in his late forties appeared. He was wearing corduroy trousers and an old sweater, and he had a gingery little mustache, thinning hair to match, and a shiny pink face.

"Nigel," said Bunny, "these are my friends, Iris Cooper and Jack Clancy. This is Nigel Carruthers, Aunt Lulu's dear friend."

"How do you do," said Nigel in a blustery way, stepping over to the bar. Thelma and Rodney stiffened, as if he were an intruder, and Nigel gave them a curt nod.

"They're sort of detectives," continued Bunny, as if we were engaged in a parlor game. "Come to see if they can find out what happened to poor Aunt Lulu."

Nigel Carruthers poured himself a whiskey and gave us a withering glance, as well he might. The way Bunny described us, we sounded like Penrod and Sam playing detective.

"I have faith in the police," he said, sitting down heavily.

"Of course," I said soothingly. "Bunny was so upset, having lost her aunt so suddenly, I felt it best to come when she asked."

Nigel made a strange English barking sound, which I took for an expression of doubt about the sincerity of Bunny's grief.

"I'd like to offer my condolences to you, too," said Jack. "I understand you were very close."

Nigel now eyed Jack as if he were the only sensible person in the room. "Thank you, young man," he said with dignity. "She was indeed a remarkable woman. She lived and breathed art."

Our eyes all fell silently on the interminable seascapes that lined the room.

"These seascapes were just the beginning," he said in his quite beautiful accent. "She lacked the confidence to fully realize her talent. I knew that the beauty of her soul could be displayed one day on canvas. I told her so. Had she lived, we would have seen a great outpouring of painting from her. Not just these seascapes, pleasant enough in their own way, but much more. Why, at the very end, I had convinced her to turn away from what she knew best. 'Are the pines not calling to you, Lulu?' I said to her."

He paused, and I reflected that "Are the pines not calling to you, Lulu?" would make a very catchy song title.

Nigel gestured expansively and continued. "Trees, sky, earth, rock. She needed a fresh approach." He bent his head down as if fighting off emotion, pressed his hands over his eyes for a moment, and said rather thickly, "But she never had a chance to really blossom. Such a waste."

"Are you an artist, too?" said Jack.

"No, I'm merely a student of life," said Nigel. "But I like to think that for Lulu, I was also a muse."

Bunny jumped up out of her chair. "Would you like to see a picture of her, Iris?" she said.

"Yes," I said. "I believe I would." I realized that I had been trying to picture Aunt Lulu, without success. Bunny led me into a large, dark bedroom. It was hard to believe, but there were more seascapes in here, as well as a large, old brass bed and a big dresser on which were perfume bottles and silver-framed photographs.

Bunny held up one of these pictures for my inspection. "Here she is in her heyday," said Bunny, pointing to Aunt Lulu caught on an afternoon some thirty years ago or so, laughing and holding up abalone shells on the beach with some other young ladies in shirtwaists, piles of hair twisted up on their heads in the fashion of the turn of the century. She had a wholesome, girlish face.

There were other, similar candid group shots, mostly taken out of doors. "When Aunt Lulu came here she tried to get in with a lot of famous writers and artists," said Bunny. "She was always talking about sitting with Jack and Charmain London at some camp fire, and a lot of other old-fashioned poets and artists, pounding the abalone meat with rocks and drinking Dago red.

"Oh, here she is in one of her getups." Lulu, looking a little older and stouter, perhaps in her forties, was draped in some strange garment, her feet bare, and holding up a spear presumably for some tableau or pageant. "And here," said Bunny, "is what she looked like more recently." This last was a more formal portrait, of the mature Aunt Lulu fingering some barbaric jewelry and staring into the camera with an intense look. She had pale eyes, severe dark brows, a stubborn square jaw, and a general air of Junoesque handsomeness. Her hair was bobbed, shot through with gray, and arranged in rows of precise waves. In fact, her hair looked a little like one of her seascapes.

Interspersed among these pictures of herself were other pictures, many of them signed, of arty-looking men in beards and slouch hats and women in roughly woven tunics and eccentric coiffures. They were, I presumed, her Bohemian friends. There were no pictures of her nieces and nephews.

"Look," said Bunny with a giggle, "she's got a few of Nigel here in his salad days." Here was a younger, athletic Nigel in tennis whites, in Tyrolean gear, with ice axe and alpenstock, and in a bathing suit, on a dock, holding up a large fish. I could see how Aunt Lulu might have found him attractive.

"How long has he been in the picture?" I said.

"He's sort of drifted in and out, over the years, I gather," said Bunny."Who knows how long they've been carrying on? But Rodney and Thelma discovered quite recently that his wife runs some sort of boarding house for moving picture people in Los Angeles. Naturally, they rushed right up here to spill it. Poor Rodney has made some bad investments, I'm afraid. And Thelma had let him invest some of her money. It's very sad, really."

"Well," I said, "whatever their financial problems, Aunt Lulu still had another twenty years or so ahead of her, presuming her health was good. I can see that they'd like to avoid having the money leave the family, but it wouldn't do them much good in the short run."

"Now it will," said Bunny. "Unless of course Rodney gets arrested."

"I can't imagine that," I said. "Thelma is his alibi."

"But the police think they're in it together," said Bunny. We were both whispering now.

"Even if they did do it," I said, before I realized how horrible it must have sounded to Bunny, "there isn't any proof, is there?"

Bunny looked stricken, and suddenly I knew why she was so unhappy. She turned away from me, but glancing sideways in the mirror above the dresser, I could see a tear brimming in her eye. "That's just it," she said. "I can't bear it. Rodney and Thelma are a little strange, but I don't want to think they could harm anyone."

"But you do want to know," I said, touching her hand. "One way or the other."

"Yes," she said in a husky whisper.

I would want to know, too, if my relatives were homicidal. And if they were, I wouldn't take any walks with them in a cliffy region.

We went back into the living room, where ill will hung heavily in the air. Rodney was scowling, and staring out the big picture window that overlooked the ocean. Thelma shifted her gaze back to Nigel and narrowed her eyes.

"How long will you be staying, Mr. Carruthers?" she said sharply.

"What kind of a question is that?" Nigel demanded.

"Quite a simple one," she said.

"The police have told us all to stay until they finish their investigations," he said. "Surely you realized that. I could ask you the same question."

Jack plunged right in. "I guess it depends on who gets the house now," he said. "Bunny tells me a lawyer is coming down with the will tomorrow."

"That's right," said Nigel smoothly.

"I suppose you think she had time to change it," said Thelma a little waspishly.

"To be perfectly frank, I think it's in poor taste to even discuss the matter," he said.

Bunny rolled her eyes. "Oh, for heaven's sake," she said, "naturally we're all thinking about it. Nigel, I wouldn't get your hopes up. Aunt Lulu made it clear we were in the will. You don't think she made a new one between the time she had that dustup with us and a few days later when she fell off that cliff, do you? Anyway, she would have to have had it witnessed."

Nigel opened his mouth as if to say something, then pulled a little at his mustache and frowned.

"Iris and I were in that car for hours today," said Jack. "I think we need a little walk and some fresh air. Right, Iris?"

"Tramp'd do you good," muttered Nigel. "Wouldn't hurt the rest of you, either. All you ever do is sit around this house, smoking cigarettes and drinking cocktails, getting soft and waiting to get your hands on Lulu's money. At least that's what Lulu told me." He permitted himself a small smile. " 'When I was their age, Nigel, I cared about life, about beauty, about art,' that's what she said."

As soon as we got into the hall, Jack grabbed my sleeve. "Bunny was right. You need two witnesses. Let's talk to the help."

We found the kitchen, where the woman who had admitted us, evidently Dolores, was washing lettuce, while a dark man in a chauffeur's uniform sat at the table drinking a cup of coffee.

They eyed us warily, as domestic servants quite naturally do when their domain is invaded. "Hello," said Jack breezily. "You folks must be Dolores and Ignacio."

The woman stopped washing lettuce and nodded.

"I'm Jack Clancy, and this here is Iris Cooper. We were pretty cut up when we heard about Aunt Lulu, and being a friend of Bunny and all, well, when she asked us to come down here and take a look around, naturally we did."

"She was a good woman," said Dolores. "We are very sad."

"You worked for her for a long time?"

"About fifteen years," said Ignacio. "We took care of her for a long time. You want to ask us some questions?" The way he said it seemed to indicate he didn't see why he should answer any of them, and he had a point.

I turned to Dolores. "Bunny says you found her," I said. "It must have been a terrible shock."

"The poor lady," said Dolores, her face crumpling, "stuck there in the rocks, with the water lapping up over her feet. I shall never forget it." She burst into tears and buried her face in her apron.

I rushed to her side, but Ignacio had leapt to his feet and got there first. He said something softly to her in Spanish. I started to withdraw, but Jack held my arm.

"Did she ask you to sign any papers before she died?" he asked. "To be a witness to any legal papers? It might be important."

Dolores let her apron fall back down and turned to her husband. She whispered to him in Spanish. He answered her quickly, then made a decisive gesture, striking the air with his hand. He turned to us. "Nothing like that," he said.

Dolores wiped her eyes and straightened herself up. They stood side by side, she looking calm and dignified, he just slightly nervous.

"How many will there be for dinner tonight?" she asked quietly. "No one told me you were coming."

"That was very thoughtless of them," I said. "But in all the confusion I suppose they weren't thinking. Please don't trouble yourself tonight. I think you should make a simple meal for yourself and your husband, and we will take care of ourselves." It wasn't really my place to direct the help in this house, but I felt sure no one else would do it, and I thought it best if I took charge. Besides, I was sure I could find something to put together—a cheese soufflé or some sandwiches. And the prospect of making dinner seemed much more pleasant than sitting in the living room pretending not to notice Bunny and her cousins squabbling with Nigel.

Dolores began to make some feeble protest, but Jack interrupted her.

"Absolutely," said Jack. "I'm sure that's what Aunt Lulu would have wanted. Turn in early. Get some rest. Iris and I can whip something up in jig time for that crowd."

That all settled, we left the kitchen. Jack clomped away noisily from the door, then to my horror, crept back and leaned against it, smiling to himself. I cringed, frozen in my tracks, sure that we would be discovered. A few seconds later, he crept back to my side.

"How could you?" I hissed. Jack seemed to have picked up some very bad habits from newspapering, although perhaps he was born with them.

"Don't you want to know what they said after we left?"

"Of course, but they must have been speaking Spanish."

"Which I happen to *comprendo un poco*," said Jack. "But of course, if you don't approve of eavesdropping, I won't burden you with—"

"Please, Jack, don't be annoying."

"Okay. He told her to keep her mouth shut. Said that the best thing to do was not say a thing about the will or they might get in trouble."

"So maybe they did sign something. How good is your Spanish, Jack? Are you sure they said 'will'?"

"If it's *testamento*, they did," he said. "That's never come up in Tia Juana, but it seems like a good guess."

"Poor Dolores seemed pretty sad," I said.

"But Ignacio seemed more scared than anything," said Jack. "What's he got to be scared about, I'd like to know."

"It's Rodney who should be scared," I said. "The police apparently suspect him, and he had a strong motive. Aunt Lulu had shouted that she was changing her will, and he'd made some bad investments and is apparently pretty hard up."

"Has anyone suggested he find work?" said Jack. "It's really quite amazing. Get a job, and generally they give you a pay envelope once a week. But I suppose he's a nerve case, too sensitive for the tedium of daily toil."

"Do you think he pushed her?" I said.

"If he did," said Jack, "he'll get away with it. That sister of his will stick by him and give him an alibi. Although, I can see her doing the deed just as easily. She's got more backbone than Rodney."

"They are really rather unattractive," I said.

"Hard to believe they're Bunny's cousins, isn't it?" said Jack.

"Not really," I said. "Bunny is charming enough on the surface, but the whole Brockhurst family is a little off."

"Good thing you didn't become one of them," said Jack. "Just think, last spring you were about to marry that dope Clarence, and these gazebos here would have been your in-laws."

"Jack," I said. "I'd appreciate it if you would give me your word never to mention that again. Besides, Clarence and I were never officially engaged."

"All right," said Jack. "The subject's closed. Unless you get engaged to some other dope, and then maybe being reminded of Clarence will stop you from making a horrible mistake. Now let's drop your personal life and get on with it. I want to get the whole layout and see just where it all happened."

"Good idea," I said. We never talked about Jack's personal life. He told me once he thought I was too good for him, which brought up images in my mind of brief, sordid interludes with chorus girls—or worse.

About half an hour later, we had a good picture of the surroundings. The house sat on a little promontory, with, on the west side, a small strip of garden with natural plants and grasses, between the house and the bluff. On the east side of the house, facing the road, there was the much larger, formal garden, surrounded by a stucco wall, which we had come through upon our arrival.

From the small garden on the ocean side, there were two paths through otherwise impassable, cliffy terrain. One led to the south, and it was this one we explored first. After a twist and turn between some pines, it led to a long and rather rickety flight of wooden steps which clung to the side of the rock and led to a boathouse below.

We went down these stairs, admiring the jade-green water below, and explored the boathouse, which had that nice salty and mildewy smell boathouses seem to have. There was a small boat there, presumably the one Nigel used to fish. It was an untidy place. Jack looked idly at a box of jumbled tools and old junk, and I examined a broken oar.

After we climbed back up, we returned through the strip of garden, past the big picture window, where we could see the others, still at cocktails, and followed the second, shorter path. This led to the lonely bluff, barren except for a single wind-pruned pine. Rather pathetically, an easel lay propped up against the tree, forgotten in the tragedy.

"Take a look down there," said Jack, driving me crazy by strolling calmly to the edge of the bluff and peering down. I inched toward him and looked over myself. Below, the water, licked with foam, churned between the rocks. I was immediately overcome by dizziness and reached out for Jack.

He took my hand and pulled me back away from the edge. "Pretty bad," he said. "The old girl didn't have a chance after she tumbled. And she might have had time to know what was happening on her way down."

"How awful," I said, suddenly overcome. "If anyone pushed her, they should certainly be held accountable."

"Not a bad way to get away with murder," said Jack, strolling over to the tree. "There's no proof one way or the other." He examined the easel, then let out a little whistle. "Her final masterpiece is still here," he said. Facedown on the rock lay a canvas. Jack picked it up. It wasn't a seascape. Instead, it was the lone pine here on the bluff.

"What do you think?" I said.

Jack squinted at it. "I'm sorry I ever said anything about the seascapes," he said. "She should have stuck by 'em."

Poor Aunt Lulu. Despite Nigel's faith in her broadening artistic horizons, her pine was stiff and unnatural looking, with the clusters of needles represented by crude green blotches. The tree looked somehow as if it were hovering a few feet above the rock, and the addition of a hefty sea gull perched in its branches had thrown the whole thing hopelessly out of scale.

"And to think," I said, "if she had stuck with those seascapes, she might have been alive today."

"That's right," said Jack. "Because she would have been facing the ocean. I guess she stepped back to get a look at her work."

"This makes things look better for Rodney and Thelma," I said. "It provides a plausible explanation for the accident."

"This is a pretty isolated spot," said Jack, looking around.

"I know," I replied. "The only way it can be reached is by this path, past the picture window. Which means that if anyone came and pushed her, then Rodney and Thelma would have seen them." I shivered. "Let's get away from here, Jack. It gives me the creeps."

"She must have fallen," said Jack, as we set off back down the path. He sounded rather disappointed.

"Of course, *The Globe* would have preferred a murder," I said tartly.

"Well, she's dead in any case," said Jack. "Given a choice between having her pushed or having her fall, naturally I choose pushed. Which leaves out everyone but Rodney and Thelma if you ask me."

"Would that make good copy?"

"Thelma's a little drab. The public likes bad women to be beautiful if at all possible. But that Rodney's got possibilities." He waved happily at them through the picture window, just as he was making these uncharitable remarks.

By unspoken agreement, we continued to walk around the house and through the front garden, so we could talk freely. Jack threw back his head and began to quote from the newspaper story he might write. "Those pale, trembling white hands, hands that have never seen a day's honest toil, could they have done this evil work, pushing a great talent to a horrible death on the cold, cold rocks many feet below?"

"Great talent?" I said.

"Well that may be stretching it a bit," he admitted. "Too bad

Nigel has the perfect alibi, and no motive," he continued. "The sex angle's always good.

"And I think the servants are hiding something," he said. "They're jumpy as cats. That Dolores could have given her a push right before she says she found the body."

We were approaching a small guest house, covered with jasmine. It was here that Nigel officially resided. "What we need," said Jack, "is a mysterious stranger to pin this on."

Just as he said this, my eye caught a flutter of movement in some shrubbery behind the guest house. I let out a little cry and found myself rushing forward. I was sure I had spotted someone there.

A second later, following the sounds of a desperate thrashing in the foliage, Jack had joined me, and together we pulled out our mysterious stranger.

She was a woman of about forty or so, with wild, coarse red hair in a long bob. The hue was so vivid I immediately suspected henna. She had rosy, white skin, large, soft blue eyes, and she wore a dress of cheap, flowered artificial silk.

"Let go!" she squealed.

Jack let her go, but I held on for a second longer. "You won't run off, will you?" I said.

"Of course not," she said, brushing me off, arranging a big, flouncy collar, smoothing down her skirt and making a pathetic attempt to tame her hair. These little gestures seemed to restore her sense of dignity, and she drew herself up to her full height and looked us in the eye.

"And you'd be that niece and nephew then," she said belligerently. Her accent, though Americanized somewhat, was unmistakably Irish.

"You mean Rodney and Thelma?" I said. "No, I'm Iris Cooper, and this is Jack Clancy."

"Who," said Jack severely, "are you?"

"I'm Mary Carruthers," she said.

"You mean Mrs. Nigel Carruthers," said Jack pleasantly. "Mother of five?"

"I am," she said.

"What were you doing in the manzanita?" I asked her.

"I was just taking a turn in the garden," she said. "It's annoying to be all shut up in that guest house all day."

"You mean Mr. Carruthers has hidden you away here?" said Jack with a certain relish. I could just imagine his newspaperman's brain churning out dreadful copy about middle-aged love triangles.

"Just until they get through with all that nonsense about the will," said Mrs. Carruthers. "Then Nigel is coming home where he belongs."

"How long have you been here?" asked Jack eagerly. I imagined he was casting her as a suspect. If anyone had a motive, surely it was Mrs. C., the irate wife, tossing the other woman off a cliff.

"What do you mean?" she asked, with a flat, suspicious look in her eyes.

"Oh, Jack," I said. "Why don't we invite Mrs. Carruthers inside the house?" I turned to her. "It's silly of you to stay out here by yourself. In fact, I was just going to put together some sort of a meal. I don't know what's in the house, but you'll be wanting dinner—"

"We can put together a respectable supper, I'm sure," said Mrs. Carruthers. "I'll give you a hand."

Presently, Jack was banished back into the living room, and Mrs. Carruthers and I were in our aprons, rather enjoying the task of putting together an improvisational meal.

I discovered two reasonably-sized fish in the icebox, but their eyes were cloudy, and when I pushed at the flesh with my forefinger, a dent remained. Even disguised in a sauce, they'd be well past it. The gathering was bound to be strained enough without bad fish.

Mrs. Carruthers had better luck in the pantry, however, and soon she was peeling and slicing potatoes. I was grating some cheese. We had decided to make scalloped potatoes, and we had also found a nice ham, some canned string beans and some apples to bake for dessert.

Mrs. Carruthers became positively garrulous, confiding in me about her husband and his abandonment of her large family.

"I knew he was no good as soon as I laid eyes on him," she said, starting way back at the beginning. "But I couldn't help myself." Mrs. Carruthers, it appeared, had been a parlor maid in England. Mr. Carruthers had been the young man of the house. She had been in her place for a matter of months before she learned she was expecting his child.

The upshot was that in an impetuous moment Mr. Carruthers made an honest woman of her, and was subsequently banished to the New World by his family, with the promise of a small income if he and his wife and child stayed away. Once he was gone, the Carruthers reneged on their promise of financial assistance, and the growing family had been eking out a poor living ever since.

"The problem is," explained Mrs. Carruthers, "he wasn't brought up to work. He's nothing but a sponger, really. Thought he was too good for us, and ran off with all his arty friends and traveled around the world, while I slaved away raising those poor children. This last time I didn't even know where he was until I got the letter from those two I thought you were."

"Rodney and Thelma Beaumont," I said. I imagined they'd sent the letter hoping Mrs. Carruthers would stir up trouble. "What did they say?"

"Just that my husband was living with another woman up here in Carmel. He'd written me once, about three months ago, and that was all I heard. All the usual promises, but no return address. I was fit to be tied. Well, I tell you, I took it upon myself to come up here and tell him just what I thought of him, and maybe tell the poor woman he deceived just what sort of a man he was. And ask him for some help with the children, too, just in case he'd found himself in a better situation."

"You were angry, naturally," I said.

"I could've killed him," she said.

"And did you meet Aunt Lulu?" I asked.

She frowned. "She fell off that cliff just before I got here," she said. "Nigel told me she knew he was married. What a depraved hussy. I can't say I'm sorry she fell off that cliff."

"I don't quite understand," I said. "You came, angry at your husband."

"Yes, and a terrible journey it was too," she said. "By auto stage to Carmel and then by taxi up to this godforsaken house."

"But you've been living with him out in the guest house," I continued.

"Well, I came to get him and bring him back home, yesterday," she said. "But he said we had to wait for the reading of the will, and he said it might cause trouble if the family knew I was here." She smiled up at me rather sweetly as she arranged the potato slices in neat rows in a baking dish. "But you discovered me, didn't you, so there's no point in my hiding any longer."

Our domestic duties completed, we proceeded to the living room, where a phonograph player was blasting away and Jack and Bunny were engaged in a frenzied fox-trot. The Beaumonts reclined in their languid way on the sofa. Nigel was brooding in a wing chair, staring into another whiskey.

He leapt to his feet. "Mary!" he said, sounding flustered. "Is your headache better?" He looked nervously around the room. "I'd like you all to meet my wife, Mary. She wanted to meet you earlier, but she was feeling a bit off."

"I never had a headache," said Mary. "Is this how you're mourning your aunt? With that jazz music and dancing?" She clicked her tongue, and Jack, looking taken aback, turned off the machine. Mary Carruthers ran her eyes over the room. "Nigel, we can use that big chair in the back parlor," she said. "I can't say I like these pictures of the sea, but maybe we could put them in the boarders' rooms."

After a shocked silence, in which it sank in that Mary Carruthers believed she was about to come into possession of all she viewed, Thelma spoke up. "These were Aunt Lulu's paintings. Her life's work."

Of course, Thelma hadn't said a kind word about the paintings before, but it is only human nature for a thing to increase in value when someone else is about to seize it.

"Oh, I suppose I've spoken out of turn," said Mary Carruthers. "I'm awfully plainspoken; I know I am." Lest there was any doubt, she added, "You must be one of the Beaumonts that wrote me about Nigel living with your aunt while the children and I were scraping by. It's a terrible shame, Nigel."

We all stood there in shock, and Nigel managed a sort of a laugh. "Really, Mary is rather—" he began by way of explanation.

"Straight and to the point," finished Jack. "Say, if everyone was like that, my job would be pretty dull. Care for a drop of something, Mrs. Carruthers?"

"I wouldn't mind," she said. "A little whiskey, please."

"She thinks she's going to get everything," said Rodney, rolling his eyes to the ceiling. "She thinks Aunt Lulu changed her will."

"My husband wrote me a letter explaining—" began Mary.

"I did nothing of the kind," said Nigel, giving her a look so dark she fell instantly silent and remained that way for the rest of the evening.

"Dinner will be ready shortly," I said brightly. Why did I insist on making everything seem normal when it so clearly wasn't? Naturally everyone ignored me, and despite my idiotic efforts to keep up pleasant conversation, dinner was a strained meal. To no one's surprise, Nigel was quite firm about dragging his wife back to the guest house immediately afterward.

"Will you be leaving after the reading of the will?" asked Rodney pointedly.

"That depends," said Nigel, "on its contents, doesn't it?" For the first time, he smiled.

"Such horrid people," said Thelma after they had left.

"I think they *deserve* the paintings," said Rodney maliciously.

"I wouldn't want my husband's dead mistress's paintings hanging around my house, even if they were Titians," said Bunny with a flounce.

"But would you take the cash?" said Jack.

Bunny giggled. "Say, would I!"

We all laughed, and that seemed to ease some of the strain we were feeling. Still, it was with some relief, soon after we had cleared the table and I had washed the dishes with Thelma, that I turned in.

I was given Aunt Lulu's room, and as I lay in bed staring across at the photographs on her dressing table, I thought about the woman who had brought me here. She had been rich, but talent had eluded her. Instead, she'd scraped acquaintance with talented people, but had they cared much about her?

No one seemed to mourn her, except Dolores. I sighed, and turned out the light, but at first I couldn't sleep. Did she fall, or was she pushed? I asked myself that question over and over again, and just before I fell asleep, it seemed there was another answer altogether, an answer that hovered just out of reach. When I did finally drift off, I dreamt of seascapes.

The next morning I rose early and dressed. I was pleased that no one else was awake. I wanted to be sure of one thing. An examination of the grounds around the house confirmed my earlier impression. There was simply no way anyone could leave the house and walk to the isolated spot where Aunt Lulu was painting, without being seen from the living room window.

I took that path out to the cliff and crept as near as I dared to the edge, looking down one more time at the foamy water churning among the rocks below.

"Iris!"

Hearing my name called startled me, and I jumped back from the cliff. It was Jack.

"Jack," I said, "there's something wrong. Those fish were simply too old."

"What?"

"Those fish Nigel caught. They're at least a week old. He wasn't out fishing day before yesterday."

"Well, no one saw him come out here and kill Aunt Lulu."

"He didn't push her then," I said.

"Then she fell."

"Jack," I said, "do you think he could have *pulled* her?"

His green eyes lit up. "Keep talking," he said.

"Aunt Lulu had a picture of him all decked out as an alpinist. And he'd convinced her to paint that tree, so she'd be facing away from the cliff."

Jack snapped his fingers. "There's some strange gear down in that boathouse," he said. "I couldn't figure it out. A pair of nailed boots and some things that looked like railway spikes."

"Can we prove it?" I said.

"We can try," he said.

We made a quick trip to the boathouse—my heart was pounding as we ran down those rickety steps, all wet with the morning mist—and examined the box again.

"Could be alpinist's stuff," said Jack.

I spotted some newspaper and picked up a crumpled copy of the *Carmel Pine Cone.* "Last week's," I said. "And it smells of fish. He stored some fish down here to bring up later."

"Here's a nice length of rope," said Jack. "Let's see if he left any trace behind on that cliff."

"Jack!" I said. "You're not going to climb up that cliff, are you?"

"Nope," said Jack. "I think I'll climb down it."

A few minutes later he was testing the knot he'd tied to fasten the rope to the pine tree that had served as Aunt Lulu's final source of inspiration.

"Will it hold?" I said, alarmed.

"I was a Boy Scout," said Jack. "Say, this'll be a swell story."

He tied the other end of the rope around his waist and edged himself over the cliff. My heart fluttered, and I squeezed my eyes shut.

"Keep your eyes open," he said, "and come over here. I might need you to help haul me up. My feet'll do some of the work."

Vertigo threatened to engulf me, so I lay on my stomach and inched over to the edge. I felt safer that way. Then, I opened one eye. Jack was lowering himself, hand over hand, down the face of the cliff, and his feet danced along the rock, seeking little toeholds here and there. If he lost his footing, he'd fall until the rope was taut, and then dangle there, bouncing against the rock. It was foolhardy.

Still, he managed quite nicely, and he was writing news copy as he worked his way down. "Your reporter plunged over the side in search of clues, hanging over the abyss, suspended between life and death, while above, plucky Iris Cooper, a mere slip of a girl, stood ready to haul him back up should he lose his footing."

"You can't lose your footing," I said. "I may be plucky but I haven't any brute strength."

He let out a laugh of triumph. "Maybe not, but your brain is hitting on all six. Know what I'm staring at?"

"Don't look down," I said.

"I'm not. I'm staring at one of those things that look like railway spikes. Someone's slammed it right into this rock here."

"Oh, Jack," I said.

"Now I'm looking down," he said. "Looks like he could have beached that little boat of his pretty easily.

"I'm coming up. Can you figure *why* he would do it? He should have waited until she changed her will. The family says he heard the argument, and she said she was going to change her will favoring him."

By the time Jack had scrambled back up—thank goodness I didn't have to pull him—I had figured out why he'd done it. Bunny had quoted her aunt as having said, in a loud voice, "Now that you've had your say about Nigel's family, I'm changing my will." If Nigel believed he was already in the will, he would have had reason to think that Aunt Lulu was planning to change it in favor of her nieces and nephews, in light of what they had told her about his wife and children.

Mrs. Carruthers had made it clear Nigel thought he was the heir. She'd told me in the kitchen that he wrote her from here with some vague promises, and referred again to the letter in the living room, when we asked her why she thought they'd inherit.

We went back to the house and called the police before anyone else woke up. After examining the cliff, they questioned Nigel, who burst into tears and said he shouldn't have hurt Lulu just as she was about to blossom as an artist.

Mrs. Carruthers hadn't helped his case. "He's a wicked one all right, with a bad temper. I wouldn't put it past him," she told the police with her usual brutal frankness when they asked her opinion. After they left, she turned to Jack and said, "I don't hold with all this divorce. Marriage is a sacrament, and with a name like Clancy, I'm sure you're a well-brought-up Catholic lad and know what I'm talking about. But do you think they'll hang him? It might be a relief, to be quite honest. My star boarder, Mr. Clemson, a very nice gentleman, ever so elegant, a dress-extra he is, has led me to believe that if I were free he might not be averse to asking for my hand."

The unflappable Mrs. Carruthers's monologue was interrupted by the arrival of Aunt Lulu's lawyer from San Francisco. With all the excitement, what he had to say was almost an anticlimax, but it gave Jack a nice finish to his story.

"I told your aunt," he said severely when we were all settled in the living room, "that there was no need to discuss the terms of her will with anyone. She simply laughed and told me that she was in the habit of telling everyone who had some hopes of being mentioned that she had left it to them. She said it insured good treatment from everyone. This lamentable practice has made my duty painful."

Poor Aunt Lulu, I thought. Her habit of buying friends had killed her.

"Well, who does get the money?" Bunny asked. Rodney and Thelma leaned forward.

The lawyer took out the document with a flourish. "The gist of it is, she has left everything," he said solemnly, "to her faithful housekeeper and chauffeur, Dolores and Ignacio Sanchez."

He coughed and continued. "With one exception." He put on his glasses and read aloud. "But to my nieces and nephews"—here the lawyer rattled off the names of all present and of Bunny's two brothers, who were abroad—"I leave something more precious. My life's work—my seascapes—to be divided equally among them." He replaced his glasses in a little case. "I have already spoken to the legatees," he said. "Mr. and Mrs. Sanchez have said you may stay here until after the funeral, and Mr. Sanchez says he will help you pack up the pictures so that you can take them with you when you go."

Before becoming a writer, K. T. Anders won the New Jersey Drama Critics' Award and the Florida Critics' Carbonell Award for her acting; she has appeared in numerous plays, television series, and commercials. The author of Legacy of Fear, The House at Blessing's Cove, *and several short stories of espionage, she has abandoned the KGB and British Intelligence, now that the Cold War is over, to write fiction that reflects the twin themes of deception and betrayal—as they apply to ordinary people.*

In "A Simple Matter of Training," a long-suffering, long-married spouse wonders whether you really can train an old dog to do new tricks.

A SIMPLE MATTER OF TRAINING

by K. T. Anders

HE DID IT every year. In the end it was only playacting of course, but he made it as real as possible for himself. It had become his annual Passion Play, done with meticulous attention to detail, complete with all the props.

He'd loved her once, of that he was sure. A dim recollection lingered of strawberry-scented summer days and firelit winter evenings, of lusty nights and tender mornings. But the plain truth was that she didn't wear well. In the last two decades, she'd turned churlish. After forty-five years of marriage, the bloom, as he and his friend Harry were fond of saying to each other, was definitely off the petunia.

He conceded that perhaps it wasn't all her fault, that he might share a small portion of the blame. Although her lumpy figure no longer lit the flame of his libido, and he'd heard everything she had to say nine times over, what did he offer in return? A paunch and two chins. And the same old punch lines. So, more likely, it was simply The Way Things Turn Out To Be—some twisted sense of humor on the part of the Divine that decrees that the seminal lover of youth should erode into the yokemate of old age.

He wasn't the type to walk out on her after all these years, so he endured. It wasn't easy. As the boredom set in, as the impatience grew, he retreated into his own world. In the face of her waspishness, he began to fantasize.

He would kill her.

He'd done it a dozen ways in as many years. He found he was really quite good at it. It was impossible to do it more than once a year—he was too thorough. He had to research, to plan, to procure the necessary equipment. It had to be the perfect murder—perfectly concealed—which left him an innocent, grieving widower. Each year he fully executed his scenario up to the moment of death. Then, in that last second, he always stopped. At the moment when he held the ultimate power over her, he always let her live, relishing his success. Each time he would revel in the euphoria of his beneficence. These were his golden years.

And she, of course, never knew a thing about it.

This was his thirteenth year. He rather liked this year's method. It was cleverer than the time he'd used the herb garden, less trouble than the rattlesnakes, more intellectually satisfying than the curare (that really had been beneath him, but he'd had other things on his mind that year—he'd had to close his accounting business and settle all his financial affairs for his retirement, so he'd allowed himself a lapse in creativity).

This year was his *coup de grace*, fascinating because she was involved unwittingly in the process. The key this year was behavioral training, the conditioned reflex. He was molding her behavior so that he could manipulate her. It was as basic as the old stimulus-response formula used by Pavlov in his experiments with dogs: just as the animals learned to salivate at the ring of a bell that signaled food, so his wife had learned a predictable, consistent response whenever he gave her the stimulus. Yet she was blissfully ignorant that she had "learned" this reaction. Yes, he thought, this year was a beauty.

He always set the murder for November or December; that gave him ten months to plan and two months to choose exactly the right time to strike. Today was November 13, so he still had plenty of time. The moment would arrive, as the moment always did, out of the blue. His genius was that he could recognize it.

Today had been a typical Saturday afternoon. His wife, Eugenie, was at the kitchen table with Agnes Tribble, the busybody from next door. Every Saturday, Eugenie provided Agnes with coffee and several pieces of fresh bundt cake in return for the intimate details of the lives of the rest of the neighborhood. This modest investment filled her cup of gossip to overflowing, and after savoring it, she doled it out, a drop at a time, to her bridge club on Monday.

He was in his refuge in the basement, working on his model trains, his other passion since his retirement five years ago. He was something of a local celebrity, with three railroad lines curving around the subterranean den, whistling through tunnels, rumbling over bridges where rivers of real water ran, stopping at a station in a city of skyscrapers or at a hamlet in the country. It wasn't a store-bought layout; he'd designed and made everything himself. Two years ago the *Morning Gazette* had done a feature story on him, and since then the local Miniature Railroad Club, of which he was president, had met in his basement on Monday nights.

He sat at the side of his diminutive world spread across three huge plywood tables and pushed the buttons, watching the freight train stop at exactly the right spot under the coal bin so the tiny black nuggets coming down the chute into the coal car wouldn't spill onto the tracks. Imagination had to take the place of the stoker who fed the steam engine, but that was all right. Imagination had to take the place of lots of things in life. He pushed the button that sent the engine and coal car into the freight-yard siding to dump the cargo at the end of the tracks behind a small warehouse.

Suddenly he frowned. The coal car was supposed to rise at one end to send its tiny load sliding into a neat pile on the ground. It was his newest design, but something was wrong. As the front end of the coal car rose, the whole car flipped, spilling tiny nuggets across the tracks. He shook his head and reached for the car.

Somewhere, his balance calculations were off. The procedure was fashioned from his observations at Harry's lumberyard, where the supply train arrived monthly to dump its load of gravel into Harry's back lot.

"Willard, could you come upstairs?"

Eugenie's voice scratched across his concentration. Eugenie had never called him Will, like his friends or his old partner in the accounting firm. Well, perhaps she had when they were first married; he couldn't remember. In fact, he couldn't actually remember marrying Eugenie. It seemed she'd been there all his life, like some bodily appendage, although the picture on the mantel clearly showed him as a young man standing next to a delicate woman in a long white dress.

He hit the button that dispatched the freight train out of the yard into the hilly countryside; the blast of its whistle echoed throughout the basement, sending a ripple of rebellious pleasure through him.

"Willard, I heard that. Why can't you ever come when I call?"

He sighed. "Yes, Eugenie."

She was waiting at the top of the stairs like a prison warden, arms folded across her bosom, toe tapping the linoleum. He ducked past her into the kitchen. With a sniff and a pat at her thinning gray hair, she turned to face him across the room.

"Willard, I've got to go into town. I need to get my hair done and get a manicure for my bridge game on Monday."

"That's fine, Eugenie. I'll be here." He gave her a placid smile.

"Willard, you can take a few minutes away from your fool trains to do something for me for a change! I can't drive with this arthritis in my knee acting up. You'll have to take me."

He glanced longingly at the open basement door. "Can't you call a cab?"

Her look would have withered a flower bed. "That's needless extravagance, Willard. My God, is it too much to ask that you take one hour out of your day for me?"

He took a breath. "I'm working on my coal car," he whispered.

"What?" Her voice slid unmelodically up the scale.

The temptation was too great; it was the perfect opportunity for a training reinforcement session.

"I'm working on my coal car," he said softly. Then he gave her the stimulus: he bowed his head to stare at his shoes.

That simple act of timorous defiance always produced the same response: oblivious to everything around her, Eugenie would march toward him like a drill sergeant, stand six inches in front of his face and unleash a tirade until she got her way. It was the bowed head that did it. He knew it drove Eugenie crazy to think he had the nerve to challenge her. Slowly, month by month, he'd worked on her, training her into perfect predictability. Now he had only to whisper and duck his head—she would come to him like a trained dog.

Today was no exception. He stole a quick glance upward as she steamed across the kitchen, hands on hips, eyes snapping. He fought the tug at the corner of his lip, but kept his head firmly bowed, studying his shoelaces.

"I am your wife, Willard. I'm more important than your damn coal car. And if you don't believe it, try having your coal car cook your dinner." It was only the opening salvo, and she continued at a fierce decibel level for a time, although he couldn't tell how long because he was marveling at the similarity between man and dog, or rather woman and dog. He'd learned to retreat under her barrage into his own cocoon of serenity and silence, and he'd gotten so good at it that he could block out everything around him, existing in a kind of limbo until she was through. Yes, he thought, he had only to wait for the right situation.

Silence had descended upon the kitchen and he knew she'd wound down. He looked up.

"We won't discuss it further, Willard," she said with a sniff. Then she clumped out of the kitchen, calling back over her shoulder, "I'll be ready in ten minutes."

The ride was pleasant enough. He puzzled over his tipping coal car. Going to town actually gave him a chance to check with his friend Harry. He was sure he could fix the problem by Monday night's meeting. Seemingly unaware of his preoccupation,

Eugenie babbled next to him as she had unceasingly for years, apparently satisfied with his occasional grunts.

The beauty shop was on Baily Street, just off Main. He found a parking space out front. An hour of freedom was granted with an admonition.

"Willard, please don't go to the lumberyard. You lose track of time. I'll shrivel up at the beauty shop waiting for you to get back, and it hurts my knee to walk that far."

He mumbled something as he got out of the car and sprinted across the street.

Hands on her hips, Eugenie called to him. "Do you hear me? Tell me where you're going."

They were separated by the flow of traffic turning into Baily Street. A blue Chevy screeched around the corner, and for a second he thought the moment had arrived. A duck of his head would send her in fury across the street in the path of the oncoming car. But the Chevy sped past before he could act. He needed a stoplight or a stop sign so that he could time it exactly. It would be better on Main Street down by the drugstore. He could wait.

"I'll sit in the park," he called with a wave.

"Don't you forget me, Willard. You come back here at half past four."

"Yes, Eugenie." He watched her enter the beauty shop, hobbling a little because of her bad knee. The lumberyard was only a few blocks away. He walked as fast as he could.

Harry, the owner, called to him from across the yard. "Hey, Will! How's the railroad magnate?"

Will puffed a little at the compliment. "Fine, Harry."

Harry sold lumber, brick, stone, gravel, and assorted hardware and plumbing. In the back of the yard was the railroad dock where the freight was unloaded. Once a month, on Saturday, the freight car backed into the siding to dump a load of gravel onto the blacktop, where it formed a mountain ready for piecemeal sale. Will had studied the railcar in this outdoor classroom before making his own model.

"Got me a problem with my dumping mechanism," he said as Harry ambled toward him. "Can I have a look?"

"Sure. Come on round back."

Harry led him to his private siding, where a raised track ran behind a cement-block storage building and ended at the gravel dump.

"Got a car of gravel in this morning. Haven't dumped her yet," said Harry.

Willard looked at his watch. "You going to be dumping soon?"

"Could be. Lemme git Charley."

They reached the corner of the building, and the railcar loomed into sight, its bed piled with gravel. Harry tooted three times on the yard whistle to signal Charley, and the two men sat down to share a little railroad talk while they waited. As a teenager, Harry had tramped on a freight one summer; they passed the time with memories, then turned to Will's problem.

"You're prob'ly going up too high," Harry said as Charley came across the yard at last. "Balance is off."

"Yeah," said Will. "I'll have to recalculate the angle."

"We'll watch Charley. He don't release the back panel till the gravel is just ready to fall." Harry gestured as Charley reached his side. "Let's dump 'er, Charley. We're doin' a little research here."

Will watched intently as Charley started the hydraulic lift. The front end of the railcar began to rise as the gigantic arm underneath the carriage growled and moaned, then at last thrust slowly upward. It took several minutes. As the car neared the apex, Will called to Charley to stop, then figured the angle with pad and pencil. Harry was right; he'd been going up too high.

Will crossed to stand at the rear of the car to take notes on the action of the back panel. He looked up at the gravel, marveling at the force of gravity that held it in place.

"Willard!"

The familiar voice seemed out of place in the lumberyard, and Will looked over his shoulder in confusion. He'd forgotten all about Eugenie.

"I knew you'd be here," called Eugenie from the far side of the yard, waving her arms. He looked back at the lift, not wanting to miss the moment the gravel began to move.

"I've been waiting for you for nearly half an hour, Willard."

She hobbled across the yard toward him. Will sighed. Fool woman was always interrupting him. He gestured to her to wait and turned back to the gravel.

Eugenie had reached the far edge of the building now, fifty feet across the tracks from where Will stood. He glanced at her. Arms out to the side, fingers splayed wide to protect her fresh, blood-red nail polish, she glared at him, her face flushed under hair that had been frothed into hard curls as blue as the sky.

"Willard, why can't you ever pay attention to what I say?" she thundered.

"I'm watching the gravel," he called.

"What?" Her voice slid up the scale warningly. "Willard, you pay attention or I'll give you a piece of my mind."

Fury was written all over Eugenie's face as she geared up for the confrontation. From the corner of his eye, Will saw Charley reaching for the control pin at the back of the railcar.

That's when he recognized the moment. It wasn't just as he had planned it, with a speeding car as she crossed the street. Nevertheless, it beckoned to him with outstretched arms. He was, if nothing else, adaptable.

And suddenly he knew the thirteenth year was the charm. He would do it this year, do it for real. He would get her into position as the gravel poured out of the car, and he would leap to safety at the last moment. It would look like an accident. Harry and Charley were witnesses. It was the best murder he'd planned, and he would do it for real in the thirteenth year. His knees nearly buckled in anticipation.

"Go ahead," he called, then softly added, "I'm watching the gravel." Then he deliberately ducked his head.

He was breathing so fast his chest thumped, but he stared at the dusty brown tips of his shoes.

"Willard!" shrieked Eugenie.

He was trembling with excitement. Her voice faded as he retreated into his own world of silence. Perfect, he thought, a little shiver running down his spine. The thirteenth year has been the best yet. No more carping, no more criticism, no more complaining. He was a free man.

In his scenario, he could imagine how the evening papers would report the accident: "Local Woman Accidently Buried Under Gravel Load." Harry would testify that it was a tragic accident, that the warehouse had blocked Eugenie's view of the railcar until she walked into its path, oblivious to the danger. Sympathetic neighbors would deliver tuna casserole to his house while he played the innocent, grieving widower. He felt the familiar euphoria of a job well done.

But he had to make it look good. Because he was doing it for real this time, he had to make it look as if he had tried to save her. He would reach for her at the moment the gravel started to fall, pull her slightly off balance, then leap back in horror, barely saving his own life.

Will was aware of a change in the sound around him. This was the moment, he thought. He came out of his reverie and reached out to grab Eugenie, a beatific smile on his lips. But his arms closed on empty air. Eugenie wasn't there. She was still standing across the tracks by the edge of the building. He shook his head in confusion. What had gone wrong? The sound of her voice was drowned out by the squeal of machinery and a rumble that instantly grew into the thunder of Zeus as twenty tons of gravel poured down the length of the railcar, coming and coming in an unstoppable avalanche.

When the police arrived to dig out the body, Eugenie was too distraught to talk; Harry handed her his handkerchief as she sobbed on his shoulder. The lieutenant turned to Harry for the details.

"Will seemed to be taken by some kind of fit," said Harry, shaking his head. His words were punctuated by renewed wails from Eugenie, and he gave her a consoling pat before continuing. "He called out 'go ahead,' so Charley and I thought he'd moved out of the way. Eugenie hollered at him, but Will just stared down at the ground mumbling. Poor Eugenie kept on yelling, but it was as if he couldn't hear her. Suddenly he stuck both arms out in front of him, shaking his head with a funny kind of smile." Harry paused as Eugenie hiccuped. He gave her another little pat on the shoulder. "Then the gravel came down," he said to the officer. "It made this here mountain where Will was standing."

During the next week, sympathetic neighbors delivered tuna casserole to the grieving widow. And Harry came round a few times to give his condolences. Agnes Tribble, of course, was a great comfort, and in return for a few pieces of fresh bundt cake, she helped Eugenie with the sad task of cleaning Willard's belongings out of the house.

"Do you want to keep this?" she said one day as she pulled a dog-eared book from the back of Willard's closet. "It's by someone named Pavlov."

"Throw it away," said Eugenie. "I already read it."